T0283068

A

DARK

AND

SECRET

MAGIC

A DARK AND SECRET MAGIC

a novel

WALLIS KINNEY

alcove
press

This is a work of fiction. All of the names, characters, organizations, places and events portrayed in this novel are either products of the author's imagination or are used fictitiously. Any resemblance to real or actual events, locales, or persons, living or dead, is entirely coincidental.

PUBLISHER'S NOTE: The recipes contained in this book are to be followed exactly as written. The publisher is not responsible for your specific health or allergy needs that may require medical supervision. The publisher is not responsible for any adverse reaction to the recipes contained in this book.

Copyright © 2024 by Wallis Kinney

All rights reserved.

Published in the United States by Alcove Press, an imprint of The Quick Brown Fox & Company LLC.

Alcove Press and its logo are trademarks of The Quick Brown Fox & Company LLC.

Library of Congress Catalog-in-Publication data available upon request.

ISBN (hardcover): 978-1-63910-989-0
ISBN (ebook): 978-1-63910-990-6

Cover design by Lucy Rose

Printed in the United States.

www.alcovepress.com

Alcove Press
34 West 27th St., 10th Floor
New York, NY 10001

First Edition: October 2024

10 9 8 7 6 5 4 3 2 1

To my sister, Shirley. This book was always for you.

AUTHOR'S NOTE

A Dark and Secret Magic is a celebration of the autumnal season and an homage to all the traditions and media surrounding American Halloween. At its heart, it's meant to be a cozy escape into a world that is a little more magical than our own. However, some darker elements are discussed within the story, so I have included content warnings for readers who would like to be aware of them. I will also keep an updated list of warnings on my website, should others be brought to my attention in the future.

Content warnings: death of a parent/grief, bloodletting, nonconsensual kissing by villain, body horror.

CHAPTER ONE
Somebody's Coming

The liminal era begins a week before Halloween. It's my favorite time of year, when half the trees are barren, and others burst with leaves the color of glowing fire coals. The garden and forest give their final offerings for harvest before the dormancy of winter creeps in. The air turns frigid, but beams of sunlight stay warm, and as the new year approaches, it brings all the traditions and celebrations that unlock the lovely longing of nostalgia. It's during this week that my magic grows strongest.

I should have been in bed hours ago, but the crackling fire to my left and the dozing cat in my lap make it impossible to move from my antique reading chair. Minutes pass, the content silence broken only by hushed feline snores and the soft stretch of cotton thread pulling over my crochet hook. Tonight's crafted creation is a little white ghost with a friendly smile and blushing cheeks. I've been in a bit of crochet frenzy since decorating my cottage for Halloween. The living room is adorned well enough for the holiday, with orange and black garlands draped on my mantle, cotton spiderwebs around my light fixtures, and a cast-iron cauldron hanging in my fireplace. But the kitchen still needs some festive touches.

I sew a second tiny black felt eye onto the ghost's face and smooth the edges with the tips of my fingers.

"Too cute," I say, admiring the pear-sized figurine in my hand.

A soft little mew escapes from Merlin. He looks up from my lap with droopy, displeased eyes.

"Sorry," I whisper.

He shakes out his ears, his collar chiming. With a lazy stretch, he rises and jumps off my lap, resettling onto the dark green loveseat on the other side of the living room.

"You've got a lot of attitude for a cat that's scared of mice," I say to the black pile of fluffy fur.

He gives me another look of consternation before laying his head down and going back to sleep.

Rolling my eyes at his dramatics, I carry the newly crafted ghost to the kitchen window. It looks right at home on the sill, next to my other crocheted decorations: a pumpkin with curling green vines, an oversized candy corn, and a small black cat modeled after Merlin. With this figurine tableau and the homemade wreaths of dried maple leaves I've placed in the windows, the kitchen decor is finally coming together.

The clock on my mantle whirs and clangs, three soft tolls that chastise me for still being awake. As the echoes of the last chime fade away, the gnarled hickory broom propped against the wall of my kitchen tips forward, crashing against the wooden floorboards.

Merlin lets out a startled cry, bolting off the couch and out of the living room.

A knot forms in my stomach. My mother's old adage about fallen brooms comes to mind.

"Somebody's coming."

Shaking off the nagging phrase, I place the broom back in its proper corner and survey the front of my cottage. Dark wood walls, pristine kitchen, messy desk, herbs that need organizing. All is as it should be. Outside the kitchen window, the night is silent. Up the hill from the cottage, Goodwin Manor looms against the night sky, glittering stars reflecting in its large windows. I moved out of my family's ancestral home a decade ago, out from under my mother's loving and ever watchful eye. These days, the emptiness of the manor casts a surreal shadow on my childhood. Every day that passes, those younger years slip further away, never to return. And yet, the building that witnessed all those moments still stands, my memories echoing within its walls.

Across from the hill, surrounding my cottage, is Ipswich Forest. The trees are frozen against the sky, not a single wisp of wind disturbing them. As if they are waiting for something.

Witches all have our ways of fortune telling. Miranda, my older sister, says the sea glass she collects from distant shores whispers to her. My younger sister, Celeste, divines from tarot cards and the movements of planets. As a hedge witch, premonitions come to me shrouded in the mists of dreams. But when I'm awake, I watch the forest. And tonight, with the trees in their silent vigil, the woods unnerve me. A few miles behind the tree line is a graveyard, the final resting place of every Goodwin mother for the past four hundred years. Including mine.

I have not been to it since she was buried in June.

Crash.

I jump, a hand flying to my heart. The broom has fallen over again, its wooden handle pointing directly at my front door.

"What are you trying to tell me, you pesky thing?" I ask, picking it up and placing it on the kitchen table. Perhaps the bristles have gone wonky? I should trim them tomorrow when I have a free moment. It's much too late to start another task now. With a final cursory glance out my window, I look toward the forest, where a dense fog is rolling in. Something just behind the tree line disturbs the creeping cloud's slow expansion.

My heart gives a shuddering beat against my chest. An old woman in a long white sleeping gown similar to my own walks through the swirling mist. Silently, I move forward, pressing my nose against the window. With every exhale my breath fogs the glass. With every inhale, it clears. And the woman draws closer.

Margaret Halliwell.

An elder of my coven and a sea witch like Miranda.

With a breathless curse, I grab a woolen coat off the stand and throw it over my nightgown before ripping open my front door and running barefoot into the cold.

"Mags? Are you okay?" I call out. She stops walking and stares at me, her gray hair floating in the windless fog.

"Hecate," she says. Her voice flat and strange.

"I'm here," I say breathlessly, reaching her. I shrug off my coat and hold it out for her, but she makes no move to take it. "What's wrong, Mags? How did you get here? Are you unwell?"

As a hedge witch, it's one of my duties to care for the sick members of the Atlantic Key, the coven I was born into. With just over one hundred and thirty witches, their needs keep me busy. At almost eighty, Margaret's health has been failing for a while now. Every two months for the past year, I've made her a tin of hawthorn balm to help combat her chronic fatigue. I sent the newest dose just a few days ago.

"He calls for me, Hecate. I have to go," she whispers.

My heart gives a pang.

"It's okay, Mags. We'll get you home," I say gently. Her husband passed away a few years ago, and Margaret is at an age where past and present are starting to merge in her memory.

She holds one of her wrinkled hands out to me. I hesitate. I so rarely touch people, finding more discomfort than solace in that level of closeness. Even my patients are used to my light-handed work. But it would be cruel of me to deny her this small sympathy. I smile and place my hand in hers.

The pain is immediate. A tugging vacuum-like sensation twists my stomach. Every hair on my arms stands on end, my skin begins to prickle and sting, and my ears swell with pressure. I try to pull my hand away, but Margaret's grip has turned viselike, her fingers clutching into the skin of my wrist. The intention of her magic coils around me, squeezing like a constrictor snake and burning cold.

"Mags!" I choke with the effort of speaking. "What are you doing?"

"You are not what you should be, little girl." Her voice is not her own. It comes out in a deep, rasping hiss. "That is deeply disappointing."

"Release me!" I shout, tugging violently to escape her grapple. Panic rises in my chest. Even at this time of year, even at my strongest, I don't possess the kind of magic to fight an elder of my coven.

Margaret gasps and the pressure around me eases slightly as her eyes clear.

"I have no more time," she whispers, her voice returning to normal. "The veil weakens as Samhain approaches. The King Below tests you. Find your mother's book, and you'll know why she named you a hedge witch."

The fog closes in around us, and shadows ripple through the vapor. The pain is a roaring train in my ears now. The sting erupts into a blazing fire. I scream and wrench my wrist from her. A ripping sensation flashes across my belly, and I fling backward, tumbling to the ground.

CHAPTER TWO
Six Days Until Halloween

Drizzling rain patters on the window. The Massachusetts sky is still asleep, and the morning fog is a long while from burning off. Merlin purrs on the pillow next to my head, his little paws stretched out onto my arm. I stare up at the wooden planks of my bedroom ceiling, with no memory of having fallen asleep. Absentmindedly, I rub my wrist. No stinging, no fingernail marks on the skin.

"'The King Below tests you . . .'" I mutter, the epithet unfamiliar to me.

I'm no stranger to vivid, peculiar dreams. But last night's was particularly cryptic.

"Find your mother's book and you'll know why she named you a hedge witch."

In the Atlantic Key, tradition dictates a girl wait until her thirteenth birthday to choose her magic. But my mother chose my path the day I was born. As the sun set that Halloween, she swaddled me in a forest-green blanket, named me Hecate Goodwin, and proudly announced to the women gathered around her that I would be a hedge witch. An ancient practice, I would be the first in any coven in almost two centuries. This sent rattled whispers scattering among the women of the Atlantic Key.

Why had Sybil Goodwin done it?

What could a simple kitchen witch want with a hedge witch for a daughter?

How could a girl with no choice ever truly belong to her craft?

That particular whisper haunted me throughout childhood, an ever-present specter of doubt hanging over me as I trained. And with no living hedge witch to mentor me, I had to rely on the scattered knowledge of my mother and other coven members. But now, at almost thirty-one years old, I have grown used to hedge craft, isolating as it may be. How disappointing for my subconscious to bring up old wounds. Hadn't I gotten over my stolen choice long ago?

"Strange dreams as Samhain nears. Not the best omen for the New Year," I whisper, letting my wrist fall back to the bed. Merlin nuzzles his face against my neck, his whiskers tickling my skin. The sound of rain against the window strengthens. Perfect weather.

I want to stay in my bed, take Merlin into my arms, and grab the book on the side table. It's a collection of Arthurian romances thick enough to lose myself in. But today is a workday. I have to tell myself this three more times before finally rising from bed.

In the pantry at the back of the cottage there is a large glass cabinet that holds my latest concoctions for the Raven & Crone, the apothecary I co-own in Ipswich. Autumnal scented-potpourri sachets that smell of cinnamon and maple bourbon, several new salves, and thirty bottles of liniment oils that are particularly useful for soothing spider bites, disinfecting wounds, and relieving muscle pain. Each item is tagged with a price and a Raven & Crone sticker.

I load all the supplies into a basket, quickly change into work clothes, and feed a demanding Merlin. The sight of my broom on the kitchen table and a completed ghost figurine on the windowsill stops me in my tracks.

So those moments had been real? Then when had I gone to bed and dreamed of Margaret? Confusion gnaws at me as I leave the cottage.

The air is cool, but not biting. Still, to protect my ears from the chill, I tuck the hood of my olive-green rain jacket over my head as I ride my bike into town.

No cars drive past on this sleepy morning so I have the road to myself. The trees above me are a brilliant wash of autumn fire. A low-lying fog blankets the canopy tops, blotting out pockets of the chromatic foliage. My bike flies over asphalt, the tails of my rain jacket whipping around me, snapping in the wind. I can almost trick my mind into thinking I'm on a broomstick, flying hundreds of feet in the air through thick moonlit clouds. Tickled by the thought, I let out a delighted laugh.

By the time I reach Main Street in Ipswich, the fog has burned off, and traffic overtakes the road, forcing me to dismount and head the rest of the way on the sidewalk. Workers decorate streetlamps with orange and black streamers and place festive lanterns on thin wires that hang over the road. Hay bales are gathered in front of restaurants, and store owners organize pumpkins in their window displays. Ipswich never disappoints once Halloween is on the horizon.

I lock my bike on a tree near the road, unhook the basket, and head into the Raven & Crone. As the apothecary door swings open and the chiming bell announces my entrance, the air fills with the scent of a thousand herbs and candles. Rebecca Bennet, the store manager, is on a ladder next to the front door, hanging decorations in the window. I stop and watch with a frown as she pastes a jolly Santa to the glass. There is also a small Christmas tree with delicate ornaments hanging from its branches tucked into the corner, along with a little pile of wrapped presents.

"Are we going to have this debate again, Rebecca?" I ask, amused.

Rebecca, in her crisp black T-shirt and dark wash jeans, looks down at me from the top of the ladder.

"It's to appease the churchgoing folk, Kate," she says with a grin. "We get to be the spooky shop all year because we go so hard for Christmas."

Rebecca is in her late forties, about fifteen years younger than my mom. But our families have always been close. Her mother, Winifred Bennet, and mine are . . . *were* best friends. Rebecca, a garden witch, mentored me in herbalism once my mother tapped her own knowledge dry. And when I turned twenty-eight, Rebecca and I opened the Raven & Crone together. With her ability to grow the healthiest plants and my recipes that put those plants to medicinal use, our little apothecary has thrived these past three years.

"I have new potpourri today and liniment, thirty bottles," I say, holding up my bike basket, letting go of the decoration debate. No need to hash it out again this year.

"Excellent," Rebecca says, emphasizing the first syllable. She climbs down the ladder and takes the box of supplies from me. "These will be gone by the end of the week."

"I hope so," I say, laughing. "That would pay for my groceries through Christmas. Merlin has recently become accustomed to an expensive wet food that's threatening to put me out of house and home."

Rebecca snorts. "Or instead of buying something for your *cat*, you could get yourself a nice birthday gift. This Saturday is the big one, after all." She eyes me expectantly and I have to actively work to suppress my grimace.

The women of the Atlantic Key get our magic from ancestral bloodlines. But magic, if unharnessed, will eventually dissipate. That's why members of our coven focus on one area of magic, committing to it at thirteen years of age. The more we practice, the stronger we become. For the past few generations, however, our collective powers have weakened. When my grandmother was a girl, to prevent this loss the elders began enforcing a Containment. Upon a witch's thirty-first birthday, she undergoes a ritual that removes her ability to perform any magic beyond that which she has practiced extensively. It allows her to devote all her intention to her chosen craft and prevents the Atlantic Key's power from dwindling over time.

"You are ready for your birthday, aren't you?" Rebecca asks after I'm silent for too long.

"Of course," I say. "I just . . . it's my first birthday after losing Mom. It will be weird."

She gives me a sympathetic nod and a sad smile.

That excuse is certainly partially true. But I can't admit to Rebecca that my bigger reason for hesitancy is that it will be Rebecca's own mother, Winifred Bennet, performing my Containment. Winifred, the leader of the Atlantic Key, is a meta-magic witch, able to manipulate the very fabric of magic itself. Of all the sanctioned crafts allowed by our coven, meta-magic is by far the most dangerous, especially for the witch who practices it. In recent years, the strain has started to show in Winifred. She's become erratic and unpredictable, and I would rather have a peaceful, quiet Halloween.

Rebecca's attention moves off me as an elderly couple walk into the Raven & Crone. She greets them brightly, and I slip away toward the back of the store. I pass soaps, candles, salves, and rock-sugar treats as well as more spiritual items. Incense burners, crystals, and fertility aids all line the back wall.

"Ginny," Rebecca calls over to her teenaged daughter, who is sitting at one of the tables in the back. "Scoot your stuff over and give Aunt Kate room."

Ginny, who has the same abundant, curly black hair that all Bennet witches share, glances up from the book she's reading.

"Hi, Kate," she says, gathering her schoolbag, various books, and dozens of writing supplies off the tabletop. "What did you think of Malory's prose?" she asks as I sit down.

"I haven't jumped into it yet," I answer honestly as I set my empty bike basket and leather satchel down on the table. Her teenage disapproval is cutting. She'd loaned *Le Morte d'Arthur* to me four days ago.

Ginny, who has been a practicing book witch for two years and merely needs to hold a book in her hands to know its contents, can never understand why it takes anyone more than an afternoon to finish a novel. It seems even I will receive no leniency from her, even though the volume of Arthurian legends she gave me is over eight hundred pages long.

"Well," Ginny clips, "will you be done by Halloween? Because I have another friend waiting to read it."

Ginny's favorite threat is that of her "other friend." Even when I used to babysit her as a toddler, she would never share her toys.

"Sure." I nod. My plans for the next week are sparse enough to make the promise semi-reasonable.

I sit down at the table beside her and pull out my Herbal from the leather satchel. From one of the pockets, I grab a deep blue glass fountain pen with stars etched in the body, a gift from my sister Celeste. My Herbal opens on its own as I uncap the pen.

Ginny looks over the edge of her novel, eyeing my leather-bound spell book with a slight trace of envy in her eyes.

"Grandma still won't make me one, you know," she says, realizing I've caught her staring.

"I do know and I'm sorry," I say. Winifred creates all the spell books for the women of the Atlantic Key. The books are infused with her meta-magic, adapting to the needs of the witch they belong to. They are our diaries, reference books, and records of our magical practice. But Winifred refuses to make spell books for book witches, a rule she didn't even break for her granddaughter.

"Your grandmother told me once that book witches have a rather bad habit of using the enchanted paper to write novels they never finish, but edit endlessly until the pages run black with too much ink."

Ginny scoffs. "I don't see why I have to be punished for the ill behavior of others."

I give a meaningful look toward her hands. Her ink-stained fingers hint at late nights spent scribbling on whatever blank sheets of paper she can find. She frowns and pulls her hand under the table, away from my sight.

"Whatever," she mumbles.

Biting my lip to hide a smile, I turn back to my Herbal. Its brown leather binding, with a large maple tree reflected over a pond etched on the front, looks brand new, just as it did when I received it on my twelfth birthday. Even after all this time, dozens of kitchen mishaps later, it still smells like my father's favorite armchair. The only mark of change is its thickness.

"The pages come as you need them," my mother had told me once when I fretted about running out of room. I had been comparing my Herbal, new and thin at the time, to her Recipe Book, which was bigger than my small arms could carry.

The pages of my book keep turning on their own until they settle onto the page I had wanted. My daily to-do list.

* *Morning routine (dress, feed Merlin, etc.)*
* *Brush M.*
* *Deliver liniment and bundles to Raven & Crone*
* *Four-hour shift at R&C*
* *Journal entry*
* *Evening routine (one hour each of reading, needlepoint, crochet, and herbalism)*
* *Prep breakfast for tomorrow*
  – overnight oats with cinnamon and fruit
* *Make tomorrow's to-do list*

Crossing off several of the tasks I've already completed, I add *Trim broom bristles* to the bottom of the list.

Ginny flips through the book in her hands for a few moments, but it's not long before her eyes are back on me.

"What is it, Ginny?" I ask.

"Do you ever get tired of it?" she responds quietly.

"Tired of what?" I put my pen down and look at her, abandoning my Herbal for the moment.

"The repetitiveness. The same to-do list every day. Gathering ingredients, coming here for your shifts, going back to your cottage alone. Never leaving Ipswich, never really seeing anyone. Isn't it exhausting?"

Teenagers really have perfected the art of brutal honesty.

I don't answer immediately; a customer is perusing the decks of tarot cards next to our table, and it gives me a few moments to collect my thoughts. Despite the bluntness of the question, Ginny's tone wasn't cruel. She's been going through a pining phase the past few months, longing for a romanticized version of a faraway, interesting life. The question has more to do with her than with me.

"I don't find it tiring," I answer. "Gathering ingredients, creating all the inventory for this store—it's all part of my craft. That would be like asking you if you ever get tired of reading." I give her a friendly smile.

Ginny shakes her head, giving me a hesitant but defiant look.

"But I choose my craft, Kate."

And there it is. That which sets me apart from all others of the Atlantic Key.

"So did I, technically," I say, fiddling with the glass pen in my hands. "When I was thirteen, the coven gathered at the edge of Ipswich Forest, and I declared my craft before the elders. Just like you did." The memory of that day would never fade. The pitying whispers as we all walked down the hill from Goodwin Manor. The coven's scrutiny making me squirm. I could feel the forest's disapproval too, the way the trees loomed over us in foreboding judgment, recognizing me as an imposter, a girl only playing at being a witch.

"Why *did* you choose it?" Ginny asks. She's not the first witch to pose the question, nor the first to make it sound simultaneously like a question and accusation. Why had I played along with my mother's meddling? Why hadn't I ultimately chosen to follow the traditions of the coven instead? Unfortunately, the answer to her question will disprove my earlier attempt to lump us together.

"My mother bade me to," I answer honestly, clearing my throat awkwardly as Ginny's eyes go wide.

I'd resisted at first. I'd planned to run into the woods in protest until I was allowed my own choice. But, at my first sign of defiance, my mother had grabbed my hand, gently but intently, and placed it on the maple tree that marked the forest's edge.

"Do as I have bidden, Hecate," she had whispered into my ear. As an elder of the Atlantic Key, my mother's direct bidding was steeped in ancestral magic, impossible to ignore without incurring the coven's wrath.

I had obeyed. Unwilling and unready, I chose the path my mother commanded.

"But either way," I say to Ginny, "I'm glad that she did. I'm very suited to the demands of my craft." It's for this very reason that, despite my hesitance over Winifred Bennet's participation, I'm looking forward to my Containment. After all these years, *I* will be the one truly choosing.

Ginny purses her lips, unconvinced.

"You don't ever get lonely?" she pushes.

"I have Merlin," I offer, which only causes her to roll her eyes. "I am alone, yes. Such is the lot of a hedge witch, existing on the boundary of things, never fully integrated. But that's okay. I am fine to be alone with my thoughts."

This isn't entirely true. Since my mother's passing last summer, I've increased the frequency of my visits to the Raven & Crone. Without them, I would go days without talking to another person. In those long stretches of isolation, it's too easy to become acutely aware of the cavity my mother left behind.

"But hasn't there ever been someone you felt improved the silence? Someone you would want to bring across the boundary with you?"

I quirk an eyebrow at her. "That book you're reading is a romance, isn't it?" I guess. Ginny often assumes the personality of whatever story has currently captured her attention. Before I can sneak a glance at the cover, she slams her ink-splotched hand on top of the book, obscuring any identifying information. My goodness. She's worse than Celeste was at this age.

"Fine. If you must know," I say. "There was someone once. A man my age I knew about a decade ago. Charming, funny, respectful. Gloriously handsome, with the most intoxicating scent—cinnamon and rain. We were fast friends. And even faster enemies."

Ginny's eyes, which have been giddy over the prospect of my long-lost romance, crinkle in confusion.

"Unbeknownst to me, he was a hexan of the Pacific Gate." I say this last sentence with all the intonation of a schoolgirl telling her friends a scary story around a campfire. While every coven across the country has its eccentricities, only the Pacific Gate refuses to restrict even the most abhorrent forms of magic. Magic that corrupts the practitioner, requires dangerous amounts of intention or sacrifice—even magics whose only uses are pure evil—are allowed. The Pacific Gate is anathema to the Atlantic Key.

Ginny's slack-jawed expression of horror is delightful. Hopefully that will teach her not to ask meddling questions.

She squints at me, possibly noticing my subtle smirk.

"I think you're lying," she says, jutting her chin out.

"Maybe I am," I say with a casual shrug, returning to work in my Herbal.

With my to-do list attended to, it's time to fill out my daily journal entry. The Herbal, sensing my intention, flips to the back section that holds my diary. A fresh blank page waits for me to start writing.

October 25th—
Odd dream last night. Subconscious messages?

My hand pauses. I should check in on Margaret Halliwell sometime this week. Dreams are finicky things and always open to interpretation, but still. I rub my wrist again, remembering the painful sting of her touch and the strangeness of her words.

"Ginny," I say, setting my pen down again. She looks at me warily.

"Have you ever heard of someone called the King Below?" Maybe somewhere in her thousand-book collection there might be a reference, a thread for me to follow.

She frowns, considering.

"Not off the top of my head. Do you want me to do a recall?" Her eyes gleam with intention. She loves a good research topic, a reason to deep dive.

The door to the Raven & Crone chimes as several more customers walk in. Rebecca greets them warmly, and I'm reminded of the duties to the shop that I'm neglecting.

"No need," I say quickly.

"Really, I don't mind. I've been meaning to forget this book anyway," Ginny says eagerly, holding up the book in her hands as a sacrifice. I was right: it is a romance.

Book witches have the ability to remember anything they have ever read, but they must give up other knowledge to do so. Like all crafts, their magic requires sacrifice. If she were to do a recall, the book in her hands would slowly be consumed, the ink disappearing until every page was blank. Ginny would also forget all its contents. She looks at me hopefully, eager to practice her craft. But there is no reason for it, given that I'd most likely made up the King Below in my subconscious imagination.

"Some other time," I whisper as Rebecca leads a customer toward the back. Ginny frowns, disappointed. At only fifteen, she needs an adult witch to supervise anytime she practices magic of that degree. I stand up from the table and help Rebecca with the checkout. An old woman holds several bags of our turmeric powder.

"This will stain anything it touches," I warn her as I place the yellow powder in a brown bag with the Raven & Crown logo embossed on the front. "But I recommend it in a pumpkin seed hummus. It will be a great addition for this time of year. And so good for the heart." She smiles her thanks before paying Rebecca.

"Ah. What I wouldn't give for some of your mother's Pump-Up Pumpkin Seed Hummus," Rebecca says wistfully next to me. "I haven't had a decent workout since I ran out of my last batch."

"I'll make you some," I offer. My mother trained me in kitchen magic. She felt all witches should know the basics of that craft, though neither of my sisters had ever shown any interest in it.

"Oh! Would you? I didn't want to ask, but that would be amazing." Her voice giddy.

"Sure, it's no problem." I laugh at her excitement. "I don't have anything to do this week anyway."

"Except read *Le Morte D'Arthur*," Ginny interjects, giving me a piercing glance.

"Right," I say after a beat.

Rebecca gives me a look. "And planning for your birthday," she reminds me with a disapproving tut.

"You sound just like Grandma whenever you make that noise, you know," Ginny says to her mother.

Rebecca's lips purse, her face suddenly a mirror image of her daughter's.

"How is Winifred?" I ask, doing my best to hide my smile.

"Crazy as always," Rebecca says with a flick of her hand. "Though I'm sure she'd love to see you. Why don't you go to the festival?"

I shake my head. The Ipswich Fall Festival is held at the Bennet farm every year. Attending has been an annual tradition for my mother and me since I was a child.

"I don't think so. Too many memories. Besides, I'll see your mom at the coven gathering this Saturday."

"I understand." Rebecca gives me another of her sad smiles before a look of realization dawns on her face, and she closes her eyes for a moment.

"Oh. Kate. You should call your sister today," she says.

"Celeste? Why? Is everything okay?" I don't like the worried look in her eyes. The last I'd heard from my little sister, she was yachting off the coast of Grand Cayman, acting as the personal astrologist to some hot-shot actor she swore was nicer than I'd believe. My mind runs away for a moment, fearing the worst for her. Maybe there'd been a hurricane I hadn't heard about.

Rebecca shakes her head. "No, not Celeste. Miranda."

"Why would I do that?" I ask after a moment. Rebecca knows my older sister and I have never been especially close. Her lips purse again, but her eyes are still sad.

"Today is going to be hard for her. I heard from the elders a few hours ago. Margaret Halliwell passed away last night."

CHAPTER THREE
When a Stranger Calls

Ominous clouds close in over the forest by the time I get back to my cottage. I'd been spared a rainy ride home from the apothecary, but more storms are on the way. Merlin greets me and I give him a few distracted pats while sitting at my desk. It is wooden, creaky, and filled with dozens of small drawers and hidden holes to squirrel away everything from writing supplies to forbidden treasures. Various recipes, order forms, and other papers are scattered on the surface. I pile them up and stuff them inside one of the cubbies. I open my Herbal back to the to-do list, crossing off my visit to the Raven & Crone. But it's impossible to decide on another task. Rain starts tapping against the roof and then begins to pour down in heavy sheets, the discordant weather a reflection of my buzzing mind.

Margaret Halliwell is dead.

I can still feel her papery fingers around my wrist. That pain, that ripping sensation when I'd jerked away from her, had felt so real. Had my unconscious mind somehow known she'd passed on? Why else would such a dream come to me?

I lay my head on the desk, my breath fluttering the edges of my Herbal. The leather book twitches and pages turn of their own accord, settling on an old recipe.

"Pumpkin Pomegranate Punch Pick-Me-Up," I murmur, lifting my head and reading aloud. "Let your troubles dissolve in bubbles." I smile at my book. The punch is a delicious drink my mother made whenever any of us had a particularly bad day. It was one of the first recipes of hers that I decided to copy down into my own book. Celeste once drank so much of this punch after a breakup that she'd floated two inches off the floor, a giggling mess. It had taken Mom, Miranda, and me several hours to get her settled down.

"Thanks for the recommendation," I say, "but I don't have any champagne on hand." I also have zero interest in carving an entire pumpkin to serve the punch in, as is required for the intention to work. But I don't mention this to my Herbal; no need to hurt anyone's feelings.

The pages flip again, a little more forcefully this time.

"Ghost-Be-Gone Gin and Tonic," I read. "For all sorts of hauntings, literal and metaphorical."

I grimace. Even if it hadn't been a dream, Margaret hadn't been a ghost. Spirits were ethereal, invisible forces across the veil that separates the living from the dead. I'd seen Mags. I'd felt her touch.

"I don't like what you're implying," I say. "And why are you trying to get me drunk, huh?"

My Herbal shudders, and with a groan, the cover snaps shut. My wooden desk shakes a bit from the impact. I bite my lip, knowing I've upset it.

Merlin nips lovingly at my ear and then lets out a warning chirp, staring at the door.

I glance that way, just as everything around me goes quiet. A distant intention reaches out to me. Then, the sound of a wave crashes against the door.

I sigh. Miranda.

A Dark and Secret Magic

I walk to my door and open it. A small box, wrapped up in brown paper, sits on my welcome mat. A bright white envelope is tied to the top with string. The letter is slightly wet and smells of salt. It's been ages since Miranda has reached out, and it's especially odd she would contact me today, so soon after her mentor's passing. I set the brown package on my desk as I read the letter.

Darling Hecate,

As I know you enjoy the solitude of your little cottage, I believe you are unlikely to have heard the news. I am sorry to inform you that elder Margaret Halliwell sailed into the next life early this morning. Of course, this could not have come at a worse time. Margaret was this year's host for the Samhain gathering, and now all the plans have been flung into the abyss. She really did not time her departure well. A more perfect storm could not have formed. There will be no funeral, thank goodness. Her body has been given to the sea, as she requested. With no living children, her Book has been sent to the coven's archives. Her affairs were in order, as she had several boxes addressed to members of the Atlantic Key. You included. I did find that strange, that she would leave something to you, but we both know her mind was a bit addled. Either way, I have sent along the box.

Breaking from my reading, I study the package on the desk. Margaret left something for me? She and I spoke very little before she got sick last year; she always preferred Miranda over Celeste and me. I unwrap the box, hesitant. It's wooden, made from mangrove, with a stormy ocean scape carved into the lid. A small yellow sticky note is taped to the top, with *Hecate Goodwin* written in Margaret's elegant scrawl.

The lid of the box creaks as I lift it. Inside are the six tins of the hawthorn balm I'd made for her the past year. All untouched.

"Oh Margaret," I whisper sadly. It seems she hadn't been interested in my help after all. Such a shame. I will have to burn the contents of the box. These balms had been made specifically for her. If I give them to anyone else, the intention might get confused. My hand hesitates, hovering over the last item inside, a small glass vial full of a dark brown liquid. A murky sort of water, swirling with sediment.

"What are you?" I wonder, pulling it out of the box and turning it over to inspect further. There are no identifying marks. I look at the back of the sticky note with my name, hoping to see a line of explanation. But the other side is blank, leaving no clue. How strange.

Perhaps Miranda knows what it's meant for? I pick up my sister's note again and continue to read from where I left off.

This week is in absolute disarray. I have written to the coven and volunteered Goodwin Manor for the New Year celebration. That announcement caused quite a few waves, but everyone is pleased. Obviously, this is a very inconvenient task to take on, but I am determined to do my duty as a witch of the Atlantic Key.

Please open up the manor house and have it ready. Celeste and I will arrive the night before Mischief and depart after the festivities of Halloween. It might be nice to be together on our first Samhain without Mother. All our old traditions could help heal the wounds of grief. And if there is time, we will try to find a moment to celebrate your birthday.

Let me know how quickly you can get the Manor open. I will send a guest list and menu in a few days.

I have to say, with Mom and Margaret gone in one year, I do sometimes feel the world is against me. I just pray this week is one of smooth sailing, but I don't have high hopes.

All my love,

Your sister,
Miranda Helenia Spence Goodwin

My eyes grow wide as I read. My sisters will arrive Thursday; that's less than five days to prepare the kinds of Samhain celebrations they

A Dark and Secret Magic

are used to. They will want the pumpkin display, the dumb supper, the cocktails, the Halloween feast. Not to mention the coven-wide celebrations that take place after sunset on Samhain. There is no hope of finishing everything on time. I set the letter down on my desk and look over to my broom, still resting atop the kitchen table. Somebody's coming, indeed. About fifty somebodies.

"Thanks for the warning," I grumble to the broom. Any sympathy I might have had for my older sister has evaporated. Only Miranda can make her mentor's death seem like an inconvenience done deliberately to annoy her.

All thoughts of Margaret's apparition and the box she sent me have been relegated to the back of my mind. I need to clear my head. With the storms outside, it would be unwise to head into the forest. My next best option is to cook.

I prep a pan of chickpeas and wild mushrooms to roast in the oven. I add lemons, garlic, and rosemary for extra hits of flavor. My mother's voice echoes in my head as I chop the herbs.

"What is this, Hecate?" She points to a plant with dozens of spindly green needles shooting out from a long thin stalk.

"Rosemary," I say.

"Very good." She nods. "And what is rosemary's purpose?"

"Making gravy taste good?" I answer after a moment. My mother laughs.

"That certainly is one purpose, yes. Anyone—witch, hexan, or mortal—can use rosemary to imbue a meal with lovely flavor. But it has other purposes too. Rosemary is for remembrance. In the hands of a trained witch, rosemary can feed and amplify her intention to honor her ancestors. Do you understand?"

I shake my head. My mother picks up the rosemary stalk, her voice even and patient as she speaks.

"Intention is what feeds magic. The desire to have something done and then increasing the chances that it will happen, all through our intention." She hands the herb to me so I can study its leaves.

23

"That is what magic is, after all. Turning fortune in our favor. Increasing the probability of your desired result. In the Atlantic Key, we call on our own intention and that of the witches that came before us. Their power remains though their spirits have passed. That power runs in your blood." She tickles my nose with another rosemary stalk, and I let out a surprised giggle.

"But," my mother says, "a sacrifice is required to feed that power. Otherwise, it would feed on you."

My eyes widen at the ominous thought. My mother laughs.

"Don't be afraid, dearest. The only witches in our coven that have to worry about that are the ones who practice meta-magic. Luckily, everything in this world can feed intention. Plants, animals, technology. If you can touch it, see it, or imagine it, it can amplify your ability to do magic. As a hedge witch, you'll work with nature. Herbs and plants will help you channel your intention. It's important to know what you should reach for when you're practicing your craft."

She points again at the other herbs.

"Sage for wisdom. Dried rose petals for love. Thyme, parsley, oregano. All things that can be found in any kitchen. Write this down, Hecate."

The edges of the vegetables and herbs have charred, beginning to burn, as I wipe tears from my eyes. I struggle to breathe through the sudden onslaught of grief brought on by the memory of my first lesson in magic. Four months after her passing, and the longing to hear my mother's voice again is still as sharp as broken glass.

Sniffling between soft sobs, I sear a chicken breast on my stove top and boil a box of store-bought pasta in water as salty as Ipswich Bay. When the chickpeas are fried and the charred mushrooms have cooled, I assemble a plate of pasta, chicken, and vegetables. The final touches are a ball of creamy burrata cheese, aged Parmesan, fresh butter, and balsamic vinegar drizzled over the entire dish.

Sharp and salty from the vinegar and parmesan, refreshing from the lemons and mozzarella, and earthy from the herbs and mushrooms. Even through my blocked nose, still a bit stuffy from crying, the flavors are stunning in combination. Each bite is a perfectly timed movement in a symphony. I force myself not to lick the plate clean, instead setting it on the ground for Merlin, who happily slurps away.

I brush him by the fire for longer than usual, allowing the flickering flames to hypnotize my sadness back below the surface. By the time I finish, Merlin's purrs have given way to soft snores, his paws kneading the skin of my legs as he falls asleep. I grab the book Ginny loaned me off my side table and haul it onto my lap. Merlin wakes at the movement and jumps off me, curling up closer to the fire.

"You're going to get singed if you're not careful," I warn him. He looks at me with half-closed eyes before turning his face back toward the flames.

"Suit yourself." I laugh and open the book. An hour passes as I read, curled comfortably into the leather chair.

When the clock strikes eight, I prep my breakfast for the morning. Tucked away in one corner of my kitchen is my mother's Recipe Book. Once again, Margaret's words echo in my mind.

"Find your mother's book, and you'll know why she named you a hedge witch."

I set the bowl of overnight oats in the fridge and pull the Recipe Book out of its cubby. It's heavy in my hands, the cover starting to show age, with the weathered etching of a bubbling cauldron on the front.

"Don't be jealous," I say to my own Herbal, still on my desk, as I begin to flip through pages. With my mom gone, all the personality of her book has disappeared. If there is something in here to discover, I'll have to find it myself. Pages full of words I've read a dozen times since June. Recipes, to-do lists, diary entries. Just like mine. After half an hour, I slam the book shut, frustrated. The only difference between our books are the medicinal concoctions mine includes. And that several days are missing from my mother's diary section.

The missing entries are scattered, random, and barely occur twice a year. The skipped dates are a little odd; she was a prolific diarist. But it wasn't out of the realm of possibility that she had days where she was too busy to write. Besides, even on the days she did write, there is no grand answer, no reason for naming me a hedge witch.

"It was just a dream," I say to Merlin. "Not every dream is a prophecy."

Putting my mother's book back in its cubby, I settle again into the chair by my fireplace and pull out some needlework, deciding I've had enough crochet for the week after last night's adventure. My current needlework project is a shawl of silvery stars I'm embroidering for Celeste's birthday. Nine passes, ten passes, eleven passes. My eyes grow heavy and my wrist sore as I count out my final row of stitches. As I cut the final silver thread, Merlin jerks awake and bolts to the front door.

"Did something out there startle you, little wizard?" I ask lazily. His ears are perked, his head tilted. He lets out a soft chirp. A strong rapid knocking on the door breaks through the sound of the storm.

My eyes flicker to the broom on my table as I anxiously wrack through my brain. No babies are due in town that I know of—at least none whose mother wishes for a midwife. Anyone sick would likely wait until the storm cleared. Could it be Miranda, demanding to know why I haven't responded to her letter? No. Not even she's that insistent.

Quietly, I rise from the chair and grab my sharp fire poker from its hook. From one of the cubbies in my desk, I grab a silk sachet full of rue leaves and slip it into my pocket. I walk to my door and peek through the small viewing slit. A tall figure is standing on the stoop, draped in shadow and dripping wet from the rain. Cracking open the door, I peer outside. The light from the fire casts a dim glow on the shadow's face. My breath leaves my lungs as I catch the scent of cinnamon and recognize the man on my porch.

"Hecate Goodwin." He grins at me through the rain. "Just the witch I was looking for."

CHAPTER FOUR

An Ancient Duty

I haven't seen Matthew Cypher in ten years. Days before my twenty-first birthday, leaders from nearly a dozen different covens had gathered in Ipswich to discuss a group of teenagers who were practicing magic dangerously in the Midwest. The leaders had stayed at Goodwin Manor for a week as they strategized how to deal with the rogue members of the Michigan Six. I spent that time running around the kitchen, cooking from my mother's Recipe Book while she, Margaret, and Winifred hosted the congregation.

On the third day, Matthew and his father, Malcolm Cypher, had shown up to the council uninvited. Before I'd known who he was, Matthew and I forged a quick friendship as the only two twenty-somethings of the group. I snuck him down to the—at the time—derelict gatekeeper's cottage that sat at the edge of our property. We'd split a bottle of cinnamon mead from my mother's pantry, and I'd told him of all my plans to convert the cottage into a true home of my own once I turned twenty-one.

When my mother found us tipsy among the dust motes of the abandoned cottage, she'd been furious with me. It was then that she told me the truth: Matthew was not some harmless hexan from the southern or Rocky Mountain covens; he was the heir to the Pacific Gate. I've never forgotten the smug smile on Matthew's face as his deception came to light. He's wearing that same smirk now.

"Aren't you going to invite me in?" he asks, his grin only widening at my shocked face. His dark chestnut hair looks black against the rainy night, but his eyes, glacial lake blue, are just as vivid as I remember.

"What do you want?" I ask him through the cracked door, still gripping my fire poker.

"Sanctuary," he says bluntly.

I scoff. "You can't be serious?"

"Are you or are you not the hedge witch?"

"That duty is archaic," I protest. There is no way I will offer housing and protection to a hexan from the Pacific Gate. "What are you even doing in town, Matthew?"

His head perks, amused surprise flashing across his face.

"Invite me in and I'll tell you." He smirks again. My eyes narrow at the smug look.

"I think not," I say firmly. The ghost of my twenty-year-old self smiles in satisfaction as I shut the door in his surprised face.

My small victory lasts only a moment before a flurry of turning pages calls my attention toward my desk. My Herbal, making its opinion known as always, flips open to a most inconvenient page.

The Duties of a Hedge Witch

Though she will exist on the boundaries of society and coven alike, a hedge witch's role is a vital one. A source of healing, sanctuary, and hope, she is to offer shelter, aid, and an ear to those who need it.

It's the first page I ever wrote in my Herbal. I always disliked it, seeing the small paragraph sitting dead center in an otherwise empty page. My mother had made me write the paragraph dozens of times, dissatisfied with my messy handwriting and the hasty sketches I drew to make the page feel fuller. Even after I was able to produce semilegible script, my Herbal continued to deem the page unworthy. As soon as I finished writing the words, the paper would come loose from the binding of the book and scatter into ash.

"Winifred made yours more temperamental than usual." Mom had laughed after the six or seventh attempt.

"A temperamental spell book for a temperamental witch," Miranda had sneered.

Eventually my mother poured a teaspoon of her piping hot Seal-It-In Spun Sugar on the page to prevent the Herbal from discarding it. The crystalized scorch mark is shaped like an accusatory finger, pointing at me in disapproval as I consider the page.

"Fine," I grumble, rolling my eyes.

Stomping back over to the entryway, I throw open the door. Matthew is leaning against one of the wooden posts of my porch, running a hand through his dripping hair. He looks exhausted, muddy, and soaked through, as if he's been walking for miles. There is no sign of a car nearby, and it is a long way into town.

A part of me does feel for him when he looks up at me hopefully, all smugness gone from his expression. Still, I shake my head.

"Hedge witch or not, I am never required to put myself in direct danger," I say firmly. He is still a hexan of the Pacific Gate. And given how we'd last parted, how could he possibly expect me to let him into my home again?

Matthew's mouth opens, and he squints at me, almost in bewilderment, before closing his eyes and giving a soft laugh of disbelief. When he opens them, he stares at me intently and leans in toward the door.

"Well met, Hecate. A curse upon me, I swear I mean no harm to you." His voice is barely a whisper, but the power of it sinks all the way to my core.

An irrevocable oath.

After receiving such a promise, it would be a direct violation of my magic to deny him shelter.

"One minute," I say, resigned. I quickly close the door again and run toward my stovetop, grabbing my olivewood salt keeper. I sprint back and sprinkle a line of coarse salt across my entryway. Another one of my mother's wisdoms: *A line of salt prevents evil from entering your home. A broken line reveals dark intentions.*

I open the door to meet his confused but amused face.

"I warn you now, any mischief and I'll enact a curse that will follow your children and your children's children for the next two hundred years," I say, stepping out of his way. He needn't know how empty the threat is. I couldn't even curse warts onto a toad.

He laughs and holds his hands up as he crosses my threshold. "I don't bite the hands that feed me."

The wooden floor creaks beneath his waterlogged shoes. But the line of salt remains undisturbed. My shoulders relax slightly, and I close the door, muting the noises of the storm.

Matthew stands in the entry and takes in my cottage. His eyes flick from the roaring fire to the lumpy upholstered sofa covered in chunky knitted throw blankets, to the dried herbs hanging from the ceiling.

"Cozy," he says, looking at the crocheted decorations and wreath in the kitchen window as he unbuttons his wet, woolen gray coat. "You've done well with the place."

"It does the trick," I mumble. It's strange having him here. The last time we'd stood in this room together, it had been little more than a dusty ruin. I'd told him how this cottage was my place of refuge from my family. How I would spend countless afternoons here after my father got sick with leukemia. How the derelict walls were my escape from the sadness of the manor after he passed. Miranda and Celeste both hated the cottage, convinced it was haunted by a long-dead groundskeeper, a rumor I had started myself to keep them away from my sanctuary. The cottage, even in its ruined state, was the place

I loved most in the world. The place I wanted to be whenever I was away from it. It was my home.

I'd told Matthew all of this. As I spoke, he had looked at me with such interest, such care and understanding, that I had been convinced I'd made my first true friend. At the time, I thought we bonded over a shared desire to find a sense of belonging, a sense of home. But looking back on it, he must have seen my loneliness and vulnerability as weaknesses. And he'd delighted in playing along to fool me.

Matthew gracefully drapes his coat over his arm. Underneath, he is wearing slate pants and a deep midnight-blue V-neck sweater. The edges of a baby-blue collared shirt are visible at his neckline and wrists. He is taller than I remember, the longer I stare at him, the more space he takes up. He smirks, noticing my gaze.

"I can hang that for you," I say, averting my eyes toward his coat.

"Thank you," he says as I reach for it. It is soaked through, heavy. For a moment our hands brush. I flinch away, trying to hide how my hands shake with nerves. He is unusually warm to the touch, despite coming in from the storm.

"Would you like something to eat?" I ask as I hang his coat on the stand near my door. Blessedly, my voice is not nearly as shaky as my hands.

"Thank you." He smiles in relief, eyeing the leftover dinner still on my stove. I take the broom off my small table, and usher him to sit.

I assemble a bowl of the leftover meal and place it in front of him, along with a fork and a sage-green cloth napkin. Merlin jumps up onto the table, intending to inspect this new source of food. I scoop him up in my arms.

"Anything else?" I ask, holding too tightly onto Merlin as I force myself to look at Matthew. I want nothing more than to leave the front of the cottage and barricade myself in my room. A Pacific Gate hexan. The heir to that coven, no less. I grew up hearing horror stories of the forbidden magic that is allowed to run rampant on the other coast. And now I've welcomed the second-highest-ranking member to my dinner table. Five minutes ago I had been dozing off by the fire. *How did this happen?*

"Some salt, please," Matthew replies. "Preferably a variety that hasn't been sprinkled over your front threshold. If you don't mind."

I force myself not to immediately glance toward my door. Merlin takes my surprised distraction as an opportunity to escape my arms.

"I think you'll find the meal is seasoned well enough, actually." I try to make my voice stern, but it has the same subtle softness I've never been able to fully chisel away, even in my angriest moments.

"If you say so." Matthew grins. He piles a portion of the pasta and burrata cheese onto his fork and takes a bite.

The change in his expression is immediate. Now it's my turn to smirk. Even lukewarm, this recipe is always outstanding. The emotions on his face shift as every new flavor hits. Initial surprise morphs into astonishment, which in turn becomes appreciative curiosity. And still, beneath all that, there are echoes of sadness in his eyes. The edges of my grief must have spilled over into the dish as I cooked it.

"Wow," he breathes before taking another bite, bigger this time.

"Still think it needs salt?" I ask.

He has the decency to look chagrined. "Can all Atlantic Key witches cook like this?"

"Only ones trained by Sybil Goodwin," I answer honestly. He takes another bite before leaning back into his chair.

"I'll never forget the food the last time I was in Ipswich. There must have been three dozen witches and hexans crammed into your house, all fighting for time to speak to the congregation. Madhouse. The only peace came at mealtimes. The Texan Hexans ate out of the palm of your mother's hand."

"I remember," I say. Chill-Out Chili served with Butter 'Em Up Dinner Rolls. As soon as the southern coven had arrived with their blustering, aggressive attitudes, we had shifted the menu around. It had taken all the chili powder in our pantry but had done its intended job. Or so I had been told. I'd been exiled from the house before I got to see its effects. *Exiled because of Matthew,* I remind myself, determined not to get too friendly. My mother had seen to it that both Celeste and I were removed from the Manor for a few days after my disobedience. Miranda, on her honeymoon, had missed the drama. We went to the Bennet farm, where Rebecca kept a watchful eye over us, and we in turn entertained a five-year-old Ginny with small shows of practical magic and tarot readings. By the time we were allowed to return home, the other covens had left to carry out judgement on the Michigan Six.

"My father forbade me to touch another of your mother's meals after that first dinner." Matthew laughs.

"That was wise of him," I say. He grins.

I'm surprised by his trust as he takes another bite of food. Perhaps he doesn't realize how extensively my mother trained me in kitchen magic. Regardless, the pasta I made tonight is perfectly safe. But he doesn't know that.

"I was very sorry to hear of her passing last June," Matthew says, studying me as I study him. He looks at me with a sincerity I don't trust. It has to be my own residual grief still present in his meal. I turn away from him and start wiping my counters with a clean rag, swallowing repeatedly to banish the lump in the back of my throat. He doesn't push the subject further. The only sound for the next few minutes is his fork scraping against the edges of his bowl.

I put away pots and pans as he finishes his meal. Every so often, I twist my head to stare at him out of the corner of my eye. He is the glaring anomaly in my perfect home, a mess I can't wipe away with my rag.

"So, Matthew Cypher . . ." I say when there is nothing left to clean.

"Yes, Hecate Goodwin?" he says in response, patiently waiting.

"Kate, please," I correct him.

"Kate, then." He smiles.

"What is a hexan from the Pacific Gate doing in Ipswich? Have you come to ruffle the feathers of all the women of the Atlantic Key? Or just me?"

He grins. "That wasn't my reason for coming. Though I would be lying if I said it wasn't entertaining to see how easy it is to ruffle you all."

I let out a little huff of annoyance, but he isn't wrong. We can be a flighty, jumpy bunch.

"Do you think my presence will be noticed?" he asks.

I nod. "If you're seen, it will be the talk of the coven."

"Well," he says casually, "I do intend to be seen. So I guess we have that to look forward to while I'm here."

I frown at his use of *we*, as if he and I are now on the same side simply because I am allowing him to shelter in my home for the night.

"You didn't say why you were here," I remind him.

He nods. "No. I didn't."

I glare at him for a moment, though I know it doesn't look nearly as threatening as I would like. Matthew chuckles.

"I've come to collect some ingredients I need."

"What?" I scoff. "You traveled all the way to New England, seemingly spontaneously, given your need for sanctuary, just for a few ingredients?"

"Well, some are very rare ingredients," he offers. I frown in disbelief.

He relents. "I did leave in a hurry—you're right. My father and I had a small . . . disagreement. I thought it would be a good idea to get away for a bit. I'm in need of some plants that grow near this coast anyway, and I knew there was a hedge witch who could provide me sanctuary." He tips his head, acknowledging me. "Coming here was the choice that made the most sense."

My frown deepens. "My sanctuary is not meant to shield people from petty family drama."

Matthew tsks. "It was a *bit* more than petty drama," he says.

"So, I'm housing a fugitive of the Pacific Gate?" That thought is deeply unappealing. With my luck, half of Matthew's coven will show up on my doorstep in the morning, looking for their wayward heir.

He shakes his head. "I'm no fugitive. My father's anger flares fast, but it dies just as quickly. I'm hoping by the time I've done all I need to do here, he will have moved past our disagreement."

"Well, at least tell me the ingredients that you need." I say. If I can get him his supplies, then perhaps he can leave and wait somewhere else for his father to calm down.

Matthew's lips twitch, and I suspect he knows exactly why I made that demand.

"One of them is night-blooming ipomoea harvested on Samhain."

I stifle the groan inside me. Moonvine. I have some in my garden at this moment. But it will be useless to him unless picked in six days' time.

"That's irritatingly specific," I say.

Matthew shrugs. "My craft tends to be demanding."

"And what is your craft?" I ask bluntly, curiosity flaring. I'd never asked ten years ago.

His eyebrows shoot up in surprise at my question. The energy of my cottage shifts. It's Matthew's powers mixing in the air of my own, confusing me, throwing me off balance. I had forgotten how palpable his presence could be.

"That's quite personal," he teases.

"Well, you know I'm a hedge witch," I grumble, embarrassed by my faux pas.

"True." He grins, then hesitates for a moment, and I can almost convince myself I see a flicker of uncertainty before he speaks again. "I study shadow magic."

The euphemism is not lost on me, and my whole body goes cold. He's a necromancer!

Shadow magic is rare, almost as rare as hedge craft. It is also one of the darkest magics a witch or hexan can practice. Of course, it is forbidden to members of the Atlantic Key. I can only imagine how my mother would have reacted, knowing I was harboring a necromancer.

Miranda too would be horrified. Celeste . . . well, Celeste would probably overlook his coven connections and spend the entire night flirting with him. He was exactly her type. Tall, dark hair, gorgeous blue eyes, with an incredible jawline. And powerful.

I turn away from him and walk back to my kitchen counter, willing myself not to react to what he has told me or blush at my own thoughts.

I can feel his stare on the back of my neck.

"Like I said, easily ruffled," Matthew laughs softly behind me, but there's an edge to his tone.

I had been reaching for a coffee mug, to make him something warm to drink, but I grimace at his taunts. Let him freeze. What do I care?

"I'm going to bed," I say abruptly, turning around. He looks at me in surprise but rises from the table.

"Of course," he says. "I'm sure you've had a long day."

He has no idea.

"The guest bedroom is this way." I point toward the hallway door.

"I remember," he says.

I try not to react to the casual way he references our first meeting, but my neck heats. I allow him to take the lead, not wanting my back turned to him at any moment.

The guest room is cleaner than it was when he was last here. Rotten floorboards replaced with strong wood planks, the walls cleared of dust and cobwebs, but it is still the sparsest room in my cottage. A queen bed, one small side table, and a tiny chest of drawers with some guest towels inside that have never been used.

Matthew looks around the room in approval.

"This is perfect, thank you," he says. In any other circumstance, I would laugh. The bare-bones room is hardly perfect.

"Do you need dry clothes? Pajamas?" I ask. His sweater and shirt are bone dry, but his pants are soaked below the knee.

"No, I don't wear clothes when I sleep," he says, his grin lighting up the darkness. He is trying to get a rise out of me again.

"How interesting. Neither do I," I shoot back quickly, refusing to be caught off guard. A little thrill shoots through me as I catch his eyes widening. "But unless you want to wash your own sheets, I suggest you keep your clothes on tonight."

"As you wish," he mumbles.

"Goodnight, Matthew," I say, pleased at having successfully shut him up.

"Sleep well, Kate," he whispers as the door creaks shut.

For half a second, I stand still, my mind reeling over the situation. Pulling the rue sachet out of my pocket, I bend down and hold three fingers to the guest room door.

"I ask for your protections," I whisper quietly, drawing intention from the inherent evil-repelling qualities of the plants in the pouch.

Slowly, I draw a long arching circle around the wooden frame and let my body fill with panicked energy. Then, with a violent motion, I slash through the invisible circle I've drawn and wedge the rue pouch just under the threshold. If Matthew opens this door, an alarm as loud as a banshee scream will ring in my mind. It's a simple ward that will last only until dawn, but I feel better.

Then, as fast as possible, I change into a clean nightgown, brush my teeth, and climb under my covers. It takes over an hour for my mind to calm down from the strange turn the evening has taken, but eventually I do fall asleep, all the while knowing that the safe light of dawn cannot come soon enough.

CHAPTER FIVE
What Nightmares May Come?

The field near the manor bursts with spring wildflowers that blow in the sea breeze. The grass tickles my feet as I run through the dew with Mom and Miranda while Celeste chases us. My sisters are both young, Celeste no older than six. She claims furtively that she touched Miranda's hair and is no longer "it." A fifteen-year-old Miranda laughs and snootily says that hair doesn't count. Tears well up in Celeste's eyes, and she runs away. Mom gives Miranda a look of disapproval, and they both rush after Celeste.

I want to join them, to console my little sister. But my legs don't move, trapped in the vines that run all along the field. I grab at them, trying to free myself. A few break away, but there is a particularly thick vine that is tougher to snap. With both of my hands, I grab hold of its snaking stem, where it is curled over my right ankle. I yank as hard as my arms are able. It begins to pull through. As it does, I spy movement twisting through the field. The vine wrapped around my ankle has also twined itself into the ground all around the grassy area, like a strand of thread in embroidery work. I pull and pull until the vine is free.

The ground I disturbed begins to grumble and shake, unstable now that the thread holding it together has been removed. A fissure erupts below me, and chunks of earth drop away into nothingness. With a scream, I fall. But my arms catch on the edge of the cliff face that has formed in our front yard. Below me, a gaping chasm stretches down into absolute darkness. I scream for my life, my wild eyes searching for my family. Mom is across the field, picking up Celeste and comforting her. Miranda strokes her hair, apologizes. They cannot see or hear my panic. Despair settles over me, but still, futilely, I scream for them.

The ground rumbles again, trying to shake me loose off the solid earth. Somewhere in the abyss beneath me, dark laughter echoes. I shriek in fear one final time as my fingers are pulled from the cliff edge, and I fall backward into hell.

CHAPTER SIX
Five Days Until Halloween

I bolt upright. The barest hints of dawn light gild the edges of my windows. The sheets around my legs are a tangled mess. A sign of a restless night.

"Strange dreams again," I mutter, climbing out of bed. At this rate, I will be thoroughly exhausted by Halloween. My hands shake as I tie my hair into a low ponytail with a green silk ribbon. Whenever I am this unsettled, there is one tried and true cure. The forest. Merlin is curled up on his chair, still fast asleep, and takes no notice as I leave. I light my fire before grabbing my herb basket and walking out of the cottage.

It's misty this morning as I approach the woods. The dull, scattered light washes out all the red tones of my hair, turning it the color of late summer straw. Yesterday's storm brought a drop in temperature, and with it, the full throes of fall. It will not rise above fifty degrees until spring. Before I enter the forest, I place my hand on the maple tree I dedicated my craft to.

"I ask to walk these woods and take of your bounty," I say in a hushed tone.

Gnarled limbs greet me, and the approving spirit of the forest thrums in the bark. I slip past the tree line, venturing deeper into the wild green. The memory of my nightmare causes me to walk with lighter steps than normal. Thankfully, the forest floor remains solid as I traverse the natural roads that exist between the trees, breathing in the morning air. The verdant smell of moss growing on the bark of ancient white pines returns my mind to me, and roaming deer make their way past without flinching or taking much notice of my presence.

Surrounded by silence, I gather whatever offerings I can find. Pinecones and other small sticks that will be good kindling through the rest of the week and months to come. The weight of my basket grows as I harvest crab apples, chokeberries, nettle, and even a few sprigs of winterberries. Despite its shrouded canopy and general gloomy weather, this forest never fails to provide.

As a young witch in training, I'd forage among the roots with Celeste, my constant raven-haired shadow, who was frightened of the woods. She would wait at the edge of the tree line, sniffling softly until I came back to her, my hoard in hand. Nettles for soups and teas, knotweed, dandelions, and acorns for tinctures and pies. Maple syrup in the spring thaw and berries and mushrooms all throughout the warm summer.

I always had a natural talent for distinguishing nutritional plants from deadly ones, though my mother encouraged me to gather any and all things that I found.

"The poison is in the dose . . . and in the intention," she used to say with a wink whenever I handed her wild foxglove or hemlock. I never saw her cook with them, yet their glass containers in the pantry would slowly empty out every year.

As the morning mists begin to lift, I come upon a pile of bones and feathers scattered around the base of a tree. A small bird left its nest too soon and has been made prey. Unusual for this time of year. Its tiny skull is picked clean of flesh, but it's unfractured. Gingerly, I pick up the skull. It's strange in my hands, the stinging feeling of a limb fallen asleep. Cold and hot all at once. I grimace, still unused to the energy of death. It's a rare sensation. In my practice, life surrounds me, vibrant and thriving. Death is emptiness and heaviness all at once. There had been a day, as a teenager, when I'd found a young fawn among the trees, recently dead and scavenged. My mother had been with me, and when I went to inspect the bones, she grabbed me roughly by the shoulders and scolded me.

"You must never touch the dead, Hecate," she had demanded. It was a lesson she'd drilled into me many times before. "It could interfere with your magic."

When I'd rebelled, wrenching from her and making another move toward the bones of the fawn, her free hand came down and struck my cheek with a sharp crack. It was the only time in my life that she ever hit me.

Never touch the dead. It was one of her most sacred rules.

And it was one I had broken the day she died. In the very moment that I'd lost my mother, I'd been introduced to the writhing electric wrongness that was death energy. I hadn't realized at first, when I saw her sprawled out on the kitchen floor, a pot of boiling water unattended on the stove. I try not to remember the way my hand had begun to sting when I'd touched her still-warm cheek and stared into her lifeless eyes. A stroke. Dead before she hit the ground. Almost two decades of studying medicinal magic, and there was nothing I could have done to help her.

I inhale sharply, my head spinning. I try to bring myself back into the forest. Into the present. I place a shaking hand against the cool earth, digging my fingers beneath the layer of pine needles. The life energy of the soil, the connection of the tree roots below, calls out to me. First, a feeling of welcoming joy, a celebration of the living force being recognized. But beyond that, there is a nervous unsettled thrum. An off-kilter beat that rises from the ground and pulses into my blood.

"All will be well," I whisper, both in hope and incantation.

I take a deep breath, inhaling the life all around me, marred only by the stinging signal of the tiny pile of bones. After a few moments, a few counted breaths, my mind calms.

I place the skull back down, letting the bird rest, and gather my heavy basket onto my hip. It's time to return. Merlin will be desperate for breakfast by now. I walk barefoot across the forest floor, using my hands to ground myself into the trees and find my way home. As I come out of the woods, I freeze. A figure stands in my garden. Matthew Cypher.

Somehow, in the haze of my nightmares and anguished memories, I had completely forgotten him. I survived the night with a necromancer in my house.

I'm almost impressed with myself. But I quickly rebuke that train of thought. I "survived" nothing. Matthew has been a perfectly acceptable houseguest.

His blue eyes are vibrant in the mist. He is in the same clothes as last night, though they are wrinkle-free.

"Good morning, Kate," he says. For a brief second, his gaze travels over my body. But then, his head snaps away; he lets out a small cough and becomes very invested in my bed of New England asters.

A slow wave of embarrassment crawls along my skin. The damp morning has made my nightgown stick to the curves of my body, the fabric almost see-through. I clutch the herb basket to my chest, giving Matthew a curt nod, and rush quickly inside.

"Well done, Kate," I murmur in exasperation upon reaching my room. "While you're at it, go ahead and do a strip tease for customers next time you stop by the Raven & Crone."

As I berate myself, I quickly change into slim black pants and a red, orange, and gold checkered flannel shirt, leaving no button undone. In the time it takes for my embarrassment to fully subside, I brush my teeth, wash my face, and braid my hair into a series of plaits that twist together and cascade down my back.

Matthew is sitting in my reading chair by a crackling fire when I finally emerge. Merlin is curled happily on his lap, purring. I stare at the scene with some bemusement. Merlin is typically an aloof cat when it comes to humans other than myself and Celeste. He only barely tolerates Miranda, and yet here he is sleeping soundly as Matthew pets him absentmindedly. I watch the unusual pair for a few moments before letting out a quiet cough.

As soon as Mathew sees me, he moves to stand, but I stop him.

"No, stay where you are," I say. "Merlin won't appreciate being jostled. He seems very comfortable." Matthew slowly lowers back into the seat. Merlin stretches out lazily from the movement but doesn't open his eyes.

"Good morning again," Matthew says.

"Good morning," I offer back. "Enjoying my fireplace?"

And my chair? And my cat?

"Very much so. I see you took my advice," he says, gesturing to the iron plate behind the flames. When I'd showed him this cottage in its dilapidated state ten years earlier, Matthew offered several suggestions for how to improve it, including a way to get the ancient hearth to efficiently heat the front room.

"Several people told me to get a fire plate when I started renovating," I say walking into the kitchen, refusing to let him take exclusive credit. He smirks.

As soon as I grab a small tin of wet cat food, the clinging of a jingle bell rings out, and soft paws thud against wood as a scampering Merlin arrives at my feet. He mews until I set his bowl down.

Matthew laughs quietly as he rises from the chair and joins me in the kitchen. He watches as I pull out the large bowl of muesli from my fridge. I also grab a bowl of strawberries, a couple of figs, and a cinnamon stick from one of my many spice racks.

"I have a bike you can take into town," I say curtly to Matthew as I use my pestle to grind the cinnamon in my mortar. "Ann McAlister runs the Ipswich Inn. Rooms are rare this time of year, but Ann always holds one for emergencies." And she owes me a favor. I'd cured her eldest son's acne in time for prom two years ago.

"And Rebecca at the Raven & Crone Apothecary can help you get some rarer ingredients. She might even have some Samhain-harvested moonvine from last year." I send out a little prayer that she will come through and get this man on his way. "Also, Ann's husband is a mechanic. He can tow your car."

Matthew lets out an amused breath. "I don't have a car that needs towing."

I pause preparing breakfast for a moment and look at him.

"Then why . . . ?" I stop myself.

I had assumed he'd broken down on some muddy rural road and hiked all the way to my door. He looks at me expectantly, as if guessing the train of my thoughts. He must have traveled here by more magical means. I'm curious but refuse to give him the satisfaction of asking. If he wishes to be mysterious and strange, then fine. I will not go out of my way to indulge him.

"All right. But you'll be needing a room at the Ipswich Inn. So, the offer to borrow my bike stands."

"You've certainly planned my day out for me." The amusement has not left his voice.

"Well, I assumed you would be eager to gather your ingredients and get home." Now that I know he works with shadow magic, I don't want to think too hard about how those ingredients will be used.

"An understandable assumption," he agrees. "But I should give my father a day or two to cool down."

"What did you two fight about, anyway?" I ask. It had to be something serious, to send Matthew to the opposite end of the continent. For the quickest of seconds, the good humor vanishes from his eyes, but it's back just as quickly as he flashes me a bright smile.

"Let's just say differences in ideology," he offers. Before I can roll my eyes at his constant evasion, he continues. "Nothing that won't eventually be forgiven. But as I said, he'll need a few days. And I certainly don't see the point in bothering with a local inn. Can I not just stay here?"

The knife I am using to slice the strawberries almost slips from my hand, and my heart begins to race.

"Last night was an emergency, and I fulfilled my duty to you. But I'm too busy this week to continue playing hostess." My voice stutters a bit through my surprise.

Matthew studies me. "Oh? Big plans for Samhain?"

"Yes, actually. If you must know," I say, "my sisters are coming home for the holiday and will expect all the bells and whistles that accompany its traditions. I'm going to be spending all week opening up the Manor, getting supplies, cooking, and decorating. And I would prefer not to leave someone alone in my cottage all day." I hadn't thought of Miranda's note since Matthew arrived yesterday. But I'm not technically lying. And yet, as I say it all aloud, the enormity of the project weighs down on me.

I gather up the berries and spices and stir them into the bowl of muesli. For a final touch, I arrange a single sliced strawberry into a sunburst in the center and drizzle a small spoonful of honey over the top. I hand Matthew the bowl, which he takes eagerly.

"Why would having me stay here alone be an issue?" he asks. I instinctively bristle at the pushiness of the question, but the inflection in his voice suggests he is simply curious. Still, I'm defensive.

"For starters, the last time I invited you to this cottage, you spent the entire afternoon lying to me."

Matthew's eyebrows shoot up in surprise. "I never lied to you," he says, mystified.

I scoff. "You told me you were a Texan hexan!"

He shakes his head and holds up a finger. "Ah, see we disagree there. You *assumed* my affiliation. I never claimed to be of that coven."

"Well . . . you . . ." I stutter for a moment. Of course I had assumed that was his coven. Most covens are matriarchies. And the hexans from the Rocky Mountains all have a certain . . . granola look to them. Texas was the obvious choice. I never would have dreamed that members of the Pacific Gate would show their faces on the East Coast, not when their rivalry with the Atlantic Key stretches back so many years.

"You never corrected me," I finally say. "I kept asking if you liked to ride horses! And at one point I think I even requested you describe Texas to me." My cheeks warm at the embarrassing memories. Matthew looks sheepish, but he can't seem to help the grin on his face.

"If I recall, I told you I love riding horses, which is true, and I answered honestly that I thought Texas was a lovely state, if a bit hot."

I groan in annoyance at all these technical truths. Matthew puts a hand up.

"I surrender. I'm sorry. You're right, I behaved badly. I was curious about you and was worried you'd reject me if I corrected your assumption about my coven."

And I had. The moment my mother found us and told me Matthew was heir to the Pacific Gate, I'd fled.

"Regardless of all that, I don't like having my home invaded. I wouldn't be able to stop worrying about you being here while I'm out and about. And I can't be distracted while trying to get ready for the celebrations."

"I could always assist as a sort of payment," he offers. "And if I'm helping you, then I'm not left here all alone. An idea which seems to torture your psyche."

He gives me a crooked grin before taking a bite of the muesli. The teasing in his eyes disappears as he eats the oats appreciatively.

"Assist how, exactly?" I question with a grimace.

"With decorating and prepping," he says as if it's the most obvious answer in the world.

"How could you possibly help?"

"We do celebrate New Year's in the Pacific, you know," he says sardonically before taking another bite.

I have no response for him. It's not every day a necromancer offers to help you carve pumpkins and dust an old house. Before I can think of something to say, he continues.

"Besides, you shouldn't be forced to take on all the work yourself. Not when you should focus on your birthday."

I shake my head. How could he possibly still remember that detail?

"I've always had to share the spotlight on my birthday. This year will be no different." I begin tidying the kitchen, nestling dirty dishes into the sink.

"But you're turning thirty-one this year," Matthew insists.

"Yes. I know."

"Don't you need to prepare? Aren't you nervous?" he pushes.

"Why should I be?" I respond. He sets his bowl aside.

"I don't know," he says. "It's your coven with all the rules regarding magic. I would be nervous if my craft was about to be taken away from me by a power-hungry meta-magic witch."

Is that what this is about? The Containment? I want to laugh.

"The Containment doesn't take away magic we *want*. It lets us focus on what we know we're good at. By blocking unnecessary avenues to magic, our chosen craft strengthens. It increases the likelihood that our intention works."

Matthew shakes his head, and his dark hair rustles with the movement. "I could never imagine being so restricted."

"Well, I could never imagine being so scattered and unspecialized. So, I guess we each have our own way of viewing things," I shoot back, crossing my arms.

"Perhaps." He frowns.

The word hangs between us as we stare at each other. Merlin is nibbling happily from the bowl of muesli that Matthew abandoned. Neither of us admonish him. We are locked into each other, neither one willing to be the first to break.

The tension is interrupted by the familiar sound of a crashing wave knocking against my front door. I jump and Matthew rises immediately from his chair.

"Who's there?" he calls out, forcefully.

"It's fine," I assure him, rushing past to the front of the cottage. "It's just my sister. She's always had a flair for the dramatic."

He grabs my arm before I can open my door. "Wait," he urges. I do, mostly shocked into compliance at the touch.

Matthew softens his grip but keeps one hand around my arm as he looks out the small window on the side of my cottage.

"It isn't your sister," he says tensely. His eyes scan the forest and the hill that leads up to the manor house. "There's no one there."

I laugh and pull myself free from his grasp. He reluctantly lets me go.

"Trust me. That was Miranda. She always needs to be certain her will is known." If you caught her on an especially bad day, there was the risk that she might use her Siren song against you, one of the many tools in her kit that she uses to get her way. I open my door, and sure enough, there is another letter on my stoop, damp and smelling of salt. The scent is more potent today. Fishier. I sigh. She's annoyed with me. I rip open the envelope and read the contents.

Hecate,

I have yet to hear from you confirming the plans for the end of the week. Are you not aware that this is urgent? Please let me know you are alive and that things at the Manor will be in order for Celeste's and my arrival! If it would be easier for you, we could stay at your cottage, even though you know I detest it. Twenty-four coven members have already said they will be present for Samhain. I expect more to confirm in the following days and will send updates so you can adjust the menus accordingly. Get back to me ASAP on this. Not kidding around.

~Miranda Helenia Spence Goodwin

Despite myself, I let out a few short giggles at Miranda's note. Matthew walks up behind me, and I don't try to hide the letter from him as he reads over my shoulder.

"She's a bit demanding, isn't she?" he says with slight horror. All the tension has left his voice.

"If I were brave, I would ignore this letter and the twenty panicky ones that will follow. Let her figure the holidays out for herself," I say. Matthew looks at me in conspiratorial delight.

"So do it. It would be no more inconsiderate than what she's expecting of you." For the first time since I saw him on the doorstep last night, my attitude toward Matthew Cypher warms ever so slightly. It is a rare occurrence in my life for someone to side with me against Miranda. With Matthew smiling at me, gleeful mischief in his eyes, I'm sorely tempted to follow his suggestion. Especially given the threat of Miranda staying at my place. Our energies never mix well in close quarters. I wouldn't be surprised if the cottage burned down by the end of her visit.

"I can't. Celeste would be devastated if I canceled," I say eventually, smiling as Matthew gives me a sad, mock-disappointed pout.

"However, does your offer to help still stand?" I ask, a strike of madness or genius hitting me.

"I'll do anything you require of me." He breaks out into a grin.

That's all the confirmation I need. I walk over to my desk, grab a pen, and flip my sister's letter over. On the back of the damp fishy paper I write,

Miranda,

The Manor will be ready for your arrival Thursday night. The cottage is not available. I have a guest staying with me.

Kate

A Dark and Secret Magic

I roll the letter up and wrap it with a string of dried elderflowers until almost no paper is visible. I light the silver-ash candle I keep on my desk and hold the letter over the flame, waiting. The fire is shimmery white, almost opalescent, and cool. It takes only seconds for the entire parcel to ignite and disappear from my hand like flash paper.

"There," I say, resigned. "No stopping them now." I never really had another option, but there had been something comforting in procrastinating my response.

"You can always change your mind," Matthew assures me.

"No need for that. I love this time of year and all the traditions that come with it. And now I have you as my excuse to keep Miranda from invading my actual home."

"I can stay here then?" he asks, pleased. I nod. His smile only grows. "I'm surprised," he admits. "With the salt line and the rue underneath my bedroom door last night, and all the talk of the Ipswich Inn, I didn't think I had a chance."

"Having a hexan of the Pacific Gate sleeping across the hall from me is a much less frightening prospect than playing hostess to Miranda," I confess.

Matthew laughs happily, and my own smile is involuntary. "And, my cat trusts you . . . so that's something, at least," I add.

As if on cue, Merlin brushes affectionately against Matthew's legs. I roll my eyes at him. Matthew bends down and gives him three long stroking pets.

Another thunderous watery crash echoes around my door. I groan in exasperation. Matthew wrenches the door open and scoffs as he bends down. He holds up the soggy yellow Post-it note that is stuck to my welcome mat.

That wasn't so hard now was it?
What do you mean you have a guest? Who is staying with you?

~Miranda Helenia Spence Goodwin

"She seems lovely, your sister." Matthew smirks, crumpling up the note and beckoning me outside the cottage.

"I am glad for the company to weather her demands," I admit as we walk.

"Even despite how strange said company may be?" he teases.

"Yes, very strange." I laugh. The horror I had felt last night over Matthew would be nothing compared to Miranda's mortification once she discovers her hermetic sister is housing a practitioner of the forbidden crafts.

CHAPTER SEVEN
Toil and Trouble

With washed-out red brick and a subtle Tudor Revival influence, Goodwin Manor stands three stories tall at the top of a large hill. It has been in our family since the late nineteenth century and has more windows and chimneys than one can count. The lawn is perfectly manicured despite the lack of a gardening service for several decades. The manor looks over the painter's palette landscape of Ipswich's autumnal forests from the back and a view of the glistening blue-black ocean from the front.

I unlock the back door, and we walk inside the dark, silent house. The living room is a ghostly scene, every couch and cushion covered with white and gray sheets.

"There's nothing quite so strange as walking into a place once full of laughter and life and finding it silent." I voice the thought before I have time to censor it.

"Well, there's no one better than a hedge witch to bring something back to life, right?" Matthew says next to me, his voice and eyes soft.

I laugh quietly. "If only that were within my reach. Besides, isn't that more your expertise?"

He gives me a quizzical look but shakes his head. "Shadow magic can't create life."

"Pity," I murmur. I move forward and begin yanking bedsheets off the furniture. After a moment, Matthew joins me in the chore.

When he learns exactly how the sheets need to be folded, I leave him in the family room and make my way to the kitchen. Shimmering copper cookware lines the exposed brick walls. I pull one of my mother's small sauce pots from the rack above the island and fill it with water. As it boils, I check all the appliances and dust the breakfast table. Once the water is roiling, I lower the temperature and drop in some dried spices from my mother's cabinet.

Nutmeg, allspice, bay, cinnamon, vanilla, and black tea leaves. With each new addition, I imagine the wooden floors and walls of the house absorbing the aroma of fall and welcoming in the changing energy of the new year.

The kitchen is spotless now and Matthew has made quick work of the family room, library, and dining room. All the furniture is uncovered, and every shutter has been flung open, allowing bright sunlight to stream in. The downstairs, dusted and aired, already looks transformed. With the scent of the simmer from the kitchen and the familiar October breeze from the windows, this could be a year ago. Back when the manor still had life. I almost expect my mother to walk into the living room and start giving us directions.

"What next?" Matthew asks from the dining room. He is staring out the window that looks on the side garden.

I catch my breath, leaving past years behind.

"The upstairs beds need to be made, and then decorations," I say, leading him out into the foyer and up the grand curving staircase. I sniff the air as we climb, pleased that my simmer pot has already begun to spread its scent to the second floor.

We head to Celeste's room first. The deep blue and antique gold room is full of her brass astronomical equipment and still smells of incense, even though she hasn't called the manor home in over four years. Matthew strips the cover sheet off her bed as I run a dust rag over the astrolabe she keeps on her side table.

"Are you still close? With your sisters?" he says aloud, watching as I carefully organize the zodiac figurines that line the shelf above Celeste's bedframe.

"You ask a lot of questions," I say.

He laughs. "A trait I inherited from my father, I'm afraid. He questions everything. Most suspicious man I've ever met."

"Another feature you have in common," I say lightly with a smirk. Matthew pauses his work and looks at me. I bite my lip.

"Sorry," I murmur, embarrassed by my rudeness. But he surprises me by laughing again.

"No. That was funny." He smiles. "And for what it's worth, I understand if you're suspicious of me."

"Oh, I most certainly am," I admit freely. Matthew seems unsurprised by this answer.

"So, your father is naturally suspicious . . . what about your mother?" Matthew knows an endless laundry list of facts about me. I'm eager to balance the scale. He doesn't seem bothered by my intrusive question.

"My mother's lovely," he says. "A very calming balance to my father's eccentricities."

"How so?" I wonder, continuing to dust.

He looks up at the ceiling as if wracking his brain for an answer.

"Well, when I was a boy, my father would play this game with me. Three truths and a lie?" He looks at me, questioning if I've heard of it.

I nod. I'd played it more than once with Miranda. She always seemed to win.

Matthew continues.

"He wanted to make sure I could tell when someone was lying to me. And that I could lie under pressure, in turn."

I grimace, though I'm unsurprised given what he's already said of his father and what I know of the Pacific Gate. They seem a paranoid, unsettled sort.

"My mother, though—she hated that game. Refused to play it with me."

He fiddles with the lace edges of Celeste's cover sheet, perfectly folded in his arms. I've abandoned my cleaning, watching him.

"I'd ask her to play Three Truths and a Lie, to practice. But instead, she'd insist on playing her own game: Four Absolute Truths." He smiles so softly it's like a whisper. "Then she'd prattle off three random facts, different every time, like the Earth is round, spiders are smaller than humans, candy corn is delicious." He laughs. "After that, she'd wrap me up in her arms and tell me her fourth absolute truth, the same one every time."

"Which was?" I ask. He looks up and meets my gaze.

"I love you," he says after a moment.

My heart clenches. What I'd give to hear my own mother say those words again, to see her walk through the bedroom door and tell me all would be well. I swallow. Matthew is staring at me, a pained expression in his eyes.

"I'm sorry," he says like he knows exactly where my mind went.

I clear my throat and walk over to Celeste's window, throwing open the dark velvet drapes so that sunlight can stream into the room. I stare down toward the side yard, my mother's garden blooming with autumnal foliage.

"This room is done. Once everything else is finished up here, we should pick some flowers from the garden to put in the bedrooms," I say, grateful my voice doesn't break.

Matthew shifts his feet, uncomfortable. "You may have to do that task alone. I'm not a good gardener."

"You wouldn't have to plant anything," I say, amused. "Just take a pair of kitchen shears to the overgrown purple sunflowers."

"Even so. I'd likely do more harm than good," he says somberly as I lead him out of Celeste's room and toward Miranda's.

"My craft, the intention I invite around me, makes it difficult to grow things. Life, struggles to flourish," he explains. "But I've always loved the sight of a healthy garden. As a boy, I would watch my aunt as she tended to her roses and pumpkins. I'd marvel at the transformations that would take place almost every day. But the more I practiced shadow craft, the less the garden changed. When my aunt eventually realized I was the cause of the stagnation, I was asked to stay away."

We fold Miranda's cover sheet together. My heart clenches again, and despite all my misgivings, I pity him.

"I'm sorry you were kept away from something you loved," I say.

Matthew stares at me strangely, as if confused by my sympathy.

"I don't know what I'd do if I couldn't walk through a garden every day," I say. Realization dawns in his eyes.

"Ah yes, well." He clears his throat. "I adapted quickly." He flashes a grin toward me.

"I'm also impressed at the intensity of your power," I admit. A hexan so connected to shadow craft that life struggles to flourish around him is a terrifying thought, but I try to keep my nervousness to myself.

"What's on the agenda for the next few days?" he asks, changing the subject as we finish uncovering Miranda's bed.

My mind turns back to the mental task list I'd been forming.

"Well, first we will have to make our way to the Bennet Farm to pick up pumpkins. Then I'll have to carve the pumpkins, which I'm admittedly dreading," I say, shaking my head. The pumpkins were always the chore that haunted me the most.

"Miranda and Celeste arrive on Thursday. There will be a dumb supper that night. Mischief night we usually spend preparing for Samhain. Though I'm sure Celeste will convince me to pull a prank or two. Saturday, we will go into Ipswich for the morning parade. Coven members will arrive at the manor in the late afternoon. And I'll spend the rest of the evening listening to dozens of women regale me with their marriage, health, and financial woes." I regret the sardonic tone that escapes me, but Matthew laughs.

"That's certainly an exciting way to spend your birthday."

I shrug. "It's my duty as a hedge witch."

"That's not the role of a hedge witch," Matthew says incredulously. I look at him blankly.

"Sure it is," I say. "I'm to offer shelter, aid, and an ear to those who need it. Be it person, animal, or plant." They are the very words my mother made me repeat over and over again that first year of my training. The very words my Herbal rejected until I knew them by heart.

"And?" Matthew says with another confused laugh, but this time it's almost nervous, as if he's hoping I'm joking.

"And what?" I say, bewildered.

His eyes flash toward me, studying my face, and I notice his grip tightens on the sheet in his hands.

"Hedge craft, first and foremost, is the balance between life and death energies. A hedge witch is guardian to the living and the dead alike."

I'm speechless for a moment.

"Hedge craft has nothing to do with death energy," I insist coolly. The very idea of an Atlantic Key witch meddling in such magic is absurd. What an absolutely wild thing for him to claim, as if my mother hadn't spent my whole childhood protecting me from exposure to death. As if the very feeling of death energy doesn't make me sick with its stinging rottenness.

Matthew blanches at my words. "Have you not been taught your craft?" he asks. A heavy sort of horror replaces the confusion in his eyes. "Did your mother show you nothing other than her kitchen tricks?" His voice becomes more agitated with every word.

I can feel my flush the instant it happens. My heart rate rises, and for a second, I'm thirteen again, standing in front of the coven and forest, convinced I'm not ready. I try to shake the memory off as my face grows stony.

"My mother's recipes were not *tricks*. She taught me everything she knew; I studied how to preserve and keep life. I learned to heal and protect."

"Admirable pursuits, yes," he says. "But not the entire picture of your craft. Did you ever learn Binding or Shadow Walking? Siphoning? Guiding?"

"No," I say firmly, not understanding any of the words he used. "That sounds like shadow magic. Which is forbidden."

"Not to a hedge witch!" he implores. "Good God! You have been left completely unprepared." He sounds panicked, but I don't care. I can barely keep my own voice from rising when I speak.

"My mother devoted herself to me and my sisters. I won't let you stand here, in her house, and insult her ability to train a witch. She was one of the thirteen elders of the Atlantic Key and one of only three witches in the whole coven who actually had any significant power, which she used to help people. Every golden strand of happiness in this town can be traced back to a meal she cooked at some point in her life."

Matthew grimaces. His eyes are hard and serious.

"Do you include yourself in that count?" he questions quietly. The tone of his voice makes me want to shiver.

"What count?" I ask, confused. I want to look away from him, but my eyes do not stray from his gaze.

"The three witches with significant power in the Atlantic Key. Do you count yourself as one of them? Do you believe yourself to be powerful?" he asks almost fiercely.

The question sits in the pit of my throat. "I'm a good healer. Great, even," I say.

He shakes his head.

"Answer the question, Kate," he insists.

It's not a simple question. Power can mean so many different things. Because of the Containment, Atlantic Key witches are very successful at their crafts. But most of us practice smaller and specialized magic; very few of us would be able to attempt anything on a large scale. Miranda certainly had never been able to conjure a tempest in all her years as a sea witch. But powerful compared to members of other covens? To Matthew, whose shadow craft is so strong it can cause whole gardens to wither at his mere presence?

"I can do more than most in the Atlantic Key," I say. "I have my mother's training to thank for that. But no, I'm not significantly powerful. Not the way she was. Not the way you seem to be."

Matthew's mouth shuts closed into a thin line, and his eyes widen in horrified anger.

"You're wrong," he says, looking out the open window toward the ocean. "And the fact that your own mother let you think so is—"

"What's it to you?" I interrupt, cutting him off as anger boils through me. My whole body has gone cold and hot within a matter of seconds.

His eyes flash back to meet mine. "Whether you are properly trained or not is of importance to every member of every coven. It's unforgivable. You have been left defenseless!" He looks aghast.

"Defenseless?" My head is spinning. "Against what?"

He opens his mouth to speak but closes it again sharply. He breathes but the pause doesn't seem to calm him. When he finally speaks, he is just as agitated as me—more so, even.

"Against all that you have been exposed to since the moment you declared yourself a hedge witch."

The air in the room is so thick with our separate intention that it is hard to breathe. My hands ball into fists, and something around Matthew sparks and crackles. I turn on my heel and storm out. Miranda's door blows shut behind me as I leave. Whether it was Matthew, the wind, or me, I can't tell.

"Who does he think he is?" I whisper to no one in particular as I stomp up the stairs to the third floor.

With more dramatic flair than I intend, I rip down the cord to the attic. The folded ceiling ladder opens with an almost violent crash. I let out a defeated breath as it shakes and trembles. I can't let too many negative emotions fill up this house. I'll never be able to purge them by Halloween. The coven members would be brawling with one another after a single cocktail. I take a few deep breaths and close my eyes, letting the anger seep away from me slowly.

I let other, happier things fill my mind. I think of sitting over a large pot of bubbling caramel. Listening to my mother's old record of Halloween music. Dancing with Celeste and Miranda to "Coolest Little Monster." The scent of spiced apples, sugar, and natural cleaning solutions.

I open my eyes as calmness washes over me, and I release a breath and climb the ladder.

The attic is dim at first, but after turning on a lamp, the whole room fills with warm orange light. Antique furniture, trunks filled with family treasure and trash, and dozens of sturdy cardboard boxes all fill up the floor space. Dust motes float through a single sunbeam coming from a small widow's watch window that looks out to the sea. In the corner where the holiday decorations are kept, there are roughly twenty boxes in total, ranging in size and shape. Inside are yards and yards of pumpkin garlands, orange and purple lights, spiderweb tablecloths, and every sort of Halloween knickknack imaginable. There are also boxes full of larger, heavier decorations, like cast-iron cauldrons and the metal broomstick lamps we use to line the front driveway.

"Oh, yikes," I whisper. In my anger, I had forgotten that this isn't a one-person task. Mom and I usually took an entire afternoon carrying down these boxes on the last day of September so we could focus solely on decorating come October 1st.

With a groan, I grab a plastic storage tub near me and lift. I'm unsteady for a moment and catch my hip on the pile of boxes directly behind me. A small box slides off the top and lands with a thud behind one of the antique trunks. My stomach drops at the muffled sound of glass breaking.

"Aw, crap," I mutter.

Gingerly setting the tub in my hands down first, I reach behind the trunk, grasping for the fallen box. I struggle to get a grip around its edges as it's wedged itself between the wall and the trunk. There is also something else back there, firm and leathery, just off to the side.

I get my arm under both the box and the foreign object and slowly work them out of the crevice. The box pops free, and I recognize it immediately as the container for a lovely crystal pumpkin my father gave my mother a few months before he passed. It was the last decoration my mother packed away every year. I want to cry. It's very likely shattered. Before I can properly mourn this piece of my childhood, my eye catches a glint of brass. The second object I pulled up, now resting on top of the dusty trunk. It's a book, large, about the size of my Herbal, and held together with a leather strap and a brass buckle. The whole thing is bound in a deep brown leather with faint red embellishments that are hard to make out in the dim light of the attic. This is not a decoration I recognize.

I unbuckle the strap, struggling to manipulate the leather, and flip the book open to the middle. The pages are all browned with age on the edges and crinkly, as if they've been long exposed to humidity. But they are blank. I flip through the entire tome, blank page after blank page.

Something creaks behind me. I turn quickly, my heart jumping.

There's nothing there but boxes and dust. I don't know why I'm suddenly so tense—I'm not doing anything wrong. Before I shut the book, I flip to the front, curious to see if this indeed was simply a fancy prop my mother purchased at a Halloween store. Maybe somewhere on this tome there is a little sticker with "Made in China" printed on it. The first page is large and yellowing, just like the rest. Only this one has words. Right in the middle of the page, written in a bright red ink:

The King Below shall never again know my secrets.
Sybil Goodwin

The nostalgia I'd felt from the crystal pumpkin is dwarfed by a wave of melancholy that rushes over me at the sight of my mother's signature. A soft sob escapes my lips as I touch the edge of her name. The sob switches to a gasp as the still wet ink smears onto my fingers, and the rest of the words melt into rivulets, spreading to the edges of the paper and finally disappearing, as if the book absorbed the ink. The front page now sits as blank as all the rest. I stare, openmouthed and fascinated.

"What on earth?" I whisper to the surrounding dust.

I flip through all the pages again to see if any other strange writing has appeared, my mind racing.

"Kate?" Matthew's voice calls out behind me. I let out a short yelp and turn around. He is standing at the edge of the ladder. He looks at me apologetically.

"You're crying!" He looks horrified. He strides over to me, eyes never leaving mine. I realize for the first time that my cheeks are wet with tears.

"No, I'm fine," I say, turning quickly back to the book. I shove it behind some boxes before standing up just as he reaches me.

"I'm sorry," he says. "I was very insensitive."

I shake my head.

"No, it wasn't that. I'm just a victim of my own clumsiness," I say, grabbing the crystal pumpkin box. I unhook the cardboard edge and pull the top open. Sure enough, inside lies the shattered remains of my mother's favorite trinket. There are a dozen larger chunks but countless shards and fragments. Matthew gingerly takes the box from my hands and inspects the contents.

"Is it important to you?" he asks, looking back up to my still tearful eyes. I nod.

"My father gave it to my mother the Halloween before he died. He had blood cancer. For many years, even before I was born," I explain. "He got better for a little while but died when I was four."

"I remember," Matthew nods. Of course he did. He seemed to remember every solemn secret I'd shared with him the first time we met.

I break from his gaze, focusing on the broken memento in my hands. "It used to catch the sunlight by the living room window and throw orange-tinted rainbows all over the ceiling. Mom and I would lie on the floor and find shapes in their patterns, pretending they were messages from Dad." Any other day I would have cried real tears over such a loss, but my mind is too busy wondering over the tome I've just hastily hidden.

"Surely you can save it?" Matthew suggests.

I examine it again before shaking my head. "I have an adhesive recipe that can make quick work of clean breaks. But it's useless for something that's been partially pulverized. I'll have to throw it out."

He stares at the contents in the box quietly for a moment, his dark head bowed away from me. Eventually, he lifts his blue eyes to mine and smiles softly. The usual smugness that accompanies this look is not present. "Let's take it back to your cottage once we're done and see if anything is salvageable."

I take the box back from him. "If you insist," I say, knowing there is not much to be done. I struggle to swallow the lump in my throat. My head is racing with thoughts and questions, but I can't investigate the book further with Matthew in the house. I will have to wait until I'm alone to look inside it again.

CHAPTER EIGHT

What We Do With the Shadows

By the end of the afternoon, the storage boxes are empty, every trinket is in its place, and each tiny lightbulb in the house glows orange. Black lace shades cover table lamps, and orange garlands are draped across fireplace mantles. Pumpkins, comical witches, and ghost figures are stuffed in all available nooks and crannies. Glowing jack-o'-lantern lights twist around the main staircase banister. Every flat surface has a candy bowl waiting to be filled with chocolates, caramels, and sour sweets. The manor finally feels like home again.

I send Matthew to fill tiny dishes with candy corn and place them in my sisters' bedrooms. While he is occupied, I run up to the attic and grab the mysterious book, placing it inside my canvas bag, hiding it underneath a pile of fake spiderwebs and woolen pumpkins.

"Dinner will be around seven," I say to Matthew as we walk back into the gatekeeper's cottage. Merlin chirps at us happily from the kitchen. "I have some things I need to work on . . ." I gesture vaguely around, hoping he won't ask any probing questions.

"I have some work as well," he says, the corners of his mouth tugging into a grin.

The tome is burning a hole in the side of my canvas bag. I leave Matthew in the kitchen and rush toward my room. Merlin scampers after me.

I wait for him to run inside before locking the door.

"Can't risk being interrupted," I whisper to him conspiratorially. He jumps up onto the bed and stares at me, his orange eyes glowing in the dark room.

After a few steadying breaths, I dump the contents of my bag onto the bed's woven quilt. Merlin chirps as wool pumpkins, cobwebs, needles, threads, and scraps of paper all fall around him. Finally, with a soft thud, the leather tome lands on my bed.

I grab it eagerly and open it to the first page. My eyes widen at the sight of shimmering red ink. The words have returned.

The King Below shall never again know my secrets.
Sybil Goodwin

Now that I've already seen my mother's name, the shock of grief is not as intense, and I focus on the sentence above her signature. The King Below. The name Margaret Halliwell invoked in my dream. The name I thought my subconscious invented. Softly, I let the tip of my index finger brush against the words again. The ink is cold and smears against the paper. I quickly pull my hand away and watch as the red liquid spreads across the first page, as it had back at the manor. It bleeds to the edges of the tome and then disappears as if sinking into the paper itself.

I stare at the blank page in wonder. There are ways to extract secrets from people. All I have to do is cook up a course of my mother's Spill-Your-Secrets Spaghetti.

One bowl of that, made just right, and anyone would tell me their most protected thoughts. But a *book* with secrets? I've never seen anything like it. And I can't very well make a book eat spaghetti.

I light the candle that I keep on a stool near my bed. The match hisses as I strike it, casting shadows all around the room.

"Maybe there's a trigger?" I say to Merlin. He quirks his head, his collar letting out a single soft chime.

I hold the book up to the candle and turn it over and over, inspecting the binding and seams, looking for any sort of secret release that will bring the ink back. The cover smells like real leather, and the paper inside is thick and rough, but nothing is mechanically unusual. I close and open the book several times, waiting to see how long it takes for the red ink to return. But my mother's handwriting doesn't grace the page again.

"Well, that was a bust," I murmur. I sit on the bed and think, my hand still running along the spine of the book on the off chance I missed something. Merlin nuzzles my arm with his forehead.

"Maybe it's time to bring out the big guns, huh, buddy?" I say to him as his scratchy tongue licks my fingertips. I give his head a pet and lay the book down on my quilt.

I walk over to my small vanity and pull open the drawer with the false bottom.

Buried among packets of rare herbs and dusty crystals is a silvery opalescent chain with a talisman hanging on one end. It is a brass lacework cage welded around a carved moonstone, a gem particularly adept at detecting different forms of magic. It glows in different shades, depending on the type present. Celeste gave it to me for my thirtieth birthday last year. Ever since she found success in the world of celebrities and influencers, her gifts have become rather extravagant. I've never really found use for it before this moment, other than as a piece of ornate jewelry.

I walk back to the bed, clutching the necklace in my hands, the moonstone dangling toward the ground. I open the book and gently lay the talisman across the blank first page. Less than three heartbeats pass before the milky white stone begins to darken in color, first turning a very pale blush and then quickly deepening to a ruby red.

Blood magic.

The air rushes from my lungs. I snatch the talisman up and make a protective sweeping motion across my chest before I shove the book off my bed. It lands upside down on the floor, several of the yellow paper pages bending inward. The moonstone turns a dull forest green in my hands, sensing the resonant hedge craft that's always on me. My breath comes in short gasps as I press my back up against my bedroom door, staring at the tome. What on earth was a book steeped in blood magic doing in my mother's house?

What had she been hiding?

There is a quick and urgent knocking on the door behind me.

"Kate? Is everything all right?" Matthew's hurried voice is muffled through the wood.

God. Why won't this man let me be?

"Yes! Everything's fine!" I call back. I open my door to his surprised face. His eyes begin to scan my dark room, but I squeeze out and shut the door quickly, stuffing the moonstone into a pocket in my pants. I'm eager to put space between the book and me.

Matthew frowns. "I heard a noise. Are you sure you're okay?" he asks.

"Absolutely. I knocked my bag off the bed accidentally. I'd stuffed it full of decorations for the cottage, so it hit the floor pretty hard."

Matthew's frown deepens.

"Kate," he says, leaning toward me. I hold my breath.

"If I told you that you can trust me, would you believe me? Despite what I am. Despite where I come from?" He stares at me, assessing me or searching for something, I can't be sure. I begin to blush under the heat of his gaze.

"It was just my bag," I answer, my voice firm.

Without giving him a chance to respond, I duck away and head out into the front room. I want to lose myself in my kitchen and not think about all the kinds of forbidden magic that I've brought into my cottage. Housing a necromancer is one thing—the Atlantic Key can't punish me for honoring Sanctuary. But being in possession of a tome protected with blood magic? That's a different beast.

Although, for all I know, maybe it's not a coincidence that I found such a book the day after Matthew showed up. Maybe he's behind it? Maybe he planted it in the attic somehow?

The thought makes my skin crawl.

"I was thinking of whipping up some dinner," I call over my shoulder. "Are you hungry at all?" The question comes out too loudly. I can hear the nervousness in my own voice.

I stop when I get to my table.

My mother's crystal pumpkin, the one I had shattered in the attic, sits atop one of the plates. It shimmers in the lamplight, intact. Only the green curling stem remains cracked off, sitting to the side. I bend down to examine it. The edges of the pumpkin are perfect, forming together seamlessly; every tiny, fragmented shard has been accounted for.

I turn around. Matthew stands at the doorway, watching me.

"You did this?" I inquire with a quiet whisper.

He nods.

"How? I thought you weren't good with creation."

"I'm not," he says. "But fixing that wasn't an act of creation. The pieces were already there. One of the first lessons of shadow magic is learning to reverse destruction."

I stare at him and then at the crystal.

"But why fix it?" I ask. My hand trembles as I run my fingers over the pumpkin's rind.

He cocks his head as if the answer should be obvious. "Because it's precious to you," he says.

Guilt flushes through my cheeks. I can't believe I'd just been mentally accusing him of sneaking forbidden magic into my mother's house.

He walks into the kitchen and stands close beside me. "I left the final piece for you," he says, pointing to the stem. I give him a questioning look. He responds with a knowing smile. "Lesson number two of shadow magic. There's power in placing the final piece."

I'm strangely bemused by his kindness. Sitting atop my work desk is a small clay pot filled with a special adhesive, my magical Mending Medley. I grab the pot and a small paintbrush from a cup on my desk. Matthew watches me quietly.

Dipping the brush into the shimmering copper liquid first, I then draw it along the edges of the spiraled green stem. Placing some adhesive along the top of the base as well, I join the two pieces together. The temperature of the crystal grows warmer cupped in my hands. It heats almost to the point of discomfort against my skin. Then, slowly, the heat dissipates. Only when the crystal cools to the original temperature do I pull my hands away. The pumpkin is in one piece, with a thin bronze scar near the top serving as the only evidence of its temporary destruction. Matthew runs a finger softly around the shimmering edge of the adhesive.

"It may not be as seamless as yours. But there is power in remembrance," I say with a smile, echoing his words back to him. He laughs quietly.

"It's all the more beautiful for it," he says. I stare at the trinket and realize I agree. The bronze line is a record of the pumpkin's history, proof of what it has survived.

I should be angry with Matthew for practicing shadow magic in my home, but I can't bring myself to be upset, not when this is the result. I carefully pick up the crystal pumpkin and walk it over to one of the kitchen lamps. As it comes into the direct light, it illuminates the kitchen walls with hundreds of translucent orange sparkles.

"Lovely," Matthew says behind me.

"I can't thank you enough," I say, turning to him. "For this, and for your help today."

He smiles. "It was nice to see that house come alive again. Your sisters are lucky to have you."

My heart gives a soft thrumming pang. Merlin mewls at my feet. I scoop him up and give him a large snuggle. He smells like pumpkin pie.

"Are you hungry?" I turn to Matthew. Merlin thinks I'm speaking to him and gives my neck a small nuzzle.

"Famished." Matthew nods.

"Sit then," I demand.

"As you wish." With a barely suppressed grin, he follows my orders and fluidly takes a seat at the table.

I set Merlin down carefully and walk over to my stove, lighting the burners and placing a pot of water on top. Matthew's eyes are once again on the back of my neck. For the first time since he arrived, I don't want to rush away and escape from his gaze. This necromancer who terrified me last night has shown himself to be nothing but considerate, gracious, and kind.

And a little cocky . . . I remind myself with a slight smile.

But I can't grow complacent. I think back to the question he'd asked before I'd run into the kitchen.

Am I capable of trusting him?

I'm astonished that a part of me wants to. But for all his generosity, there's still a lot he hasn't told me. I'd trusted him once, when we first met. And I'd been proven wrong then. I also can't ignore that he'd come to my door seemingly out of nowhere, with a story about needing rare ingredients, yet he was more than happy to waste his first day in Ipswich otherwise occupied. It didn't add up.

My mind elsewhere, I grab a packet of ravioli, a bushel of Brussel sprouts, and a brown package of bacon tied up with twine I'd purchased from the butcher a few days before. My plan is to brown some butter, sauté the bacon and sprouts, mix all these ingredients together, and call it a day. I need something simple but hearty—my brain can't focus on much else—and this meal always does the trick.

The ravioli goes straight into the water, already boiling thanks to my less than stable emotions. I begin to chop the Brussel sprouts in half, my hands shaking slightly. One especially pesky sprout keeps rolling away from me. I let out a frustrated laugh as it slips my grasp for a third time.

"Allow me." I freeze as Matthew's hand wraps around and steadies my own as he grabs the errant vegetable. He neatly slices it in half with the knife. I look over my shoulder, his face dangerously close to mine. He lets go, but not before gently pulling the knife out of my grip.

"I'm perfectly adept in the kitchen," I say with a slight huff once I've found my breath. Matthew smiles, continuing to chop the greens.

"Of that, I have no doubt. But I want to pull my own weight," he says.

Mollified, I watch him for a few moments. He makes quick work of several more sprouts. Longer pieces of his dark hair dangle in front of his face as he looks down at the cutting board. One of his cheeks has a slight dimple when he smiles. It's adorable.

Enough, Hecate, I berate myself.

Turning my attention back to the meal, I move rapidly through dicing the meat, throwing a liberal helping of butter into a searing-hot saucepan. The butter melts almost instantaneously, turning a lovely shade of golden brown. Matthew tosses the halved Brussel sprouts into the pan, where they hiss and pop as they begin to fry. The bacon goes in next, the grease melting and crisping up the sprouts even further.

"Pasta water," I say to Matthew. He grabs half a ladle of the foaming water from the pot and adds it to the brown butter sauce, giving it a little more substance.

"Is the pasta ready?" I ask. He nods and grabs my spider spoon, using it to catch all the ravioli that are floating to the top of the pot. He transfers them to my sizzling frying pan and I toss the dumplings to coat them with the glistening butter sauce.

Within minutes, the meal is ready. Matthew spoons the ravioli into individual dishes while I place a loaf of pumpernickel beer bread and some honey butter onto the table.

Matthew sets both dishes down and ushers me toward one of the empty chairs, pushing it in for me. He sits beside me and immediately takes a bite of food. There is a gracefulness to the way he eats, spearing ravioli, sprout, and bacon all on his fork and chewing appreciatively.

"I should be smarter and always make sure you take a bite first," he admits with a quick wink. "But your cooking is too good to resist."

"I'll confess, I've been surprised by your inherent trust in me," I say, smiling despite myself.

"Well then, we are both full of surprises," Matthew grins. "I half expected you to kick me out the second you saw the resurrected pumpkin."

I laugh. "The thought crossed my mind, but I didn't want to seem ungrateful."

He laughs as well, taking another bite.

"Besides," I say with a shrug, "what you did to the pumpkin isn't so far off from what I do when someone in Ipswich comes to me with a bad scrape or broken bone."

Matthew stares at me for a moment before speaking. "Would the rest of your coven think the same? Or would they reject me if they could see what I do?"

I shake my head.

"Every woman in the Atlantic wishes she had such talent for practical magic."

That gets another laugh out of him, referring to his shadow magic as a simple, practical craft.

"Then why is there animosity between our two covens?" he asks.

"Because you aren't only fixing broken objects, are you? Shadow magic is control over bodies long unoccupied or, even worse, the resurrection and enslavement of souls that should be left to rest." Most covens forbid necromancy, but it is an especially insulting craft to the Atlantic Key, where reverence and respect of our ancestors' spirits is paramount. The few times my mother spoke of necromancers, she wove tales of corrupted hexans and witches digging up the bones of their long-dead forebears to make them serve as powerful thralls. She always said that ancestral magic is a gift that must be given freely, not forcibly stolen.

Matthew looks thoughtful, considering. "I won't argue your point against disturbing resting souls. But what's the harm in using what they leave behind? Why should the untapped potential go to waste?"

I shake my head. "You don't ask permission."

He raises his eyebrows. "That's quite the assumption. And that's quite the standard to have when, if I recall correctly, your own mother rarely asked permission before enforcing her will over her own guests."

He's not wrong. And I hate that. I can't bring myself to respond. I take a bite of dinner instead. It's good, salty from the bacon and sprouts, softened by the mild cheese of the ravioli. I chew on it thoughtfully.

"What are you thinking?" Matthew asks, after a moment of silence.

"I'm thinking that you have caught me in a trap of my own hypocrisy," I admit with a slight grimace. Matthew leans back and smiles his classic grin. I realize for the first time that it isn't necessarily smugness that lights his face, but amusement. As if he is fascinated and entertained by the whole world around him.

"Hecate Goodwin, you are nothing like I first believed you to be," he says.

"Really? You are exactly as I thought you would be, Mr. Cypher," I lie. He laughs happily.

"I think you're secretly warming up to me."

"I think not," I lie again. He is undeterred, taking several more contented bites of dinner. Memories of meals my mother cooked occupy my mind. All the marriages she helped foster, all the children born nine months after she prepared a fertility meal, all the opinions swayed. She really had blanketed the entire village of Ipswich in a veil of her own control. But it was always for good. To help and heal and protect.

But she was hiding something. I bite my lip at the thought of the book lying at the edge of my bed frame, bent and abandoned. And the warm vermillion from the moonstone.

"Find your mother's book, and you'll know why she named you a hedge witch."

"If I told you that you can trust me, would you believe me?"

I stand abruptly from the table. Matthew stops eating and looks at me, concerned.

"Everything okay?" he asks, moving to stand as well.

"Yes. Keep eating," I hold up a hand to prevent him from leaving his seat. He eases back down but keeps his eyes on mine. "I . . . I'll be right back." I turn from the table and leave the kitchen, heading to my room.

Inside, the book is still on the floor, exactly as I left it. My hands shake a bit, refusing for a moment to pick up the tome.

"You carried it all the way down the hill from the manor, Hecate. You didn't grow a third ear then, and you won't now," I whisper to myself.

Still, I take one of my shawls off the chair where Merlin usually sleeps and wrap it over the book. The bundle is heavy in my hands as I walk carefully out of my room, suddenly afraid that one wrong step might cause the book to burst into flames. Or dissolve into blood.

Matthew stands up from the table when I return.

"What's wrong?" he asks. No doubt my fear and confusion are etched on every corner of my face.

Words don't come to me. Is this really the right choice? I had worked hard to hide the book from him this afternoon. But now, after he has fixed a pretty glass trinket and complimented my cooking, I'm preparing to reveal it all? I almost step back into the shadows of the hallway, but our eyes meet. There is no amusement on his face, only concern. One of his hands is outstretched and brushes up against my arm as if he instinctively wants to steady me. I lean ever so slightly into his touch, bemused by the relief it gives me.

"I found this in my mother's attic today," I say, unwrapping the shawl from the book. The dark leather of the tome is rough against my skin. "I've never seen it before. It was well hidden. I think it's magically bound. But I can't figure it out."

Matthew's brow furrows.

"May I?" His hand leaves my elbow and reaches out toward the book. I let him take it. Gingerly, he inspects the binding, the brass buckle, the spine. Then he flips it open to a random page and runs his fingers all along the handmade paper. "The craftsmanship is impressive. What makes you think it's magically bound?" he asks.

"Flip to the front," I instruct softly. He does as I say and breathes in sharply. I sneak a glance. Sure enough, the scarlet red words are back on the first page.

"Gwaed. Magic of the blood," he whispers, looking at me. I nod solemnly. "Your mother's?"

"I don't know why she would have this. It doesn't make sense." But it must be hers. Mags had spoken of a book. What else could this be?

"This writing. It's in her hand?" he asks. I nod again. He lets out a long slow breath.

"What do you think it is?" I pressure.

Matthew studies the book some more before looking back at me. "I can't say for certain what this book is. But the writing on the front is heavy magic, a kind I've seen before. Simple but powerful. A protective charm has been placed over the pages. Only the blood of the book's owner can unlock its contents. No one else can access it."

"Is that why the ink disappears every time I touch the signature?" I ask. Matthew's face pales at my question. I take a step back in alarm.

"You touched these words?" he whispers urgently.

I nod, startled by the panic in his voice.

He snaps the book shut and slams it onto the nearby coffee table, making me jump. He turns back toward me, placing both his hands on my shoulders.

"You have herbs here, yes? Any premade pastes for drawing out poisons or venoms? On the off chance a hiker stops by with a snake bite?" He speaks calmly, but his grip on my shoulders is deathlike.

"Y-yes, of course," I stammer.

"Good." He says. "I need you to sit down and tell me where I can find them." He leads me firmly to one of the quilted chairs in my living room.

"Pantry. At the end of the hallway. There's a glass cabinet against the back wall. All poison control mixtures are in the yellow ceramic pots—" I haven't even finished my sentence before he leaves me and runs to the back hallway. I sit, suddenly exhausted, and listen to the sound of Matthew rummaging urgently through my supplies.

While he's gone, I take account of myself. My head feels fine, my breathing isn't labored. My pulse is quicker than normal, but I attribute that less to any dark magic and more to the general stress of Matthew's reaction. Less than a minute passes and he is back by my side, setting down several of my most potent poison controls.

"Is this entirely necessary?" I ask, almost laughing. But the seriousness of his gaze silences me.

"With which hand did you touch the ink?" he questions quietly. I lift my right hand up. He grabs it, roughly at first, but his grip gentles when I let out a surprised breath. He inspects my palm and fingertips carefully. The heat from his hands warms mine as he traces my lifeline. I shiver at his touch, not realizing how cold my skin had become.

"You'll need to trust me, Kate," he says. He reaches into his pants pocket with his free hand and brings out a small leather case, no larger than a snuff box. He releases my hand for the shortest of moments to flip the case open and grab the object inside. A small but deadly sharp silver pocketknife with a spine made from pale bone. He grips my hand gently again before I can pull away.

"Are you going to explain to me what's going on?" I demand, trying to get free of his grip.

He tightens his hold on my wrist. Not enough to hurt, but just enough to prevent me from wriggling away.

"Blood magic is one of the most powerful crafts," he says. "But it's also the greediest. That wasn't an ordinary protection charm. There's no such thing as 'ordinary' with Gwaed. Charms and curses are two sides of the same coin in that craft. You've likely been infected. I need to draw it out."

I stop struggling immediately. Matthew looks at me, waiting, his hand still gripping mine. I manage to nod my acquiescence.

He spreads some antiseptic paste all over my palm and fingertips. The scent of eucalyptus is intense, burning my nostrils. He holds the blade of the knife up to my hand and presses the tip against my pinky finger. A tiny bead of scarlet-red blood forms. He has cut me so gently that I don't even bleed enough for gravity to pull it downward. He repeats the process on my ring and middle fingers, and again, scarlet beads form anticlimactically. His shoulders relax slightly.

But when he presses on my pointer finger, I let out an involuntary cry. Pain shoots through my hand, but not pain from the knife. It's an icy-cold searing that pierces through to the bones of my finger. I watch with horror as a thick black sludge pools from the tiny wound.

Matthew's eyes dart to mine, flashing regret. He wastes no time with calming words, instead, he holds my hand close to his lips and whispers things that I can't hear over the blood pounding in my ears. His breath warms the back of my fingertips as black liquid continues to pour from the newest wound. Matthew takes the knife and makes several small slashes underneath the first. The black blood pours from these cuts as well. He grimaces and makes one final slash right at the base of my finger where it meets the palm. Several drops of normal bright red blood seep out.

"It's not nearly as bad as it could have been," he says to me, his grimace fading into relief. "The infection hasn't spread very far."

He turns back toward my hand and continues to whisper. I realize it's not that I can't hear him. He is speaking a language I don't recognize. Welsh, perhaps? A twinge of annoyance at my own helplessness pesters me as he works. But there is nothing to do except watch. At one point, it almost looks like shadows pour from his hands and wrap around my finger. But I blink and the darkness is gone.

Finally, all the cuts begin to bleed red, and then cease soon after. Matthew wipes away the droplets of blood that have collected on my wrist with a damp cloth. He then applies a soothing balm all along my hand. Milk thistle and jewelweed. Gently, he uses his thumb to massage the ointment into my skin. I revel in the feeling of warmth returning to my fingers.

But despite his tenderness, I can't ignore the stinging of the cuts forever.

"Allow me," I tell him after a little while, slowly pulling my hand away and dipping my fingers into the soothing ointment. I softly massage the medicinal cream into my skin, humming several low notes as I do. The vibrations travel all through my body but I direct them toward my hand, sighing with relief as they work with the ingredients of the cream and begin to feed intention and energy into my wounds. Matthew watches, his eyes widening, as the cuts in my skin go from raw and open to thin pink lines, to hardly any marks at all.

"Amazing," he breathes when I am done. "Truly, phenomenal."

I hold my hand up for both of us to inspect. The only signs of the ordeal are several patches of skin around my pointer finger that are a tinge redder than others. But that irritation will soon fade.

Matthew takes my hand into his, drawing it closer in curiosity. "I could never manipulate living flesh so perfectly," he says.

I shake my head and laugh at his phrasing. Nothing like a necromancer to dehumanize the skin.

"Have you ever tried?" I ask.

His eyes are wide as he looks at me. "I'd likely do more harm than good. If not to the subject, then to myself."

"Even so, it's thanks to your expert surgery skills that I'll walk away without a mark," I say. "Deeper cuts and wounds are harder to heal so seamlessly. There are a handful of people in Ipswich who have scars similar to the pumpkin over there." I look over at the crystal sculpture Matthew fixed. The bronze highlighted crack shimmers in the candlelight.

He doesn't respond, just continues to study my hand. His fingers run over my knuckles, his thumb brushes against my wrist. My skin is extra sensitive after the magic that has coursed through it. His touch sends shivers up through my arm.

"Did the ink come into contact with any other part of your body?" he asks suddenly. I shake my head quickly.

"You swear?" he demands to know.

I have half a mind to roll my eyes and tell him I licked the book. But this isn't the time for jokes. And I don't want that bone knife anywhere near my tongue.

"I swear," I say firmly. He searches my face before acquiescing.

"Okay," he says. "So, now we need to know what your mother was so desperate to hide that she dabbled in blood magic to protect it."

I shake my head, bewildered. "She enforced the avoidance of forbidden crafts more than any other elder."

Matthew's eyes turn sympathetic. He is still holding my hand, but no longer in such a way as to inspect it. No, now my palm rests on his, our fingers nearly intertwined.

Hesitantly, I pull away. He stares down at his own hand and stretches it softly. Merlin has hopped up on my chair and is pawing at my forearm, worry in his eyes.

"It's all right, my sweet thing," I say, grabbing a hold of him and bringing him close to my face so I can kiss the top of his furry head. He immediately begins to thrum with a loud vibrating purr.

"If the book really does belong to my mother, perhaps my blood will unlock it? I only touched it before. I never gave it blood," I suggest, scratching Merlin under his chin.

"And thank goodness for that!" Matthew exclaims without humor. "If you'd offered your blood to it, I shudder to think what could have happened."

"Would it really have been so severe? My mother and I share blood."

Matthew shakes his head. "Gwaed doesn't work like that. Blood is unique to an individual. Your trying to open it would be no different than if I had tried. Only your mother's blood can resolve the protection."

I frown. This magic is so foreign to any that I'm used to. To me and mine, bloodlines are continuous, our greatest source of power.

"My mother is gone, though," I say.

"Which is probably why the infection stayed so localized," Matthew says. "I was barely able to sense the magic surrounding the book until I saw the inscription. It's weak. If your mother had been living and maintaining the protection, the curse might have eaten you from the inside out within an hour."

I shudder, suddenly understanding the urgency with which Matthew had acted. Still, why would my mother possess something so evil? What was inside that book that needed such extreme protection?

"If we wait long enough, will the magic eventually fade?" I ask.

"The curse? Maybe. But not the lock. Unless you know of someone who specializes in spell removal, that book is protected indefinitely."

The answer comes to me almost immediately. "Winifred," I whisper.

"Sorry?" Matthew questions after a moment. I turn to him.

"Winifred Bennet. She's the coven's meta-magic witch. She might know how to get inside this book." I don't know why I hadn't thought of her sooner. "I'll go to her tomorrow. She lives on a farm outside of town. She and my mother were close, so she might agree to see me," I say to him. His eyes narrow, considering.

"We'll go together, if that's all right with you," he finally says, smiling when I agree without hesitation.

The truth is, I want Matthew with me after all that has happened tonight. I am not sure my meeting with Winifred will be a peaceful one. She can be erratic at the best of times. There's no predicting how she might act if I come to her and accuse my mother of dabbling in forbidden magic. But perhaps she won't be surprised at all?

I stare at the tome's cover. I should have recognized Winifred's handiwork on the leather etchings the moment I found it. Similar hash marks make up the design of Mom's Recipe Book, Miranda's Navigator, Celeste's Star Chart, and my Herbal.

Winifred is the only witch within eight hundred miles capable of creating an item like this. She might even be the one who cursed it in the first place. Perhaps my poor mother is innocent, after all. But either way, tomorrow I will confront the most powerful witch in the Atlantic Key. I'll need all the backup I can get.

CHAPTER NINE
Styx and Stones

The trees around me are thick, and the damp chilly air reeks with of decay. It's dark—whether from the dusk or the dense woods, I'm not sure. I place my hand on a nearby oak, hoping to ground myself, to gain a sense of direction. But when my hand touches the rotten trunk, it cracks apart and pieces of it fall away. Glass. I jump back quickly to avoid the sharp shards. With no shoes, I walk gingerly around the disintegrated tree and pray my bare feet don't slice on the scattered glass.

I walk to a different tree and try to ground myself again. It shatters at my touch as well, the muffled sound of slivers of glass plinking against the forest floor.

My heart starts to race. If I can't connect with a living tree, I'll never find my way out of these woods. The darkness around me grows heavier, pressing in tightly. Somewhere in the forest an owl lets out a long shriek, the single sign of another living creature. Part of me wants to run, but I do my best to keep a steady and slow pace, frightened of disturbing any more vitric trees.

I walk until I come upon a black flowing river, too wide to easily jump across. Every drop of moisture in my throat evaporates at the sight of the water, a powerful thirst demanding to be attended to. I sprint toward the river, falling to my knees at its murky bank, and try to cup some of the dark water into my hands. It slips away from my palm like mist, impossible to catch. My throat grows drier, my thirst more desperate. I lean down to drink straight from the river, but the water's surface dips away from me. I lean farther still, dreaming of even a single drop of moisture to quench the cracked desert of my throat. But I go too far and lose my balance, toppling into the black.

The water rushes into my ears and mouth, a welcome sound from the deafening silence of this forest. I don't struggle to breathe despite being submerged, my lungs accepting the liquid without any protestation. Maybe I'm finally safe? The thought lasts half a heartbeat before I see the faces. Thousands of them rising up from the deep below, screaming in silent horror, staring at me. With a start, I see Margaret Halliwell among the hoard. Her ghostly figure reaches out toward me. I kick and scramble, trying to swim back to the surface, but icy fingers grip my ankle.

I bolt awake and frantically push the bed quilt off my legs. My ankle stings, as if scratched by invisible nails, but there are no marks on my skin. Breathing heavily, I scan the darkness of my bedroom, half expecting the ghostly figures to have followed me into the conscious world. But there are only the wooden walls of my cottage. I am alone.

CHAPTER TEN

Four Days Until Halloween

The home fries in my cast-iron skillet are crisping up perfectly when Matthew walks into the kitchen. The cottage is bright and airy this morning. All the windows are thrown open, welcoming in the pristine blue sky and fresh air. It's cold outside, but the sunlight streaming through the trees gives off enough warmth to keep the shivers at bay.

"Have a seat," I call over my shoulder to Matthew. "Breakfast is almost ready." One of the dining chairs scrapes against the floor behind me as he settles in.

"How did you have time to make all this?" he asks, bemused. The table is already covered in dishes. Parmesan scrambled eggs paired with smoky paprika ketchup; a citrus salad with cinnamon syrup; an apple spice coffee cake with sugar streusel on top and whipped maple yogurt in the center; and finally the steaming, crispy potatoes with garlic, chives, and caramelized onions that I'm finishing up. I place the potatoes on the table and pour two cups of black coffee from my French press.

"I woke up a bit earlier than normal," I answer semi-honestly as I sprinkle a dusting of cardamom into the coffee. Matthew accepts one of the mugs gratefully. "We need a hearty breakfast. There's a long day ahead of us."

He stares at me in disbelief. The various serving dishes sit on the table between us, a massive feast inappropriate for only two people.

"A *bit* earlier?" he questions.

I don't meet his gaze.

I've been awake since four this morning, unable to fall back asleep after my nightmare. I'd headed to the kitchen to whip something up in the hopes of luring myself back to sleep. My ever-helpful Herbal had autonomously flipped to a recipe for Pass-Out Pie, a suggestion I ignored. When a freshly brewed pot of de-stimulating tea failed, I found myself furiously whipping together batter, slicing apples, chopping herbs, and making pumpkin hummus, with Merlin asleep at my feet.

I load a dollop of the whipped yogurt onto the coffee cake and take a bite. The tanginess of the yogurt pairs perfectly with the spiced apples strewn throughout the cake. For a brief moment, terrifying dreams and mysterious books are far from my mind. I take a sip of my coffee, letting the cardamom transport me somewhere far away. I let out a long, slow sigh.

"Is everything all right?" Matthew asks after piling some eggs onto his plate.

"Just mentally preparing, that's all," I answer quietly, watching steam rise off my mug.

"Is she really that frightening?" His brow furrows.

I look up at him. "Winifred? No. And yes," I admit. "Have you ever been around a meta-magic witch?"

He shakes his head. "No. It's a rare choice for people in the Pacific Gate. Their life expectancy is too short."

I nod. It's a miracle Winifred has lived as long as she has. The Atlantic Key meta-magic witch before her didn't make it to fifty. In other covens, they are lucky to see thirty-five.

"I've known Winifred since I was a baby," I explain to Matthew. "She was almost like a grandmother. But it's always disconcerting, being in the same room with her. She can drain a witch or hexan's magic within minutes, excommunicating them, leaving them unable to access intention. It doesn't matter how close you are to someone like that—the unease never fully subsides."

I hadn't minded too much when I was younger. I'd trusted Winifred with my life. But a meta-magic witch's power eventually turns unstable until it ultimately consumes them. Winifred has held on, but the cracks have begun to show as she approaches her mid-seventies.

"I don't know what to expect from today," I acknowledge to Matthew.

He sets his fork down and gives me a steadying look.

"What's the first thing that needs to be done? Once we approach that, all other plans will fall into place."

I think for a minute. If we are going to head to the Bennet Farm, we will need transportation.

"I should ride my bike to the Raven & Crone. We'll need a car to get to the Bennet farm, and Rebecca lets me borrow her truck sometimes."

"You don't need to ride your bike into town all alone just to get a car," Matthew says.

"I don't mind. I should stop by the shop anyway, to check in."

"Well, could I come with you?" His tone is casual, but I don't miss the tension in his jaw.

I stare at him for a moment, unblinking.

"I only have the one bike," I say slowly.

"We could walk," he offers. "Or I could ride around on your handlebars," he says with a grin.

I laugh. "It's five miles. Either option doesn't sound very comfortable. Let me just get Rebecca's car and come pick you up."

"I don't mind the distance," he pushes back. "And it's a beautiful day to spend time outside."

He's not wrong about that. The sky has become even bluer over the course of breakfast.

"How far is the Bennet farm?" he asks after a moment. "Could we not just walk there?"

"It's *seven* miles. And I need Rebecca's truck for the pumpkins."

Matthew gives me a questioning look.

"The Bennets have the best pumpkins in Massachusetts. And I need a hoard to properly decorate for Samhain. Two birds, one stone."

"All right then." He looks at me, satisfied. "So we walk into town, visit your apothecary, borrow a car, and head to the Bennet farm. Doesn't sound so vast to me."

I smile as I realize what he has done. I'm much calmer now that all the tasks are laid out in an orderly fashion.

"Since we'll be in town anyway, we should stop by Maitland's Boutique. They have a menswear section, so you could pick up some clothes for the rest of your stay," I add.

He's dressed in his blue ensemble again this morning, and it looks just as clean as it did yesterday, but surely he would like to change at some point.

"Perfect," Matthew concurs. "And since we are multitasking, is it possible your apothecary has certain rarer ingredients on hand? I do need to acquire those at some point."

"You know," I reply with a grin as I take another bite of the coffee cake, "it just might."

* * *

The chime of the Raven & Crone clinks daintily as I walk inside with Matthew. My feet ache a bit, not used to walking such long distances in my suede boots. And my arms are sore from carrying half the bags from Maitlands. After the two-hour walk into town, we'd spent a good chunk of time picking out ensembles for Matthew that will hopefully last him through Halloween. He has changed into a pair of dark-wash jeans, a black turtleneck, and a camel leather jacket.

"Kate!" Rebecca calls to me from behind the main counter. Her curls are twisted into a bun with a candy corn–patterned silk headband holding back the flyaways. A pair of beaded spiders dangle from her ears. Ginny stands next to her, ringing up customers. Rebecca gives me a quick wave as I unravel the scarf from around my neck. Her hand pauses in the air as she sees Matthew walk in behind me.

"Hi, Bex!" I smile and give her a small wave in return. Her mouth drops open ever so slightly as Matthew and I walk toward her together.

"Rebecca, Ginny, this is Matthew Cypher," I say, setting down my two shopping bags next to the counter. "He's staying in town for a few days as my guest." Rebecca's eyes widen. If the Atlantic Key didn't know I was hosting a mysterious visitor by now, they would within the hour.

Ginny gives Matthew a cursory glance as she hands a pile of change to a customer. When the man leaves, she pulls a book out from under the counter and flips it open to read. Her mother, on the other hand, stares at Matthew with interest.

"Very nice to meet you," Rebecca says to him. "Welcome to the Raven & Crone. Please don't hesitate to ask if there is anything I can help you with." Her voice is an octave lower than normal, her eyes heavy as she stares at him.

"Actually, that's why we stopped by," I say. "May we borrow your truck? He wants to see the festival." No need to incite Rebecca's curiosity by also telling her we plan to speak to her mother. To sweeten the request, I pull out a small glass container of the pumpkin hummus I promised her.

"Oh! Thank you!" Rebecca's face lights up as she takes the covered bowl from me. "And of course. You know the truck is yours whenever you need it."

"Thank you," Matthew bows his head in appreciation. "I made Kate promise to take me to all the best Halloween haunts in town."

Rebecca flushes as he speaks. "Well," she breathes, "there is no better place to celebrate than Ipswich. We can't get enough of Halloween!" She laughs happily, patting me on the shoulder, but her face falls as she glares uncertainly at the Christmas decorations she has strewn around the store.

"Excellent." Matthew grins brightly. Rebecca's hand freezes on my shoulder as she smiles tentatively back at him. A large group of customers walk into the store, a family of adult women who begin fawning over our lavender display. Rebecca makes no move to greet them. She continues to smile blankly at Matthew. He shifts uncomfortably and looks toward me. I stare at her, an odd squirming feeling roiling around my stomach at her clear attraction to Matthew. Even Ginny, who isn't easily distracted while reading a book, gives her mother's odd behavior a sideways glance.

"He also needs some herbs," I say, forcing Rebecca's focus back to me. "The list should be in your ledger."

"Of course," she says, finally taking her eyes off Matthew. From under the counter, she lifts her own Herbal. Where mine is dark and simple, hers is an explosion of green embroidery over white leather, with golden hardware.

"Come with me, Kate." She beckons me behind the counter and opens the door to the back room. She ignores my confused look, jerking her head in an insistent manner for me to join her. Matthew begins to follow, but Rebecca holds up her hand.

"Sorry, you'll have to wait out here. All requests from the ledger have to be reviewed in private," she says to him regretfully. He frowns but doesn't follow us into the storage room. Rebecca leads me to the very back. The door to the rest of the store is still open so she can keep an eye on the floor, but we are well out of earshot.

"What are you doing?" I ask, mystified. She's never secretive over her spell book.

She doesn't answer me. First, she sticks the bowl of hummus in the small refrigerator we keep in the stockroom. Then, she flips to the back of her Herbal, where the order ledger is kept. Members of the Atlantic Key write notes directly to her so their orders can be promptly filled. We simply address an order to her in our own books, and a copy will appear in the back of her Herbal.

"Ah yes, I see the newest entry," she hums as she skims a finger down the page. She begins reading the list I jotted down into my own Herbal before Matthew and I headed out. "Smoked barberry root bark, damiana, crystalized juniper berries, and mugwort powder." She looks up and gives me a pointed glance. "Is someone brewing a love potion?" Her tone is teasing, but there is an undercurrent of curiosity and a note of concern.

I let out a breath of relief. Damiana is a dead giveaway for love magic, but it has other uses too. I don't remind her of that. Better to let Rebecca draw her own incorrect conclusion.

"I honestly can't say," I admit. I'd thought it a strange collection of ingredients when Matthew had dictated the list to me earlier, especially when also considering the Samhain-harvested moonvine. But I hadn't bothered asking him what his plans were for the herbs. I prefer not to know.

"Who is this man, Kate? He's staying at your house? Is he even a hexan?"

"He is," I say casually, answering two of the three questions.

"Which coven?" She looks at me, impatient, but I shake my head.

"I can't say that. He invoked sanctuary."

Her eyes widen. "Well, that doesn't instill confidence, does it?" she whispers with high-pitched urgency. She looks toward the main room, and my eyes follow hers. Matthew's back is angled away from us, his face in profile as he looks over the rest of the store. One of his hands taps at the wood countertop.

She nudges a shoulder into me. "So, it's really just been the two of you, alone at the cottage?" she whispers.

"Mm-hm," I say absentmindedly, distracted by the starkness of his side profile. A strong nose, dark eyelashes, and a sharp jaw. Rebecca gives a slight snicker.

"He is quite handsome, isn't he?"

"Oh good Lord." I sigh in exasperation. "Do we have the herbs or not, Bex?"

She snaps her Herbal shut. "Of course, we have them. What kind of establishment do you think we run?" She turns toward the apothecary cabinet we keep in the back for coven members and begins pulling at the drawers.

"Send him in," she says over her shoulder. "I need to give specific brewing instructions for some of these."

I shake my head but go back out into the main room. Matthew turns to me, a slight smile on his face.

"Rebecca wants to see you," I say.

"For brewing instructions?" he asks, his grin widening. I grimace. How much of our conversation had he heard?

"And probably to interrogate you a bit," I say too sharply. He laughs.

"Excellent. I hold up very well under scrutiny." He gives me a wink as he heads behind the counter. I roll my eyes at his departing back but can't ignore the flip in my stomach.

I let out a long, stuttering breath and close my eyes. "Keep it together, Goodwin," I whisper.

"Talking to yourself is a bad habit to start at your age," Ginny says beside me. I slowly open my eyes. She is still standing at the register, reading her book. The words are hardly legible as she has scribbled countless notes in the margins and between the lines of text.

"Shouldn't you be in school?" I point out. She shrugs.

"Those who dictate other's behavior would be better off regulating their own. If you'd like, I can give you the sources that state I have no moral, ethical, or legal obligation to be in school today."

I grimace again. An argument with a book witch will either be the most interesting conversation of your month or an inescapable labyrinth.

"Some other time," I say.

"Yes," Ginny says, "perhaps we can discuss after you finish *Le Morte D'Arthur*?" She looks up from her book with an expectant and rather condescending look.

"Oh." I shake my head. "I'm sorry, Ginny. But with planning the coven celebrations, I won't have time to finish it by Halloween."

She is unsurprised. "Well, I'd like it back then. My folklore shelf feels wrong without it. All the books are getting upset."

So much for her "friend" who needed it. I add *Return Ginny's book* to my ever-expanding mental to-do list. It seems I am haunted by books this week.

Ginny gives me an impish look.

"Your gentleman friend seems nice," she says.

"He knows how to make a good first impression," I admit.

Ginny nods. "And I couldn't help but notice the distinct scent of cinnamon when he walked in." Her look is prying, excited, and a little nervous. I stare back at her, keeping my face steady and unbothered. Admitting to her that Matthew is exactly who she thinks he is would be breaking sanctuary.

She rolls her eyes at me when I refuse to play her game.

"Still curious about your King Below?" she asks, trying another tactic to elicit a response from me. I turn my eyes to the wooden counter, busying my hands by arranging our natural lip balms so all their labels face out.

"Maybe," I admit. "Why? Been doing research on it in your free time?"

Ginny shakes her head. "No." She twists one of the curls by her ear, a dead giveaway that she's lying. "But my offer to recall still stands."

I look around the store. No customers are ready to check out. Matthew and Rebecca are still chatting in the back room. Interest sparks in Ginny's eyes, however hard she might be trying to deny it. Knowing her, she spent the past two nights furiously scanning through all her books for any mention of the King Below. She could just tell me what she found. But she wants the excuse to practice her craft. I really shouldn't request this of her. Shouldn't distract her with my own mysteries and problems.

"Okay," I whisper quickly, giving one final glance toward the back room. Rebecca is laughing while Matthew speaks to her animatedly.

Ginny smiles widely.

"Excellent!" she coos. She reaches under the checkout counter and pulls up a yellow tea candle from the storage boxes underneath. From the pocket of her brown and mustard tartan dress she pulls a small lighter in the shape of a tiny book. With a flick, she ignites the lighter and holds the flame to the candlewick until it catches. She stares at the flame for a few moments, focusing her breath. Then she flips her book to the back and rips out the final page. She puts on the tinted spectacles that hang from a chain around her neck and stares at the torn paper, holding it up to the candle. It begins to smoke and then bursts into flames. Behind the glass, Ginny's eyes glaze over in a dusty, inky haze. I look around the store. No one has noticed the oddity occurring at the cash register.

"The King Below," Ginny whispers, her eyes unfocused, gazing into the beyond. "Not many mentions of him in my collection. Mostly just references to references."

My stomach sinks. A dead end, then.

"But I will find him eventually . . . Ah," she breathes. "That makes much more sense." Her eyes blacken even more behind the lenses. She teeters for a second. I place an arm on her shoulder, steadying her as she travels through the labyrinth of her own mind.

"What is it?" I ask.

"It took me a second to notice the connections," she whispers, "but I see him now. He is spoken of in many places, given many names. He keeps watch over the land below and ushers souls to their final resting place once they cross the veil."

"Are there any stories that you can recall directly?" I push. Ginny nods and begins to speak. Her voice takes on a dreamlike quality.

"The King Below, or a version of him, appears in several Western European folktales. One Welsh tale is particularly specific." She fiddles with the burnt paper in her hands. The pages in the still intact book on the counter are beginning to lose their ink.

"Second book on the fourth shelf. Page three hundred and fifty-nine. A raven-haired wizard in the woods discovers his forest is dying. First, the leaves all fall off their branches at the height of summer. Then the flowers on the forest floor wither away. Death seeps out from rotten stumps and consumes any living thing within reach. The wizard knows it is only a matter of time before Death comes for the local village. He finds a medicine woman who knows the forest as well as him. They believe their combined powers might be enough to defend their lands. Binding themselves together, they intertwine their magic and forge a talisman meant to beat back the borders of Death. A key that locks it away. They fight bravely, but the wizard is overwhelmed by necrotic energy. Realizing all will be lost if she doesn't contain the onslaught of Death, the medicine woman throws up a barrier of fog and dreams."

"The veil," I whisper. Ginny nods.

"The boundary she creates keeps Death in its place. But in her haste to protect the forest and the village, she also trapped the wizard on the other side of the veil. He still holds the key they created, which gives him a command over Death. But he is trapped, a prisoner among the dead."

She leans against me; the extended spell is beginning to exhaust her.

"Folktales diverge here at the end, depending on the country of origin. Some say the wizard went mad from loneliness, eventually turning into a trickster deity that lures innocent villagers into deadly bargains. Other tales morph into a parable explaining the seasons. So long as the medicine woman lived, the wizard was able to walk half the year among the living, though he brought Death and Winter with him. But when her time came and she herself passed into the land below, he became trapped forever."

"Is he dangerous?" I ask, my stomach in knots.

Ginny is quiet for a moment; her black eyes shift back and forth.

"I'm not sure?" she says, uncertain. She grimaces, as if the admission tastes sour in her mouth. "He's bound by very specific magic. He can only affect the world of the living through those he bargains with."

I can hear Matthew and Rebecca wrapping up their conversation.

"That's enough, Ginny," I say quickly, taking the burnt paper out of her hands and placing one of my cool fingertips at a pressure point just under her ear. "Come out of your mind. Be here."

Ginny shudders and the inky haze in her eyes floats away, like clouds on wind. She reaches up to remove her glasses.

"Fascinating," she says, wiping the foggy lenses on her sunflower-yellow cardigan. "Why the sudden interest in a figure from the Late Middle Ages?" she asks.

I sigh and shake my head.

"Things are afoot, Gin," I whisper. She gives me a confused look, but the fire of interest lingers in her gaze. I straighten quickly as Matthew and Rebecca come back through the door. Matthew holds a small basket full of glass bottles packed with dried herbs and powders.

"Are you good to go?" I ask him, my voice too chipper.

He nods. "Very well stocked and well educated. The customer service at this establishment is impeccable." He grins at Rebecca, who gives him a beaming smile. It seems he passed whatever test she put him through.

"I hope you two have a great time at the festival," she says, digging into her skirt and handing me the keys to her truck. "Have some of the cider for me."

"Looking forward to it," Matthew says.

The dainty chime rings again as he holds the door open for me. Rebecca's large red pickup truck is parked on the street outside the Raven & Crone.

"Would you like to do the honors?" I say to Matthew, tossing him the keys.

He catches them easily. "As long as you navigate," he agrees.

We climb into the cab of the truck, stuffing the bags of his newly acquired clothing into the passenger footwell. The leather of the seats is cracked with age, but the car is nice and clean and, happily, full of gas.

Matthew sets his basket of herbs between us. I spy the damiana and juniper berries and try not to guess what shadow magic they will be used for.

"That was a very successful trip," Matthew says. "Rebecca is an interesting woman."

"I think it still would have been easier if I'd just gone to the apothecary myself and then picked you up. She will tell the whole coven about you. We'll be lucky if we keep the fact that you're from the Pacific Gate a secret."

"I don't see the need for that," he says, starting the car. The engine roars to life and he pulls out of the parking spot. "And I'm glad I came. I enjoyed the walk into town. I've always thought Ipswich was charming." He grins as we drive down Main Street.

Sunlight is streaming, reflecting off the glass windows and metallic cars. Every store front has finalized their Halloween display with pumpkins, witches, and ghosts, crowding the sidewalks. Zumi's, the local coffee shop, has a chalkboard sign advertising their Autumn Spice and Caramel Cloud Lattes. Groups of people walk with strollers up and down the sidewalks, chatting with one another as their children babble nonsense to themselves. One infant, already dressed in costume as a tiny little pumpkin, naps under a soft blanket in her bassinet.

"And besides," Matthew says, "how would you have survived, leaving a stranger unattended in your beloved cottage all morning?" He gives me an amused sideways glance. I roll my eyes.

"I would have managed through the pain somehow," I say. His grin widens. "But you aren't really a stranger anyway," I add, just to be difficult. This seems only to please him further. His eyes crinkle in amusement.

"It's this turn, right here," I say quickly, remembering I'm supposed to navigate. Matthew flips on the blinker, and the ticking sounds like a countdown as he makes the turn onto County Road. Off to the Bennet Farm. Off to see the meta-magic witch.

CHAPTER ELEVEN
Fright Fest

The road becomes gravel, crunching beneath the truck tires as we make our way to the Bennet farm. Workers are still out in the corn fields as we drive past, taking advantage of the last hours of autumn light. Slowly, the farm proper comes into view. The farmhouse itself is not too large, a wooden exterior painted dark green, and a wide wraparound porch with rocking chairs facing every cardinal direction. The meadow that surrounds the farmhouse has been transformed, as it is every year, for the festival.

Hundreds of people stroll around, some in costume, and all others in classic New England flannel and tweed. Large sugar maple trees, their leaves a burst of bright red, are wrapped up in lantern lights. Dozens of stalls sit in a large semicircle outside the barn, some selling candy apples, others popping kettle corn. Five food trucks from local vendors are parked along the grass, their owners frantically taking orders and throwing specialty tacos and bahn mi sandwiches onto piping hot grills. In the center of the meadow a large stage has been constructed. A local guitar player I've seen perform at Zumi's is strumming and cooing to the audience sitting on the dozens of bales of hay strategically placed nearby.

Matthew pulls the borrowed truck into a dusty parking area, squeezing between two sedans with out-of-state plates.

"You ready?" he asks as he shuts the engine off. I stare out at the festival, watching all the children begging their parents to go into the hay maze.

"I think so," I answer honestly.

My mind races between a dozen conflicting thoughts. Winifred was my mother's best friend. But I haven't spoken to her since mom passed. Would she hate me for prying into this? She's the most powerful witch in the coven. She could curse my magic away, if it pleased her to do so. Hell, I am going to trust her to remove some of my magic this very week. What if I anger her today and she purposefully ruins my Containment? But I need answers. Why did my mother have that tome in the Manor? What secrets did it hold? Why did it look like it was made by Winifred, herself? That question alone was enough for me to open the truck door.

"Well, well, well. Look what the black cat dragged in," a warm and drawling voice greets Matthew and me as we reach the ticket booth. A man leaning against the booth, dressed in raggedy denim overalls, tips his patchy hat toward me.

"Hi, Jack." I smile. Jack Handler is the Bennet farm foreman and Winifred's longtime companion. "How's the festival this year?"

"Busy as always. But that's how we like it. Are you here for the festivities or to pick up your pumpkins?" Jack can be all business sometimes, but he talks to me directly and doesn't question me about Matthew.

"Both," I answer.

"The usual thirty-one?" Jack confirms, waving over a teenage boy in a festival T-shirt and dusty blue jeans. "Billy will take care of you and help you load up everything. Let me know if there's anything else you need!"

The boy named Billy runs over, breathless, and waves as Jack introduces him. Even he does a double take at Matthew.

"Thanks, Jack!" I grin before remembering why we have actually come to the farm. I reach out to stop him as he begins walking away to greet other festival-goers. He turns back toward me in surprise. In a low voice I ask, "Is Winifred around? I have some things I need to discuss with her."

Jack throws his head back and laughs. "You need to get in line, Kate, like everyone else."

I'm slightly disappointed. I hadn't expected the royal treatment, but it stings all the same, considering all I've helped Jack with over the years. The reason he still has hair is because of my Follicle Stimulating Salve. But he's right. Winifred Bennet is always in high demand this time of year.

"Any advice on how to get in said line?" I ask.

"Buying pumpkins certainly helps," Jack chortles. "But once you're done with that, talk to Grace over at the cider booth. She'll let you know about Winifred's availability." He gives a little nod to Billy, tips his hat toward me a final time, and walks off toward the maze.

"Right this way, folks," Billy says, gesturing for me and Matthew to follow him to the pumpkin patch.

"How powerful is this Bennet witch exactly?" Matthew bends and whispers in my ear as we walk. I get goose bumps on my arm as his breath hits my neck but I keep my eyes forward.

"Winifred is the most sought-after citizen in Ipswich," I explain. "Not everyone in town knows that witches live among them but everyone knows if you need something, Winifred can get it done. The fall festival is the only time of year she'll even consider taking visitors. Her schedule fills up quickly over the course of these five days."

"Even for other witches?" he asks, incredulous.

"*Especially* for other witches," I say.

We walk together through the gate of the pumpkin patch. Several small children are running up and down the rows between the gourds, begging their parents for every new variety they come across. A husband takes pictures of his wife and baby, posing together among the vines.

"How would you rate your pumpkin-picking ability?" I ask, turning to Matthew.

"I'm better at carving them," he admits.

"Lucky," I say, "I've never been good at that." I look toward Billy, who has recruited two more helpers, and smile. "I need thirty gourds in total, of all different sizes. And, this is very important, they need to be as round as possible, all a similar shape. No big bruises or flat parts." Miranda always had a discerning eye for pumpkins. If I pick a bad batch, it will give her endless fodder for complaints.

The three boys grimace. This close to Halloween, the best pumpkins have already been claimed. But they run off toward the back fields which aren't as picked over.

"So what do we do?" Matthew asks, watching the boys run.

"While they are doing the hard labor, we can find a warty devil."

I snort at the confused look he gives me. "It's what my mom always called the pumpkins I wanted to take home. I never cared about the perfect pristine ones like she did. I've always liked pumpkins that look almost moldy in their discoloration. The ones covered in bumps and knobs. Plus, no one ever wants those, so they are easy to find late in the season. Like that." I point out one near Matthew. It's sickly green, with a long neck and bulbous bottom, and absolutely covered in warts. He appraises it and then looks at me skeptically.

"And why exactly are these warty devils so near and dear to your heart? Do you have a soft spot for misshapen, mangled, and rejected things?" The tone of his voice is hard to place. He's both teasing me and genuinely asking.

"No, not really," I answer honestly. "It's just that it takes a lot of skill to make a perfect jack-o'-lantern look scary. You have to be a pretty talented carver. Warty devils are so ugly that half your work is already done for you before you even start."

Matthew throws his head back and laughs loudly. Several of the people inside the patch look toward us with bemusement. Ignoring the onlookers, Matthew bends down and plucks the ugly green pumpkin from the vine.

"Your devil, madame." He presents it to me.

"Thank you," I say, laughing as he bows with a little flourish.

He looks at me with mock seriousness. "We should probably get out of here before I cause the rest of the vines to wither and decay. I don't think your meta-magic witch will appreciate me killing off her crops." He glances around at the pumpkins at our feet, as if half expecting them to immediately fall away into rot.

I look off into the distance. Billy is bossing around several other farmhands who are frantically pushing a wheelbarrow around the outer patch of pumpkins.

"All right," I say to Matthew, clutching the warty devil to my chest. "I could use some kettle corn anyway."

The line for the popcorn booth is next to the pumpkin patch. We each grab a bag of the cheese and caramel mix and lean against the fence at the festival entrance. Matthew surveys the grounds. The corner of his eyes crinkle as he scans the horizon intently. He seems worried.

"Looking for something?" I ask, popping a piece of caramel corn into my mouth.

He shakes his head. "I'm simply taking in the sights."

Right.

That worm of distrust wiggles its way back into my mind.

"They don't have fall festivals in Washington?" I quiz, barely preventing myself from rolling my eyes.

He laughs. "I live in Oregon, actually. And yes, they do. I used to take my little sister every year."

"Used to?" I ask nervously, imagining a rather tragic backstory for him.

He flashes me a good-humored smirk. "She's twenty-five now. And married. She's got a kid on the way, so I assume in a couple of years I'll be chaperoning my niece or nephew around the festival grounds, buying them candied apples and trying to keep them from throwing up on the rusty old carnival rides."

"That sounds very . . ." I lose my train of thought for a moment.

Matthew raises an eyebrow at me.

". . . normal." I finish. He laughs.

"What exactly were you expecting?"

"I'm not sure," I admit. "I can never be certain with the Pacific Gate; you're so shrouded in secrecy. I half thought the festivals you'd attend would include ritualistic animal sacrifices and dark dealings among sorcerers."

"And so what if they do?" he responds. "Similar things must happen this time of year in your coven."

"I think not," I huff.

"I'll remind you: we came here tonight specifically to seek out a deal with another witch over an object shrouded in dark magic."

I open my mouth to speak, to claim it's not the same, but the proclamation rings false even in my mind. His words sting in their truth, but at least there is no animosity in his eyes.

"How about your family? Did you come to the Fall Festival often?" he asks, generously changing the topic, noticing my sudden distress.

"Yes," I say. "It was tradition. Mom would load us all up in the car, and we'd roll the windows down and blast the stereo. It always took exactly three rounds of 'Monster Mash' to get to the farm." I smile at the memory of our discordant voices trying to drown one another out.

"Once we got here, Mom would pick out the pumpkins, and Miranda would convince Celeste and me to do the haunted hay-bale labyrinth with her."

Matthew looks incredulous. "How would *that* go?"

"Poorly," I say, laughing. "Celeste would get scared almost immediately, and Miranda always ended up accusing me of cheating my way to the middle of the labyrinth."

Matthew scoffs. "Did you climb up the walls or something?"

"Not exactly. I'd use my powers." I hold up my right hand in explanation. To be fair to Miranda, she wasn't entirely out of line in her complaints. "Part of hedge craft is grounding oneself in the environment. It's how I can travel through the Ipswich Forest and never get lost. If there's something living connected to the land, I can touch it and gain a sense of direction."

Matthew grins. "And you used your grounding to sense the middle of the maze?" he guesses correctly.

I nod. "It always surprised me when it worked. The hay used for the labyrinth is harvested weeks beforehand. I never once felt a spark of life among the bales. And yet I still could always ground myself. I could always get a very weak signal, pointing me in the right direction. So, there must have been some final ember of life among the dried grass."

Matthew looks out toward the labyrinth. The hay bales are stacked nine feet high and take up the entire western back field of the farm. The sun is starting to set over the tallest portions of the maze.

"What if there wasn't a final ember?" He turns toward me. The edges of his jacket are dusty from leaning against the fencing.

"What do you mean?" I ask.

"What if you weren't using life magic in those moments? What if you were tapping into a different power?" His voice is low and quiet as he speaks, keeping our conversation private. But his eyes are alight with something akin to excitement. He continues. "What if you were instinctually adapting your training, which allowed you to ground even among dead plants? You might have been doing shadow magic."

My mouth drops open at the claim.

"That's not funny," I say, actually rolling my eyes this time.

Matthew wraps a hand around my arm gently, leaning into me.

"I'm not making a joke," he insists seriously. "You're the hedge witch. It's what you're meant to do."

"You said as much when we decorated the manor. And I'm telling you now, you're wrong." Every time he has made similar comments, unease twists in my chest. He has to be wrong.

Luckily for me, the conversation ends, as Billy and his two helpers approach us with a wheelbarrow filled with pumpkins. All three of them are sweaty and pant from the exertion. I pull myself away from Matthew and survey their load.

I'm impressed by the job the three boys have done, considering the time of year. Several of the gourds have unfortunate depressions near their stems or on their sides, but for the most part, they are nice and round.

"Are you planning on biking these home, Ms. Goodwin?" Billy asks uncertainly.

"I don't think the wheelbarrow would stay straight if I tried." I wink at him. He blushes a deep red. "We brought that truck over there."

Billy perks up as I point out Rebecca's truck in the makeshift parking lot. "Oh well, we can load these up for you if you want to enjoy the rest of the festival," he offers.

"That would be incredible. Thank you for all your help," I say as I hand him and the other two boys a tip. They all grin widely at the extra cash and begin pushing the wheelbarrow toward the parking lot. I smile back, hiding the sense of queasiness in me, my mind still chewing on Matthew's continued claims about my magic.

"And now the meta-magic witch?" he suggests from behind me. I shake my head.

"No. Now, Grace," I say matter-of-factly. I can't dwell on the shadow magic argument. There are other tasks at hand.

I lead Matthew toward the table at the edge of the hay labyrinth. Grace Harper, a middle-aged blonde woman with permanently sunburned skin and an all-denim wardrobe, collects payment from a young couple for their two pumpkins. On the table before her is a cash box, a dozen or so plastic cups, a large thermos, and a "Free Cider" sign. Several people stand around the table, chatting and drinking out of the red plastic cups.

Matthew walks up to the table, and he takes no notice of the admiring stares that follow him as he fills two of the cups with the steaming caramel-colored liquid from the thermos. He hands one cup to me before taking a sip of his own. My hands growing warm from the heat, I take a small drink, and my heart is filled with maple, spices, nostalgia, and home.

"This is phenomenal," Matthew says after several long drinks.

"It's my mother's recipe," I say to him under my breath. It is a well-known fact around town, but Grace doesn't like people mentioning it.

"I've added my own twists to it," Grace says loudly, shooing away a couple who has been lingering. She turns and gives me a soft glare. Not quite resentment but also not friendly.

"And it's fantastic," I assure her, taking another sip, knowing all too well that the only difference between her cider and my mother's is that Grace made this batch in a cast-iron Dutch oven instead of my mother's suggested copper-lined stockpot.

"Mm-hm." Grace's lips are pursed. "How many pumpkins is it this year, Goodwin?" she barks more than asks. Matthew stiffens beside me but Grace pays him no mind.

"Thirty-one," I answer. "And I'm told you're the woman to see if I want to meet with Win?" I bite the inside of my cheek to keep my tone friendly.

Grace shakes her head. "Farmer Bennet barely has a moment to eat, let alone a moment for you."

"I could come back tomorrow? It's critical that I speak to her though." I say.

"You and everyone else in town," she scoffs. "Her book for the week is completely full. You could try next year." She grins at me smugly. For a moment my whole body flashes over with angry heat. I quickly have to remind myself that Grace doesn't know about the Atlantic Key. To her, I'm another lonely Ipswicher who wants to pay a premium price for superstitious advice.

"There's always the carving contest, right, Grace?" a voice pipes up behind us. Matthew and I both turn to see Billy shuffling awkwardly on his feet.

"What contest?" Matthew asks the boy. There are daggers in Grace's eyes.

Billy keeps his head down, avoiding looking at her. "The pumpkin carving contest that's held every night. The winner gets either their choice from the baked goods booth or a free meeting with the farmer." He points to the stage where the guitar player had been strumming earlier in the afternoon. Currently, seven tables are set up on the platform, each covered with newspaper, carving tools, and a lovely jack-o'-lantern pumpkin, waiting to be carved.

I turn to Grace with questioning eyes. She shrugs.

"He's technically right."

"Well then, that solves the issue. We'll compete in the contest," Matthew says to Billy. I turn quickly to him.

"No, let's not," I plead. "I'll see her on my birthday this Saturday. I can ask her about it then."

Matthew shakes his head forcefully. "No, you deserve answers now." He pulls me away from Grace's booth, his jaw set in tension.

"I would very much enjoy causing that woman a particularly nasty night," he says through his teeth as we walk past several teen girls convincing one of their friends to go on the haunted hayride.

"Don't waste your magic or emotions on Grace. She's been a pill her whole life. It wasn't personal," I say.

He nods but keeps walking briskly away, one hand wrapped around my arm, pulling me along. I grip his arm tight, to keep from falling over as we approach the stage.

"Well, well, well," Jack says as we get closer. "Going to try your luck, you two?"

"Only if there's space for us," I say as Matthew finally releases me. I send a quick prayer that all seven pumpkins have been claimed.

"You have perfect timing, there are two spots left," Jack replies, his happy voice booming across the stage.

"Oh. Can't we work together?" I ask, looking nervously toward Matthew. If I'm going to have any chance of doing well, I'll need a partner.

Jack shakes his head. "No teams. Sorry!"

Well, damn. "Guess I'm waiting until Saturday," I laugh. But Matthew shakes his head, a sly smile on his face.

"Don't you worry. This means we have twice as much chance of winning as everyone else."

"You won't be thinking that once you see my sorry attempt to carve," I mumble. He and Jack both laugh.

A crowd is gathering. Billy and a few other festival workers are corralling an audience for the contest. Several other hopeful contestants are climbing up onto the stage, staring at the choices for pumpkins. Matthew hops up onto the platform and holds a hand out for me. I reach out to him, and he grabs me firmly around the waist, lifting me up onto the stage with him. I'm impressed by his surprising strength.

"You okay?" he asks me quietly, studying my face, which I'm sure is showing every ounce of my discomfort. A large crowd staring at me, a competitive event, and pumpkin carving. It's like all my weird stress dreams from high school have come back to haunt me.

But I don't tell him any of this. I just nod and try to breathe.

He's standing so close to me that my nose fills with a spicy aroma. Cinnamon and rain. I relax. For a brief moment he draws his hand up and down my shoulder in a reassuring pattern, and my skin underneath my sweater heats from his touch. All thoughts of contests, shadow magic, and mysterious tomes start to fade from my mind. Matthew's eyes meet mine. My grip on him tightens. But just as quickly, he pulls himself away from me, and I am left missing the weight of his hand on my arm.

"You're going to be great," he says, leading me across the stage. We walk together toward the tables of pumpkins. Each of the seven jack-o'-lanterns is identical in color, size, and ribbing. No doubt an intentional choice. I half wonder if Winifred had Rebecca plant these for her.

The stage is almost full now. I'm bemused by the collection of people who are standing up here with us. Clearly this is no ordinary pumpkin-carving contest. Where there should normally be groups of friends and families laughing and enjoying the activity, instead there are members of the city council, a local news anchor, and even one of the candidates for mayor. The candidate smiles at me meekly as I stare at her. I wonder what she hopes to ask of Winifred.

The last two free tables are on opposite ends of the stage and my stomach sinks even further. I start my trek to the other end but

Matthew holds up a hand and stops me. He turns to the mayoral candidate, who is next to one of the empty tables, and smiles.

"Would you mind terribly switching tables with us?" he asks her. His voice takes on a smooth, friendly quality, with an ever so slight hint of huskiness. He offers her no other reason or explanation. I almost laugh at his naiveté. But to my shock, she smiles at Matthew and abandons her table for the one on the far end of the stage.

He turns and gives me a smug wink when he sees the surprise on my face, inviting me to take the table next to him. I hardly hear Jack as he announces to the crowd that the contest has begun. Corny spooky music begins playing overhead, and the audience begins talking among themselves as the contestants pick up their tools.

I turn my back to the crowd, pretending to inspect my pumpkin, but my blood is rushing through my head as a distasteful thought crosses my mind.

"Did you just use compulsion on her?" I hiss at Matthew. It wouldn't be the first time he'd cast forbidden magic around me. But it would be the first time he'd done so against another person.

If he's offended by the question, he doesn't show it. But I hear his low chuckle as he spins his gourd around, checking for imperfections.

"Honestly, Kate, be serious," he whispers back.

"I am," I insist. "That woman has been on local access shows for months running nasty dirty ads against her opponents. She's not exactly known for being amenable."

Matthew rolls his eyes in exasperation. Out of the corner of his mouth, he defends himself. "I can't compel living people. Has the possibility that I have a natural charm ever occurred to you?"

I think for a few seconds.

"No," I answer simply, knowing full well it's a lie. Matthew chuckles again but offers no further response.

I look over my pumpkin in earnest now. I'm relieved to see a long scar around its stem. The top has already been carved out, and to my delight when I pull the stem off, the guts and seeds have all been removed. It won't change the outcome of my final result, but at least I won't have to get elbows deep inside the orange stringy goo.

The sounds of the festival come back to me now. The sun is setting and there is a warm glow in the chilly air. Screams come from the labyrinth, and the scent of fudge, cider, and hay wafts over the evening breeze. Mathew and the five other contestants are hard at work, sawing away at the flesh of their fruits. The back of my neck is burning with embarrassment. I wonder if anyone in the audience is perplexed by the woman standing perfectly still at the end of the stage.

Trying not to think too hard, I pick up one of the several serrated tools placed by my pumpkin. I search for the flattest spot possible on the skin, hoping to make things a little easier on myself, but it's perfectly round, pulled straight from a storybook.

I plunge the sharp tool into the flesh of the pumpkin and start to saw back and forth, trying to form the first eye of my jack-o'-lantern. What I meant to be a triangle ends up as a lopsided dismal parallelogram. I try not to panic and attempt to copy the same shape for the second eye.

I spend too much time trying to get the eyes to match. By the time I'm done, fifteen minutes of our allotted half hour has been used up, and I'm left with two very strange oblong holes right in the center of my pumpkin. Gritting my teeth, I continue to work. The only thing keeping me from fleeing the stage is the hope that Matthew has some ounce of artistic ability running in his veins. Otherwise, I don't see the point of going through with the humiliation of it all.

Once or twice, I look at his work out of the corner of my eye. He has started to form a lovely forest scene all the way around his jack-o'-lantern. The trees are carved like friezes. He is working intently on something I can't see, but I'm more optimistic. I smile, even as my hand slips and I accidentally carve a giant slash across my pumpkin's lip. I'm not nearly this clumsy when sewing up a human injury. Then, again, people are much easier to deal with than pumpkins.

The burning on my neck grows hot. What I thought was simple embarrassment is something more. I abandon my carving and turn around, looking for a source of the sensation. My eyes guide me to the farmhouse. To a window on the second floor. It's blacked out, but I am suddenly certain we are being observed. Is Winifred on the other side of that glass? Is the burning a warning or an acknowledgment? I try to remember the way it felt only moments before. Had it been painful, vindictive? Or a greeting? Whatever it was, I feel nothing now as I try to stare through the window into the house.

"Aaaaand *TIME*!" Jack's voice calls out. He congratulates each of us and hypes up the audience as he passes us each a tea light to put inside our pumpkin.

"Shall we start on this end of the stage?" he asks the crowd, pointing to the grumpy mayoral candidate. The crowd cheers. The candidate gives a tight smile and turns her pumpkin to face the audience. She's carved an American flag into the face. While internally groaning at the cliche, I admit I'm impressed by her work. The lines are a little sloppy but the fifty pinpricks of light where the stars should be is a nice effect.

"And what's the name of this artwork?" Jack asks her. Her smile freezes and she looks at him uncertainly. All the contestants look around at one another. None of us knew we were meant to name our pumpkins.

"Sp-spooky Freedom," the candidate says, forcing a grin.

The crowd claps politely, if a little unenthusiastically.

Jack goes down the line. There's a typical smiling jack-o'-lantern with much cleaner lines than mine. A cat in a witch's hat. A vampire. And a particularly interesting candy-corn pumpkin, skin sliced away in different thicknesses to create the candy's white-yellow-orange gradient effect with the fire glow inside. That one is my favorite so far.

"And now for our newcomer. What's your name, newcomer?" Jack asks, holding out his microphone.

"Matthew Cypher," Matthew says with a tolerant grin and a glance toward me.

"All right, folks. Matthew has created a spooky forest for his entry," Jack says to the crowd excitedly, examining the swirling, glowing orange treetops and branch work so delicate it resembles lace.

Matthew shakes his head. "The trees are just the back of it," he says.

With long, elegant hands, he spins his pumpkin around on the table for the audience to see the other side. There are several gasps, and my own breath abandons me.

Right on the center of his pumpkin, nestled among tall and twisted pine trees, is a perfect mini replica of my cottage. Each little roof shingle and window crack is accounted for. The doorway and windows glow with firelight, and the brightest part of the pumpkin is the white-hot smoke rising from the brick chimney. A detail likely missed by everyone in the audience is the kitchen window. Carved behind it is an almost imperceptibly small pumpkin, the crystal heirloom Matthew fixed for me last night.

"Gorgeous. Just gorgeous," Jack tuts. "And what's the title?" he asks.

Matthew's blue eyes meet mine as he considers.

"Home," he finally says out to the crowd. There is a muttering of approval rippling through the packed area, and then a sudden rush of applause. Pinpricks hit the back of my eyes. I look away from Matthew, not wanting him to see how easily affected I am by the sentimentality.

"Truly impeccable," Jack admires. "And finally, let's see what Kate Goodwin has to offer." He walks to the end of the stage and holds the microphone out to me. I clear my throat of emotion before I speak.

"Nothing that can top the previous entry, I'm afraid," I say into the microphone, earning a couple of chuckles from the crowd. I spin my pumpkin around, and the laughs from the audience only increase.

"Oh. Wow." Jack looks a bit horrified by my creation. The microphone hangs limply in his hand.

"The title of my work is *Pablo*," I say to the crowd, with a wry smile. "As I was clearly inspired by the unique art style of Picasso." The laughter grows as they applaud politely. What would have brought me burning shame ten minutes ago causes nothing but amusement now. My head is still swimming from the loveliness of Matthew's carving, and I have no room for embarrassment anymore.

Jack congratulates each of us again and asks the audience for a final round of applause for all the contestants before he grows dramatically quiet.

"It's never easy to single out a winner at these contests," he says solemnly. "I have no doubt you each tried your very best." I don't miss the uncertain look he gives my pumpkin as he says this.

"But there can only be one winner. Which means I must disappoint six of you tonight." He shakes his head with faux regret one final time before pulling a golden certificate out of his overall pocket with a flourish.

"Tonight's winner of the Bennet Farm Pumpkin Artistry Contest, is the submission *HOME*!" He walks quickly over to Matthew and presents the award as the crowd around the stage breaks into enthusiastic applause. Matthew beams at me as he graciously takes the golden certificate from Jack.

The crowd slowly dissipates. The other contestants grumble unhappily as they climb down the stage stairs, until Matthew and I stand on the stage alone. I walk over to him, admiring his pumpkin up close. I'm amazed further as the tiniest of details come into view. He's managed to even carve the correct wood grain of my door into his image.

"Do you like it?" he asks, watching me as I run my fingers lightly over the glowing kitchen window. I nod emphatically.

"I wish I could keep it forever," I say with a slight smile. But we both know that in less than a week this pumpkin will shrivel and cave in on itself, taking all the beauty with it. "How did you get every detail so correct?" I breathe, fawning over it.

Matthew is silent beside me until I pull my eyes away from the pumpkin. He shifts imperceptibly on his feet, almost uncertain in posture.

"Ever since I was last in Ipswich, I've revisited that cottage many times in my mind. And in my dreams," he says after a pause. "I've often thought that I've seen it so frequently I could draw the exterior from memory. It's nice to be proven right."

My heart pounds quickly as he stares at me. I can't stop thinking about how close we are standing to each other. I can't stop glancing at the beautiful carving he made. I can't stop breathing him in. Cinnamon and glorious rain.

But I know he's hiding something from me. Even through all his smiles and kindness, unspoken secrets linger in his eyes. My face falls as confusion and suspicion enter my mind once more. I look down at my feet.

Matthew takes his hand and cups a finger underneath my chin, lifting my gaze back to his. My face burns from his touch.

"I'm on your side, Kate," he whispers.

I frown. "My side against what?"

He takes my hand and gently places a gilded foil certificate in my palm. I look down at it.

Redeem for One Meeting With Winifred Bennet

Right. The meta-magic witch.

"Shall we get you some answers?" Matthew suggests quietly, studying my face.

I swallow, my mind reeling, my skin still warm from his touch, but a chilly breeze brushes across me, and I remember why we're really here.

We leave the stage and walk toward the farmhouse. My eyes flit up to the black windows of the second story. For a moment, the setting orange sun glints off the glass, blinding me.

By the time my eyes adjust, the noise of the festival has dipped perceptively. Excited chatter and entertained screams still echo across the meadow and through the maze, but it's as if every tenth person has fallen silent. And I see why: a figure has emerged from the farmhouse. Standing on her front porch, her wild and curly black hair spiraling all around her face like a spider web, is Winifred Bennet. She is nodding as Jack whispers in her ear. Her gray eyes meet mine. The last time I'd seen her, my mother had just been laid to rest. Not much about her has changed in the past four and a half months. Still, my stomach clenches with nerves as we approach.

"Now, hold up one minute," Grace, who is sitting on the stoop, stops us before we make it to the steps of the front porch. "Only he can go in," she says, pointing to Matthew. "That ticket was for one meeting. It's not a two-for-one deal."

"Enough," Winifred snaps at Grace. "Don't ever speak to a Goodwin woman that way again, Grace." Her eyes seethe with annoyance, and she puts a hand up in quick condemnation before Grace can protest. Then she turns to Jack.

"As I was saying, Sweetness, if Hecate or either of her sisters call on me in the future, there's no need to make them jump through the usual hoops. They get access, just as Sybil did." Her eyes meet mine again, and she smiles warmly.

"Whatever you say, doll," Jack rasps happily. Winifred pats his arm a few times and then shoos him away.

"Now, I believe I owe this young gentleman some of my time." She smiles at Matthew. "Come on in, you two. Let's get out of this cold air!" She beckons us to follow her through the screen door of the farmhouse.

Matthew and I look at each other, and for a moment each of our faces reflect the uncertainty of the other's. But we've come this far. It would be foolish to back away now, especially knowing we've caught her on a good day. I take a breath and step forward, with Matthew quickly following behind me.

"Good, good. Come in, come in!" Winifred says, ushering us through her threshold. "Not you!" she snaps as Grace tries to follow us through as well. She closes the door quickly on Grace's shocked face.

Before I can gather my bearings, the sound of the front door lock clicks into place.

"Now, Hecate," Winifred says, turning to me. The smile on her face vanishes. "Do you want to tell me exactly why you've brought a necromancer to my farm?"

CHAPTER TWELVE
The Meta-Magic Witch

I freeze at the question and the coolness in her gaze.

"There will be no further discussion until I am at ease," Winifred says, giving me a pointed look. Matthew steps between us, blocking my view of her.

"My name is Matthew Cypher, ma'am. We met about ten years ago, during the Michigan Six convocation. Kate has honored me these past few days by acting as my host while I stay in Ipswich." He reaches out a hand to Winifred, but she shakes her head, refusing his greeting.

"My memory hasn't abandoned me, boy. I know who you are," she scoffs. She looks him up and down in a stern appraisal.

"It's so like a hexan to praise the honor of an Atlantic Key witch and yet exercise none himself. Forcing sanctuary. In this day and age? Barbaric." Her eyes shift back to me. My thoughts jumble, unsure what to do or how to get her back to a better mood.

"Well met, Winifred, a curse upon us, I swear we mean no harm to you," I say, hoping the oath will soothe her worry.

She gives me a resigned look.

"Fine," she snaps and walks slowly past the two of us as she murmurs her general disapproval. Matthew shifts as she moves so that he is always between her and me. She uses a cane to support herself—that's a new addition since the last time I saw her. It thuds firmly against her hardwood floor, somehow lending her more authority than she already has. She lowers herself into a quilted chair in the front sitting room, letting out a long groan as she does so, and shifts around on the fabric, finding the perfect position.

"Now, what do you want?" She looks up at Matthew expectantly.

He doesn't miss a beat under her judging gaze. "I competed for this meeting with the intention of letting Kate take advantage of it," he says.

"Really?" Winifred's eyebrows raise in surprise. "You ask nothing of me?"

Matthew shakes his head. "No, ma'am."

Winifred frowns before shrugging. "That makes my life easier, I suppose. What can I do for you, Hecate? Sit down!" she insists, pointing at a small couch across from her chair.

I walk forward but Matthew steps with me, still blocking my path to her.

"It's fine," I say, resting a hand on his shoulder. His brow furrows, but he steps aside all the same. Winifred snorts, amused, I assume, that Matthew thinks he could stop her from getting to me if she wanted.

I walk over to the couch and look around at the house I used to know so well. The sound of the floorboard creaks, the odor of pungent incense, the subtle silent crackle of Winifred's magic in all the walls. It's all at once familiar and alien to me. A place I know intimately and yet haven't seen in years. I sit down slowly on the loveseat and look at my mother's closest friend.

"Win . . ." I pause. How do I explain myself? I look to Matthew, standing tall next to me. He gives me a reassuring smile. I take a deep breath.

"I was visited by Margaret Halliwell the night she died," I say. Winifred squints in confusion.

"Impossible," she says, shaking her head. "Margaret was bedridden, practically comatose. I was with her that last day. She did not leave her house."

I swallow.

"I believe she came to me after her moment of death. As a wraith."

Winifred's eyes widen, and the air in the room suddenly crackles with her energy. The room grows dark as Matthew's intention bears down and surrounds me, shielding me from whatever attack might come from the meta-magic witch. I grip the edge of the couch, ready to fling myself in front of him if Winifred loses control.

"Oh, calm down you two," Winifred snaps. The crackling in the air stops as she regains control of herself. The lamps in the room glow brightly again as Matthew slowly retracts his magic. "I was surprised, that's all." She looks wistfully at the front door. "I shouldn't have locked Grace out. I could use a glass of whisky right about now."

I wrap my arms around my stomach to keep my torso from shaking with nerves. The rough warmth of Matthew's hand rests down on my shoulder.

"A wraith you say?" Winifred gives me a pointed look, her lips pursed. I nod. "Did this vision speak at all?"

"She said the veil was weakening. She said someone called the King Below was testing me. And she told me to find my mother's book to understand why she named me a hedge witch."

"A very talkative wraith, it seems," Winifred grumbles. "And you're certain this wasn't a dream? It's not uncommon for members of the coven to sense the moment an elder passes. If you were asleep, you may have been particularly susceptible to that psychic release. What?" she snaps angrily, looking at Matthew. My eyes fly to him; he's scowling at her.

"Lying does not become you," he says through gritted teeth. I look back to Winifred. Her temple is pulsing as she gives him an irritated look.

"Do not pretend to understand me, boy."

"Win," I interject, needing to have her ire directed away from Matthew. "I thought it was a dream at first as well. But the past few days have convinced me it was real."

"How so?" she asks.

"I found a book. At the Manor. I think it was my mother's. The book Margaret told me to find."

"And?" Winifred looks at me stony-faced. "What did this book say?"

"Well, that's the thing. It's sealed with a complex magic. All it says is 'The King Below will never again know my secrets.' The rest of the pages are blank."

Winifred lets out a deep breath. "Well then, perhaps that's for the best." She sighs.

My stomach sinks at that response.

"I was hoping, for my favor, that you would drain away the Binding magic, so that I might see what's inside those pages." I ask the question, despite knowing her answer will not be the one I hope for.

"Why on earth would I do such a thing?" Winifred scoffs. I study her face, taking in her total lack of surprise over what I have told her. Annoyance, frustration, and even some worry etch the lines of her face. But no hint of surprise.

"You already know about this book, don't you?" I guess, my voice hardly more than a whisper.

She purses her lips but nods, folding her hands onto her lap.

"Your mother came to me a few years after Miranda was born and asked me to make another book. I wondered if there was something wrong with the Recipe Book I'd made for her. She assured me there wasn't but claimed she wanted to get started early on Miranda's." Winifred shakes her head at the memory.

"I thought it unusual at the time. I don't start working on spell books until a witch is closer to her thirteenth year. But Sybil was my best friend, so I made one for her. It was beautiful too. Leather from one of my favorite steers. Wood binding from that oak tree outside. Took me months to carve magic into those pages but it was one of the most powerful I've ever created. Each sheet of paper brimming with intention. Miranda would have been lucky to have it." She pauses, her eyes lost in previous decades and previous choices. Then they clear and flash to me.

"I didn't know the book's true purpose until after you were born. When your mother named you a hedge witch, Margaret and I confronted her. We wanted to know why she took your choice away."

"Did she tell you?" I ask. My heart races, I'm nearly leaning off the couch as I wait for her to answer.

"No," she answers bluntly, and my shoulders sag. "No, she didn't. But in the course of our interrogation against her, Margaret found the book I'd made all those years ago. And to our surprise it wasn't empty, waiting for Miranda to claim it. It was full of horrible, forbidden magic."

Her eyes flit toward Matthew, daring him to be offended. He stands at my side, his jaw tightly clenched, but he makes no comment. She turns back to me.

"I was disgusted, of course," she says. "She was on track to be an elder of the Atlantic Key, and there she was with an artifact of the forbidden crafts. I didn't know what to think."

"What kind of magic was in the book?" I ask, horrified by her story.

"I will not speak on it," Winifred says tersely.

"Well, what did she say when you confronted her?" I push, exasperated.

Winifred lets out a sharp bark of laughter.

"She tried to make us understand. Told us she'd never been happy only being a kitchen witch. She said the Containment had ruined her life. Prevented her from reaching her full potential. That she had to search out sources of power beyond the natural gifts of our ancestors. Margaret and I didn't want to hear any more after that. We left."

"I don't believe this," I whisper quietly. All the blood rushes from my head, and the room tilts as I try to breathe past her words. Winifred looks at me with aching sympathy.

"Some witches are never happy with what they have. Luckily for you, Sweet Pea, that's never been a flaw of yours." I can tell she is trying to compliment me, but the words burn against my chest. Content Hecate. Quiet Hecate. Stagnant Hecate—making endless to-do lists in her cottage at the edge of the woods.

"You said she sought out other sources of power?" I force myself to say, to get back on track of the conversation. "Was the King Below that source?"

Winifred's eyes widen, but she tilts her head.

"I'm unfamiliar with that name. If she ever mentioned it, I have forgotten. But between you and me, Sybil wrote down lots of nonsense. I wouldn't put it past her to have made up such a figure."

She's lying to me. I can see it in the way she grips her cane. Feel it in the perturbed shift in her magic. Matthew's annoyed huff beside me all but confirms my suspicion.

"But Margaret said the name. And Ginny—"

"Do not!" Winifred says, her voice suddenly in a screech. "Do not get my granddaughter involved in this. I forbid it!"

The magical command from the elder twists around me, turning around my mind in a confused flutter. A direct bidding. But there is no way for me to follow the order since Ginny is already involved. If Winifred senses her command failed, she gives no indication.

"The book—" I say, once again trying to redirect the conversation.

"Enough, Hecate," Winifred snaps. "I am shocked at your behavior. You should have reported the wraith sighting. Such an omen is disastrous this close to the New Year. And you should have destroyed the book the moment you realized it was forbidden. Where is it anyhow? Have you brought it with you?" She scans my body, giving the leather satchel at my side a suspicious glare.

"No," I answer simply, thanking all the fates that I'd had the foresight to leave it at the cottage. If I had it on me and Winifred directly bade me give it to her so she could destroy it, I'd have no choice but to obey. And then all my hopes of getting answers would go up in smoke.

"You will bring it to me," Winifred says casually. A command but not technically a bidding.

"I will not," I say, jutting my chin out in defiance.

I shouldn't have said it. I know that even before the words leave my mouth. It's a deadly mistake.

There is a heartbeat of silence after my rebuke; and then Winifred loses her composure.

Her magic plunges into me like crackling, freezing electricity. All my muscles tense as her magic invades my own. I let out a cry, trying to push her out, but it's no use. Winifred's meta-magic scours through my veins and energy, filling all my empty spaces and then emptying out. Repeatedly. Over and over. Scorching my psyche. I cling to the couch to keep from slumping to the floor as my vision blackens. I am utterly at her mercy; she could strip me of all that I am in this moment.

"Enough." Matthew's command is said calmly, quietly even. But the change in the room is sudden. The meta-magic dissipates from my skin and mind immediately. I gasp as my lungs fill with air and my vision returns. I feel nauseous but otherwise intact.

Winifred sits in the same position as before, so it takes me a moment to notice how the scene has shifted. A silky black cord encircles her neck. It floats, not quite touching her, but pulls itself tighter, getting closer and closer to her skin. Winifred reaches up to rip the cord away before it can trap her.

"I wouldn't do that. Even a single graze can infect you," Matthew says, staring at her unblinkingly.

"What is this?" she breathes. Her eyes are wide as she looks at him, and I'm shocked by the fear on her face.

"Leftovers of a curse I pulled out of Kate last night. A curse her mother's book inflicted on her." His voice is clinical, almost bored. I stare at the black cord in amazement. He had saved that writhing nasty piece of blood magic?

"Get it off me," Winifred says through gritted teeth. "I bid you to remove this at once." Such a direct command from an elder would be impossible for an Atlantic Key witch to ignore. But Matthew stares at her, unbothered.

"Are you capable of behaving yourself?" he asks, in a low and quiet voice. Winifred nods quickly. After a beat, the black cord untangles around her neck. Matthew opens his hand, and the curse slithers down across the floor and up to meet him. Like a snake's shadow, it disappears into his sleeve. "Apologize," he demands, still looking at Winifred.

I look between them, in shock. Completely at a loss.

"I'm sorry, Sweet Pea." Winifred turns to me, her eyes misty. "That was wretched of me. Your mother would be so disappointed. I swore to her I would always protect you, and now look at what I've done."

I turn my face away from her. However sincere her regret, I can't quite forget the feeling of having been so invaded. Matthew is by my side instantly.

"Are you all right?" he rushes to say, cupping my chin, attempting to lift my face to meet his eyes. But I flinch away from him. Slowly, he lets his hand drop. I try to ignore the flash of hurt that crosses his eyes. "Can you still feel your magic?" he asks tensely.

Winifred stands from her chair. She sniffles and wipes at her eyes. "I didn't take anything from her. I would never do that."

"Isn't that exactly what you plan to do this Saturday?" His calm facade cracks ever so slightly as he says this. There is real anger in his eyes. Winifred stiffens.

"The Containment is for the good of the witch. More so for Kate than anyone else. She'll finally be protected," she says, a stray tear falling down her cheek. I want to scream in frustration. She is echoing the same mysterious sentiments that Matthew has been saying for days. I bury my face in my hands, trying to block it all out.

"You'll be taking away half of who she is supposed to be. It's a betrayal," Matthew says.

This accusation proves too much for Winifred. I can feel her intention pulsing in grief-stricken confusion. She lets out a strangled whimper and hobbles away through the French doors that lead to her kitchen, a series of sobs escaping from her.

I want to warn Matthew. To insist he be quiet. He got the upper hand on Winifred and is lucky that she has fallen into a delicate state. But if she swings back, if the winds of her mind change again, she could still strip him of his craft while barely breaking a sweat. She could do to him what she had almost done to me, and we don't need an inter-coven war on top of everything else.

Matthew and I are alone in the room together. A grandfather clock ticks loudly in a corner by the fireplace, I hadn't noticed it before, but now it's deafening.

"Kate, I need you to tell me if you're all right." He's calm again but insistent.

"We should leave," I rasp. "She could gather herself at any minute. She won't let you walk out of here, knowing what you could do to her. I've never seen her look so afraid. She'll never forgive you."

"You forget I'm not restricted the way your coven is. I've studied defense against magic like hers."

I shake my head. So hubristic. "Have you ever seen someone excommunicated, stripped of their magic, Matthew?" Finally, I lift my eyes to meet his. Though I'm looking at him in defiance, he lets out a relieved sigh.

"No, I haven't," he admits, holding my gaze.

"And you don't want to. We should leave," I reiterate. I never should have brought him here.

"No, please not yet." Winifred's soft voice comes from down the hallway. Her skirts rustle as she hurries back into the sitting room. She has composed herself, but the regret of her earlier actions is set deeply into the lines of her face. I stand up, steadying myself on Matthew's arm. He welcomes my grip, clasping me tightly with his free hand.

Winifred walks up to me but pauses a few feet away, recognizing she's not welcome any closer. She holds a vial out to me.

"What is it?" Matthew asks.

The liquid inside the vial is a silvery translucent blue. Like pure seawater around northern glacial fjords. It reminds me of Matthew's eyes.

"Tranquilum," Winifred says. Her eyes flutter over me, examining me. Tentatively, her magic reaches out and prods the edges of my own.

"Stop that," I hiss at her, surprised by my own bravery. She flinches back but looks at me with pleading eyes.

"I can see the stress in your aura. Something's eating away at you. You're not sleeping well are you, my dear? Nightmares?"

I don't respond, not surprised that she'd been able to detect that. She nods, taking my silence as confirmation.

"The Tranquilum will take the bad dreams away. There's no sleep more peaceful and steady. There's enough in here for two nights. I can make some more and send it to you or bring it on your birthday. But you should take this vial now. You need to get some sleep. Please, Sweet Pea."

The repeated diminutive breaks me. For a moment I am sitting with Rebecca on the front porch swing, watching mom and Winifred walk the fields, the insects of summer buzzing around me. The farmhouse and all its crackling magic feels like home. I know I shouldn't, that it will put me into her debt, but I grab the vial out of her hand.

"Thank you," I whisper. She nods and then her eyes fall to where my hand is wrapped around Matthew's forearm, his other hand clasping us together.

"I don't suppose I can warn you against falling for him, can I?" she says, looking at me again.

I stiffen, pulling away from Matthew.

"You always assume too much, Win," I respond coolly.

"Do I?" she wonders, her delicateness fading. "Maybe ask him sometime why he never came back to Ipswich after he and his father gate-crashed the convocation, hm?"

"Goodbye, Winifred," I say, desperate to get Matthew away before her eyes alight with fire once again. I turn and leave, trusting the creaks in the floorboard to tell me Matthew is following.

I burst out the front door of the farmhouse. The night sky is pitch-black, but the festival is well lit. The sounds of gaiety fill the air and are exceptionally jarring after the events that unfolded inside. Both Grace and Jack are sitting in rocking chairs on the porch, waiting. A long line of Ipswich citizens has formed outside at the edge of the stairs. They all look at the open door hopefully.

A low wailing comes from inside the house, and Jack rushes past me to comfort and assist his lover. Grace has a look of horror on her face at the sound of Winifred's tantrum but quickly falls into her role.

"All right, everyone, Farmer Bennet is done with meetings for the night. I know—I'm sorry—we will try to find a time to reschedule you."

I don't hear what else she says as I walk briskly away from the house and the fair. Matthew doesn't stop me until we are all the way to the truck, which is now loaded with large orange pumpkins and my single warty devil in the back bed.

"Kate, stop," he says before I can open the passenger door.

"Why do you still have it?" I say, whirling toward him as my frustration finally breaks. There are a million things that I want to scream about, but this is the one my mind has latched on. "Why do you still have the curse? After all your talk of trust! You're going around hoarding deadly blood magic abominations?" I want to stamp my feet and beat at his chest. It's only my desire not to mimic Winifred's erratic behavior that keeps me from throwing a full tantrum.

"I wasn't going to sit there and let her attack you," Matthew says defensively.

"That doesn't answer my question," I insist.

Matthew sighs. Speaking slowly and calmly, which only infuriates me more, he explains.

"What would you have me do, Kate? Release the curse into the woods behind your house and hope that it infects an unlucky deer before it follows the urge to come back and finish the job it started with you?"

I stare at him, unsure how to answer. Sensing my hesitancy, he continues. "Blood curses don't go away once they leave their target's body. They fester whether or not they are infecting someone. And they will always return to finish the job if given the opportunity. I have to keep it tethered to me until I can find a way to destroy it."

I groan and put my head into my hands. Margaret's wraith. My mother's book. And now this. I am being haunted by all that is dark and secret. I long for my Herbal and its Ghost-Be-Gone Gin and Tonic recipe.

"Kate," Matthew says softly, "I promise, I will destroy it as soon as I can."

I lift my head away from the sanctuary of my palms. "Fine," I breathe. "Please just take me home." I don't give him time to respond, jumping into the cab of the truck and slamming the door shut.

The trip to the cottage takes longer than it had earlier in the day. Matthew drives gingerly in the darkness. Even so, the pumpkins roll around comically in the back of the truck bed. We ride mostly in silence until Matthew looks at me from the corner of his eye.

"So, are you not going to ask?" he says.

"Ask what?" I question, holding my hands up to the heating vent of the truck's cab, hoping to bring some warmth into my fingers. My whole body has slowly gone cold ever since Winifred invaded my magic.

"Don't you want to know what the meta-magic witch was referring to? About why I never came back to Ipswich."

"Oh," I say lightly. "I figured the climate didn't suit you." There's more sass to my voice than I intend, and Matthew smirks.

"The truth is I do want to ask," I admit after a few moments, "but I also know that Winifred wants me to. So I'm keeping my mouth shut. I've always been more spiteful than is good for me."

Matthew laughs out loud at that, and I manage to crack a smile as well. We drive in silence for another few miles. It's a dim night made even darker by the spindly tree branches that stretch out over the lane we're driving down.

"I was banished," Matthew says softly after a while.

I sit still for half a heartbeat, convinced I didn't hear him correctly.

"What?" I ask, incredulous.

"I tried to return to Ipswich a few months after the convocation. I couldn't get closer than Salem." He laughs as if the memory amuses him.

"Why would you have been banished?

His smile becomes mischievous but contrite. "I suppose I overstepped my welcome."

"And now?" I question, "After ten years of banishment, how are you able to be here?"

His smile fades as he parks the car in the small drive outside my cottage. It's quiet in the cab of the truck as the engine goes silent. No crickets are chirping in the woods this evening.

"Banishments end when the witches who cast them die. Two witches were involved in mine." His voice is soft, apologetic.

I suck in a breath. "I see." My mother. And Margaret.

"If it's any comfort, I deserved it," Matthew says. "I knew your mother was upset with me for running off with you that first afternoon. And my father *did* warn me not to eat anything more from Sybil Goodwin. But when a kitchen witch offers you a slice of warm banana bread, how are you supposed to refuse?"

I know exactly what recipe he's referring to. Ban-Ban-Banana Bread. It's moist and rich, with a chocolate base and gooey, melty caramel chunks mixed throughout. A sweet cream glaze decorated with dried banana chips always graced the top. Mom made it all the time when I was a kid, though she never added the black pepper, briny sea water, or chrysanthemum petals that were the key ingredients for its magical effect.

"So your first instinct once the banishment was lifted was to come and bother the daughter of the witch who cursed you?"

He turns to me.

"That's not why I came," he says seriously. "And am I really such a bother?"

He has a whisper of a smile on his lips, but his eyes are sincere, curious. I feel his breath against my cheek and realize how closely I am leaning in toward him.

"No," I answer honestly. He smiles and there is a note of relief in his expression.

"I'm glad," he admits, turning away from me and pulling the key out of the ignition. Before he steps out of the car, I reach over and grab his jacket, stopping him. He turns back to me.

"Why are you here, Matthew?" I ask. My chest feels lighter the moment I voice the question I've been holding in for so long. He looks at me for several heartbeats.

"I had a lot of reasons for coming."

"Well, tell me one, at least. And please not the excuse about the herbs. That was the most bogus story I've ever heard." I expect him to laugh, but he doesn't; he just stares at me.

"I needed to see you," he says after a moment.

I don't say anything, but I'm certain he can hear the rapid pace of my pulse. He looks out the front windshield, toward my cottage.

"The Pacific Gate, we have our own rituals that take place on Samhain. As soon as I felt the banishment lift, I volunteered to come to the Atlantic to gather the necessary ingredients. My father was furious. He didn't think I should be wasting my time with it. But I had to come back, to see this place, to see if you'd found what you wanted. I thought about the day you showed me the cottage. I couldn't wait to see it again. To see *you* again. I left my father behind in a seething rage. I've never been a patient man," he admits with some chagrin.

"I traveled through the night, through the rain, only to be met with your wariness and barely concealed hostility." He gives me a lopsided smirk. I glance down at my hands, my own turn to feel chagrined.

"But it didn't matter. Because you had built all you wanted. And I was happy for you. Proud too."

I want to cry. I've spent days assuming the worst about him. And here he was, confessing only innocence.

"I have two more questions," I say, my breath shaky.

"I will try to answer them," he says, looking at me with some unease.

"First, as a necromancer, can you call on spirits to haunt someone? Or send them a message?" I ask.

Matthew nods slowly. My stomach drops.

"Did you send the spirit of Margaret Halliwell to me? To warn me about the King Below?" My biggest fear ever since I'd found the tome in the manor was that Matthew was somehow wrapped up in all this mystery and intrigue. His arrival was too perfectly timed not to be.

Matthew shakes his head emphatically. "That wasn't me," he insists, staring straight into my eyes. And I believe him.

I let out a deep breath of relief.

"Okay," I say with a smile, letting go of his jacket.

He steps out of the cab and walks around the front, to open my door for me. I will my heart to stop beating quite so quickly, but it refuses to listen. My head throbs from my rapid pulse. Somewhere out in the forest, a howl breaks through the trees, sending nightbirds scattering and rustling the canopy. Matthew takes my hand as I get out of the car. I barely have time to register the touch before he leads me, quickly, into the cottage.

When we enter, Merlin gives me an earful, annoyed by how long I've been gone. He runs from my touch, wanting to punish me by withholding affection.

"Great," I grumble. "Now my cat hates me."

"No, he doesn't," Matthew coos, bending down and scooping Merlin up into his arms.

"Right," I smirk, watching the two of them snuggle as I head into the kitchen. A wave of exhaustion hits me from every angle. I want nothing more than to fall into my bed and enter a dreamless sleep. The vial of Tranquilum feels heavy in my pocket, the promise of a peaceful night.

Within two minutes, I have a kettle on the stove and a mug in hand. From my cupboard I pull out my favorite blend of Somnia tea. Matthew sits at the kitchen table, still holding Merlin, and watches as I prepare the nightcap.

"Would you like some?" I ask him as the kettle begins to whistle.

"Please," he says. I sift the loose leaf tea into two metal bubble-shaped strainers and pour boiling water into each cup. I place one of the mugs in front of Matthew and take a seat at the table.

"What's next on our adventure list?" he asks as I uncork the vial of Tranquilum in my hands.

"Well, we can leave the pumpkins for tomorrow. It will be a dry night," I say. I'm not certain of the weather forecast, but I don't want to spend the next hour moving all the gourds into my front room. "Tomorrow I have to carve them all for the grand display. I'm sure you can imagine how well that will go." I shudder at the foreboding task. If Matthew thinks my pumpkin carving tonight was bad, he just needs to wait and see how monstrous my creations become ten pumpkins in. "As for the more mysterious element of our week, I suppose we need to find another way to get rid of the magical barrier on the book now that Winifred has refused."

Matthew takes a sip of the tea. "Any thoughts on how we might do that?" he asks.

"Zero," I say, tipping the vial into my cup. "You?"

I don't know how he answers. The last thing I remember is the drip drip drip sound the Tranquilum makes as I put it in my tea.

CHAPTER THIRTEEN
Something Wicked This Way Comes

My feet are damp and aching, and my lungs burn from exertion. I've been running. Sweat drips down my slick forehead and evaporates rapidly in the freezing night air. I'm shivering and hot all at once. I'm not in my bed—I'm not even in my cottage. I'm in the forest.

And I'm not dreaming.

With rapid breaths I turn and turn, trying to gather my bearings. I walk over to an older trunk and tentatively place my hand on its mossy bark. I breathe in relief as it doesn't shatter beneath me. But that relief fades as my energy connects with the forest around me.

I'm at least four miles from my home. I don't know how I got here. As I attune to my surroundings, all the sensations, from my aching lungs and scratchy throat to the cuts and bruises on my legs, come into focus.

A Dark and Secret Magic

Dawn is closer than midnight, but the sunrise sky is still at least an hour away. If I keep myself grounded, keep my hands on the trees, I can make it out of the woods. I can—

A snapping twig interrupts my thoughts. I press myself up against the pine I have grounded to. There is a small hollow in the trunk, tantalizing in size. It's almost big enough for me to squeeze into, but not quite. Still, I try to make myself as small as possible. Another twig snaps, and my heart stutters. I stop breathing immediately, despite my burning lungs begging for oxygen. My icy breath, fully vaporized, floats away into the sky and is gone forever. Another snap.

I turn my head slowly to look toward the sound, praying my eyes meet those of a deer or some small ground vermin. I scan the darkness, and for a moment, there is nothing. But then, one by one, lights blink out from the abyss. It takes a moment to realize they're not lights, but eyes. Six of them, glowing red like firelight. Deep, guttural growls build from such a low vibration that it seems the forest itself is shaking. The growls grow louder until sharp deafening barks surround my tree. The forest erupts at this. Shrieks from owls, frantic running from nocturnal prey and predator alike, howls that echo around for miles. An intense carnal fear breaks me from the tree, and I run. The canine barks transform into squealing yips and ferocious roars, and the ground around me booms. Whatever these creatures are, they are chasing me.

I run blind at first, in a primal panic. My feet practically fly across the moss-laden forest floor. The hellish beasts are falling behind. I'm losing them.

After a minute of mad-dash sprinting, I throw my hands out toward any tree I pass by. I have to gain some sense of direction. Though my hands connect on the trees for less than a second, my stomach fills with dread. I am being chased farther and farther away from home. I'm not outrunning the creatures. Their movements are not random; they are calculated.

They are herding me.

I would sob if I wasn't conserving every ounce of breath to fuel my sprint through the forest. I dash between old-growth trees, trying to find a pocket to escape into, to circle back around and head toward the edge of the woods, toward safety. But the three creatures have me flanked. Flashes of fiery eyes and visceral growling drive me deeper into the dark. I'll never make it home now. True exhaustion is closing in on me as every cell in my body sputters and coughs out its final bits of energy. I beseech my spirit and the spirit of the forest for any little ounce of magic that might save me. Tears stream down my face as my legs give out underneath me.

I fall face first into the mossy dirt. The forest floor pushes its way up my nose. The cuts and scrapes on my feet sting.

These are my final moments. Celeste. Miranda. My mother. Their faces flash through my mind. Though I don't have breath for it, a long, loud primal scream of despair escapes my lips.

And suddenly, there is warmth as all the trees surrounding me burst into flame, banishing the shadows. I suck in a few desperate ragged breaths, squinting as my eyes adjust to the brightness.

The creatures that were herding me continue to let out whines and barks. I can just make out the edges of their giant silhouettes on the other side of the fiery pines. But they don't draw nearer.

Either fourteen trees all underwent simultaneous spontaneous combustion, or the creatures have brought me where they wanted me. The trees crackle and burn, and smoke fills my nose. I'm too tired to cough, and I feel dizzy, sleep crawling back up through my subconscious to drag me under into an eternal rest.

Somewhere in the distance I hear painful whines and keeling. Yips and roars and snaps. Trees fall over all around me, from the fire, from other damage—I'm not sure.

The darkness comes first, then the silence. The flaming trees extinguish almost as quickly as they had lit. Smoke lifts from the ground, and my lungs fill with blessed cool air. The forest is silent for half a second: no more growling. Soft thudding gets louder and closer to me, and then there are warm hands turning me over.

"Kate! Kate, can you hear me?" Matthew's panicked voice fills my ears. His face is close to mine as I am pulled off the forest floor and into his arms. The relief that fills my body is the sweetest, most intoxicating high. A hand caresses my head, my cheek. He repeats himself. "Can you hear me?"

I squeeze my eyes shut. Tears fall from them, but no sob escapes from my ruined throat.

He cradles me to his chest.

"I've got you. You're safe. I won't let him take you from me," he whispers.

His warm hands push strands of sticky hair away from my face. I cling to him, leaning my head against the crook of his neck. For a long while I'm convinced that he's rocking me on the forest floor, like a child. But when I manage to open my eyes for a short moment, I see the ground moving beneath us. He's carrying me out of the woods.

"What—" I try to speak, but my voice comes out as the smallest rasp. Matthew shushes me.

"Don't talk. Rest. I've got you," he says, his voice lulling me to sleep.

CHAPTER FOURTEEN
Three Days Until Halloween

When my eyes open, my first thought is that no time has passed at all. The sky outside the window is an inky black, the same color it had been in the woods. My next thought is the pain. My arms and legs feel as if they weigh a hundred pounds each. My mouth is sandpaper dry, and an annoying stinging covers my entire body. The only source of comfort is a softness against my cheek. Merlin is purring, curled up on my chest, his little face plopped onto my chin. I kiss his forehead lightly, only to wince as my chapped lips crack from the movement.

Merlin perks his head up, orange eyes shining in the dark. The tiniest little mewl escapes from him.

"I know. I'm sorry," I croak, my throat raw from screaming. Wincing again at the movement, I sit up. Several objects thud around in the bed as I shift. A couple hot water bottles and cloth packets filled with warm aromatic herbs. My feet are wrapped in gauze and smell like aloe

and tea tree oil. The scent is immediately familiar. My phoenix salve—
made especially for burns and cuts.

Standing up, I sway, unsteady on my feet. My body aches but at
least I'm not cold. My hair is dry, combed, and braided, and I'm
dressed in warm flannel pajamas. If not for the pain, I could convince
myself that none of it had been real. Just another round of
nightmares.

Merlin hops off the quilt and runs out of the bedroom. His collar
jingles quietly as I follow him down the short hallway and into the
living room.

The entire front of my cottage glows in soft, flickering light. Every
surface—the coffee table, my writing desk, the windowsill with my
crocheted figurines—all are covered in jack-o'-lanterns. More than
two dozen pumpkin faces stare at me, some grinning cheerfully, some
scowling, some holding back mischievous secrets. Nearly every pumpkin we brought back from the Bennet farm is carved to a state of absolute expressive perfection. And their internal flames cast shadows that
dance throughout the room.

I follow the sound of soft scraping to the kitchen. Matthew sits at
the table, a couple untouched pumpkins piled onto the table beside
him. The muscles of his right arm flex as he uses a flat head scraper to
pull the seeds and stringy flesh out of another pumpkin. Merlin skit-
ters past me and jumps up onto the table. Matthew relinquishes
his project for a moment to give the cat a couple of scratches under
his chin.

"Hey, buddy," he whispers, "you're meant to be watching over
your mistress."

"A job he takes very seriously," I say quietly, grimacing at the pain
in my throat. Matthew is out of his chair and in front of me before I
finish the sentence.

"You're awake." His smile is laced with piercing relief. "You've
been asleep all day. How are you feeling?" He scans me from head
to toe.

"Confused," I admit with a croak. My hand flies up to clasp the sharp stinging and pressure in my throat.

Matthew walks over to my stove, where my cast-iron kettle sits. "That's understandable." He lights the burner. "Sit down and rest. I'll try to make you something for your throat."

He heads back to the table. On the edge of the weathered wood surface sits my Herbal. He thumbs through a few of the pages, looking for something.

I don't sit. I know exactly what I need. Inside the cupboard beside my spice cabinet are my teas, those for pleasure and those for intentional purposes. I grab my most powerful blend of cinnamon spice tea and the last bottle of sage honey I have. I make a mental note that I will need to resupply before the first snow falls.

Matthew stops thumbing through my Herbal and watches as I scoop the cinnamon tea into a tiny delicate bag and tie the top with string. The kettle lets out its musical whistle as I grab the copper mug meant specifically for this concoction and carefully ladle two teaspoons of the sage honey into the bottom. A bag of tea goes above the bed of honey, along with boiling water. The bag spins in the current, and a deep orange color seeps out from it. The honey slowly dissolves as well. All the while, I focus on the fiery scratchiness of my throat and imagine the relief this tea will bring. I use the handle of my thin wooden spoon to give the drink a good mix, to ensure everything is incorporated together.

I take a few deep breaths to steel myself for what's to come. It's hard to let cold air into my throat. I position the cup near my nose, so I breathe in the spicy steam. That is irritating too, but at least it's warm. I turn away from Matthew so he won't see me grimace.

I brace myself and then take the first gulp. The pain is almost immediate. My throat erupts in fire, and my eyes water as I hold back the cough that my body so desperately wants. The liquid pours over what feels like a thousand tiny cuts in the back of my throat, all the way down my neck.

But just as quickly as the burning comes, it fades. My throat is still thick and scratchy but less irritated than before. I take another gulp. Fire again, but less intense, and it fades even quicker. Another gulp—this one is almost manageable. Another and I can finally enjoy the flavor of the tea, warm and spicy. And it doesn't hurt quite so much to breathe anymore. My muscles relax their tension as the pain in my throat subsides. When I set down the empty cup, all that's left of the pain is the tiniest of tickles. I'm relieved. If I'd had an infection, the tea would not have been quite so effective. The damage to my throat must have been irritation from overuse. I can't say the same for my hands and feet. Now that my sore throat has been addressed, I'm aware of the stinging underneath my bandages, and vividly reminded of the night before.

"What happened yesterday?" I ask, turning to face Matthew. He has been watching me this entire time. At my question, his face turns apprehensive, unsure. He shakes his head and sits down at the table. I walk over and join him. My warty devil pumpkin is in front of me, uncarved.

"Was it all real?" I question, not meeting Matthew's eye. I'm almost afraid of the answer.

"Yes," Matthew says roughly, almost angrily, which confuses me.

"Too bad," I whisper. "I was hoping vivid hallucinations were a nasty side effect of whatever was in the sleeping draught Winifred gave me. Guess not."

"Don't let her off the hook so easily. She's partially to blame for what happened. Trying to make a hedge witch not dream? She's a fool." Matthew is insistent. I meet his eyes and see the anger blazing in his gaze. I look away quickly, blushing in shame.

"I shouldn't have taken it," I say in a small voice. I've never walked in my sleep, but I've also never indulged in sleep aids either. I should have been more careful. But Matthew scoffs.

"How could you know it would trap you inside your head and put you in such a vulnerable state? Don't put this on yourself for a single second," he urges. "No, no I should have known," he mumbles. I realize now that his anger isn't directed at me.

"Well, don't blame yourself either," I say, offended and, despite myself, slightly amused. "You're not my guardian."

His eyes flash up to mine with such surprising sorrow that I immediately stop laughing.

"Aren't, I though?" he asks softly, more to himself than to me. Inside that confounding question there is so much regret and remorse that I can hardly decipher it. All I can think to do to comfort him is to reach out and take his hand in mine.

For a moment, he lets me, and our fingers intertwine. His palm is warm and rough against mine. He looks at me, his eyes questioning, hesitant, but the softest of smiles graces his lips. I give his hand a gentle squeeze. At the first moment of pressure, he rips his hand away, breathing in sharply.

"I'm sorry," I say, drawing my hand back toward myself.

"I'm fine. It's fine," he says quickly, dragging his shirt sleeve over his wrist, but not before I catch sight of the red tinged bandage he is trying to cover up.

"You're hurt!" I say, aghast.

"Nothing serious," he tries to assure me, but I shake my head.

"I'll be the judge of that. Let me look."

Matthew sighs deeply but doesn't argue further, rolling the sleeve up again. There is a loose bandage wrapping up his forearm and even further, past where the sleeve can roll.

"What on earth?" I breathe, moving closer to inspect it, but Matthew flinches. "I'll be gentle, I promise," I assure him. He remains tense but doesn't move away from me this time as I softly, very softly, lift one of the bandages. Underneath, there are angry welts and a long, curving gash that extends beyond this first bandage and into the ones surrounding it. This is really, really bad.

"Okay," I say calmly, keeping my alarm to myself, "I need you to remove your shirt so I can get a better look at the entire wound."

He hesitates for a moment, looking at me warily. I meet his gaze firmly, letting him know there is no room for discussion. Reluctantly, he uses his good hand to unbutton his shirt. He shrugs one arm out easily but struggles with his injured one. I assist getting the fabric off of him, placing one hand on the small of his back. He shivers slightly at my touch but doesn't complain. Candlelight flickers across his bare chest. His muscles are tense from either the cold or pain, I'm not sure.

It takes immense effort to maintain my outward composure once the extent of his injury becomes clear. The bandages wrap all the way up his arm and around his left shoulder, down toward his collarbone. I wonder at the suffering he must have endured tending to his wounds all by himself. As well as the pain he must have suffered while taking care of me. And to then spend God knows how many hours carving nearly thirty jack-o'-lanterns? For a moment, as the candlelight and shadows flicker across his entire body, I am simply awestruck by him.

As tenderly as possible, I unwrap the gauze from his shoulder. The angry red welts and irritated skin that begin at his wrist run all the way up to the top of his shoulder in a long and deep gash. I can tell from the smell of tea tree oil that Matthew tried to use my phoenix salve on his wound. But this is too severe for that topical ointment. If this gash isn't immediately addressed, it will likely get infected. This requires Mending.

"Wait right here," I say to him. "I need to get some items to clean out the cut and get you fresh bandages." He doesn't answer me but nods softly.

Merlin patters behind me toward the pantry, but I shake my head.

"No, you go sit in his lap and distract him," I say. He chirps in agreement and heads back to the kitchen to be with Matthew.

I walk into my dark pantry and flick on the dim overhead light. The pantry is in disarray; nothing is where I left it. Some bottles are shifted around or on the completely wrong shelf, and others are toppled over. It takes me several minutes to find everything I need, but eventually I walk back into the front room with my arms full of ointments, fresh gauze, and a bowl to hold any discarded bandages. Before heading into the kitchen, I make a quick stop at my desk and grab my bottle of Mending Medley.

Matthew uses his good arm to push the pumpkins on the table away, making space for me to set down all my supplies. I cut away the rest of his soiled bandages, and my worst fears are confirmed. The gash along his shoulder and arm is incredibly deep. And nearly a day old.

My first step, as with every Mending, is to slowly roll a charged white quartz along the irritated skin. Matthew makes no noise of complaint—doesn't even flinch as I move the rock over the shallow parts of his injury. But the moment it grazes the edges of the deep gash, he jerks away and inhales sharply.

"I see you raided my pantry," I say with forced amusement, to distract him.

"Yes," he says through gritted teeth. "I know I left it in a bit of a state. Sorry."

I shake my head. "No need to apologize. I'm impressed with your herbalism skills."

"Be impressed with yourself then," he says, his voice even now. "The instructions in your Herbal are clear and organized. I would have been helpless without them."

"I'm surprised the book cooperated with you. What diagnoses and treatment did you manage to pull from it?" I tease, moving around to face him as I roll the crystal over the front of his shoulder.

A trace of a smile hits the corner of his lips as our eyes meet; he knows what I'm doing. But his smile disappears quickly as he speaks.

"The most pressing one was your hypothermia," he says. "You had almost no color. Your lips were blue." As he says this, absentmindedly he cups my chin with his good hand, and softly runs his thumb over my bottom lip. Heat radiates across my face from his touch. His eyes find mine, and I'm taken aback by how tortured they are. "I found your herbal compresses and filled the bottles with hot water infused with fleece-flower root, valerian, and fennel."

"Very impressive," I say, barely managing to keep my voice even as he brushes his fingers against my lips. He has conveniently skipped over the part where he must have dried my hair, taken me out of my soaking wet nightgown, and dressed me in flannel pajamas, all while bleeding from the wound on his arm.

I set the crystal down on the table and move around again to address his shoulder. I pick up one of my many antimicrobial salves and dip into it with clean fingers.

"This might sting," I say with a soft warning. He nods again and braces himself against the table.

"It felt like hours," he admits softly as I begin to press the salve onto the edges of the gash.

"What did?"

"Waiting for you to be warm again," he says. "For color to return to your cheeks. Once I was certain you weren't going to freeze, I got to work on all the abrasions. Ow," he hisses as I pass over a particularly jagged area of the wound.

"Sorry," I say, pulling my hand away. I survey the wound again. "I have to use my adhesive to make sure this heals correctly. But it will leave a distinct scar. Is that okay?" I ask. He nods his assent.

I reach for my ice-cold clove oil. I pull the stopper out of the jar and slowly tip it over the very top of his shoulder. He inhales as the freezing ointment pools onto him, but as the oil drips down his shoulder and into the crevices around his wound, I can see the muscles of his back and shoulder begin to relax.

I put on some thin gloves so the numbing oil doesn't affect me. "Can you feel this?" I ask him, softly prodding at the skin of his upper arm. He shakes his head.

"All I can feel is the cold," he says in amazement.

"Good," I say, satisfied. "That means it's working." Now that his injury has been sterilized and numbed, it's time to Mend. I grab the Medley and dip a small ceramic spoon into the shimmery copper liquid.

"You might notice a little pressure and a little heat, but the cold should keep any burning at bay," I say.

With one hand I press together the very end of the gash at his shoulder, getting the edges of the skin and muscle as close together as possible. Then, I pour the adhesive into the wound and watch as it settles and stretches into place, bonding with the skin on either side. I hum, letting my intention flow through my hands and into Matthew. This will be a slow process, and I will use up all my Mending Medley. I repeat the same steps with the next section of the injury, slowly working my way down his arm. For the intention to take hold, I imagine the adhesive properties of the Medley stitching the fractured tissue back together, creating healthy bonds and restoring the flow of energetic life to the skin. The mixture heats under my hands and gaze.

The only sound in the room, other than my humming, is Merlin's purring and the soft whispering flicker of the pumpkin lights around us. Matthew makes no complaint as I work, but every time my skin grazes his, he shivers.

"So," I say as I work, "you were saying about abrasions?"

Matthew lets out a breath and continues. "Phoenix Salve for the scratches and irritation. Goldenseal for the bites."

"Bites?" I say, confused. I pause with the adhesive in my hand. I look down toward my arm and pull my pajama sleeve up to the elbow. My arm is covered in scratches and bruises, but no bites. I run one of my fingers along a small thin scratch on my arm that itches annoyingly.

"Mostly Merlin's handiwork," he whispers.

"What?" I stare at him, bewildered.

"Your feet are covered with claw scratches from him as well. Along with a few bites," Matthew says, watching me out of the corner of his eye.

"No," I shake my head. "Merlin would never hurt me." As if on cue, the black cat lets out a long, sorrowful mew.

"I think he was desperate," Matthew explains. "I woke up last night to him scratching and howling hysterically outside my bedroom door. When I picked him up, he was covered in forest debris and shivering. The back door of the cottage was wide open. The diversity of bites suggests he initially tried to wake you as you journeyed into the woods. First little love nips, trying to get your attention as you walked.

Then, when he realized you were unconscious, deeper and more intense swats and bites. When those failed, he came back for me."

"And then what?" I ask, incredulous. "You ran out into an unfamiliar forest to find me?"

He nods solemnly. "It's been a long time since I felt fear as strongly as I did last night," he whispers quietly. "Yes, I ran into the woods, with no hope of direction. But then I heard you scream. I could hardly breathe from the dread, but at least I knew what direction to Shadow Walk."

"Shadow Walk?" It's the second time I have heard him use that phrase.

"It's the ability to travel long distances quickly by crossing through the veil and back."

I shake my head. "I never knew such a power was possible."

"It's rare. The only magics that utilize it are shadow and . . . hedge." He looks up at me warily. I purse my lips but don't respond. Instead, I turn back toward his arm. I can't let my intention wander too much or the Mending won't take.

For the next half hour, he sits in silence as I work. I hum quietly, helping the wound stitch back together, and keep my eyes focused on his arm. But I notice every time his gaze shifts toward me again.

Finally, I pour the last scrapes of the Mending Medley from the bottom of the container onto the shallow edges of the wound near his wrist. I prod the top of his shoulder, pleased to find the adhesive up there has already settled, forming a seamless bridge and seal. Matthew's whole arm shimmers in the candlelight, his copper scar radiating like frenetic lightning from his shoulder down to his wrist.

I grab the gauze, take a clean crystal, and quickly graze it along the edges of the cloth. Then I wrap the gauze around Matthew's wrist, all the way up his arm, and around his shoulder, meditating and imagining the skin healed, warding off infection and pain.

I study the new bandages, pleased with my work. Slowly, my mind leaves triage mode, and I am left in terrible awe by the size of his injury.

"What did this?" I wonder quietly.

"Hellhounds," Matthew answers, as if that is a perfectly acceptable response. I want to laugh, but the seriousness with which he says it keeps me quiet.

"Hellhounds? Coming after me?" I ask.

Matthew nods.

"Why?" I breathe. I can't imagine it. I hadn't even known such creatures existed before last night.

"Because you're the hedge witch," Matthew says, standing and reaching for his shirt, currently lying on the kitchen table. He looks at the wrapped bandages with appreciation and moves his arm easily about, seemingly free from pain.

I want to groan.

"You keep saying that, you know. And it never actually explains anything."

Matthew begins buttoning his shirt. "I know," he says apologetically. "It would all be easier to explain if you had been properly trained in your craft."

I flash with anger at his words. I walk away from him, toward the back of my kitchen, and set down the empty bottle of adhesive, admittedly a bit too loudly. The fact that he can move his arm again should be proof enough that I'm not the imbecile he so clearly perceives me to be. But I take a breath instead and turn to face him again. Last night should be proof enough to me that there are things I hadn't been warned about.

"Then tell me. What exactly about hedge craft has been hidden from me?" I ask.

Matthew abandons the effort of buttoning the top few buttons of his shirt, giving me a wary look.

"When we decorated the manor," I continue at his hesitation, "you were upset I didn't know how to Shadow Walk. You also mentioned other shadow magic—Binding, Siphoning, and Guiding?" I scrunch my nose up as I try to remember that contentious conversation. "What are those?"

He considers his words for a moment.

"Binding is a form of communion with long-gone spirits," he says. "Any ten-dollar psychic on the side of the highway pretends to talk directly with the dead. Only a hedge witch can actually do it. Siphoning is the ability to transform life energy into that of death, and vice versa. Guiding is the act of leading a spirit from this world into the next when their time has come. It is the most critical duty of the hedge witch."

I sag against my kitchen counter, under the burden of all my confirmed fears. Once again, I'm thirteen years old, hesitating at the edge of the forest with my mother's hands pushing me forward. There has been so much I was never taught. Even through this feeling of defeated exhaustion, I am angry. My mother violated all our coven's traditions to name me a hedge witch and then spent my entire life hiding half my magic from me? What was the purpose of it all?

"How do you know all this?" I ask Matthew, trying to ignore the stabbing feeling of betrayal in my chest.

"The Pacific Gate has known of you since the day you were born. You were the first hedge witch in centuries. I grew up hearing about the girl in the east who would take up the mantle and walk the boundary of life and death. Where I am from, you are revered. Is it any surprise that I joined my father on his trip to Ipswich ten years ago? I had to see you for myself."

"I'm sure it came as a nasty shock, then. To find a run-of-the-mill witch, incapable of doing anything of significance." I laugh hollowly.

A brief look of frustration crosses Matthew's face, and suddenly he is crossing the room, coming straight toward me. My legs root to their spot. He stops right in front of me, our chests nearly touching. His body heat warms the surface of my face. I smell the cinnamon and rain of his skin, his copper scar glowing underneath the gauze. He lifts his bandaged hand up and reaches out to me. My vision swims in surprise, and I stop breathing. Wondering, anticipating, unsure what is about to happen. But he stops, his hand just in front of me.

"This is not the work of a 'run-of-the-mill' witch," he insists in a low whisper, twisting his arm around to show the extent of the bandages. "This is a miracle." He speaks slowly, reverently.

I shake my head. "Even so, I can't do all the things you say I am supposed to do."

"But that isn't true," Matthew says in a rush. His hands grip onto my shoulders. "You Shadow Walked last night, however inadvertently. You said to Winifred that the wraith spoke to you. Only a hedge witch could hear those words. Even if you weren't taught these talents, the magic is there, desperate to be used."

"But why would my mother name me a hedge witch and then keep all this from me?" It was nonsensical. And if these elements were really part of hedge craft, how was it a sanctioned practice in the Atlantic Key?

Matthew opens his mouth to speak but then shuts it just as fast, a frustrated look on his face.

"That I can't say. Your mother's choices were her own," he answers.

My frustration intensifies.

"I need to get inside the book, Matthew," I say, glancing over to where the tome sits, still on the coffee table, from the night Matthew removed the curse from my hand. Margaret's warning, Winifred's evasion. My mother's silence. Everything points back to the book. The desire to remove the blood magic charm has flamed beyond curiosity. Every ounce of my intuition is focused on the need to know what is inside those pages.

Matthew's hands drop from my shoulders.

"I understand," he says. "I wish I knew a way to help." His forehead crinkles as he frowns, and his eyes flit back and forth as he considers different options.

"I think I know someone who can," I say, moving away from him. At my desk in the corner of the living room, I tear a scrap of paper out of my Herbal and strike a match to light my silver-ash candle. I pick up a pen.

A Dark and Secret Magic

Ginny,

I need to meet with you. I need to know more about the King Below. And charm removal.
When?

—Hecate

I roll the paper up and wrap it in dried elderflower before holding it above the flame. Winifred's bid not to involve her granddaughter floats through my head. But since she hadn't worded it quite right, there is room for evasion. I cling to that loophole desperately and push the paper into the flame. It bursts into smoke, disappearing from my hands.

"What time is it?" I ask over my shoulder.

"Ten minutes to ten," Matthew answers, walking over to me.

"Excellent," I say aloud. Ginny will be up for at least four more hours. No true book witch goes to bed before three. "I can stay up and wait for a respon—"

I haven't even finished my sentence when a draft blows in through my fireplace. *Le Morte D'Arthur* in my reading chair flips open from the wind. Dark, scratchy writing appears on the inside cover. Matthew and I both lean over the book and read the messy script.

Midnight. Salem Library. Ask for Laurie.

CHAPTER FIFTEEN
The Witching Hour

Rain thrashes against the windshield as we drive into the library parking lot. There is half a tree's worth of windswept orange leaves plastered to the side of Rebecca's car. The library is large, out of place, even for downtown Salem. There are over a dozen cars parked, *a lot for midnight on a Wednesday,* I think to myself.

We exit the car, and I let out an ungraceful scream as the rain pelts my face. Laughing, Matthew grabs my hand with his good arm and pulls me forward. We run through the rain, into the colonial brick building. Warm air rushes around us once we get through the glass doors. There are long tables arranged in an open central room, with rows and rows of bookshelves in every direction. Hushed whispers echo quietly around the room, along with Matthew's and my labored breaths from running, but for the most part it's quiet. A sandy-blond-haired man sits behind the reception desk.

"Hello," I say in a hushed tone.

The man looks up from his desk and smiles. His tired eyes go wide when he sees Matthew. I look at Matthew's recently bandaged arm, but thankfully it is hidden beneath his shirt. No sign of the healing cut and glowing adhesive. The receptionist's eyes dim in disappointment after a moment, once he sees Matthew's hand grasping mine. I blush and try to pull away, but Matthew tightens his grip ever so slightly. Not so much a command as an invitation. I let my hand settle into his, enjoying the warmth.

"How can I help you two?" the receptionist, whose name card reads "Michael," asks in a whisper.

"We're looking for Laurie," I say. The man's eyebrows rise in surprise.

"Oh," he says. "She doesn't get many visitors. Her office is down and to the left, at the very back of the archives."

We thank him and make our way toward the other end of the building. Around my shoulder is a knitted grocery sack. Inside, wrapped in several scarves, is the cursed tome. I cling to the bag as we walk past shelves covering American history and sociology. We turn down a darkened hallway lit by a single lamp that swings from its fixture despite no air vents in the vicinity. The only door looks like it goes to a janitor's closet. I look to Matthew uncertainly. He shrugs, equally confused.

I reach out and knock on the closet door. It swings open, and Matthew and I both take a step back as a young woman with the largest pair of glasses I've ever seen steps out. She has cool brown hair in tight curls piled into a sloppy bun, and she is wearing a long gray dress with a pocket watch dangling from a belt tied around her hips. Ten small clockwork rings adorn her fingers. I recognize her from some of the past Samhain gatherings, a time witch.

"You're early," she says sharply, looking both of us up and down.

"Laurie! Good to see you," I say, holding out a hand. "I'm here to meet with Ginny. She said to ask for you."

Laurie stares at my outstretched hand for a beat before looking back up at me, her eyes magnified behind her giant glasses.

"You're early," she repeats.

"Sorry," I say, a bit taken aback but getting the sense that we have offended her.

"No use apologizing. Ginny must not have told you how things operate here. May I have your name and coven affiliation? I need to write it down in my Time Table."

"Oh yes, I'm Hecate Goodwin." I say.

"Coven affiliation?" she asks, pulling out a palm-sized leather journal and a quill pen from the pocket of her dress.

"Atlantic Key," I mumble quietly, embarrassed for assuming she'd know who I was.

"Really?" Laurie's head pops up from her book and she gives me a closer look. "Have we met before?"

"Once or twice," I admit. She shakes her head.

"Sorry about that. I can't remember a human face to save my life."

"It's fine." I smile. My mother told me once that time witches use memories as sacrifices to practice their craft. It makes sense that my few unimportant interactions with Laurie are no longer embedded in her mind.

"And you?" she says, turning to Matthew.

I tense but he answers her question in a relaxed tone.

"Matthew Cypher of the Pacific Gate."

She pauses her scribbling, giving me a questioning look.

"I vouch for him," I say firmly.

"All right then," she grumbles, writing his name down in her book. "We still have a few minutes, but come in. Better to wait out of view." She beckons us into the small room behind her. Matthew and I walk in, side by side. It's cramped with the three of us in there. We stand around a small coffee table with two large hourglasses on top. The room echoes from the ticking of discordant, unsynchronized clocks. The walls are covered with time tellers, their minute and second hands moving in hypnotizing patterns.

"Don't stare at those!" Laurie says to me urgently. I rip my eyes from an intricately carved cuckoo. "Don't want to get lost in time, do you?" she asks.

"No?" I say in a hushed, uncertain whisper.

She holds out a finger, and I don't try to talk further. Her right wrist nearly bumps against the edge of her nose as she studies her diamond-encrusted watch.

"Just two more minutes until midnight. No speaking, please. I need to concentrate."

Matthew gives me a smirk as we stand awkwardly in the dark room. I itch to say something, to ask where Ginny is, but Laurie's pointer finger is still up, a beacon of silence.

After a long bout where the only noise is the incessant ticking of clocks, Laurie lowers her wrist.

"Ten more seconds now. Look here, please." She points to one of the hourglasses, filled with pitch-black sand. "You will have thirty minutes."

"Thirty minutes?" I ask, dragging my gaze to her.

"Eyes on the hourglass!" She snaps her fingers at me and points toward the coffee table. Matthew snorts at her tone. I nudge him with my elbow but keep my eyes where Laurie has directed.

"It's time," she says. With elegant hands covered in rings, she lifts the hourglass and turns it over and then sets it back down onto the table with a thud.

"Oh good! Right on time," Ginny's voice breaks through the silence. Matthew and I both turn toward the sound. My mouth drops open. We are no longer in the small cupboard. The room has become a spacious study bursting to the brim with overloaded bookshelves, a writing desk, and several large leather chairs that smell heavily of cigarette smoke.

I turn around. Laurie and the cupboard are gone, replaced by a brick wall. A marble console table sits against it, with the hourglass on top. Black sand slowly pours through the bottle's neck into the bulbous bottom.

"Ginny?" I ask, turning back to look at her. She is dressed in a tweed jumper with dark brown stockings and a beige turtleneck, standing in front of one of the bookshelves. She eyes Matthew with interest and turns to give me a knowing smile, but her face falls.

"What the heck happened to you?" she demands to know, taking in the bandages on my feet and legs.

"Long story. What is this place? Where are we?"

Ginny looks around. "We are still in Salem Library," she says. "These are the archives of the Atlantic Key. Only elders and book witches are allowed in here. But Laurie owes me some favors. It's normally her job to protect the room from non-coven members." She gives Matthew a smirk.

"Protect it how?" I ask, still marveling at the space around me.

"I don't know exactly. She puts it either in the recent past or distant future. She's told me several times, and I always forget." She waves her hand, as if the details are irrelevant. I turn to Matthew, exasperated. He laughs at my expression.

"You don't think this is a bit peculiar?" I ask.

"Time witches are peculiar folk," he says.

I turn back to Ginny. "Does your mother know you're here so late?"

"There is no 'late' in the witching hour. And you're wasting your sand," she says, snapping her fingers and pointing toward the hourglass behind me.

"Right." I cough. "Well, first I have something for you." I reach into the knitted grocery sack and pull out *Le Morte d'Arthur*. Ginny smiles, pleased, and holds out a hand. I give her the book, and she strokes it lovingly.

She takes it from me eagerly and places it on a writing desk, next to several other books on medieval folklore.

"I'm glad you reached out. I've been looking more into the King Below ever since I did my recall for you. My own library wasn't enough, so I had to come here. Laurie's been nice enough to hold it open for me all day."

I expected as much. Once Ginny is on the scent of a good research topic, it's difficult to get her to come up for air. The room we are in is in a state of disarray matched only by Ginny's room at Rebecca's house: papers strewn about; books piled high in different corners; a large tote bag with pens spilling out of it, lying much too close to the burning embers in the fireplace.

"Find anything new?" I ask.

"Yes," she says. Her face turns grim. "Nothing good, though."

"Well, that's comforting," I grumble. She looks contrite as she picks up one of the books on folklore. The pages are scribbled over in inks of a dozen different colors—Ginny's own note system that I've never been able to make sense of.

"It took me a while to figure him out. But there are dozens of references to the King Below in books collected by the coven as well as in the journals of our ancestral mothers." She points to a section of the bookshelves where hundreds of bound leather tomes are crammed against the wood, their spines cracking from age and confinement.

"Margaret Halliwell's Navigator is the most recent addition to the collection. Her whole book is written in code, but it didn't take me too long to crack it." Ginny smiles smugly, always endlessly proud of her mental prowess.

I tense with anticipation. "Did you read her diary entries? Were there any mentions of my mother?" Winifred had said that she and Margaret had confronted my mother after my birth. Maybe Margaret had written about the encounter. I cling to a small hope that perhaps her version of events will paint my mother in a better light than Winifred's. My hopes are dashed as Ginny shakes her head.

"No," she says. "Her diary entries weren't very personal, mainly just descriptions of the ocean currents she encountered during her daily swims. But there was one specific page I found fascinating."

Her eyes flash with intention, and the pages of the Navigator flip wildly before settling in her hands. She holds the book out to me and Matthew.

From the Records

Amelia Williams: b. 1626, d. 1657. Hedge witch
Sarah Bennet: b. 1662, d. 1699. Hedge witch
Frances Langmore: b. 1757, d. 1792. Hedge witch
Abigail Browne: b. 1795, d. 1809. Hedge witch—TKB?
Hecate Goodwin: b. 1993. Hedge witch

"I went into the records myself to confirm this list," Ginny says. "The Atlantic Key used to consistently have a hedge witch among our ranks."

"Here," I point at the witch who came before me on the list. "Margaret made a note: TKB."

Ginny nods. "I had the same thought. The King Below. I went looking for the journals of all the witches listed here. But the archives won't give them to me." She shoots a sullen and offended look at the stuffed bookshelves. "So I checked the journals of other coven members who were alive at the same time as Abigail Browne. Several members wrote of her sudden death. It was preceded by horrible nightmares. She kept complaining to her mother of a silver-haired man chasing her through the forest in her dreams."

"The King Below." I shiver. Ginny nods again.

"Apparently he used to wreak quite the havoc on the Atlantic Key in past generations."

"I thought he only affects those who make deals with him," I say to Ginny, reminding her of our conversation at the Raven & Crone.

She nods hesitantly. "He cannot touch most living creatures. His dominion is typically over the dead."

There is a silent but deafening *but* at the end of her sentence.

"Typically?" I ask, resigned.

Ginny's eyes flit with uncertainty. She opens another one of the old books on the writing desk and skims her eyes over it. "Well, given the secondhand accounts from many of the journals, despite his restraints, he may be able to interact with . . . a hedge witch."

I plop down into one of the leather chairs.

"Of course," I say with a laugh. An aching sadness blooms in my chest as I imagine the plight of the poor women who came before me. Girl, in Abigail Browne's case. She had only been fourteen when she died.

"It's still a little complicated," Ginny rushes to say. "He is bound by the rules of nature. But a hedge witch is more at risk by the very nature of her powers and the origin of the King Below's existence. Especially now, as Samhain nears and the veil weakens."

My breath catches at how close her words resemble those of Margaret Halliwell.

"How much worse can it get?" I ask her. She quirks her head.

"Worse?"

"What else can he do to me? Last night, I was attacked by hellhounds. Can it get worse than that?"

Ginny's eyes go wide, and she makes a sweeping motion with her hand, a protective sigil.

"Using hounds on a living soul?" She whistles in horror. "That skirts dangerously close to breaking the rules that bind him. He's risking incurring nature's wrath. Which means he's getting desperate."

"What does he even want with me?" I ask.

Ginny sighs. "I can only guess," she says.

"Then guess," Matthew prods her, his voice gentle but firm. She picks up a different book, a notebook, and holds her hands over it. It flips to a page in the middle.

"A hedge witch can be his counterpart on the living side of the veil, just as that first medicine woman was," Ginny says, skimming her notes. As she reads, she takes a pen that had been shoved into her hair and underlines a new sentence. "Their interconnected powers maintain the boundary between the lands of the living and the dead. The hedge witch guides spirits across the veil, and the King Below accepts them into his realm so they may rest.

"When the veil is healthy and both guardians play their part, the King Below can walk in the world of the living from Samhain to Beltane. But as we've seen, yours is an uncommon craft."

"And apparently I'm not even practicing correctly," I say bitterly.

Ginny continues. "My guess is that the King Below is weak after working alone for so long. He plans to make you *his* hedge witch. He'll have you help him maintain the boundary so he may regain strength and be able to travel between worlds again." She sets her notebook down and walks over to the shelves of journals. She pulls one out and opens it to a page near the back.

"There are some notes in the oldest ancestral journals that suggest the Atlantic Key might be the descendants of the medicine woman from the folktale. I'm sure you're a tantalizing prize for him. Original bloodline and a practitioner of hedge craft."

"Why come for me now, though? I'm almost thirty-one. Why wait all this time?"

Ginny shrugs. "Perhaps he didn't have a choice. His influence in the living realm is limited for most of the year, save for the weeks around Beltane and Samhain. And even then, he must conserve his powers wisely. Or maybe you've been under some form of protection until recently?"

Mom.

All these years, she'd lied to me and protected me. And now, without her, I'm defenseless. Just as Matthew had said. I suddenly feel very, very alone. I lean forward and put my head in my hands. I stay like that for a long while. Eventually, I feel a warm hand touch my shoulder.

"Kate." Matthew's voice is soft. I turn to face him.

"Did you know all of this?" I ask him. He stares at me, his mouth in a hard line.

"There have been . . . rumblings in the Pacific Gate. Rumors. I needed someone else to confirm them to you, though." He speaks slowly, choosing his words carefully. His eyes scan the walls of the room.

"So, is that it, then? Some ancient death guardian is coming to drag me to the underworld?"

"I won't let that happen," Matthew says to me.

"Good luck," Ginny scoffs, still reading through the journal in her hands. "Once the sun sets on Halloween, his powers will be at their maximum."

"As will Kate's," Matthew says firmly.

"Is there any way to appease him?" I ask Ginny. The idea of my sisters and the whole coven being in danger, and the idea of Matthew trying to intervene, has made my hands go clammy.

"Well, you could always agree to be his hedge witch." She laughs nervously.

"No," Matthew growls from his chair.

"What exactly would be the outcome of that?"

"It's not a notion worth entertaining!" Matthew argues. I turn to him and raise an eyebrow. He shuts his mouth but continues to scowl darkly.

"Based on his behavior in the stories, it would be a disaster," Ginny breathes. "He'd likely use your powers and vitality to walk the land of the living for six months every year. Striking devilish bargains and wreaking havoc in mortal lives. And let's not forget that not a single witch on Margaret's list saw the age of forty."

"Is there anything I can do? To protect myself?"

"He's a creature of darkness. He operates in shadows. As long as the sun shines, he cannot get to you."

"And when the sun goes down?" I prod.

Ginny's face is grim. "Protective barriers on your home. Charmed sachets. Call on the ancestors. Anything to bring good luck." She cracks a small smile, but it doesn't reach her eyes.

I slump back slowly into the leather chair.

"I should write to Miranda, tell her and Celeste not to come for Samhain. No one from the coven should come," I whisper, my voice shaking. Matthew rises from his chair and walks to me. He kneels down beside me and takes my hands into his. Ginny watches us with fascination.

"Look at me," he urges. I meet his gaze. "Nothing is going to happen to you or your family. Nothing." His eyes are dark and serious. His voice unwavering.

"Are you not listening, Matthew? I'm a sitting duck. Actually, it's worse than that because my magic is all tied up together with the very creature that's hunting me. And now that my mom's protection is gone, there's no hope."

"That's not true," he insists. "You have your powers. You have your sisters. Your coven."

"I can't bring them into this," I say.

"You already have," Ginny reminds me.

We both stare at her and she shrugs. "Don't get me wrong, I'm happy to help. I don't think I'll be much use in an actual confrontation, but any if there's any information you need, I will do my best."

The bag at my side grows heavy at the reminder.

"Did you manage to look up charm removal?" I ask.

"No, I was too busy," she says regretfully, looking at all the books strewn across the desk and floor of the study.

I pull the cursed book out of the sack.

"This book—don't touch it!" I say as she reaches a hand toward it. She draws back. "It's steeped in a curse made of blood magic. The curse prevents any of the words inside from being seen. As a book witch, is it possible you could still read it?" It was my last single thread of hope.

Ginny looks thoughtful.

"Maybe. Open it up and let me see." She leans forward as I gingerly flip to the middle. The pages are as blank as ever. Ginny stares at it for a long time.

"There is . . . something," she whispers.

My heart leaps.

"Really! You can read it? What does it say?" I ask quickly. She leans away from me and shakes her head.

"I can't read it. But I can feel the words. The book wants to be read. It's definitely not blank." She scrunches her nose. "Why don't you just ask Grandma to remove the curse?" she says after a moment.

"We already did," Matthew says quietly, still beside me. Ginny smirks.

"And she refused? Interesting," she says, tapping her fingers on one of the books by her side. "Well, I didn't have time to look anything up. But Grandma always says if a meta-magic witch is out of your reach, use water from the River Styx to wash away blood or shadow magic."

My stomach sinks. Water of the River Styx is one of the most powerful ingredients a witch can have in her cabinet. The name is a euphemism: water from a section of river in which someone has recently drowned, but it's incredibly rare. It seems every time I get close to opening my mother's book, another obstacle gets put in my way.

"It's a shame Margaret isn't still alive. Any sea witch worth her salt would have water—" I stop talking, realization dawning on me.

"Kate?" Matthew asks, staring at me. "Your sister Miranda? Would she have the water?"

I shake my head and laugh.

"It doesn't matter if she does. I already have some."

CHAPTER SIXTEEN
The Grimoire

"I can't believe I had it this entire time," I say aloud, holding the vial up to the lamp near my desk. Flecks of waterlogged soil float around in the murky mixture. The vial Margaret left me in the mangrove box with her unused tins of Hawthorne balm. Water of the River Styx.

"Amazing," Matthew says beside me, also inspecting the vial in my hands.

After waiting out the rest of our half hour in the library, and receiving a very curt goodbye from Laurie, Matthew and I had made our way back to my cottage through the pouring rain.

"Margaret used her final moments on this plane of existence to tell me to find my mother's book, all the while knowing she was leaving me the very key to unlock it." I look at him in amazement. "But how could she have known I would find the book?"

He looks at me with a soft smile. "Things that need to be found tend to show up. Especially when witches are around."

I smile back at him, but my stomach feels frozen.

"Are you ready?" Matthew asks. I nod and walk toward my fireplace, clutching the River Styx water against my chest like a talisman.

I sit by the hearth, fanning out my long skirt around me. Merlin curls up into the folds of the fabric. Matthew sits by my side. I pull out the cursed book from the knitted bag.

The heat of the flames does little to warm me. The cold I feel is internal. Dread.

I uncork the vial and look at Matthew expectantly.

"What?" he asks, concerned.

"Hold out your hand. It's time to make good on your promise," I say. He looks at me for a moment, searching my eyes for meaning before understanding dawns on him.

"Must I? It's proven itself quite useful."

"Hand," I insist.

His hand automatically lifts up toward me and that inky black shadow begins to pour out of his skin, wrapping around his wrist. Up close I can see the curse for the true horror that it is, blood and necrotic magic wrapped up into one. Slivers of it thrash against his skin and small tendrils try to reach out for me before being subdued by the shadow magic.

I take his hand in mine. Matthew clenches his mouth tightly shut, concentrating on keeping the curse under control, subduing any way-ward tendril that reaches out for me. With my thumb, I unstopper the vial. It uncorks with a gasping pop as the seal breaks. Oxygen rushes in, and the water inside the vial begins to bubble. I hold it over his wrist, where the majority of the writhing curse sits.

"Careful," Matthew warns.

"Water of the River Styx can't dissipate magic inside a witch or hexan. This won't hurt you," I say impatiently.

"I know that," he insists. "I'm warning you not to spill. Other-wise, you might not have enough for your mother's book."

I bite my cheek to keep myself from rolling my eyes. I focus on the task at hand. I tilt my wrist at the most discreet and perfect angle so that one single drop of the murky brown water separates from the vial and falls onto the black coil. I half expect some piercing shriek or wail, but the magic simply dissolves away into a faint mist. We both stare at his now empty wrist for a few moments before I release his hand.

"Well," I say, "at least we know this stuff actually works." I close the stopper on the vial with a satisfying snap.

I set the cursed book on the ground. The light from the fire casts dancing shadows across its cover. Merlin gets up from his spot on my skirt, climbs slowly into my lap, and curls into a tight ball of fluff. Matthew waits patiently, but I can't bring myself to unstopper the vial again.

"Are you all right?" he asks.

I nod. "Winifred said when she last saw this, it was full of darkness. That my mother was using forbidden magic." I look up at him with wide eyes. "How can I face that, if it's true? How can I face you? Especially considering everything I've said to you since you've arrived."

"Would you prefer to be alone?" Matthew asks hesitantly.

I shake my head.

"Good," he breathes. "I don't know that I'd be capable of leaving you right now."

I smile.

"Alone would be much worse." I say. "Besides, if the book retaliates, I'll need you close, to bind the blood magic again."

Matthew nods and settles in, waiting.

I open the book. The shimmering red ink, the blood, sits on the first page.

The King Below shall never again know my secrets.
Sybil Goodwin

I yearn to trace her handwriting again, but instead I uncork the vial, and the water begins to bubble. Before I have time to talk myself into another paralysis, I let my wrist twist, and the vial tip. The murky water splashes down onto the pages of the book. The paper darkens as the blood ink smears, swirling with the water and then disappearing entirely.

The fire crackles as we stare at the pages, watching for several minutes as the water evaporates and leaves the page dry. Nothing appears on the parchment.

Perhaps I didn't have enough water? Maybe Matthew had been right: I shouldn't have wasted even a single drop on the fragment of the curse he bound to himself. I steal a glance toward him. His glacial eyes are on me. My stomach clenches as I touch a shaky hand to the book and slowly turn the first page.

My heart leaps. Where once there had been blank parchment, now there is an incantation in a language I don't recognize, but I can tell what it is by its form and structure. An evocation. In my mother's hand. Written in the same bloodred ink as the curse. I bite my lip and turn the page. This one is covered in a scratchy, chaotic handwriting quite distinct from my mother's elegant scrawl. And it's in English. I read the words aloud to Matthew, dumbfounded the longer I speak.

> *This tome is a sacrifice and offering to the witch Sybil Goodwin, who called upon this Crown for the gift of Gwaed. She has entered into sacred contract and will never utter words of what has transpired, lest she be reaped. She earned the right to this sacred and ancient magic by the seal of a bloody kiss and the solidified promise to name the next Goodwin daughter a hedge witch.*

I pause at these words as blood drains from my face. I look up to Matthew, whose brow is furrowed and grim. I take a steadying breath, trying to slow my whirling mind down, and continue to read.

> *With Our blood and Hers, this tome is born and sanctified. The bond between us is made eternal in the honoring of the mother's promise. Her blood is Our blood. Her life is Our life. Those who would seek to prevent Her from fulfilling Her duty will be met by Our eternal wrath.*

Along the margins of the page are sketches of a cloaked figure with long silver hair draped in shadows, his face turned from the reader's eye.

"The King Below," I whisper, reaching to trace the edges of the figure's cloak. Matthew's hand shoots out and quickly yet gently stops me.

"Careful," he warns. "Remember what happened the last time you touched the ink. There might be other curses on the rest of these pages."

He's right. The vial of Styx may have removed the initial curse, but it might not have been enough to remove any others hidden within the book. I turn the page again, careful not to touch the writing.

I find a list of ingredients. Castor beans, water hemlock, black onyx crystals, squirrel blood—every forbidden ingredient I know and several I've never heard of are written on this page. Even more horrifying are all the uses listed in the adjacent column next to each ingredient. For affectation, page twenty-eight. For accretion, page sixty-three. For compulsion, page one hundred and seven. Quickly, I turn to page one hundred and seven.

There are sketches on this page of twisted, drooping faces with a glaze about their eyes. Ingredients for spell work. Intention setting. Ritual casting instructions to curse someone's blood and take control of their will. The instructions are in that same scratchy, untethered hand as the dedication at the beginning of the book. But all along are my mother's notes in the margin, crossing out some words, adjusting ingredient amounts. My eyes finally see the sketches of the drooping faces clearly. They are faces I recognize. Roger Strode, the Ipswich town pastor. Grace Harper's brother John, a local doctor. Worst of all, with burning betrayal, I recognize the eyes and smile of the final sketch: my father.

My throat begins to close up, my breath stutters, and my eyes begin to swim with tears that try to block out the awful reality. Winifred had been telling the truth. My mother didn't just use blood magic to protect this book. The book itself is blood magic. An instruction manual. A Grimoire.

Everything my mother had ever railed against, everything she ever told me was evil and wrong in the world—it was all right here in this book. She was a liar. A hypocrite. She'd made a pact with the King

Below. And she had sacrificed my chosen path so she could manipulate the town to her will. My whole life has been forfeit to her whims.

A soft whimpering sob escapes my lips. Suddenly, the book is gone from my view, and strong arms are wrapping around me.

"Matthew, I think my mother killed my dad," I croak.

"No. No, she didn't," he insists.

I nod fervently. "The doctors said it was leukemia. But what if it was something else? She poisoned him with one of those awful curses in that book, didn't she?"

"Enough. Enough for now," he whispers into my ear, drawing me into him. I throw my arms around him, bury my face into his neck, and sob.

CHAPTER SEVENTEEN

Two Days Until Halloween

I don't dream that night, only drift in some sort of endless fog. A clap of thunder finally wakes me. It's morning but the sky outside my front room windows is still heavy with storm clouds. I'm lying on the couch that's pushed up against my living room wall, a quilted blanket draped over me.

Matthew is across the room. He's asleep, reclining in the chair next to the fireplace. His breath is steady, but he doesn't look peaceful in his rest. His face, as handsome as ever, even with an unshaved five o'clock shadow, is drained of energy. He looks burdened under an invisible weight. The shimmering bronze of the scar on his arm has dulled appropriately overnight, but it still peeks through the ragged edges of the bandages underneath his shirt.

Physically, I feel leagues better than I had yesterday. My feet no longer sting, my throat is back to normal, and my joints don't ache. But my head hurts, and my face is puffy and raw from crying. My soul feels as if it has a wound as deep and savage as the one on Matthew's arm. I want to close my eyes, burrow under my quilt, and stay hidden away. But both my sisters arrive tonight and expect a full dumb supper to be waiting for them.

The thought almost makes me laugh. How can I keep these two competing realities together in my head without letting them drive me mad? How can I stress about pumpkin carving in one thought and contemplate my mother's evil deeds in the next? Not to mention that the King Below has sent hellhounds after me, wanting to claim me and drag me down into his realm.

The worst of it all is my mother's betrayal. I have the overt suspicion that she wasn't the only person in my life who kept secrets from me. Winifred clearly knew more than she let on. Why else would she have reacted so violently when I mentioned involving Ginny? Matthew, in all his goodness, isn't free of my paranoia either. He knows things, things he refuses to say. He leaves my questions half acknowledged or gives answers so vague they are rendered unusable. Who else is lying to me? Miranda? Celeste even? Hell, what if Merlin is the mysterious King Below in disguise?

"Stop it, Kate," I whisper, covering my eyes with one hand. "If you suspect the cat, that officially makes you a crazy person."

Slowly, I pull myself off the couch and tiptoe quietly into the kitchen. A chilly October morning plagued by thunderstorms and bad thoughts has only one cure. I walk around all the carved jack-o'-lanterns that are placed on every surface of this room and grab my mother's Recipe Book from its corner. My hand shakes as I flip through its pages until I find the recipe I'm looking for. My mother's recipe for So Cozy Salted Caramel Hot Chocolate.

Coughing quietly to fight the lump in my throat, I get to work, following the recipe exactly as written. Milk, cream, caramel, cocoa powder, and spices, all go into a large stockpot. I stir and stir until the ingredients are blended together. Merlin wakes up and jumps onto the counter next to me, watching with twitching eyes as my wooden spoon makes endless circles in the melting drink. I add the last of my gold flake reserves and several shots of whisky, all while imagining the warmth from my fireplace filling the cottage and keeping the storm from seeping its dampness and misery into the walls.

The drink is done when the air around me grows thick and warm and smells like whipped cream.

Matthew is still asleep in the chair as I place a pumpkin-shaped mug down softly on the side table for him. I grab the quilt I'd left on the couch and drape it over his legs, moving gently so as not to wake him by accident. Taking a sip from my own cup, I relish the warmth that radiates out from my chest as my mouth coats in thick chocolate and caramel. It's an effort not to inhale the rest of the drink, because I want so badly to banish the ice still lingering in my heart. But I know not to consume this heavenly mixture too fast. Otherwise, I'll be in for one hell of a stomachache.

I set my mug down on the coffee table to cool and move to stoke the fire. But I abandon the chore quickly. Lying next to the empty fireplace is the Grimoire. Right where I left it the night before.

My stomach flips at the memory of Matthew's arms around me as he pulled me away from the nightmare of those pages. I'd buried my face in the crook of his neck, soaking his already ruined shirt with my tears. I wince, wondering if I'd caused him pain as I clung to him, shaking. But he'd never complained. Just sat with me, stroking my hair and murmuring soothing words I hadn't listened to.

I scowl at the book, contemplating how best to burn it. How could one stupid object make me spiral so out of control? And why should I let it have any more impact on me?

Grabbing my long matches, I strike one and watch the tip burst into flame. I hold the Grimoire in my other hand and stare at it until the match burns out. Letting out an annoyed breath, I strike another match, determined to light the tome on fire and be done with it. But once again, I hesitate.

I blow out the match and open the book to the same page that overwhelmed me last night, and my eyes immediately find the drawing of my father. Against Matthew's warning, I trace the edges of the sketched face.

A memory comes to me. A conversation I'd overheard as a very little girl, out of my room long past bedtime. My mom had been sitting in the Manor's kitchen with Grandmother Goodwin. I'd been hunting for snacks but stopped outside the kitchen door as I heard their tense conversation.

"You must stop this, Sybil. A witch who lies to herself can never succeed. Magic without truth is meaningless." My grandmother's prim voice shook as she spoke.

My mother, who was beginning to show with Celeste, replied softly.

"That's the great thing about being a witch, Mom. We get to decide what is true."

I'd never heard the rest of their conversation. My father had found me outside the kitchen. He'd swept me up into a fit of giggles and took me to his study, where we'd split a cup of my mother's hot chocolate. It was one of the few memories I have of him.

My heart aches at the memory of his laughter. Had it all been a facade? All those years of love and devotion. Had my father been a victim of Compulsion? Forced to sire children for my mother and donate his family fortune to the Goodwin estate?

No, that couldn't be. Thralls of Compulsion are dead-eyed and humorless. My father had been so full of life and love before he got sick. So Affectation then? My closest encounter with that sort of magic had been when Miranda accidentally sang her Siren song to her prom date. He'd followed her around in a lovesick haze but only for a single night. Affectation of the blood, on the other hand, is more permanent. It inspires long-term obsession, lust to the point of insanity.

That doesn't make sense either. My father hadn't been crazed or erratic. But here he was, included in the drawings of what I could only assume were my mother's victims. My mind turns back to the darkest of possibilities. Perhaps my father's blood-borne illness had not been natural.

I turn the page, then the next and the next. More ritual instructions, more spells, over a dozen ways to kill someone by turning their blood against them, each entry more violent than the last. I'm queasy. How many different people's blood stain this book? I turn to another page near the back. It's not like the others. A diary entry is written in a wispy black ink, still my mother's hand, but quite distinct from the red pigment that fills the rest of the Grimoire. The date at the top of the page makes my heart race. February from the year I was born. It's one of the missing days from her diary in the Recipe Book.

"Of course," I breathe. Merlin puts a gentle paw on my leg. I look at him. "She would journal in here when writing about forbidden magic. She couldn't risk anyone reading her Recipe Book and knowing what she was getting up to."

Merlin nudges his nose against my arm. I scratch him between the ears and begin to read.

February 25th—

William grows sicker and is refusing treatment. I have gone to doctors, begging them to keep helping him. Our pastor won't stop trying to get him to accept this fate, no matter how often I tell him not to. And nothing I cook makes any difference. He gets worse and worse. I don't have the power. It is only because of Winifred that I have this new chance. I promised her I would not waste this opportunity. And I won't. For the sake of William. For the sake of the little girl growing inside me. For the sake of our family.

I read the entry twice, my eyes flitting over the sentences, the words coming to me in bursts.

"Winifred." I seethe quietly, unsurprised by the confirmation of her involvement but furious all the same. Another diary entry waits on the next page, dated four years from the last.

May 31st—

William is gone. It's my punishment. A few days after I told Him that I would not honor our bargain, that I could not do that to my daughter, William caught a fever. No matter what I cooked, no matter how I tried to use Gwaed, His wrath overcame it all.

And I must live with the consequences. Miranda puts on a brave face for me; I know she's trying so hard to be strong. But Rebecca says she cries when I am not around. Hecate is angry, as always. And I weep for innocent little Celeste, who will never know her father. I'm at a loss. I can make no move to protect Hecate without fear of further retribution. I am locked and bound with threads I can't untangle. At least here, in these pages, my thoughts are now safe. I take the lessons he taught me and turn them on him. The King Below shall never again know my secrets.

The next page has yet another entry, this one only a year after the previous.

June 13th—
    He's growing weaker. I'm certain of it. My dreams are more erratic, less specific. And since Beltane, I'm rid of them entirely. I might not have to face him again until the week before Samhain. To think! Freedom may be closer than I realize.

Another page, another entry. Dated from the year I turned thirteen.

May 2nd—
    I can't express how thrilled I am with Hecate's progress. She's a natural talent and shows true passion for her craft. It seems to be enough for her. I've worried for years she would feel the emptiness, the half of herself missing when we started her training. But I have kept her far from death, far from His influence. We are so close. I will fulfill my end of the bargain this Samhain. After thirteen tumultuous years, Kate will be named a hedge witch. And as long as I do as I technically promised, the rest of my family will be spared from his wrath.
    We just have to outlast him. He can't have many more years left. And even if he does, once Kate goes through her Containment,

once she loses access to the death magic she never learned, he will no longer be able to use her. This plan will work. It must.

I will always be vigilant, though. I am no fool. There are certain to be those out there who realize what I have done. And I have no doubt they would rather she fulfill her role.

"Kate?" Matthew's voice breaks me out of the hypnosis of my mother's Grimoire. I snap my eyes up to him. "Are you all right?"

"Yes," I say quickly, shutting the book. "I made you a drink to warm up. It's nasty outside today." I point to the mug of hot chocolate on the side table next to him.

"Kate." Matthew's voice is soft as he ignores his drink and stares at me. I burn underneath his gaze, and yet I can't bring myself to look away from him. "What else did you find?"

"You were right," I say quietly.

"I often am," he replies with a smile. "But about what this particular time?"

I don't have it in me to smile back.

"She didn't kill my father. She was trying to save him." I look down at the book again, my eyes sweeping over the subtle red pattern that swirls around the brown leather.

"That's a good thing, isn't it?" Matthew asks. I nod hesitantly.

"But it all feels so pointless. My father didn't live. I know now why she named me a hedge witch, but it doesn't change anything."

The fire crackles between us.

"She also wrote that the King Below was weakening," I say after a minute.

Matthew nods. "Ginny mentioned the same."

"Yes." There was so much to consider, a thousand moving pieces that all feel just out of reach. And barely any time to make a plan. I pinch the bridge of my nose, my head suddenly throbbing.

"What do you need? What can I do?" Matthew asks. He gets out of his chair and sits down next to me on the floor, taking my hands into his. I lift my eyes up to him.

"I need . . ." I pause. The clock on the mantle strikes ten in the morning, reminding me of all that must be done for the day.

"I need to go to the grocery store," I admit with an amused huff, standing up and setting the Grimoire on the fireplace mantle. The situation may seem absurd, but now more than ever, the time has come to call on the protection of my ancestors.

"We have a dumb supper to prepare for."

CHAPTER EIGHTEEN
The Dumb Supper

"Oh, Kate, it's stunning!" Celeste beams as she steps into the foyer of the manor. She removes the silk scarf around her neck and drops her Armani and Hermes luggage onto the marble floor. Miranda walks in a moment later, wearing a knit sweater and with her wild red curls neatly twisted into a bun. Her green eyes scan the interior of the house in apprehension. She pauses at the mantle in the living room, where photos of the three of us in our childhood Halloween costumes are lined up in a row, an orange garland snaking between us. Her lips purse.

"Not quite how Mom used to arrange it. But it is lovely, Hecate." Miranda's smile turns sweet.

Celeste squeals and claps her hands "The fabulous three. Together again!" She gives me a hug, which I return without complaint. She releases me quickly, as if suddenly remembering that I am the sister who doesn't like to be touched.

"Welcome home," I tell my sisters with a smile. I am proud of the Manor this evening. I have channeled all my heartbreak and fear into a cooking and decorating fervor. All the lamps are switched on, and dozens of candles are lit around the first floor. The scents of rosemary, thyme, and garlic waft from the kitchen. The dining table is set for six, with black lace table runners and crystal goblets twinkling in the lamplight. *Spook Along With Zacherley* is playing on the phonograph by the liquor cabinet.

"The pumpkins on the lawn are to die for!" Celeste says, grinning. "Your best work ever!"

"Thank you," I say with a slight smile as I grab Miranda's and her luggage and begin hauling them up the grand staircase. I'm grateful that Celeste has packed light. But Miranda has a massive roller bag that I have to lug up the stairs one step at a time. Lord knows what she has in this thing—she's only staying three nights.

"What time is dinner?" Celeste asks when we reach the second floor.

"At midnight, like always. Is that enough time to get ready?" I say, setting their bags down.

"Absolutely," she agrees. She then takes out her phone and snaps a selfie next to the cobweb-covered grandfather clock at the top of the stairs.

"It's a little bit of a rush but shouldn't be a problem," Miranda says with a thin smile. "And did you get my final headcount for Saturday? It's crucial that there is enough food for everyone," she says to me.

"Yes. Fifty-seven," I say, not mentioning that her note with the headcount hadn't even arrived until a few hours ago. Typical Miranda, she demands excellence from others but is constantly tardy in her own tasks. "Do you need help to your rooms?" I ask.

"No, I've got it. Thanks, Kate," Celeste says, collecting her bags.

"Yes, if you please," Miranda says.

Celeste rolls her eyes and gives me a wink as she heads down the hall to her bedroom. I grab Miranda's roller bag and begin dragging it to the other end of the hall. She follows behind me, her stilettos clacking against the wooden floor. Her bedroom door opens with a creak that makes me cringe. I should have gone over the hinges with a lubricant before she arrived. Oh well.

She walks into the room and appraises the decorations. Several of Mom's Halloween bears are placed on the pillows of her bed, and spiderweb candelabras line the mantle of her fireplace. I've scented the room with caramel and sea salt potpourri.

She turns to me and smiles. "Really nicely done, Kate. Thank you. I will be quite cozy."

"My pleasure," I say, putting the bag near the vanity. "See you in about an hour." I head to her door.

"Wait," she says. I stop and turn back to her. She hesitates, as if unsure she wants to ask the question on her mind. "You never did answer me. When I asked about your mystery guest?"

Her eyes try to wiggle answers out of me.

"Well," I say as I walk out the door, "if we're lucky, he might be joining us for the dumb supper."

"He?" Miranda exclaims as the door shuts behind me.

Inside my old bedroom, it's dark. I switch on the desk lamp, which casts a ghostly glow over the walls. Of all the rooms in the house, mine is barest, since all my prized possessions came to the cottage with me. Inside the closet hangs a single black dress. The same dress I've worn to the dumb suppers the past five years. The same dress I wore to my mother's funeral this summer. For the tenth time today, I swallow an angry sourness that bubbles in my throat.

I take the dress off the hanger and lay it on my old bed. The sleeves are see-through black lace, the only instance of embellishment. I change out of the mossy-green sweater I wore for my sisters' arrival and slip the black dress over my head. It reaches all the way down to the floor in a pure jet column with a sweetheart neckline. I spend some time wrestling my hair into pinned-up curls. As a final touch, I clasp a bright green scarab beetle hairpin into the back of my bun. My mother gave me the pin on my sixteenth birthday "for luck." I squeeze into my one nice pair of heels and dab on a Guerlain perfume Grandmother Goodwin always wore.

"Spirits, be with me," I whisper to the empty room.

Once I'm dressed, I walk back down to the first floor and give a final check on all the food in the kitchen. Everything looks perfect. The grandfather clock strikes midnight, clanging throughout the house. Miranda and Celeste's doors both open upstairs. The record on the gramophone keeps spinning, but the music stops and the house falls silent as the clock finishes chiming the hour.

"You look nice," Miranda says to me as we meet in the entryway. She looks stunning in a form-fitting mermaid dress covered in silk fringe. Her red hair is up, styled very similar to mine. The bodice of her dress is a lingerie corset with an attractive halter that accentuates her long neck. Dozens of thick silk cords fall from the neckline and wrap around her shoulders like a web.

"Not as nice as I do," Celeste announces from the top of the stairs, with a happy laugh. She is wearing a velvet black ballerina gown with tulle and Swarovski crystals in her petticoat that sparkle as she descends to the first floor. An extravagant multistranded pearl necklace hangs from her neck. In her short raven bob is a headband with a giant black bow in the center. Even at twenty-seven, I can't help but still see her as the four-year-old who shadowed me around the estate constantly.

"You both look lovely," I say with a smile as a knock sounds on the door. "Ah," I say, turning to open it. "Our fourth living guest."

Even though I know he's coming, I'm not prepared to see Matthew when I answer the door. He stands underneath the lamplight of the porch in a stunning black suit with satin detailing. His dark hair is perfect, as always, and his blue eyes are alight with mischief. He does a double take when he sees me, which makes me grin.

"You look beautiful," he says, his eyes sweeping over my face, my hair, my dress. From his inside pocket he produces a long-stemmed rose and presents it to me.

I can tell it was once red. In fact, it's likely he pulled it directly from my mother's flourishing garden. But its petals are dried out and crinkly now, its stem hard as crystal. Devoid of all life and yet still beautiful in its death.

"Thank you," I say, accepting the flower. It's only been an hour or so since we were last together; he snuck out the back door when we heard Celeste and Miranda's car coming up the drive. Despite the short separation, it's a relief to see him again. After everything I've learned in the past twenty-four hours, I don't know how I could get through a night of honoring my mother without him by my side.

"May I come in?" he asks after a moment. I nod and step aside, making room for him to enter. Finally, my sisters get a glimpse of him.

One of them gasps, Celeste I can only assume.

"Hello, ladies," Matthew says, stepping forward. "Thank you for letting me join you this evening. Kate has been kind enough to involve me in your New Year's traditions."

Both of my sisters are stunned into silence.

"Girls, this is Matthew. Matthew, these are my sisters, Miranda and Celeste Goodwin."

"It's a pleasure," he says with a small bow to them both. "I've heard a lot about you the past few days."

Miranda glares at Matthew, not in animosity but in the way she glares at any person she doesn't know. Celeste, on the other hand, is grinning excitedly. She's the first to collect herself.

"So, you're the mysterious guest staying with Kate? Nice to meet you, Matthew," she says, extending her hand to him. As he takes it, she cocks her head and stares at his features. "Have we met before? I can't believe I'd ever forget a face like yours. My god, you're gorgeous."

"Celeste!" Miranda admonishes her, but Celeste ignores our older sister. I try to keep my face neutral as I run through my memories of the Michigan Six convocation. Had Celeste seen him at some point?

"Oh, let me guess!" She grins, still gripping Matthew's hand. "You're one of the Texan Hexans, aren't you? I've spent loads of time in the Lone Star State. Surely, we've crossed paths there."

"I—" Matthew hesitates, his silver tongue unsure as he looks at me questioningly.

"The hour is continuing on without us. Shall we?" I say, ushering them all into the dining room, eager not to force Matthew into another lie.

"Oh, of course!" Celeste says, noticing the time on the clock. "I don't want to miss the cocktails again, like we did last year, Kate," she says over her shoulder as she walks into the dining room. Miranda follows behind her, and Matthew and I enter together. We all fall silent as we cross the threshold, doing our best not to disturb the spirits.

The dining room looks as if it has been pulled straight from a dark fairy tale. The table is covered in black lace. A range of dishes, from Victorian platters to Fiesta tableware, span the surface, each piece belonging to a different Goodwin matriarch. Miranda takes her seat at the head of the table as the oldest living Goodwin witch. Celeste sits on the right side of the table, next to one of the seats dedicated to the Departed.

Matthew pulls my chair out for me. I am sitting in the middle, the seat closest to the kitchen. It is where I have always sat at these suppers. Matthew's chair is on one side of me. On my other side is my mother's place setting. An orange crystal dessert plate is stacked delicately atop a translucent black dinner plate of the same material. A black lace napkin is draped across the plates, with a sprig of rosemary tied on top. My mother's initials are embroidered in the corner of the napkin cloth. I lightly trace the S with my fingertips, my stomach swelling with the cocktail of emotions I've been burying all day: confusion, grief, rage, longing. They all mix together until I am desperately untethered. Matthew's warm hand grabs my free one and squeezes reassuringly. He looks at me in concern. I offer him a soft smile.

Miranda's eyes are narrowed, flickering back and forth between Matthew and me. Her eyes linger on Matthew's wrist, where the edges of his bronze scar peek out from underneath his cuffed sleeves.

I withdraw my hand from Matthew's and grab the tiny silver matchbox lying in the middle of the table. Everyone watches as I strike a match on the tinder. The rush of the flame is the only noise in the silent room. I light the wick of a long black taper candle in the exact center of the table. So long as the candle remains lit, the spirits honor the ritual. The dumb supper has officially begun.

For roughly one hour, we must eat in total silence and sacrifice the best portions of our meal to the plates meant for our departed guests. Any excessive noise, and the spirits of our ancestors might be frightened off, and the blessings of Samhain perhaps reduced.

I head to the kitchen, leaving Matthew alone with the curious eyes of my sisters.

The first course is coffee and dessert, as is custom in a dumb supper. I bring out a pitcher of a strong black brew and pour the top two servings of the pot into the ancestors' cups. Then, around the table by age. Miranda first. Matthew. My own cup. Then finally Celeste, who gives me the same sad little pout she gives every year at being the baby of the group. In the same order, I place a ramekin of chocolate Earl Grey crème brûlée onto each of the dessert plates. We watch the candle in the center of the table after everyone has been served. It flickers with gentle approval. We pick up our spoons and dig in. Matthew breathes out appreciatively at the flavor of the crème brûlée, and Miranda devours her entire ramekin. Even Celeste, who normally never takes more than two bites of a dessert, finishes her serving. I clear the plates and cups and head back to the kitchen.

Next, all the goblets on the table are filled with a vintage red wine before I serve boeuf bourguignon and buttery mashed potatoes, Mom and Celeste's favorite. Celeste beams at me when she sees what I have made. Once again, we eat in appreciative silence. Despite all I learned yesterday, I actually manage to enjoy the food. These dishes are impossible not to appreciate, even when cooked by another witch. That is the power of my mother's recipes.

The next course, the appetizer, is a selection of homemade gyoza in chili oil. Our grandmother loved them, as does Miranda. She eats twice as many as Matthew, Celeste, and I. Her delicate fingers are slick with shimmery oil by the end of the course. She and Celeste both silently grin as she licks them clean. Then she remembers Matthew and uses her napkin to finish cleaning herself up.

The final dish of the evening is an autumn salad with crisp apples and pomegranate seeds. We are all so full that collectively we only manage about six or seven bites before I clear the plates away, hurrying to get Celeste her cocktails before the candle goes out.

Matthew follows me to the kitchen for this course and assists with assembling the apple cider margaritas. I cringe as he crushes the ice, hoping the noise doesn't scare any spirits and berating myself for not thinking to do that earlier in the day. But neither of my sisters shout that the candle has blown out.

Matthew carries the tray of cocktails and serves each of us in the correct order. We all quietly lift our glasses and silently toast one another. But as the four of us move to take our first drink, the grandfather clock chimes the first hour loudly. We all jump at the noise and the candle, now just a small black pile of wax in the center of the table, blows out. The lights in the house brighten. The spinning record starts emitting music again, the final verse of "Coolest Little Monster" playing throughout the room.

"Aw, man," Celeste sighs, setting her drink down disappointedly without a sip. If we continue to eat now that the candle has blown out, it would be a great sign of disrespect.

"I'm impressed. That's the longest I've ever seen a supper go. They never last that long back home," Matthew says with a laugh, setting his own drink down.

"That's funny," Miranda says, her eyes narrowing. "I thought they didn't do dumb suppers in Texas." She stares at Matthew pointedly.

Before he can respond, the cocktail glass sitting at my mother's place flies off the table and smashes into the wall behind me.

The alcohol splatters and splashes on the back of my neck. Chunks of ice and apple slide down the wallpaper. Celeste lets out a loud shriek, and Matthew rises quickly from the table, scanning the room, one hand protectively on my shoulder. Miranda and I exchange a worried glance. She rises from the table slowly and reaches into the bodice of her dress. She pulls out a velvet black drawstring bag and undoes the tie, pouring out its contents into her hand.

"By the ocean, by the riptide, by this sea glass, Mother, say what vexes you beyond the veil." Miranda throws dozens of translucent pale blue pebbles onto the dining room table. They clatter around the dishware with crystalline clinks, and the room falls silent.

"Nobody touch anything," she urges us, staring at the sea glass on the table. "The spirits need time to communicate. I will check on the glass in the morning. Then we shall know what message they have for us this New Year."

"Has anything like this happened at your suppers before?" Matthew asks quietly. His hand is still gripping my shoulder.

"No," Celeste admits, fidgeting with the bow on her head. "We get flickering candles. Maybe a gust of wind. Never something so overt." She stares at the ruined wallpaper where the cocktail glass smashed.

"Then again, we've never had a hexan at the table," Miranda says with a head jerk toward Matthew. "Maybe you're a bit of bad luck."

"I have dishes to wash," I say abruptly, standing from my chair. I can't be at this table a second longer. Matthew's hand slides off my shoulder and down to the small of my back.

"Are you all right?" he asks me quietly. I nod. But I want out of the dining room.

"Miranda, pick up the shattered crystal before someone cuts themselves," I order. Her eyebrows shoot up in surprise at my demanding tone as I head through the swinging door into the kitchen.

I twist the sink knobs and watch as steaming water pours into the soapy basin, bubbles quickly forming and filling it to the top. I grab some of my great-grandmother's china, scrape the food for the departed into the trash, and plunge the plate into the searing hot water.

The swinging door creaks open, and I smell Celeste's perfume before I see the black tulle of her dress.

"The stars are bright tonight," she says, coming to stand next to me at the sink.

"In warning?" I say with a short but quiet laugh. A little late weren't they?

"I don't think so," she says thoughtfully, her hand running up and down her long multistranded pearl necklace. "In anticipation, I think."

"Everyone is looking forward to the New Year, it seems. Even the stars and spirits." My hands are getting used to the hot water, but they have turned red from the temperature.

"It's more than that. Something big is about to change," Celeste insists. "Why would Mom's spirit smash the—"

"I don't want to talk about Mom," I say, pulling my hands from the hot water and facing my younger sister. Her pale blue eyes look at me in surprise.

"Oh. Okay." She relents quickly as the door opens again. Matthew and Miranda walk into the kitchen. Matthew carries the drink tray, which holds several of the large shards of crystal from the cocktail glass.

"Thank you," I say, reaching for it. He shakes his head.

"I've got this," he says. "I'll take it back to the cottage and see what I can do." He gives me a quick wink.

"Oh no, you're not allowed to leave yet. Not before we get to interrogate you," Celeste says with a laugh.

"Celeste, it's getting late, and it's been a long day. Can we save the questions for a later time?" I request, but she lifts a hand up to quiet me. Miranda smirks.

"Come on—you bring someone home for the holidays and expect us not to barrage him with questions? No, it won't stand. We have every right to get some answers." Her voice is good-natured, but she is determined. "Don't worry, Matthew. It won't be that painful."

"Celeste—" I warn as she pulls something from a pocket in the skirt of her black ballerina dress. She ignores me as she begins to shuffle the cards in her hands. Her beloved tarot deck that is never more than two feet from her body. They are well worn, some even ripped around the edges, from the thousands of readings she does for her celebrity clientele. Miranda looks smug over in the corner of the kitchen, her arms crossed. Matthew sets the tray of broken glass down on the kitchen island and watches with interest as Celeste shuffles. After five or six tricks, Celeste lays the deck down on the marble countertop before him.

"At your leisure, cut the deck, please," she says with a sweet smile to him.

"You know," he says with his classic cocky grin, "you could ask me the questions yourself."

"I trust this deck more than I trust you," she replies. Matthew shakes his head with amusement. He reaches out and, with an elegantly swift movement, cuts the deck in half. Celeste sweeps in quickly and reassembles it, giving it one final shuffle. As she does so, she speaks aloud.

"Stars align. What do we need to know about our new friend, Matthew? Three cards shall do for now." She places the shuffled deck back down on the marble and overturns the top card with her small, pale fingers.

A black sky with a constellation of stars in the shape of an embracing couple: the Lovers.

My eyes flash to Matthew, who is already looking at me. He averts his gaze and pretends to study the card as Celeste giggles and Miranda lets out an annoyed tut.

"Well, that's a freebie. Guess we should have guessed that card would turn up. Now that we know his present, let's see his near future." She smiles at me mischievously. I am too mortified to speak as she flips the next card. The planet Mars eclipsed by its two moons.

The Tower.

The air in the room shifts. Matthew stands up straight, a look of resolve in his eye. Miranda and I both take a few steps toward the table to see the card more clearly. Celeste remains calm, but her eyes widen at the image. She glances at Matthew.

"Destruction. Torment. Danger," she whispers. "And your ulti-mate fate . . ." The final card is flipped and placed onto the others. A constellation in the shape of a scorpion and a hooded figure with its arms wrapped around a maiden. My blood turns to ice.

Death.

CHAPTER NINETEEN
Spirits and Shadows

Celeste's hands shake as she quickly picks up the three cards and stuffs them back into the deck.

"Death is not as bad a card as you might believe. It simply signifies change. Transformation," she stutters.

"I assure you, there is no need to sugarcoat the truth for me," Matthew whispers, his eyes dark. "I'm well aware of what the card means."

Celeste glances nervously at him and then toward me.

"I'm sorry, Kate. I should have listened to you." She bites her lip regretfully. Miranda steps forward and puts an arm around Celeste.

"And that's the lesson we learn when we try to discern fate so long after sunset. Surely, it's clear that the spirits are still around, playing their tricks, trying to frighten us. We shouldn't trust these foolish cards tonight." She rubs Celeste's arm affectionately and smiles toward me, but there is tension and worry in her eyes. "Why don't we all go to bed? The hour is late, and there is much to do in the next few days."

Celeste gathers her deck back into the folds of her skirts.

"Good night, Kate," Miranda says to me. "I look forward to getting to know you better tomorrow, Matthew," she says. He bows his head to her as she walks Celeste out of the kitchen.

He watches them leave before walking over to the sink. He grabs a soapy plate from the warm water and begins to rinse and dry it off. I am still rooted to my spot, staring at the marble countertop where the three-card spread had been. The kitchen should be warm, but there is a chill on my skin.

"Matthew—" I say, walking over to him as he puts another piece of china onto the drying rack.

"I'm a shadow hexan, Kate," he interrupts. "I haven't had a tarot spread absent of the Death card since I turned thirteen." He turns to me and smiles, tucking a finger under my chin. I study his face, searching for some sign of concealment or hidden worry. I find none. His blue eyes are soft, his smile warm, and his jaw isn't clenched with tension.

My shoulders ease with relief, and I let out a small laugh.

"Of course—I should have realized," I say.

"I'm afraid your poor sister might be traumatized over it, though. Perhaps I should admit my craft to her before we leave for the night? To ease her worry?" he says with a smirk, turning back to the sink and cleaning the final piece of china.

I shake my head. "It's a miracle she didn't immediately recognize you and tell Miranda. No, I need time to prepare before we say anything about you."

"And have you decided what you will tell them about the other thing?" he asks.

"About the King Below? I don't know." I shake my head. "A part of me wants to keep them out of it."

"A decision for tomorrow, then," Matthew says, folding the dish rag over the edge of the sink and pulling the drain up. "Now, let's see what I can do about this." He grabs the tray with the broken crystal glass. "I'd prefer to work on it back at yours. Shall we?"

Together we walk out of the kitchen and through the dining room, where several plates are still scattered about along with the handful of sea glass Miranda is using for her divination. We make our way to the family room and out the door onto the back lawn.

It's a moonless night, but the first part of our path is lit by the soft glow from the jack-o'-lantern display Matthew finished setting up while I cooked dinner. Thirty-one carved faces smile and leer at us, scattered in the hedges of the lawn and casting long shadows in their midnight glow.

"We need to blow all these out," I say. "Otherwise they won't last through Samhain."

Matthew pauses and stares at the pumpkins. The still night picks up with a soft but biting breeze. A mist-like shadow moves across the lawn, and the lights of the jack-o'-lanterns extinguish one by one as it passes over them.

Matthew turns to me with a wink and holds out his free arm. I shake my head and grin, wrapping my arm around his, expecting him to lead the way back down the hill. But he doesn't, he simply stands there in the darkness, staring at me, candle smoke wafting over us into the night sky.

"What?" I ask.

"You look lovely in the starlight," he says simply, his voice low and quiet.

"Thank you," I whisper, grateful there is no moon to expose the sudden red flush that has covered my neck.

He leads me down the hillside, toward the forest and my cottage. The ground is semi-frozen beneath us as we walk. With Matthew in his formal black suit and me draped in this flowing lace gown, we look like quite the ghostly pair. The shape of my cottage on the edge of the woods grows sharper as we get closer. The outlines of the trees sway unnaturally, their top branches bending inward, as if pointing toward something hidden deep within the forest.

The unease that I'd been working so hard to keep at bay ever since we'd left Salem Library, sinks its teeth back into me.

When we enter the cottage, Matthew sets down the tray on the nearest surface. I can hold my tongue no longer.

"What about the Tower card?" I ask in a whisper. "Does that one haunt you as well?"

He doesn't answer at first, running his hand along the cracked and shattered edges of the crystal glass.

"No," he admits. "That one was less expected."

My stomach twists, even though I'm not surprised. "Do you think it was a warning? About the King Below?" My voice wavers.

Matthew studies me silently. We both know the answer, but he forces a cheerful grin onto his face. "It could be more to do with the fact that I am a Pacific hexan living among the Atlantic Key. I suppose we shouldn't be surprised that my near future looks a little grim." He laughs.

"Dammit, Matthew. Take this seriously!" I cry, annoyed by his dismissive attempt at humor. "No good ever comes from that card. And Celeste doesn't read false—"

He is standing over me before I finish the sentence. Gently he takes my hands into his and looks down at me with a smug yet softly delighted smile.

"Hecate Goodwin, are you *worried* about me?" The question is asked with amusement, but his eyes are burning into mine.

"Yes," I admit, trying to ignore the red flush returning to my neck and chest, both from my anger and from his close proximity. "If you give me a minute, I can look through my Herbal. I have a few counter-hex bags I can create that might offer some protect—"

He cuts me off again by cupping my face with both of his hands. "It's not your job to protect me," he says in a low whisper, as his fingers brush softly against my skin.

We stare at each other for a moment.

I lift both my hands to his arm and slowly unbutton the cuff of his sleeve. He looks on curiously as I push the crisp white shirt and jacket sleeve up, revealing the now faded copper scar. I run my fingers along the edge of where the adhesive has healed into his skin. It's smooth and cold, like a vein in a marble statue.

"Isn't it, though?" I ask, looking back at him.

"I'll remind you," he says, his thumb stroking my cheek softly, back and forth, "that I incurred this injury while fighting off a pack of creatures chasing *you*."

I open my mouth to respond, to thank him for saving my life, but nothing comes. All I know is that I can't rip my gaze from his. His eyes, his jaw, his lips.

He pulls my face closer. My hands brace themselves against his chest, running over the cool fabric of his shirt. My heart pounds furiously, and I am hyper aware of the quick pace of his own, beneath my fingertips. The warmth of our breath mixes in the air between us as our lips draw nearer.

SMACK!

We both jump as a loud, tumbling thud echoes through the walls. Matthew grips me tightly to him as we both look in the direction of the noise. Over by the fireplace, the Grimoire has fallen off the mantle and onto the floor. Matthew lets out a long sigh. For the briefest moment, his hands knot into my hair, and I think I feel his lips brush against my temple.

"Spirits are bothersome creatures," he grumbles into my ear before releasing me from his grip. I laugh softly, ignoring the sense of disappointment sinking in my stomach.

I walk over to the fireplace and gingerly pick up the Grimoire.

It's opened to some horrid ritual of torture, though I can't make out the language. The sketches in the margin vaguely resemble animals and humans alike being flayed alive. My stomach turns, but I find some small sick relief that I at least do not recognize any of the faces. And my mother didn't make any notes in the margins. Perhaps she never used this page. It's all I can hope for as I turn to the next page. My fingers falter. I inhale sharply at the drawings on the paper. Sketches of glowing eyes and snarling snouts, which so closely resemble my nightmare pursuers in the woods. Matthew is by my side in an instant, looking over my shoulder, to see what on the page has distressed me. I read:

Call upon the Cerberaxi.

The Hounds of the King Below. An infernal prayer and either an offering of blood or a sacrifice to shadows will draw these messengers forward. They will do your sacred bidding if you pay a high enough price.

"Will he send them again? To finish the job?" I ask aloud. Ginny had said how reckless it had been for the King Below to use hellhounds against me. Either he wouldn't risk it again and would get to me some other way, or he was desperate enough to try anything. I don't find comfort in either of those options. Especially given how dark it is outside.

Matthew straightens up.

"If he does, they won't get close to you. Not if they have to go through me first," he says.

"No! You aren't allowed to fight them again. They could kill you!" I look back at their images. The sharp claws glint off the page, I can almost hear the baying sounds they made ripping into Matthew's arm.

"Please," he scoffs, "I took down three of them within a span of thirty seconds."

"And almost became permanently disfigured in the process," I admonish him. "Had the wound on your shoulder been any deeper, you might have lost your arm."

He's chastened, but only just so.

"How did you fight them?" I ask after a moment. Perhaps if I learn, I won't be so defenseless should they come again.

"Hellhounds are made almost of pure shadow magic with only a drop of Gwaed. They are entirely too easy for a shadow hexan to manipulate. If you can get your hands on them, Siphoning is the easiest way. I drew their energy into me, essentially sucking away the very shadow magic that held them together."

I frown. "The chances of me successfully using shadow magic for offensive protection are slim."

"You have more power than you realize," Matthew says gently. "But it's a moot discussion either way. Those creatures can't get to you while I'm here."

"They got to me before," I remind him.

"Yes," he says, sighing, "but I've extended the protective barrier around the cottage, and as long as you don't drink any more of the Tranquilum, we don't have to worry about you Shadow Walking beyond it again." He says all this with self-assured confidence, but his smile wavers when he sees my shocked face and realizes what he has said.

"I . . . Kate—"

"What protective barrier?" I interrupt. My head reels. *More* magical interference that I hadn't known about? Matthew remains silent, no doubt hesitant to speak while I'm staring at him with such an aghast expression.

"Answer me!" I insist. "How long have you had a boundary up?" The fireplace flares, the heat of it washing over the back of my legs.

He is quiet for another moment. When I open my mouth to demand answers again, he speaks.

"Since the night I arrived," he answers definitively.

"Why?" I ask.

"To protect you," he says calmly.

My mind hurries over a hundred thoughts. The endless internal battle over whether to truly trust him rages inside me. He seems determined to put himself in danger to make sure the King Below stays far away from me. He's told me time and time again that I can trust him. But he hasn't even be honest about the ways he has helped. He has so many secrets, I think even he's starting to lose track.

With a slight start of surprise, I realize I don't care about his secrets. As much as I know that I should, I don't. At least, not as much as I care about—fear, really—the possibility that he might get hurt again. I might not be able to fight hellhounds or the King Below with shadow magic, but there must be something I can do. Something to protect myself. Something to keep Matthew out of the fray.

"Teach me to Shadow Walk," I say, looking up at him again.

"What?" He blanches.

"You heard me."

"No," he says firmly.

"Why not?" I cry. "Apparently I'm capable of it. I walked the night of the hellhound attack. And you said it's one of the tenets of a hedge witch. If I can learn to control it, I can outrun them."

"You won't need to outrun them, Kate. I'm not going to let them near you. I'm not going to let you out of my sight again."

"You're not thinking this through!" I insist, crossing the living room. "You can't stay in Ipswich forever. Eventually, you will have to leave. I should learn something—anything—that might offer me protection. And we already know I'm capable of it."

"Let's just get through Samhain, okay? And then we can discuss it."

I shake my head. "I'm not going to be a sitting duck for the next few days. Teach me."

"No," he says firmly. "It's too risky."

"Why?" Anger is building up in me. He's been talking of Shadow Walking since the day he arrived, and he chooses *now* to clam up about it.

"Because there are other things in the shadows, Kate, remember? Things worse than hellhounds." He speaks passionately but in a stilted way, almost unsure in his word choice.

I've had enough of his excuses. And I've had enough of feeling like I have no say in the matter. The time has come to force his hand. I leave the living room and walk into the kitchen. Sitting under my spice cabinet is the vial half full of swirling Tranquilum. I grab it.

"Kate, no!" Matthew shouts. He rushes across the living room and into the kitchen, but not before I uncork the bottle and tip several drops of the sleeping mixture into my mouth. It coats my tongue in a bitter and minty film. I have to steady myself to keep from recoiling at the taste. Matthew snatches the vial from my hand.

"Are you out of your mind?" he shouts, his eyes wide in shock as he glares at me.

It's my turn to be smug. "You said this was why I Shadow Walked two days ago. I'm recreating the process."

He lets out a long-defeated sigh and runs a hand through his dark hair, untidying it and making him look even more frazzled than he had before.

"Are you forgetting how helpless you were, Kate? You barely had any control over yourself."

"Relax," I admonish him lightly. I took a lower dose than before, but I don't tell him this. "You're going to need to show me how to Shadow Walk now, since I'm going to do it anyway," I say with a sweet smile.

For a moment, amusement flashes across Matthew's face, but he forces his mouth into a stern line.

"Fine," he says darkly. Before I can react, he grabs my hand and pulls me out of the kitchen and into the dark hallway between our bedrooms. He pushes open my door. Merlin is curled up in his chair, sleeping soundly.

"Lie down on the bed," Matthew says sharply. I don't move as he shrugs off the formal coat he had worn to the dumb supper.

"Why are you undressing?" I ask, alarmed.

"What, you're not shy all of a sudden are you?" he says sardonically. I don't answer as he sets his jacket over my vanity chair and then takes a seat at the edge of my bed. He beckons me toward him.

"We need to do this quickly, before the Tranquilum sets in and confuses you."

"And is there a reason we have to be on the bed?" I ask, staying where I stand.

He stares at me, through the darkness, for a single moment before answering. "Shadow Walking starts with projecting your spirit beyond the confines of your body. If you're not lying down, there is potential for injury." He holds his hand out to me. Slowly, I walk forward and take it. My earlier bravery has dissipated. I realize with displeasure that I'm trembling slightly.

Gently, more gently than I deserve, Matthew takes my hand and lightly pulls me down next to him, sitting on the edge of the bed.

"I need you to trust me. Can you do that?" he asks quietly.

I nod.

He places one of his hands on the back of my neck and the other at the base of my throat. There is no doubt in my mind that he has taken note of the furious beat of my pulse, the way it sputters and speeds up at his every touch.

He shifts his weight, drawing me closer to him, and then lightly leans me back until we are lying down together on top of my quilt. I feel the weight of him off to my side, the warmth of his palms on my neck and chest. My head can't focus on any one sensation long enough. I am about to intentionally practice shadow magic. If the elders knew. If my sisters knew!

"You want to focus on these two points," Matthew urges, lightly pressing on my neck and chest with his fingers. "Center the core of yourself at the top of your spine here. And then release it, above your heart."

I stare at him wildly, confused. He stifles a slight smile.

"Close your eyes," he urges. I comply, shutting out the dim room. I wait a few moments, absolutely at a loss for what is supposed to happen.

"Listen to your breath," he whispers in my ear. His deep voice is so soft but with the slightest faraway rumble. "Take note of every sensation in your body. The way the fabric of the quilt feels on your legs, the way the air in the room settles around every inch of your skin. Draw all of that awareness of yourself up right here." He presses more firmly at the base of my neck and his touch is like an anchor. Where I had been momentarily distracted by a vague itch on the top of my foot, all my attention is drawn up to where his fingers are touching me. I almost forget that any other part of me exists. My breathing is starting to slow down, and the world feels heavier than it did only moments before.

"Very good," Matthew says, his voice far away. "Now, take a moment to center yourself. Then sit up when I release you." His voice fades away from me. But I can still feel his hand on my chest, his thumb drawing small circles above my clavicle. I relish in the sensation of it, the way my skin warms under his touch.

He pulls away. For a moment I am left disconcerted by the lack of feeling, but I do not linger in it. Instead, I force myself to sit up through the heaviness, to follow his touch and find it again in the darkness.

There is intense resistance holding me down, like the weight of several lead blankets, but I force myself through it. Suddenly, I am free. The room comes into view, though I don't remember opening my eyes.

I lift myself off the bed and stare at the door in front of me, a little uncertain about the point of this exercise.

"Impressive." Matthew's voice is right in my ear, his hands coming to rest on my shoulders as he stands behind me. I inhale sharply and move to turn toward him, but he holds me firmly, keeping me in place. "No, don't turn around. If you see your body, it might shock you back to it."

"What?" I choke.

See my body? Had I done it? I look down at my hands. They look real enough. I take a small step forward; the ground holds me in place, though I do note with some interest that the wooden boards of my bedroom don't creak beneath my feet.

"Welcome, Kate. To the land below," Matthew says, and I don't miss the grim note in his voice. "Now, think of another location within your cottage. We'll go there next."

I move toward my door. No sooner do I think about heading back into the living room than a darkness passes over my eyes. When it lifts, I find myself transported, standing near my writing desk.

"Whoa," I breathe, stopping in shock at the sudden change in scenery.

"Really, quite amazing," Matthew says, once again from behind me. I whirl around to face him. He is standing beside the fireplace, which is still lit, but the flames are ghostly and strange, as if their light is shining from a different room, and not a single crackle emanates from the burning wood.

"I've really done it?" I ask, staring at Matthew. His eyes are bright and excited.

"I've never seen someone take to veil crossing so quickly," he says, beaming. "You're a natural! A true hedge witch."

"I wish I could take credit, but I have no idea how I did whatever I did," I admit, though I'm immensely pleased by his praise.

"Once you get the feel for it, it will get easier and easier. But we're not done yet." He walks over to me as he says this.

"You've already started to figure out the mist step, the ability to shift location at will. But this time we are going to aim further. Imagine yourself outside, at the edge of your garden—"

I don't hear the rest of what he says before the darkness envelops me.

When it lifts, I am not in my garden, but I hadn't expected to be. Because when Matthew said to imagine myself outside, my first thought was of my forest.

I stand among pine trees, but their familiar scent doesn't fill my nose. They look strange, brittle. Like glass. Memories of the hellhounds come rushing back along with Matthew's threat of other things lurking in the shadows. My heart begins to race as a surreal panic sets in. I've gone too far. Matthew won't know where I am. The hellhounds will find me. I need to get out of these woods. I break out into a sprint, praying I make it back to my cottage before the forest knows I'm where I shouldn't be. Twenty yards. I can hear Matthew calling my name in the distance. Ten yards. I shout back quickly, hoping he hears me. Five yards. The edge of the trees are so close, I can see the murky outlines of my cottage through the branches. I scan the area frantically for Matthew.

Hands grab my arm. "There you are."

The shriek that escapes me is like a banshee's cry, and I feel a tugging sensation in my stomach as shadows envelop me again.

The world comes into sharp relief. The air is bitterly cold, the ground hard and freezing. Where the sounds of the forest had been muted and muffled only moments ago, now the cacophony of the autumn night fills my ears. Crickets chirping, owl hoots, crunching grass beneath my feet, and the dying echoes of my screams shaking the branches of the trees around me. I turn wildly, searching for whoever grabbed me. I am alone only for a single breath until a quick swirl of shadow surrounds me. I open my mouth to scream, but it dies on my lips as Matthew steps out of the shadows and rushes over to me.

"It's okay, you're okay. It's me." He pulls me close to him, his eyes scanning the night around us.

"We're not safe. There was someone else here," I say in a rush. "Someone grabbed me."

"That was me," Matthew says.

"No," I argue. "It was before you came. They grabbed me but I screamed, and they disappeared."

"That was me, Kate," he repeats. "I grabbed you. The only reason I disappeared was because you corporealized and couldn't see me anymore."

"I did what?" I ask, breathless.

Matthew laughs.

"I have never seen a witch take so effortlessly to Shadow Walking while not even aware of it." He chuckles. "I am in awe of you, Hecate Goodwin. It took me six months to learn what you just did."

"Not exactly effortlessly," I grumble, embarrassed. "I can't even get directions right."

"An easy fix with practice." He smiles, running his fingers through my hair. "But you figured out the real trick, which is coming back to yourself. Look around. Welcome back to the land above."

As soon as he says it, I know he's right. When Shadow Walking, it had felt like moving in a dream. Everything slightly wrong, distant and near all at the same time. But now, it's all so clear and real again.

I stare at my hands. "How—" I can't even form the question.

"That is Shadow Walking. It's not simply an astral projection. It's calling your body to your spirit. Corporealization to a new location. With enough practice, you will be able to project and then materialize almost instantly."

An owl hoots and I'm hyperaware of our vulnerable position out in the open.

"We should get back inside, we should—"

Matthew shakes his head. "We're safe. *You're* safe. I told you I extended the boundary. Nothing necrotic can come within a few miles of your cottage without my permission."

I glance over to my back garden and the stones of my home, not more than twenty feet away. I'm relieved, knowing I don't have to be afraid of the forest anymore. Still, I am shaken by Matthew's display of care.

"That seems like a slight overexertion," I say quietly. The amount of intention, sacrifice, and concentration it would take to maintain such a large spell is almost incomprehensible to me. Matthew shakes his head and cups my face with both his hands. My skin erupts with flushed heat from his touch.

"Not when it comes to protecting you. Brilliant, amazing, precious you," he whispers as our eyes meet.

My heart clammers again. The thrill of my success, the exhilaration of his touch—it all erupts inside me. Burning, stunning desire. He is bent over me, his face so close to mine. I lean forward, closing the small gap between us, and press my lips to his.

The world tilts around me the moment we connect. Matthew's breath hitches in surprise. He returns the kiss, his lips yearning and hungry as they find mine over and over again. His hands, once gentle around my face, grip fiercely into my hair, pressing me closer. I lean into the pleasure of it all, slowly wrapping my arms around him, letting myself be consumed by the scent of cinnamon and rain that has exploded around us.

My hands clutch at his back. Pent-up tension ripples through his shoulders and releases itself in the passion of the kiss. One of his hands remains swept up in my hair, the other trails down the side of my body. He wraps an arm around my waist and clutches me to him. I gasp, breathing sharply in the brief moments of reprieve. I want it to never end. But my head begins to swim, half from the pleasure, half from a desperate need for air.

Reluctantly, Matthew gives me one final slow and delicate kiss before pulling away. He rests his forehead against mine.

"You have no idea," he whispers, his breath ragged, "how badly I have wanted to do that." He buries his face in my hair and nuzzles my temple.

I huddle against him, shivering both from the cold and from his touch.

"Are you all right?" he asks, pulling away to look me over.

I nod and slowly lift my hand to his face, letting my fingers brush softly over his cheeks, his nose, his lips. He closes his eyes appreciatively at my caress.

"I think . . ." I pause, considering my words, not quite sure how to express the soaring emotion filling me in this moment. "I think the whole world might have rearranged itself." I shake my head and laugh, embarrassed. But Matthew cups my chin with one of his hands and lifts my gaze to his.

"I know exactly what you mean," he says softly, "because mine rearranged years ago."

I'm transported in time. Back to ten years before. Back to when we were two friends standing together in a dust mote–filled beam of light inside the abandoned gatekeeper's cottage. The way he had looked at me before my mother found us. The same way he'd looked at me when he showed up on my doorstep a week ago. How he had sent his magic out to greet me like you would an old friend or lover. How his eyes had filled, not with smug mischief as I'd always believed, but with awe and adoration.

He is looking at me in that same way now, at the edge of Ipswich Forest. It all clicks together, his behavior since we met. His protection, his help, his support. Even through all the secrets, that constant undercurrent of care and attention. There are still so many questions to be answered. But those can wait until tomorrow. For now, I just want to exist in this moment. This moment in which I simultaneously know I love him and know he has loved me for a third of my life.

CHAPTER TWENTY
One Day Until Halloween

Thick, gray, drizzly mist greets me through the window when my eyes open. It looks positively dreadful outside, but I am bundled up cozily beneath several quilts. My only source of discomfort is my long lace sleeves, which have been rubbing against the scratches healing on my arms all night. I never got the chance to change out of my dumb supper dress before the Tranquilum finally took me.

The bedroom is dark except for the diffused misty light slowly brightening outside. The cottage is settling around me with content and quiet creaks. A pair of chipmunks race their way across the roof, their tiny feet pattering on the ceiling. Behind me, I hear soft, rhythmic breathing. I turn over and see Matthew lying beside me, still dressed in his suit from the night before.

Sound asleep, he looks incredibly peaceful. His chest rises and falls in slow rhythm. Everything about him is softer in this light. The curve of his jaw isn't as severe as it is in the nighttime, and his lips are in a resting position with a natural upturn I've never noticed before. Stubble covers the bottom half of his face.

With delicate fingers I lift a hand to his cheek and softly follow the edge of his jaw, feeling the prickliness of his unshaven hair tickle my palm. From there I lightly draw my hands over his nose, his forehead, just under his thick black eyelashes. I am quite in awe of how truly, stunningly beautiful he is.

Suddenly, his lips break out into a grin. He lazily reaches up and grabs my hand with his own. He takes my fingers, which have been running over his temple, and draws them down to his mouth, where he places several soft kisses onto my palm and wrist. He lets out a content sigh and then opens his eyes.

"Good morning." His voice is husky and rough.

"You slept in my bed," I point out.

Though, *on* might be a better descriptor. While I am completely curled into quilts, Matthew is uncovered, the pants of his suit and his once crisp shirt wrinkled.

"Apparently so," he chuckles, looking around my room. Merlin eyes us sleepily from his little embroidered chair. "Though I will remind you," Matthew says, "that you asked me to."

I scrunch my eyes and think back on the night before. I vaguely remember some general pleading on my end, though it all exists behind the fog of the Tranquilum.

"Did I at least stay put after falling asleep? No more Shadow Walking?"

"You slept quite like the dead, funnily enough." Matthew grins. "I did think to check your pulse once or twice. I hardly slept at all." He lets out a long dramatic yawn to highlight his exhaustion.

I roll my eyes. "Well, you needn't suffer any longer. I have to get up now. Things to do."

Before I manage to wriggle my way out of the sheets, Matthew has shifted quickly, pulling me under him. I let out a quiet yelp of surprise before his lips close down on mine. And suddenly the whole world is spinning again, and I am too hot under these quilts, and the more interesting moments from the night before come roaring back into my mind.

My lips part and he deepens the kiss, firm and soft all at once. His hands work their way through my hair, gripping onto me and pressing me to him, as if he can't get close enough to me to be satisfied. I am utterly at his mercy, my limbs and body contained beneath the covers between us. But I eagerly—too eagerly—return his kisses, longing to run my own hands through his hair.

Before I am ready, he pulls away, breathless, pressing one final soft kiss on my top lip. Then he turns his head and slowly begins to run his nose up and down my jawline, his lips brushing softly against my neck as he goes. I can barely catch my breath at the sensation of it, and I can hear the grin in his voice as he speaks.

"And what could possibly draw you away from bed on a gray morning like this one?" he murmurs in my ear, still nuzzling my temple.

I wrack my brain for a moment, knowing there is an answer beyond the haze in my mind. "The safety of the children of Ipswich," I finally say with a regretful laugh. Matthew pauses in administering his affections and looks at me in surprise.

"I'm going to be honest," he says thoughtfully, "that was not the answer I was expecting. And unfortunately, it's a good one."

I laugh softly. "One of my many traditions, I'm afraid."

Before he can distract me further, I sit up and free my limbs from the quilts. Merlin chirps and hops off his bed when he sees me rise. He runs up and nips affectionately at my toes when my feet hit the cold bedroom floor.

The first thing I need to address is my clothing. I can see the irritated scratches through the pattern of lace on my sleeves.

"No special wardrobe change this time?" I ask Matthew with a cocked eyebrow. He grins.

"I considered it. But I didn't have the excuse of saving your life to make taking your clothes off an appropriate course of action. Though,

I can always assist you now, if you'd prefer?" He sits up with eager eyes. I shake my head.

"No, I think I can manage. If you wouldn't mind giving me a few minutes."

He gives a good-humored if disappointed nod before lifting himself off the bed.

"I'll be outside if you end up needing me," he says with a wink as he walks out my bedroom door. I shut it behind him with a determined thud.

With a few inches of wood now separating us, all my confidence vanishes. My heart beats rapidly, thinking back on the things we whispered to each other last night. Running over to my vanity, I gather several of the crystals that rest there. The pink quartz, which I have never really paid attention to before, now becomes my lifeline. I catch a glimpse of myself in the mirror. My hair is still braided, but dozens of thin strands have fallen out of place and are sticking out every which way. My cheeks are full and flushed, my lips slightly swollen. And my eyes are bright despite the disturbed sleep I've had this past week.

"Not last night, though," I remind myself out loud as I begin to unbutton my dumb supper dress. Last night had been perfect, spent slumbering under warm blankets in warm arms. Perhaps that is why I look so well this morning. It is amazing what good rest will do to someone who hasn't had it in a while.

I make quick work of getting ready. I don't bother leaving my room to wash up since Matthew would no doubt use the opportunity to distract me again. As appealing as the thought may be, I don't have the time. Instead, I change out of my dumb supper dress into a warm but light, pleated wool skirt and a deep plum blouse that is billowy in the sleeves. Not exactly ideal for cooking, but the shirt hugs me rather attractively. I leave my braid as is, but I wrangle the flyaway strands of hair so that they fall and frame my face nicely. After blotting on some raspberry lip stain and stuffing the pink quartz crystal into my skirt pocket, I dare to open my bedroom door.

The cottage smells like fresh coffee. Matthew sits in my reading chair with Merlin curled onto his lap, a sight I am slowly growing used to. He has changed into a knit cream sweater and dark jeans and sips from one of my ceramic mugs. On the kitchen counter, below the spice cabinet, is my French press, halfway full with rich dark coffee. I pour myself some and fill the rest of the mug with milk, watching the black and white mix and churn into shades of light beige. When I take a sip, I am unsurprised but pleased when it tastes like cinnamon.

Drizzle patters on the kitchen window. The roof of the manor house is barely visible through the rain. Wondering if Miranda or Celeste are up yet, I frown.

"What are you thinking about?" Matthew asks, walking up behind me and leaning casually against the kitchen table.

"I'm beating myself up for not being a good hostess. I should bring my sisters breakfast."

Matthew shakes his head, amused. "Your sisters are grown women. They can take care of themselves."

He's not wrong. But Mom would have been mortified at the thought of guests in her house having to fend for themselves. Ice prickles across my chest as a flash of resentment runs through me. Why should I let my mother's wishes dictate what I want? This thought is immediately followed by a gnawing guilt in my stomach and the ugly, wretched specter of grief.

"What is it?" Matthew asks gently, setting his coffee mug down on the table and walking over to me. My distress must be written all over my face.

"I'm so unsure how I'm meant to feel. About everything that has happened this week. About everything I've learned regarding my mother. About the King Below. And then there's you. I keep flitting between excitement and happiness to moments of profound betrayal, fear, and confusion."

Matthew cups my face with his hands. "I don't think anyone would blame you for being confused," he says softly.

"I still miss her," I whisper. He nods, unsurprised. "But how can I justify it? After all she did?"

Matthew sighs. "She's not the only person to turn to the taboo in times of desperation. And it's people who fear darker crafts that are the most likely to be corrupted by them," he says sadly. "That doesn't mean we can't empathize with who they were before power infected them."

"Funny to hear you defending her," I say. Matthew looks thoughtful as he carefully brushes some of the loose strands of hair away from my face.

"I think I've come to understand her a little bit more these past few days."

"Why is that?" I ask, mystified yet a little amused by this change of heart. "Now that you know she wasn't a Goody Two-shoes kitchen witch, she's more deserving of your empathy?"

Matthew laughs loudly. "Not once in my life have I thought of Sybil Goodwin as a Goody Two-shoes, even when I believed she was only a kitchen witch. I knew your mother just for a few days, but in that time it was clear to me that she would do anything to protect the ones she loved. Even if she did overdo it sometimes. Like banishing a young and innocent hexan when she realized he'd fallen for her daughter."

I flush but don't respond.

"I have no doubt that very protectiveness is what led her to seek out more power," he continues. "I can only imagine the state of turmoil she must have been in to go against what her coven believed in. To turn her back on everything they had been working for."

"Would you do it? Turn away from all you knew?" I ask.

"To protect the people I love? Absolutely," he answers definitively.

I can't quite bring myself to his place of understanding. As a hedge witch, I've always had a solitary practice. I gather with the coven at Beltane in the spring and Samhain in the fall, and that's it. But even so, the idea of betraying their ideals, what I once had thought were my mother's ideals, I couldn't find anything respectable or understandable in it.

You Shadow Walked last night! I remind myself. *And you're in love with a necromancer!*

I look over at Matthew. I will have to eventually make a choice to betray the ideals of the Atlantic Key if I want to be with him. And I do. But I can't think of the repercussions of that now. The thoughts are too dark. Instead, I wrap my arms around Matthew's neck and pull him toward me.

I kiss him without restraint, letting any fears or doubts about the next few days melt away . . . or be buried away. He grips my waist and crushes me toward him as he eagerly returns the kiss. If I could have my way, I would drag him back to my bedroom, and we wouldn't leave until Samhain was well behind us. But duty, family, and tradition keep me rooted to my spot in the kitchen. With a repressed sigh, I break away from him. His eyes are bright, his dark brown hair slightly mussed from my fingers running through it.

"Thank you," he says, his thumb lightly tracing my lips.

"Let's make breakfast," I respond, determined not to be sucked into bleak thoughts any further. He chuckles as I turn away from him and head toward my cabinets. I grab some mixing bowls off the shelves and take ginger, nutmeg, and cinnamon from my spice rack.

Matthew watches as I mix together heaps of flour, the spices, and several cups of buttermilk and pumpkin puree.

"What's this recipe?" he asks.

"Pumpkin cinnamon pancakes," I say, cracking several eggs into the bowl and whisking quickly.

"And I'm assuming these aren't only for us?" He eyes the large bowl.

I shake my head. "If I'm lucky, my sisters will be so happy with the meal, they won't mind its delay."

"How can I help?" he offers. I smile.

He heats up the maple syrup while I warm the griddle, carefully pouring the batter into pumpkin-shaped pancake molds and drawing the segments of the gourds with a cinnamon and sugar paste.

We make twenty pancakes and two cups of spiced maple syrup, which Matthew pours into a ceramic gravy boat. I cut some strawberries into quarters and sprinkle them over the pancakes. I place it all onto a platter and wrap the whole thing in tinfoil.

Despite my protests, Matthew insists on taking the food up to the manor himself.

"You're not walking in the freezing rain," he demands, taking the tray from me.

"I'm not as delicate as you think I am," I say with a huff.

"It's not about you being delicate." He grins. "It's about preventing any discomfort on your part whatsoever. For my own pleasure and peace of mind."

"That's a fool's task," I grumble. "Discomfort is part of life."

"Then a fool I shall be." He leans down and gives me a quick kiss on the cheek before snatching the boat of spiced syrup from my hands.

Before I can argue further, he drapes a coat over his head and runs out the door. I laugh as he races up the hill to the manor, the icy rain pelting off his coat, and steam drifting up from the food. When he disappears behind the hedges that line the driveway, I turn back to my kitchen. It's time to start the true task at hand, or it will never be done in time.

From my highest shelf I pull down my cauldron. It's a tongue-in-cheek reference, of course. It's my pure copper stockpot, but it's my most prized possession other than my Herbal. This stockpot has been passed down the Goodwin line for at least five generations. And every year, on the 30th of October, it is used for one specific purpose.

I place the pot on my stovetop, but I don't light the burner yet—there are supplies to gather. Clear quartz, black jade, and pyrite from the vanity in my room. Candles from my supply closet; black for protection, green for luck, and purple for wisdom. Lastly, I grab my

Herbal and my mother's Recipe Book, doing my best to ignore the third book of Winifred's design sitting on my desk, the Grimoire. I can't invite any negative thoughts in this process.

Back in my kitchen, I light the candles in a triangle around my stove and place the crystals in a circle inside that triangle. With my black salt, I draw thick, dark lines to connect the candles to one another. My burner roars to life as I pour eight cups of sugar into my stockpot. Next, the honey goes in, with a large dash of vanilla. I stir it all together and then sit patiently as the sugar begins to dissolve into the honey. After a few minutes, my door opens as Matthew enters. A cold breeze nips at my feet before he shuts away the elements.

"Whatever that is, it smells amazing," he says, taking a deep breath. I don't answer, still trying to maintain my focus on the energies of the candles and stones, coaxing them to seep into the molten sugar.

The kitchen floorboards creak as Matthew makes his way over to me. "How can I help?" he asks, placing a hand at the small of my back. I close my eyes and revel in his touch.

"You can't," I say, turning to face him for a moment. "If anyone else's intention gets mixed up in the recipe, then the spell won't take."

His eyebrows shoot up in surprise and he looks at the copper pot with interest. He hadn't realized I was doing magic. "And what spell would that be?" he asks.

"Careful Caramel Apples. Ipswich has a munchkin masquerade the morning of Halloween. All the kids parade around the main town square in their costumes and adults pass out treats. My mother and I always hand out caramel apples, spiked with a little bit of magic to protect the children on Samhain."

"A townwide protection spell?" Matthew lets out an impressed breath.

I don't answer for a moment. The sugar has turned a dark amber. I grab the heavy cream off the counter and pour it into the pot, then add several sticks of butter, more vanilla, and a few splashes of bourbon.

"It's not very powerful—it's spread too thin," I say. The mixture rises quickly, the hot sugar reacting to the cold ingredients. I stir furiously until the caramel settles down again. "It can't bend the fates in your favor, but it can increase judgment so that little kids will remember to look both ways before crossing the street to the next house."

I keep my eye on the caramel, stirring occasionally before turning the heat down. As I wait for the mixture to turn the perfect color, I prep the apples. There are four dozen mini apples, each with a clean stick pushed into its flesh. On a separate baking sheet, I cut up a handful of leftover apples into thin slices, laying them flat on the parchment paper. Matthew watches in silence, but his eyes are on me. Every so often, whenever I find myself stirring the caramel, he places a soft kiss on the back of my neck or rubs his hand over my shoulder reassuringly.

When my candy thermometer reads two hundred and thirty degrees, I pull the caramel off the heat and break the lines of salt connecting the candles. The candle flames extinguish the moment the ritual ends.

"You can help with this part," I say to Matthew, carrying the hot pot of caramel over to the kitchen table, setting it down on a trivet next to the trays of apples. He joins me and watches as I gingerly grab the first apple on the tray closest to me, lifting it by its inserted stick.

"You don't need to be shy with the caramel. Better to over-dip than under-dip. And if you spin it like this, it creates a lovely swirl." I demonstrate with the first apple, letting the hot sticky liquid rise halfway up the fruit and spinning it as I pull it out of the pot before placing it back down on the tray.

"And these?" Matthew asks, pointing to the apple slices.

"Those are for the toddlers. You can either use a fork to dip the slices or a spoon to drizzle caramel on top. Either way works. The important thing is that they are small and light enough for little hands to hold."

Matthew washes his hands and begins assisting. We work in silence for a long while. The task becomes more difficult as time wears on and the caramel in the pot thickens up. I can't heat it back on the stove, as the candles are spent and the crystals need to recharge. The result is that the first few dozen apples are lovely and perfect in their appearance, and the final dozen or so have humorously uneven globs of caramel stuck to their sides.

"I used to do this with my mother every New Year when I was a boy," Matthew says after a while, carefully drizzling caramel on the last few apple slices.

"Really?" I smile at the thought, though I struggle to imagine Matthew as any younger than in his early twenties.

He nods. "She would make candy apples. Her 'poison apples' as she called them. I would help her decorate. They were always shockingly bright red. And more sour than any other candy I'd ever had." He laughs softly at the memory.

"What does your mom practice?" I ask. I think back on what he has told me of her so far. He's never once mentioned her using magic. Matthew pauses his work and looks at me.

"Hearth magic," he answers simply.

I try to compose my surprise. Hearth magic is one of the most ancient crafts but also one of the tamest, based on protection and the creation of sacred home spaces. My great-aunt Cassandra had been a hearth witch, and my only memories of her are her throwing bags of herbs into the fireplace and calling it a day, letting the plants work their magic. Hearth craft is wholly good. Quite literally there is no aspect of the magic that could bring harm to others.

"Why are you so shocked?" Matthew asks, setting down the final sliced apple.

"I don't know." I shrug. "I didn't think there were hearth witches in your coven."

"Just because the Pacific Gate doesn't forbid any craft doesn't mean everyone chooses darker ones. The majority of my coven would fit right in with the Atlantic Key. Well, the women, at least," he adds as an afterthought.

"So why did you choose necromancy?" I question. If his coven really was as perfect and fostering as he would have me believe, what had led him toward the darkest of all the magics?

"Ah yes," Matthew says, unsurprised by my question. "I chose shadow magic," he says this pointedly, and I blush at accidentally using the derogatory term, "because I was the eldest Cypher son, and it was expected of me."

I furrow my brow.

"Who expected it?" I ask.

"My father. The coven. It is our tradition. Since the start of the Pacific Gate"

"That's ironic," I say, shaking my head. Matthew looks at me quizzically. "Well, you've criticized the lack of choices in the Atlantic Key and yet you were forced into your craft," I elaborate. Our fates have been so similar. Matthew simply laughs.

"Well, luckily I had a natural affinity for it. Unlike my father, who desperately wanted to go out to sea and never return. He has always struggled with the shadows. But not me—I found my freedom in them. I remember on my thirteenth birthday, when I was finally allowed to Shadow Walk by myself and dedicate myself to the craft. It felt like . . ." He pauses, searching for the right phrase.

"Breathing for the first time?" I finish for him, remembering all my happiest times of solitude gathering herbs in my forest. He smiles at me.

"Exactly."

The apples are all finished now. Most are lovely and glistening but a handful are clumpy and thick. They remind me of my beloved warty devil pumpkins. I carry a tray over to the refrigerator and sit it on the top shelf.

"The caramel has to set overnight. By tomorrow morning they will be perfect and the spell will be at full potency," I explain as I put the rest of the trays away.

"So now how will you spend the rest of your afternoon?" Matthew asks.

The rain shows no sign of stopping, but with Samhain tomorrow and the dumb supper behind us, there is one more task that must be completed. One I've been avoiding.

"How far did you say that protective boundary extends from the cottage?" I ask Matthew.

"A few miles. Why?" he inquires.

That will be just on the edge of it.

"We need to venture into the woods. It's time to decorate the graves."

CHAPTER TWENTY-ONE
Mischief Night Necrosis

My raincoat keeps my body dry, but I walk barefoot into the woods. Matthew walks beside me. In one hand, he carries a basket full of end-of-season flowers we plucked from my garden, and in the other, a tall black umbrella. He holds the basket almost at arm's length.

"It's okay if they wither a bit," I assure him. My feet make squelching noises as they hit a patch of mud. But I don't mind. I readjust the weight of my own flower basket. "That would be more fitting for the season anyway."

"Given how poorly your ancestors reacted to my presence last night, I don't think it's in my best interest to show up with a bunch of dead flowers for them," he says, holding his basket out one inch farther. I laugh but my breath stutters. My hands are clammy and I know I can't blame the rain. I wrap my arm through Matthew's, scooting under the umbrella with him and try to absorb some of his warmth.

"We're not far now. The gate will be visible soon." Just as the words leave me, the trees part and an old stone wall comes into view. In the center of the wall is a wrought iron gate with welded herbs and other metallic plant sculptures wrapping around the rods. I take the basket from Matthew's hands and place a single, blue-tipped lilac aster on top of a mossy stone just outside the entrance.

"This," I say to Matthew as I push the gate open, "is Goodwin Graveyard."

The graveyard is not very large. Only about thirty of my ancestors are buried here. The scent of damp earth and old stone surrounds us. Three large oak trees are the kings of this burial ground, their restful shade normally casting peaceful shadows over the graves. Today, I eye the shadows nervously. A twig snaps somewhere out in the woods. My head whips around, my eyes darting as I try to place the source of the noise.

"You're safe with me," Matthew says, taking my hand in his and giving it a reassuring squeeze.

"I know." I nod. "Let's just get this over with."

With Mom, this had always been a divide and conquer task. She would start at one end of the graveyard, I the other. Each of us, with our baskets, making small bouquets of flowers to sit on the graves until Christmas. But with Matthew, and his refusal to touch the flowers we picked, it's up to me to place a bundle at every headstone.

Cassandra, Eloise, Morgan—I read the names as I go, greeting each of them with respect. I offer them the final blooms of my garden. Multicolored purple and black dahlias, ice-white camellias, roses that blend red and pumpkin orange, all tied together with gray lace.

Matthew stands behind me as I work, his face serene, but I don't miss the way his eyes scan the forest. I am bundling four roses together to place at my great-aunt Agatha's headstone when a thorn catches me on the ring finger.

"Ow." I wince, immediately sticking the finger into my mouth and sucking the sting away. Matthew is instantly by my side.

"I'm fine," I say before he can ask after me. "Just a pinprick."

"Let me see," he says, gently taking my hand into his. My ring finger is still bleeding.

"A bit more than a pinprick, I think," he says to me with raised eyebrows.

"Please," I scoff. "It's easily dealt with."

I reach into the basket of flowers at my side and grab a bright orange calendula. I pluck a single petal from the head and wrap it around my wounded finger. I hold the petal in place with my other hand and let out a soft hum. The temperature of my finger increases ever so slightly before fading. I let the petal fall away. It floats to the mossy ground, orange and red against the earthy green.

"Good as new, see?" I say to Matthew, holding my finger out for him to inspect. The tiny cut is gone, only the barest point of pink left behind.

"I don't think I'll ever get used to seeing that," Matthew says, staring at my hand in wonderment.

"It's really so simple." I laugh. "You could definitely do it, with all your seemingly endless power."

He looks at me dubiously.

"I think not," he says with a shake of his head.

"Have you ever tried? To heal?" I push back. Truly, it boggles my mind that a hexan as talented as he would be so demure.

"No," he admits slowly.

"Let's have a little experiment, shall we?" I say. I stand up and wipe the dirt off my knees. I hold my arm out toward Matthew, exposing the still healing scratches on my forearm.

"Place your hand here," I say to him, pointing to one of the smaller cuts. "And try to heal it."

Matthew takes half a step back from me.

"Kate . . ."

"It will be fine."

"I can't just do it the way you can. I need something to sacrifice," he argues. I dangle the mostly undamaged calendula flower in front of him.

A Dark and Secret Magic

"So do I," I remind him, placing the flower in his hand. He studies it and then my arm.

"I'll have to use some shadow magic," he says softly. "Won't that bother you?"

I shake my head calmly. He lets out an uncertain breath but then places his free hand on my arm, above the scratch. He holds the flower aloft above his heart and closes his eyes.

"Good," I say. "Now focus on the energy from the flower, the healing and life it holds in its cells. The energy will call out to you. Answer it. Then direct it to the damaged skin."

I feel the heat on my forearm, tingling, almost stinging, but not painful. Matthew makes no sound, but his forehead is wrinkled in concentration. Eventually, the stinging fades. I pull away as Matthew opens his eyes. We both look to my arm, where the skin is scratch-free and baby soft.

"You did it!" I say proudly, beaming at him. "It seems you're just as quick a learner as I am." He smiles back, but there's a pained expression in his eyes.

"What's wrong? You did wonderfully," I try to reassure him. I look to the calendula flower in his hand. It's wilting, crystallizing like the rose he had given me last night. My smile fades as my eyes land on Matthew's hand.

A thin blueish-black stripe runs down the back of his hand, following the line of his veins.

"What happened?" I gasp. I grab his hand and pull it toward me. He winces and I ease my grasp as I inspect the mark. To my horror, it looks like a small sliver of his skin, about the size of my scratch, has died and turned necrotic.

"Matthew," I say in a horrified whisper.

"As I once said, if I heal, it seems to do more harm than good." He pulls his hand out of mine and gives it a stretch, studying the black mark himself.

"Will it go away? Will it heal?" I ask, my voice wavering.

Matthew shakes his head. "I suspect not. Death is death. But it won't spread. Unless, that is, you have other cuts you'd like me to heal."

His voice is teasing, but I feel sick to my stomach.

"I'm so sorry," I mumble. He reaches his other hand out and cups my cheek.

"Don't worry. Now we know. And besides, it's just another mark for my new collection." He gives me a cheeky grin and rolls up his sleeve to show off the bronze scar. It has settled into the skin and now looks almost like a metallic tattoo. The only giveaway to its true nature is the sound the raindrops make as they plink off the adhesive. He grins at me, but I can't find it in myself to return his smile.

"How many more bouquets?" Matthew asks, running his fingers along my jaw. "I'm rather eager to get you back home," he admits, his eyes sparkling. His tone is light but his shoulders are tense. The clouds above us are darkening, the rain growing colder. The sun must be getting low.

"We can leave now," I whisper. I want to be back home. I want to be warm, dry, and in bed. And I want him.

Matthew pulls away from me and shakes his head. He looks toward one of the graves pointedly. The one closest to us. My stomach sinks.

"Not that one," I say meekly.

"She's your mother, Kate." His voice isn't admonishing, but I burn under his disapproval.

"I'm not ready. We lay the garden offerings as a sign of respect. It wouldn't be real if I did it now. The intention would be misused."

He nods his understanding and I relax.

"Then I'll do it," he says simply.

"What?" I start with surprise as Matthew bends down and grabs several of the flowers in the basket.

Working quickly, he ties them up with the gray lace. The edges of the petals are already starting to wither as he walks over to the grave. He kneels, placing a hand on the headstone and whispering something

I can't hear. I stare at him, open mouthed, as he honors the witch who banished him for over a decade. The witch he has not stopped criticizing since he arrived. Despite my own anger toward my mother, my eyes mist over at his humility, his desire to see the family tradition fulfilled even when I am incapable of it.

My heart swells with so much love for him I almost have no more room in my lungs to draw breath. The only flicker of pain I feel is the sight of the dark line on his hand, a permanent injury I caused in my own stupidity. If I could do anything to undo that damage, I would.

I start at the fierceness of the thought and continue to stare at his hand, placed on my mother's grave. She too had loved a man so strongly she would do anything to protect him. Her partner of many years. The father of her children. Her warm hand to hold in the dark, cold night. My mother's name, etched in stone, looms at me. What she did was wrong. It was selfish. But as Matthew draws his hand back and stands up, a part of me finally understands her.

He turns around and I am there. He takes a step back in surprise at my sudden nearness, but I don't let him move far from me. I grab the front of his sweater, now damp from the rain, and pull him toward me. Our lips meet and all the tension inside me goes quiet. His surprise ends as he returns the kiss. He wraps one hand up into my hair, tangling it in my braid. Our lips part for a moment, and I take a deep breath, touching my forehead to his for just a moment. Our skin is feverishly hot—both of us.

"Thank you," I say to him, almost in a whimper.

"God, what spell have you put me under?" he whispers back. He kisses the corner of my mouth and then runs his lips down my neck, letting out a long, low groan as he does so. Warmth and anticipation pool inside me. One hand still in my hair, his other explores my body, along my waist. I cling to him, savoring the light pressure from his fingertips as they travel up the purple fabric of my blouse, leaving stinging pleasure in their wake. I can feel his excitement, the lustful tension in his muscles. My head lolls back, drizzling rain pattering on my cheeks. Matthew's lips find mine once again, crushing down on me.

A crow calls from the depths of the forest. The sound makes me jump. I pull away, and for a brief moment my senses return to me.

"We can't . . . not here," I say quickly. I look around in horror, at the graves of my grandmothers. Matthew laughs but nods.

"Take me home," I implore.

"Yes, ma'am," he says definitively. His eyes are sparkling once again, and the sight of his smile makes me want to fly.

He grabs my hand and pulls me away from the graveyard; the baskets of flowers and umbrella are left abandoned. His own breath is ragged, his skin flushed as we run together. Every so often, I fling a hand out to a tree just to gain a sense of direction.

As the break in the tree line comes into view, our pace quickens.

"Damn this, close enough," Matthew huffs in frustration, turning and picking me up into his arms. We kiss under the tree canopy, and the rainy forest comes alive around us. I swear I can hear the very sound of life thrumming through the veins of these woods, the sound of mushrooms and moss growing, sparking with energy.

"Matthew," I say, laughing and pulling away from his adorations, "it's only a little farther." I try to gracefully untangle myself from his arms, still keeping one of my hands clasped in his, and now it is me who pulls us forward.

The rain around us suddenly takes on the salty smell of the sea. I pause at the tree line. There is a figure standing on the back porch of my cottage.

"Miranda," I breathe, the carefree giddiness draining from me.

I step away from Matthew and walk through my garden. My sister stands on the stoop alone, holding the empty pancake tray and syrup boat in one hand, a polished black umbrella in the other.

"I thought you might need these back," she says, looking at the dirty dishes in her hand as I walk up the steps. "I knocked but you didn't answer." Her words are accusatory, as if I'd been ignoring her, despite the fact that she just saw us walk out of the woods.

"Sorry. Matthew helped me decorate the graves. We were just returning."

All my excitement has vanished, but my skin is still warm and red from the run. Miranda looks me up and down, and I become painfully aware of my partially unbuttoned blouse and mussed hair.

"Indeed," she says with a frown. She holds the pile of dishes out to me without a further word.

"Thank you," I say, shocked at her having trekked down to the cottage to return them.

"Well, aren't you going to invite me in?" she asks impatiently. "It's freezing out here, Hecate."

"Of course," I say, pushing my back door open and stepping aside quickly. I follow behind her, and Matthew closes the door behind me. We cross the hallway and into the front room. I give a small mournful glance at the closed door of my bedroom as we pass by. *If only.*

"Can I get you anything?" I ask Miranda, trying to steady my thoughts.

"A London Fog, please," she says with a polite smile, though her grip on her umbrella is white-knuckle tight.

"Of course," I say again, taking the umbrella from her and shaking it out.

"I won't be long, I just need a moment to warm myself." She walks over to the sitting room and stands near the fireplace. For a brief moment I shoot a look of panic over to my writing desk, where our mother's Grimoire is sitting out in the open. Miranda's sharp eyes are bound to notice it. But if I make any move to conceal it now, I will only draw her attention.

Matthew studies my face, trying to parse my panicked look. I turn away from him and head to my stove. I pour some milk into a saucepan and throw in a couple bags of Earl Grey tea along with a dash of vanilla extract and a few teaspoons of sugar.

As the milk warms, the cottage is silent, save for the creaking of my stove and the crackling of the fire. Occasionally, Miranda hums to herself, but the notes are too quiet to identify.

I listen intently, waiting for the moment she stops and screams at the sight of the Grimoire atop my desk. I honestly don't know if she would immediately tell the elders. How could I explain it to them? Would they believe me? Would Winifred back me up or accuse me further, demanding to know why I hadn't destroyed it after she told me to?

As I shakily pour the London Fog into one of my delicate china cups, I realize that if Miranda sees the book, there is zero chance I will celebrate my birthday without being excommunicated.

I steal a glance at Matthew, sitting on my couch near Miranda, as I walk over with the cup. His eyes are on me, his brow furrowed as he tries to discern the tensions in my shoulders.

With slight terror, I realize he won't let the elders within a hundred feet of me without a fight, if it came to that. Maybe that's how the Tower card comes into play. I want to roll my eyes. Of course, the destruction and torment would be brought on by Miranda.

I stop walking, finally registering the notes Miranda is humming, more loudly now as I approach. She is staring at Matthew. Her green eyes glimmer in the firelight, and her intention reaches out across the room, beckoning Matthew to look at her, to become intoxicated by her. Horror runs through me.

"Stop it," I hiss at her, letting the cup fall from my hands. Matthew lunges forward and catches the falling porcelain before it smashes into the wood floor. Hot liquid pours over his hand and splashes onto the tops of my feet.

"Kate?" He looks up at me, worry etched in his voice. Miranda looks at me as well, defiant.

"How dare you," I say to her through gritted teeth. "How dare you try to Siren a guest in my house."

Miranda rises from her chair. "I did it because you needed proof."

"What's going on?" Matthew demands to know, setting the cup down quickly on a side table. "Are you all right?" He turns to me.

"Look at him, Kate," Miranda urges. "Look at his eyes. They are clear. He wasn't affected by my song at all."

"So? Your attempt to gather him into your thrall failed." My relief is short-lived and replaced quickly by rage. Of all the incomprehensible things Miranda has done to me, this might make the top of the list.

"Do you know what Margaret always said about men who couldn't be Sirened, Hecate? She said those are the men with the blackest hearts. Incapable of devotion." Her tone is imploring, almost desperate.

My temples begin to throb, and it gets harder to breathe. I stare at Matthew, searching his eyes for some sign of a trick or act. But I see only his worry and confusion.

"I know what you are," Miranda says, turning to him. "The sea glass told me this morning." Out of her pocket she draws several of the stones she had scattered onto the dumb supper table. They have all turned black, like obsidian.

"He's a traitor, Hecate," she says to me while still staring him down. "The stones whisper of betrayal and lies. Deception and the stench of death. I don't know where you found this scoundrel, but you need to turn him out of your home, now."

"Don't listen to her, Kate," Matthew turns to me, his own eyes as equally desperate as hers. "Your ancestors . . . they're confused." Miranda barks out a laugh at these words. Matthew eyes her angrily. "They are!" he insists.

"Get out," Miranda hisses. "Before I make you get out." The sea glass in her hands begins to vibrate and hum, similar to the notes she had been singing before.

"Kate," Matthew grabs my face, pulling me to look up at him. "I'm here to protect you, I swear it. You can't let her banish me."

"How dare you touch her!" Miranda yells, yanking my arm to pull me away from him. Pain shoots up my shoulder as she rips me away. I let out a cry of hurt. Matthew whirls around and snatches Miranda's wrist.

"Enough," he growls. Miranda is forced to release me. I fall to the floor from the force of her tug, my whole left arm singing in pain.

Matthew's eyes are filled with rage as he stares at Miranda, the beautiful blue of his irises grows darker, morphing into an indigo-tinged black. She meets his gaze defiantly for a moment, but then her face contorts with anguish. The black sea glass falls from her hand and scatters around next to me on the floor as she lets out a long, low cry. The skin on her arm near Matthew's grip turns a bruised sort of dark blue. Her veins fill with inky shadows that slowly work their way up to her elbow, leaving necrosis in their wake. My sister shrieks in agony, her legs collapsing beneath her.

"Matthew, stop!" I sob.

Immediately, he releases Miranda. She falls to the floor beside me, cradling her decaying wrist. I stare up at him, terrified and confused. He steps away from her and rushes toward me, reaching down to gently lift me to my feet, but I scramble away from him.

"I'm sorry. She was hurting you," he explains.

"She was hurting *me*? Look at what *you've* done to her!" I shout at him. Matthew doesn't respond, but his stare is one of heart-wrenching sorrow.

"He's . . . lying . . . to you." Miranda sobs, still holding her arm to her chest. "Keeping . . . secrets."

I hold Matthew's gaze. "Be honest with me."

"I have only ever been honest with you," he pleads with me.

"You have kept things from me," I insist.

He sighs in frustration. "There are certain things . . . things I can't *physically* say, Kate."

"No. No more of that." I shake my head. "Either you tell me the full truth, or I won't stop Miranda from casting her banishment."

He stares at me in shock. I force myself not to look away, but the hurt in his eyes makes me want to sob. But I need to know the truth. He looks around wildly, as if desperate to find some alternative solution. After a moment his shoulders sag in resignation, and my heart clenches with fear. He looks at me with determination and begins to speak, choosing his words very carefully.

"Fine. I'm going to tell you my four absolute truths, Kate. You have to promise you'll believe me." His eyes bore into mine.

"No . . . don't trust him," Miranda whimpers.

I look at them both. My heart feels as if it's ripping in two.

"I promise," I say to Matthew.

He grips my shoulders and draws me into him. I don't resist despite the pain.

"First, you should not go through the Containment tomorrow. You will need every ounce of strength in you, come sunset. Second, no matter what is about to happen to me, this cottage will protect you. Sleep safe and sleep soundly, but do not leave after nightfall. The darkness is dangerous. Do *not* try to Shadow Walk tonight. Third," he pauses and takes a deep breath, gritting his teeth as if the next words are almost painful to say.

"My family and I are descendants of the King Below, sworn to serve him," he manages to say, choking on the words. My blood freezes. "When you failed to Guide Margaret across the veil, he realized the extent of your mother's betrayal and commanded my father to come to Ipswich to train you. My father refused. I came instead."

The very breath is knocked from me. I knew it. Knew he'd been keeping secrets, knew he was wrapped up in all of this. Every conversation he sidestepped, every intuition I ignored, all of it had always led to this moment. But hearing the truth aloud is so much worse than I'd anticipated. The fire behind us shudders and shrinks. Dark shadows fill my cottage, and from far off in the distance, hellhounds bark. I look toward the noise and shiver in fear.

"Look at me, Kate. Look at me," Matthew's deep voice calls me back.

"Fourth," he says as shadows seep down the walls and reach out toward us. He leans down and presses his lips to mine, gripping my shoulders tightly. My heart shatters. The kiss lasts less than a second before he breaks away.

"I love you," he whispers against my lips. A wind picks up and shadows overtake the room. My eyes try to adjust to the darkness, but it is black as pitch.

"Kate?" Miranda cries somewhere in the dark, though her voice is drowned out by the howling in the air. Before I can shout out to her, the shadows clear. The firelight emerges again, and warmth returns to the room. Silence. Miranda is still huddled on the floor. And Matthew is gone.

CHAPTER TWENTY-TWO
Metamorphosis

It is cold and dark where I am stuck. When I try to move, I hear sounds resembling the groaning and cracking of wood being stretched. Rough surfaces scratch my skin and prickly thorns poke into my scalp and palms. My eyes struggle to open. When they do, there is only black night and bright stars above me. Trees of the Ipswich forest loom tall against the sky, both the ones that thrive and give me sustenance throughout the year, and the brittle dead ones that shatter under my touch. They are mixed together, right on top of one another, shifting back and forth, undecided in their own fate.

Again, I try to move my arms, but I'm held down, tangled within a cradle of branches in one of the trees. The symphony of creaking wood starts up again and the skin on my hands is stretched painfully when I try to lift them. I hiss with pain and settle back down.

My body is covered in twisted vines and branches. I can't tell where wood ends and bone and skin begin. The green tendrils of the plant wrap around me tightly, digging into my flesh.

There is movement in the trees, I strain my eyes and lift my head from the crown of leaves that is trying to pin me down further into the canopy. A lone dark figure sits on a mound in a clearing beyond my tree. The shadow creature plays with something orange and glowing in its hands. My mother's crystal pumpkin.

I start to writhe, the leaves of my tree shaking from the movement. I need to get out and tell the creature to be careful. It's delicate. Beg him not to break it.

The creature's head snaps up and stares in my direction. I go deathly still, suddenly acutely aware that I do not want to draw attention to myself. The tingling of fear spreads up my neck. The figure stands and begins to slowly walk down the mound it had been perched on. A long inky-blue cloak billows in the starlight as he walks toward me. I close my eyes and sink into the safety of my tree. There is no escape. I can't run. All I can do is pray I remain unseen.

"Oh, but I always know where you are." His voice, like the rasp of death, caresses my ear. The cold breath that hits my cheek is biting and bitter. I only barely suppress a shriek of surprise. A moist hand and long, thin fingers wrap around my neck. My eyes flash open and I am staring into the blackest irises I have ever seen. A man of indeterminable age, with sunken eyes, and pale, icy skin is staring down at me. His white fingers squeeze around my throat, and he breathes heavily. His dark blue cloak falls over my body, slimy to the touch on the places where it brushes against my skin. Underneath his cloak he is in a full black suit. A glittering chromatic key on a long silver chain hangs from his neck.

The man pulls our faces closer. I wrench my head, turning away from him, and close my eyes, but he doesn't care. He presses his lips down near my ear.

"I've been waiting for you for so long," he whispers before biting on my lobe ever so slightly. I writhe in disgust, trying to pull away, praying this nightmare will end and I will wake up.

"Our bond is eternal, Hecate Goodwin. Dream or not, you belong right here with me. Admit it, how nice it would be to stay here—forever." His damp fingers make their way down my throat. I recoil at the sensation of their caress.

"Answer me," he hisses, and suddenly clawlike fingers dig into my neck.

"No!" I cry in pain, and lash out my legs, kicking hard at the cloaked man. He falls from the tree in a flash of silver and indigo before disappearing into a swirl of shadows. The forest grows silent for half a heartbeat before a long tolling rings out, the striking of a grandfather clock, and a guttural laughter echoes on the wind as a voice slithers over me like damp, shedding snake skin.

"Whatever you believe, you will come home to me soon enough, my darling. When the clock strikes and the sun sets, I shall take you. And finally, I will be free."

CHAPTER TWENTY-THREE
Halloween

Saturdays make the best Halloweens. Crisp, clear skies and cool weather, with a high in the forties, is always preferable. Throw in a crescent moon to grace the sky during the day and set early, leaving the night dark and ideal for ritual casting, and there could be no better conditions for Samhain. Truly, my thirty-first birthday is destined to be ideal.

If only I hadn't opened my door and offered sanctuary to a necromancer a week before. Then there would be no dark tarnish on this day.

The windows of my cottage are thrown open, letting in cool, crisp air. The forest has come alive with color, the peak of fall extraordinarily late this year. Only the pine trees are left in their evergreen. Everything else is a wash of vermillion reds and ochre yellows.

I sit at my vanity and take the curlers out of my hair. I'd nearly torn them off my head after waking from my most recent nightmare. I had thrown on a cap and run to my bathroom, where I'd taken a ripping-hot shower to wash the feeling of those damp hands off me. That dream had been so real I'd almost convinced myself I'd been

Shadow Walking. But unlike the night of the hellhounds, I have no new scratches or sores from where the tree rooted in my skin. The only mark on me is a slight bruise near my left shoulder, from Miranda's yank yesterday.

But reality or dream, it was a promise of what was to come. Unraveling my final few curlers, I try not to focus on it. But of course, if my mind can't think about the horrifying nightmare, it wants to wander over to Matthew. Both trains of thought are equally abhorrent to me.

The clock on my fireplace peals out nine chimes, and I hasten my pace, swiping shimmery emerald eyeshadow on my lids and twisting my loose curls into a wild bun, with several locks spilling over. Black stockings with spiderwebs etched out in several patches, and a green tartan dress over a long-sleeved cream blouse, are my choice of clothing for today. The final piece of my wardrobe is hung on a silk hanger in the closet. A long, forest-green cloak with gold geometric trim. A gift from my mother many years ago. As I put on my Edwardian emerald earrings that dangle and frame my face, I consider not wearing the cloak this year.

My shoulders droop. Is this how it is always going to be from now on? Will I see anything my mother ever touched and be filled with bitterness and hurt? Will every little happiness that she brought to my life be tarnished and tainted, never to be enjoyed fully again?

"You've got bigger problems, Kate," I whisper, needing the reality check. There is no guarantee I'll make it past whatever horror the King Below has planned for me today.

A knock sounds at my front door. Scooting away from the vanity, I rip the cloak off its hanger and throw it over my shoulders. As a final flourish, I fasten my moonstone talisman like a necklace.

"Come on, Merlin," I say to the cat, watching me get dressed. He spent the previous evening pawing fretfully at the guest bedroom door. I peeked my head inside a few hours before, momentarily convinced that Matthew would be in his bed, sleeping peacefully. But no, the room was empty.

Merlin gives me a disgruntled sound of displeasure as I grab the basket filled with caramel apples off of my kitchen table.

"Suit yourself. You always love the munchkin masquerade, but you're free to skip it this year if you wish. Celeste will be disappointed, though," I remind him.

When I open the door, my younger sister smiles tentatively at me. Her dark hair is stick straight, as it always is, cut sharply at her chin. In her hands she holds a picnic basket similar to mine, but hers is full of store-bought Halloween candy. She is dressed all in navy blue, and her cloak looks as if it is made of pure liquid silver. For a moment, I am reminded of my nightmare and the horrid silver-haired man in the indigo cloak. But I quickly shake the thought from my head.

"Happy Birthday, Kate!" Celeste shouts happily, her voice melodic as always. "Aw, and you're wearing last year's present. That color looks so pretty on you!" She smiles at the moonstone talisman hanging from my neck. The ornate gem has turned green, as it normally does when it detects my hedge craft. But there's something different to it now, specks of silver that swirl around the verdant backdrop. My stomach twists at the thought of some invisible magic surrounding my own, waiting.

"And is this my favorite nephew?" Celeste exclaims, looking down at my feet.

Merlin chirps happily and wastes no time jumping the several feet up into her open arms. She nuzzles him contentedly.

"Are you going to sit in my basket today, hmm?" She scratches him under his chin, and his purrs are loud enough to be heard all the way into Ipswich proper. I look around the front stoop: Celeste is all by herself.

"No Miranda?" I ask. Celeste gives me a disapproving frown.

"No, though I can't imagine you're surprised. She's too busy trying to figure out how to deal with her destroyed hand."

"Well, I'm sure she will figure something out. Shall we?" I say, closing the cottage door. After all, if Miranda believes she can just waltz into people's homes and start singing her Siren song, then clearly she can do anything, right?

It's an ungracious thought, but I'm too angry to care.

Celeste is not one to huff, but I could blister at the look she gives me. We walk down the quiet lane, our two picnic baskets swinging from our arms, Merlin riding contentedly on Celeste's shoulder. The only sounds are crunching yellow leaves beneath our feet along the long stretch of road. But I can almost hear Celeste's mind working double time as she debates whether or not to talk. Eventually, as we approach the first set of colonial houses on the outskirts of town, she breaks the silence.

"So . . ."

"Can we not just enjoy the holiday?" I say before she has a chance to speak her mind.

"You can't seriously think I'm not going to ask you what happened last night," she whines.

"There's nothing to tell," I insist. Celeste snorts.

"Of course not, no need to explain why Miranda came home with a decaying limb, right after getting into a confrontation with the heir of the Pacific Gate."

I stop and stare at her. Several children already in costume shriek as they run past us. Celeste rummages into her bucket and pulls out several miniature candy bars and begins pelting the kids' backs as they get farther away. She laughs happily as several Snickers find their mark.

"When did you remember?" I ask.

Celeste rolls her eyes. "I didn't remember. I always knew. A girl doesn't forget a face like that, even after ten years."

"So, why didn't you say anything?"

Celeste almost looks hurt by the question. "Because you didn't. I wasn't about to rat you out to Miranda."

I can hear the sounds of the parade already. It wasn't meant to start until half past ten, which isn't for another five minutes or so. But it's underway.

"C'mon," I tell Celeste, "We need to get to the front as fast as possible." We rush through gathering crowds, swatting away orange and black streamers dangling from the lampposts. Eventually, we settle at the edge of the road, across the street from Zumi's, with another crowd of adults who all gaze at our cloaks admiringly. The parade will soon make its way down to us.

I'm more eager this year than usual to pass out the apples, both because I want the chore to be done and because if an evil death deity plans on visiting Ipswich tonight, I want the town's children to have all the protection I can offer them.

"So, are you going to tell me what happened?" Celeste pushes again while we wait. She asks quietly enough, and the marching band is drowning out most other noise, but I still find myself glancing around, looking for anyone who might be listening.

"Miranda tried to Siren Matthew. Things got out of hand, and he ended up fighting her off me," I say quietly.

"Miranda did *what*?" Celeste shrieks. I shush her urgently. Before I can clarify the events of the previous evening, we are interrupted by a gaggle of college-age girls and boys who have cut across the parade road.

"Oh my god," one of the girls exclaims. "Are you Celeste Goodwin?"

Celeste needs no time to collect herself before turning to the girl and affecting a smile as she nods.

Several of the college kids squeal excitedly and begin to swarm us.

"I've been following you online for years. Years!"

"Will you read my fortune for me? Please!"

"I can't believe you're in Ipswich! Weren't you in St. Martin last week?"

"No, you dolt. She was in Ibiza," comes a cry from the back of the group.

The crowd around us murmurs disapprovingly at the mass of students blocking the road where the parade is due any minute. Celeste does her best to give each kid a moment of her attention. A kiss on the cheek here, a selfie there, all while trying to usher them away from the street. At some point she grabs my hand, and we bob and weave through the crowd, escaping her mob of admirers.

"Sorry," she whispers, but not the least bit embarrassed. "Oh, look, here come the cute ones!" She claps happily as the parade comes into sight. Ipswich parents walk their children, in full costume, all along the town square. Men on stilts and women in fairy wings dance up and down, leading the parade. Several kids spot Celeste and me. They immediately drag their parents over to us, ignoring the adults on the other side of the road eagerly holding out store-bought candy for them.

We have a system developed over the course of many years. And even though she hasn't been home for the holidays in some time, Celeste takes to it perfectly. She sets her picnic basket down so the passing children can pet Merlin. If a child is well behaved and considerate, they get a piece of her candy. If there is one who's absent-minded or a little too rambunctious, they get a slice of caramel apple. A hoard of monsters stop by to pet my little familiar. Frankensteins, vampires, superheroes, ghosts, and ghouls all take a moment to nuzzle Merlin, who plays his role perfectly. For a handful of extra-special children, he even does a full belly flop and rollover.

The morning passes in this way, with Celeste and me both too distracted to pay attention to each other. But when the mass of the parade begins to slow down, and the children are fewer and farther between, she turns to me again.

"I can't believe Miranda would try to Siren him," she whispers over the music. I give her a skeptical eye, and she shrugs in acceptance.

"Okay, I mean, I know that she enjoys the occasional man to be besotted with her. But I thought she gave that up after getting married. And to think she would try it on *him*!"

"It didn't work, Celeste," I say.

"Of course, it didn't work." She laughs. "Miranda was a fool to think it would."

"Why do you say that?" I ask, shocked. Had it been so obvious to everyone but me that Matthew was a liar with a blackened heart? A pang rips through my chest. I still can't believe how quickly I fell under his spell.

"Miranda knows the Siren doesn't work on men who are already in love," Celeste says before breaking out into cheers for a well-dressed little witch at the caboose of the parade with her parents. If my sister notices the way I have paused, she doesn't react. The crowd at the side of the road splinters off, some people gathering in the square, others returning back home.

"Shall we head back to Mom's?" Celeste suggests, packing Merlin into her basket. "There's lots to do before tonight."

I barely hear her. Revelations have come so quickly these past few days, I can't keep up. I tossed and turned last night after kicking Miranda out of my cottage. I went through each and every interaction I'd had with Matthew, playing them over in my head again and again. The crystal pumpkin, his carving of my cottage, the night of the hellhound attack. I'd been so certain of his heart. But Miranda had wounded that conviction, and Matthew's confessions all but obliterated it. By his own admission, he is a sworn follower of the King Below. And he attacked my sister.

Because she was hurting you, I remind myself. And Matthew hadn't just admitted his guilt yesterday; he'd also offered what seemed like sincere advice and warning. And he'd told me he loved me. *If what Celeste is saying is true, then—*

No. I can't fall into the trap of glimmering hope and allow myself to be tricked yet again. If he cared for me, he would have told me the truth before Miranda forced it out of him. And he could have stayed, could have explained himself, but he ran into the shadows once his deception was revealed.

"Kate?" Celeste asks after we have been walking for some time. "Are you okay?"

I've been rubbing at my temple, the bright light from the sun exacerbating a sudden headache.

"Miranda didn't mention that," I say finally.

"What?" Celeste tilts her head.

"She didn't say the part about men in love. She said only men without hearts, men who were incapable of devotion, were able to resist the Siren."

Celeste tuts angrily and mutters something I don't quite catch under her breath.

"She certainly has a lot to answer for, Kate. But I know she feels badly about what happened."

"She feels bad because she went up against a hexan more powerful than her and walked away the loser. I'm not sorry for her," I shoot back.

"I'm not saying you have to forgive her today, Kate," Celeste snaps impatiently. "Do what you want—it's your birthday. I'm just letting you know, as a third-party observer, that she was regretful this morning."

I don't respond and we walk in silence. Several times on our way back to Goodwin manor, Celeste is stopped by more of her followers. She beams with every interaction, reveling in their adoration. I am too lost in thought to pay any of them much attention.

When we walk into the manor, Merlin jumps out of Celeste's basket and begins to run wildly around the first floor, a path he has zoomed through thousands of times. I forget how much he must miss the wide-open space of this house.

Mom's Halloween record is playing in the open entryway. I look toward the large family room and notice with surprise that the doors are thrown wide open, and all the furniture has been removed. I look to Celeste with raised eyebrows.

She shrugs. "I got bored and knew it needed to be done for tonight." As she speaks, she won't meet my gaze, which makes me narrow my eyes. She has never been one to do chores out of boredom.

"Fancy a drink in the kitchen?" she offers sweetly before I can press her further.

"It's a little early, don't you think?" I say suspiciously as we walk past the dining room and through the butler's pantry.

"It's after noon." She shrugs, leading me into the kitchen. The hinged door swings shut behind us, and Celeste turns around with a flourish, looking at me excitedly.

On the center of the marble island, sitting atop our grandmother's black lace dessert stand, is the cake to end all cakes. My mother's Better Than Anything Ultimate Halloween Birthday Cake. She only ever made it for me on my thirteenth and eighteenth birthdays, since it was such a labor. Layers of chocolate apple spiced cake with bittersweet ganache between them, an absolute slathering of peanut butter frosting, and salted caramel drizzle on top for a final flourish. Even mortals who attempt this cake end up imbuing it with some sort of magic since it takes so much time and effort. A witch who knows what she is doing can easily impart good luck and protection for an entire year on whoever eats the first and last slice. Not to mention, it's utterly delicious.

"Happy Birthday, Kate," Miranda says timidly from the corner of the kitchen. She is dressed in a sea foam–green empire waist dress, and her right arm is wrapped and hooked into a makeshift sling she has fashioned from one of Celeste's Hermes scarves.

"You got it done in time!" Celeste claps her hand giddily.

"How did you do this?" I ask in awe. Miranda begins to answer, but Celeste jumps in.

"We worked on it all last night. Well, I worked last night while Miranda dealt with . . . stuff," she says, gesturing to Miranda's limp arm. "And then she insisted on doing the rest of it while I distracted you all morning. Didn't I play my part well, Miranda?" Celeste asks sweetly.

"Very well, dearest." Miranda smiles, then turns to me. "We needed to make sure you had The Cake for your thirty-first."

My throat constricts and the back of my eyes prick painfully. Not only have they made me this incredible tribute, but the kitchen is sparkling clean, which is another miracle unto itself.

"Shall we eat?" Celeste suggests. She grabs the cake stand and brings it to the breakfast nook, where three bowls of pasta are already placed and steaming with heat.

"Spill-Your-Secrets Spaghetti?" I ask Miranda with surprise, eyeing the hearty meat sauce loaded onto the noodles. It was one of our mother's best recipes and one of the only ones she ever taught Miranda and Celeste.

Miranda nods. "Yes, but I left out the taro root, so it's safe. No spilling of secrets, I promise," she says.

"Ugh, you know I wouldn't even care if it wasn't safe," Celeste says, shoveling pasta onto her fork. "All I've had to eat today is Almond Joys and a peanut butter cup. I'm desperate at this point." She takes a massive bite and sighs happily.

"I love salty food," she says through a mouthful of noodles.

Miranda and I both laugh and follow suit. The first bite of my mother's spaghetti is always the best. The familiar flavors, Cretan oregano and dark opal basil, hit me a little harder than I expect. I glance at my sisters. Both of their gazes are misty as our eyes meet. This is the first time we've shared this dish since our mother passed.

"Thank you for this, Miranda," I say quietly, setting my fork down. "It's delicious."

"Mmm." She hums in agreement. "It is good, isn't it? Not quite the same as Mom's, but still decent." A ghost of a nostalgic smile graces her face as she takes another bite. Celeste ignores both of us, still hungrily devouring her portion of the meal.

Once all our bowls are empty, Celeste clears away the dishes and, with great fanfare, places the birthday cake at the center of the table.

"Now remember, you have to have the first *and* last piece for the good luck to take effect," she says with a giggle as she cuts a gigantic piece of the cake and hands me a plate.

"I don't think I am going to be able to even finish this one," I say, staring at the layers of peanut butter frosting and caramel dripping over the chocolate spice base.

"Well, at least try," Celeste says, cutting a piece for Miranda and a small sliver for herself.

My fork sinks into the impossibly moist cake, and I gather as much of the icing into this first bite as possible. The apple spice and chocolate flavors hit first, infused with calming intentions, and I feel instantly relaxed. Then comes salted caramel, tasting of hope and good fortune. My sisters wait until I swallow before digging into their own pieces. Miranda eats hers eagerly, but Celeste only manages two bites before setting her fork down.

"Still too rich for me," she says with a hum. "And now it's time for presents!" She claps her hands and gets up from the table. She grabs two boxes wrapped in brown craft paper off the kitchen island and sets them beside me on the table.

"You didn't need to get me anything," I say. Celeste rolls her eyes.

"Since when do we not get each other birthday gifts?" Miranda asks through a mouthful of cake. "Open mine first," she demands.

I laugh and start unwrapping the present tied with ocean-blue ribbon. Inside the box is a stationery set, notecards with greenery trimming their edges, and a small bunch of dried elderflowers.

"A reminder to stay in touch. Since I so rarely hear from you," Miranda says primly.

I accept the critique. "Thank you. I was running low."

"Mine next," Celeste says, shoving the box with a silver star lace tied around it.

I untie the ribbon, and the paper falls away. I lift the top off the small box. Inside is a delicate gold ring with three tiny ornaments on the head. An anchor, a sprig of thyme, and a starburst.

"I had it custom made!" Celeste claps. "I got one for myself too—see?" She holds out her hand, and indeed there is the same ring on the index finger of her left hand. She looks at Miranda.

"You have to wait until Christmas for yours," she says.

Miranda and I both laugh. I slip the ring onto my index finger, to match Celeste's.

"Thank you—it's beautiful," I say to her. She grins at me.

"I thought it would be nice to have during your Containment, a reminder that your sisters are always with you." Her eyes get a little misty as she says this.

Miranda and I glance quickly at each other, both remembering that Matthew had warned me against the Containment before he left. I haven't decided if I will heed his supposed list of truths. But it is clear from her frown that Miranda is decidedly against him. If she suspects I might follow his advice, there could be hell to pay after this very short-lived peace.

"Miranda, maybe Win could look at your arm some time tonight?" Celeste says, oblivious to the increased tension. "She might be able to suck some of the death magic away."

"There is no magic to draw away. It's just dead," Miranda says mournfully. I bite my lip, horrified by my cruel treatment of her the night before. I had all but kicked her out of my house into the freezing cold to fend for herself. And then she'd spent the rest of the evening and this morning making me a cake, without the use of one of her arms.

"I can try to look at it," I say softly. Miranda shakes her head. "There's no need."

"Oh my god, Miranda, just let me look at your arm," I insist. I push my plate away, empty except for a few cake crumbs, and scoot my chair to the side of the table. Miranda sighs but gingerly unties the scarf holding her arm in place. I take a moment to help her unwrap the gauze. I prepare myself for a stench of rotting flesh, but none comes. Beneath her elbow all the way to the tip of her fingers, her arm is mummified. The skin has shrunken around atrophied muscles, veins protrude under the surface but are void of all color. Around her wrist are black markings in the shape of a gripped fist. I scan the surface of the dehydrated and blue skin, looking for any telltale injury that I can begin to heal. But there are none. No scrapes or cuts have affected the surface. No burns or blisters. Only death.

"Celeste," I whisper. "In the crystal cabinet in the butler's pantry, grab me the vials that read 'Winter Cherry Sap' and 'Moonseed Paste.'" They are some of my mother's strongest ingredients, which she brought back from one of her trips to the covens in India.

"And a bowl of clean water and some towels," I say more loudly as Celeste scurries away to fetch my requested items.

"Do you really think you can fix it?" Miranda asks hesitantly.

"I don't know. But I'm going to try," I answer honestly. She nods her understanding. I roll my sleeves up and stretch out my sore shoulder, being careful not to touch right along the bruise.

"I'm sorry I grabbed you so hard," Miranda says as we wait for Celeste. I shrug and shake my head.

"I'm more interested in you apologizing for using your Siren." I surprise myself with this request. Miranda's eyes widen with surprise as well, and then harden.

"I did it to protect you." She says this firmly, and though I want to fight her on it, it's clear she believes what she is saying.

"And yet you failed to mention the other reason your Siren might not have worked against him."

Miranda looks away, for once having the decency to be ashamed.

"Yes, that possibility came to mind once he gave his little confession," she waves her good hand dismissively, but her cheeks are flushed red.

"Why was it so impossible for you to believe that he might love me? Celeste guessed almost immediately." I stare at Miranda, trying to see my own reflection in her green eyes, wishing I could understand what it was that warped me so brutally in her perspective.

"I don't know," she whispers as Celeste rushes back into the kitchen, her arms full of supplies.

"Have you brought me the entire pantry?" I ask her as she lays several tinctures and bottles down onto the breakfast table. She sets a clear glass bowl filled with fresh water right next to Miranda's arm before looking at me.

"I don't know, Kate. I panicked." Celeste throws her hands up in the air in exasperation and sits down petulantly in her seat, always the shadow of the child she once was.

I smirk but turn back to focus on Miranda's arm. This won't be an easy task, I've never worked on anything so brutal. For a moment, I think about Matthew, how he has never been good around life and how I, in turn, have never been good around death.

But as I wrap my hands around the leathery, dry skin of Miranda's ruined arm, I realize perhaps that isn't quite so true. Death was kept from me. I was shielded from it for years. But I had taken to it naturally when Shadow Walking. Matthew had claimed one of the powers of my craft was Siphoning, the ability to transform life energy into that of death. But he had also suggested that process could be reversed. Maybe I could do this after all.

I try to ground myself in Miranda. Most of her body pulses with vibrant, electric life. Her arm, though, is a shadow.

However, I realize with excitement, not devoid of energy. There is no sensation of life, but I still connect to something. It's similar to the dry grass walls I'd use to guide my way through the Fall Festival's labyrinth, similar to the bones of the baby bird I'd found in the forest. I hold onto that death energy and use it as an anchor. I close my eyes and breathe deeply, sending my intention through the arm and up toward her living skin above her elbow. With each breath I try to draw the living energy back into the necrotic arm. It wrestles with me, hesitant to return to the ruined flesh. It won't be enough. Pushing down panic, I take another breath and open my mind further, searching. The clock by the door ticks loudly, the kitchen refrigerator buzzes, and the very walls of the house begin to whisper. One hundred and fifty years of our ancestors' lives have been witnessed by these walls, and echoes of their vibrant laughter and magic ring in my mind.

"I ask for your blessings to revive what has been lost," I whisper, pulling all of the energy toward me, up through the floorboards against my feet. Births, marriages, midnight spell work—all the joyful history blends together. The tragedies are there as well. My father's passing, every screaming match between me and Miranda, every facet that makes up the mosaic of life filling this house, I gather it all and direct it toward my sister.

And then, beneath the surface of her mummified skin I can feel it, the faintest pulse of life. Weaker than any I've ever felt before, but still present. With a breath of relief, I immediately grab the winter cherry sap and pour it into the bowl of water, watching as it swirls into nothingness. It would be deadly to drink, but it is without a doubt one of the strongest rejuvenators of atrophied muscle. I slowly dip the dish towels Celeste has placed nearby into the sap water, letting them soak through, and then ring them out. Placing each damp cloth gently onto Mirandas arm, I press them into her, massaging the oily water into the cracks and crevices where her skin is fully desiccated.

I repeat this process over and over again, always focusing on that tiny thrum of life in whatever few cells of her arms still work. Slowly, the thrum grows stronger until eventually all the water in the bowl has been used up. The skin on Miranda's arm is still discolored, but it is hydrated, fuller, not so completely stuck to the bone.

Celeste watches the whole process with obvious fascination and disgust. Miranda keeps her eyes averted from her own injury. Once every last drop of water is gone from both the bowl and the dish towels, I squeeze out moonseed paste into my hands and quickly rub it onto Miranda's skin.

"This is to complete your rejuvenation. You will need to apply this paste every day until the color returns to normal. Mix some aloe in to speed up the process." I say, rubbing her arm vigorously, trying to coax the blood vessels and tissue back to working order. "You must be energetic in your application," I say between breaths. "Let your arm know who's boss."

Miranda gives a polite laugh but still looks at her veiny blue arm in disgust.

"We can wrap it in bandages if that would be easier for you," I suggest. "You will need to change them every day when you switch out the paste."

"Thank you," Miranda says to me. "You've done a very fair job, Hecate." She gives me a stiff smile, and I have to suppress my simultaneous laugh and eye roll. I've given her back a limb, but I suppose "a fair job" will have to suffice.

Miranda stands quickly, almost knocking the vials still on the breakfast table completely over. "We should all be getting ready. The coven will be arriving soon," she says.

As if on cue, the grandfather clock strikes three in the afternoon. I let out a yelp. The sound of the clock so closely matches the tolling I'd heard in my dream last night, and for a moment I expect to hear the howl of a hellhound echoing around the manor.

Both my sisters stop and stare at me.

"Kate?" Celeste asks. "Is everything okay?"

I look out the kitchen window, toward the rough October sea under a crystal-blue sky. The sun is getting lower, inching toward the horizon, the threat of shadows just beyond. I set my mouth into a grim line and turn toward Miranda and Celeste.

"There's something I need to tell you," I say.

CHAPTER TWENTY-FOUR
Samhain

"No time for dillydallying, ladies," Miranda snipes at a group of witches gathered in one of the corners of the ballroom. They all snap to attention, pulling candles, crystals, and talismans out of their bags and handing them to Miranda. She runs them over to the buffet table, where I'm helping Willow Dennison, a young meta-magic witch in training, sort items.

"Here are more materials," Miranda says quickly, dropping them into a pile before walking off to welcome another group of witches that have just arrived. In the two hours since I told Celeste and Miranda everything that has happened to me this past week, my oldest sister has entered a mode of emergency triage that I've never seen from her. Messages of warning and requests for aid were immediately sent to every member of the coven, some via Miranda's waves, others using my brand-new stationery set. Witches are arriving from all over New England, armed with their spell books and charms, to face the coming threat. Miranda has organized us into a small army, assigning tasks and barking out orders like a general.

Willow hesitates, holding her small hands over the newest pile. After a beat, she picks out a single tiger's eye.

"I think this is the only thing that's properly charged. Everything else feels too depleted." She drops the stone into my hand, and I place it in a much smaller pile off to the side. It's not much. The tiger's eye, a few smoky quartz crystals from a hearth witch, a charmed horseshoe from a witch who'd taken a Texan hexan as a lover, and seven black candles that Rebecca brought from the Raven & Crone.

Willow looks at this selection, her brow furrowed.

"I could be wrong, though. Once Winifred gets here, she can go over it all again, in case I missed something."

"Kate!" Celeste calls out. She's standing with a group of witches by the large fireplace, our mother's portrait hanging above her. She waves me over to her.

I turn back to Willow.

"Trust your instincts—you're doing great." I give her red hair a quick ruffle before heading through the crowd, over to Celeste.

At least half of the coven is gathered in the ballroom, far more than the fifty-seven we'd originally expected. Music plays on the old gramophone, but no one dances. Everyone moves with hurried, fretful paces. A group of elders pours concentric salt circles around the room. Others write runes on the walls with homemade inks. Celeste reaches out and grabs my hand as I get to her, pulling me closer to her group. She's with Ginny, Laurie, and another young witch I don't recognize.

"We should get you over to the paint station," Celeste says to me, holding her hands up. Each of her palms has an eye painted in the middle, surrounded by other protective symbols. A friendly witch covered in beautiful tattoos takes me from Celeste and begins painting symbols of protections onto my hands with a shimmery sage-green paste. I look around the ballroom as she works. All these witches have gathered at a moment's notice, witches who thought they would spend the evening in celebration and revelry but are instead getting ready to go to battle. Directing the entire room are my two sisters. They guide witches to workstations and keep stragglers in line. I will never be able to fully express my gratitude to them all.

"A beautiful sight," a voice beside me remarks. "A coven coming together," Winifred says as she studies the green markings on my palm. She is trussed up in a magnificent purple gown, along with a powdered pompadour wig. The pièce de résistance of her costume is a frilled golden collar around her neck that glows in the light of the setting sun.

My shoulders tense at her nearness. My body remembers the way it felt the last time I'd seen her, when she'd ripped her intention into me and almost wreaked havoc with my magic.

Winifred gives me a knowing look and then smiles brightly at my sister.

"Well met, Celeste. And Happy Samhain."

To her credit, Celeste only gives Winifred a curt nod. She's been thrust into action the past few hours but is still clearly shaken by all I have told her about our mother and the other elders.

"Hello, Winifred," I respond after it becomes clear Celeste has no intention to speak. "It's an honor to have the coven gather in my name."

"Indeed," Celeste says after a moment. "Even those who have been dishonest with us." She looks at Winifred pointedly.

One of Winifred's eyebrows rises up in slow defiance as she looks between us. "I was surprised to receive Miranda's letter. She seemed very well informed of the situation. You've been doing your research."

"We have. As have other members of the coven," I say. Winifred's nostrils flare at my obvious taunt. I shouldn't dangle Ginny's help around like a toy, but my temper is rising beyond my control.

"And how about your little necromancer?" she asks me after a moment. "I didn't think he'd leave your side tonight."

Her blow lands as intended. Celeste scowls and I pull my hand away from the witch who has been painting it. She had looked up in fear when Miranda uttered Matthew's craft.

"Thank you," I say, dismissing her. She does not respond, quickly gathering her bags of ink paste, and leaving the three of us alone.

"Matthew left," I say. "Miranda accused him of treachery after reading her sea glass. He admitted he was a sworn follower of the King Below. And then he disappeared."

Winifred pauses.

"Well, you are lucky your sister was looking out for you, then. He was a rather good actor. Even had me fooled."

Celeste shakes her head.

"That is so not the vibe I got from him," she says with an eye roll. "I still can't believe he would just leave you."

"Celeste," I say, my voice rising, "he literally confessed to being an agent of the King Below and then disappeared into a puff of smoke in front of me."

She huffs and walks away from our corner of the room, grumbling something, but I don't hear her, distracted by the way Winifred's eyes widen and her face grows ashy.

"What?" I demand. She looks down and studies the floor.

"Are you certain he left willingly?" Winifred whispers, an unsettling shake to her voice. Had she not heard what I just said? He'd kissed me, told me he loved me, and then Shadow Walked out of my life.

Although, I suppose, that's not quite right.

Shadow Walking is distinct from what happened to Matthew. When we walked together, the darkness greeted us like a friend. But yesterday, the shadows had been writhing malicious masses, hungrily reaching out with the sole purpose to consume.

"She has entered into sacred contract and will never utter words of what has transpired, lest she be reaped."

The words from my mother's Grimoire come to my mind. Perhaps Matthew was held under a similar contract. He had said there were things he couldn't physically tell me. Is that what he had meant? That speaking the King Below's name would forfeit his right to freedom?

"The King Below took him?" I whisper, horrified. He didn't leave me. He had been reaped.

"I won't speak on it," Winifred says suddenly, taking a step away from me. A flash of fear crosses her eyes, and realization hits me instantly.

"Oh," I breathe. *"You've* entered into a bargain with him too, haven't you?" The accusation burns in the back of my throat. That's why she has been so silent on the matter. If she speaks his name, she gives him the right to drag her away. "What did he give you? What did you trade?"

She looks away from me, refusing to answer. I can't blame her for her lack of courage. My own mother had remained silent on the subject of her fiendish patron for my entire life. But not Matthew. He'd told me and had paid a steep price. The walls of the ballroom feel like they are spinning around me, the colorful costumes of all the witches turning into a blurry kaleidoscope.

"Can someone be rescued from the land below?" I ask quietly.

Winifred snaps her eyes back to mine.

"Whether they can or not is of no consequence to you. Once your Containment is over, this entire matter will be put to bed. The land below must go on without us."

This answer unnerves me. I still haven't decided if I should go through with the Containment. I've only just learned the new elements of hedge craft, and my connection to them isn't strong enough to survive Winifred's influence. I will lose everything Matthew has taught me. And from the sounds of it, I will lose Matthew too. But if Winifred is right, if this is the only way to keep the King Below from gaining power, if this will keep the coven out of danger, what choice do I have?

Then again, how can I trust Winifred?

The clock on the wall tolls the half hour, a bell on a grave.

"Seven minutes to sunset," Laurie shouts out from across the room, her eyes transfixed on her wristwatch.

Outside the ballroom windows, the fire-red forest meets a golden sea. Dark clouds are rolling in from the ocean, threatening to obscure the sunset. A cold wind swirls dead brown leaves off the ground outside. The edge of the sun touches the tops of the trees of Ipswich Forest. Only a few miles away, throngs of young trick-or-treaters have just finished dinner and are ready to set off on their evening adventure. But that childlike innocence might as well be a hundred miles away.

Real, deep fear begins to set into my core. There is no icy grip in my chest or nervous fluttering in my stomach. This fear is more primal than that. Every organ in my body thrums with a certain sense of impending doom.

"Will this work?" I ask Winifred, all resentment leaving my voice. "Will the coven's charms keep Him at bay? Will they all be safe?"

"The Atlantic Key may not be what it once was," Winifred admits with regret. "But by the grace of our ancestors, we will prevail."

I glance uncertainly toward the pile of discarded items that Willow and I sorted through. Less than a tenth of the coven's talismans hold any power at all. Celeste takes the few items worth keeping and places them inside a salt pentagram drawn on the ballroom floor. She must sense my gaze, because she looks up at me and nods.

"It is time," Winifred says. "Gather!" she shouts to the crowd.

Everyone falls silent. The coven circles around the ballroom, everyone's Halloween costumes rustling against the marble. Seventy or so witches clasp hands. My sisters stand together. Winifred leads me into the center of the circle.

"Sit," she commands. I obey, lowering myself down onto the top point of the pentagram.

"Thank you all for gathering on this All Hallow's Eve," Winifred says, slowly turning to look at every member of the coven. "We were surprised to learn of the trouble the Goodwin sisters have found themselves in."

A murmur travels the crowd, and I hold back from snorting at her blatant lie.

"But it is our duty to them and to one another to see them safely through." She gracefully lowers herself to the floor so that she is positioned in front of me.

"First, we must destroy the origin of this hateful entanglement." She holds her hands out toward Miranda. My sister looks at me almost nervously before stepping forward. From under her cloak, she presents a leather-bound tome. Our mother's Grimoire. My eyes widen. She must have snuck down to my cottage during the uproar of the past few hours. Miranda looks away as she hands the tome to Winifred.

"Let this be a reminder to all in the Atlantic Key: Do not become greedy, do not seek more than what you already have, do not invite the evil of discontent into your life as Sybil Goodwin did." She holds the book aloft for the coven to see. I want to snarl at her for mentioning my mother's name and for her blatant hypocrisy. The coven around us titters in surprise, excitement, and confusion. None of them know the true extent of the story.

Winifred slowly lowers the Grimoire down and places it on the floor, in the very center of the pentagram.

"Give me your hand," she says, holding out one of her palms. I do as she asks. She places her other hand on the Grimoire and begins to whisper at a fevered pace. I lean in closely and listen, certain the rest of the coven cannot hear her.

"Hecate Goodwin, by my powers I unbind thee from this evil. I rescind my intention that made this tome and nullify all contracts within." Winifred's words are fast and full of fervor. She continues this mantra, repeating the sentence over and over again. Members of the coven lean forward, straining to hear what is being said. But she keeps her voice low and firm, staring at the Grimoire intently. But the book remains unchanged.

"Winifred, we don't have time for this," I say hurriedly. The sun will set any minute. She shakes her head, lifting her hand away from the tome. "It will not fade," she says, her brow furrowed.

"What does that mean?" I whisper back. She shakes her head again and looks out toward the rest of the coven.

"That spell will take some time to come into effect, of course." She beams at them, her smile too wide to be believable. "Now, we move forward with the Containment."

At her words, the other elders step forward. Only ten now, with my mother and Margaret dead. They form a smaller circle around us, along the edges of the pentagram, and begin to chant. The rest of the coven hums in the outer circle. The candles in the room begin to flicker.

Winifred takes both my hands in hers. Her gray eyes bore into mine.

"Hecate Goodwin, do you renounce the right to magics beyond those that you have cultivated the past eighteen years? Do you agree to be bound to the garden, kitchen, and healing crafts that have fulfilled you for more than half your life?" Her words come out in a rush.

"Do you accept that, by forgoing all other paths, you strengthen the one you already walk?" Winifred's hands squeeze around my wrists tightly. I open my mouth to speak but pause; there's a thrumming in my body, and the sense of doom blooms into panic, increasing exponentially with every beat of my heart.

Out of the corner of my eye, the glint of light shining off the horseshoe next to me blinks away. The sun has set. I have turned thirty-one. And Samhain has begun.

Outside, a dog howls.

"The ceiling!" A witch in the circle shouts. I look up. In every corner of the grand room, inky shadows descend from the highest points on the walls.

"Hecate." Winifred tugs at my wrist, forcing me to look back at her.

"Do you consent to be contained?" she asks again. I don't answer. There is a biting breeze in the room, as if someone has opened a door and let in the bitter north wind.

"Hecate," Winifred whispers through gritted teeth. "I bid you say yes."

The effect is almost instant. My mouth opens to follow her command, acquiescence on the tip of my tongue. But I rip one of my hands from her grip and slam it over my mouth, silencing the *yes*. I won't let Winifred force my hand as my mother once did. If I agree, it has to be my choice. The room spins, from the shadows pouring down the walls and from my defiance.

"If you defy me," Winifred seethes, "you will break yourself from this coven, and I will have every right to excommunicate your magic. Now, answer: Do you consent?"

We are out of time. The King Below's minions are coming to make good on his threat from my nightmare. And yet I remain paralyzed by this decision. I want to scream in frustration at myself. Do I place my faith in my coven? Do I place it in Matthew? If I don't agree, will the King Below take me anyway? He's already proven his willingness to overstep the laws that bind him. Who's to say he won't take his wrath out on the Atlantic Key? On my sisters?

Suddenly, the choice is clear.

"No." I force the word out. The coven gasps. Winifred releases my other hand. The vibrations of panic in my body stop for a moment as I bask in this newfound clarity. But the peace is short-lived.

A series of howls and barks sound out, just outside the windows. The witches around us break into disorder, with screams and shouts echoing around the room as the shadows continue to pour down the walls. Several members break from the circle and run across my path to escape. Their footprints create holes in the circles of salt. Obsidian-like ichor seeps up from the cracks in the floorboards, twisting and writhing among the stampeding feet. A long dark tendril reaches out for me. The moonstone dangling around my neck has turned the color of pitch.

A hand swipes at the pentagram around me, sending salt, a smoky quartz, and the horseshoe flying toward the shadow closest to me. The black cloud retreats.

"Get up," Celeste says, panting. She grabs my arm and tugs me onto my feet.

"No!" Winifred says, reaching out for my skirt. I stumble backward and barely have enough time to right myself as my sister drags me across the ballroom. Black smoke pours from every crack and crevice. The main door to the exit is blocked by dozens of panicking witches.

"Over here!" Miranda shouts to us. Celeste and I both turn. Miranda holds open the door to the library that sits just off the ballroom. We rush over to her, going against the flow of moving bodies.

"Get inside," she says as we reach her, practically pushing us both into the library and shutting the door. The sound of the tumult is immediately lessened behind the thick walls. Familiar sights greet us.

Our father's favorite reading chair, the chess table, and dozens of bookshelves with his most precious novels and encyclopedic texts.

"What is happening, Kate?" Celeste asks. She clears her throat, trying to keep her voice steady.

"The King Below wants me. Those shadows were how he took Matthew last night. And now he's come to take me too," I say.

"We will hold him off," Miranda says, clutching her bag of sea glass and staring at the door in determination.

I shake my head. "It's Samhain. He can walk the world of the living at his own will."

"Yeah?" Celeste challenges, squaring her shoulders. "Then where is he? Why doesn't the chump show his stupid face?" She turns around the room, asking the question to the open air.

A howl breaks out among the screams outside, and there is a fierce scratching at the library door. Books begin to fall off shelves as black smoke pours off the edges.

"Oh," Celeste whispers meekly. The edges of the smoke flicker with orange light, and the books still on the shelves begin to ignite.

Celeste runs toward the shelves of our father's beloved library and begins hurling books off the burning shelves. The dark smoke curls up around her dress, and her cape flickers with flame.

"No!" I shout. Miranda hurls a handful of sea glass at her, the glass breaks against her back and salty water pours out in a dense spray, dousing the flames momentarily. Miranda runs toward Celeste. A tendril of smoke wraps itself around her bad arm, and she collapses with a scream of agony.

"No, please—not again," she cries. The inky clouds envelop her and begin to reach out toward me.

The library darkens further, shadows overtaking the entire room. Celeste curses. Miranda's groans of pain grow louder.

This can't be happening. If the King Below wants me so bad, then fine, but my sisters won't be part of it. I will go to him, but on my own terms, under my own control. He won't take my physical body. Not if I can help it.

I close my eyes and relax, focusing on the sensations all around my body. The scratchy feeling of the tights on my legs. The way my shoes pinch my little toes ever so slightly, the tickle of one of my curls on the back of my neck. And all that sensation, all that awareness of myself, I bring to the base of my neck, imagining a very specific set of fingers guiding me along my skin. My mind fills with images of the clearing in the forest that the hellhounds had herded me to, that place that seemed so familiar in my dream last night.

"Celeste," I call out.

"I'm here," she calls back from the darkness.

"Please try to catch me."

I take a single breath. And then I push all of my intention forward and walk out into darkness.

CHAPTER TWENTY-FIVE
The King Below

The clearing is empty, save for the trees, as I spin around, looking for signs of the dark figure who has been stalking me in my dreams.

"Hello?" I call out.

The forest is quiet, muffled. Somewhere in the distance, thunder rumbles across the sky, but I hear only its echoes. The trees around me are a mixture of old dead wood and brittle obsidian glass. And I am all alone. But the moonstone talisman around my neck is still pitch black.

Something catches my eye.

Off to one side of the clearing is a lit jack-o'-lantern sitting on the ground. His smile is happy and friendly, his candle flickering orange in the darkness.

"Who put you here?" I wonder aloud as I walk over to it.

Another light glints through the trees when I approach the pumpkin. I look out into the woods and see, with surprise, that two rows of lit jack-o'-lanterns form a path deeper into the forest.

"All right, then," I say, almost amused by the surrealism of the scene. I follow the path of the pumpkins, my shoes padding quietly. After a few steps, I kick them off and ground my feet on the forest floor, taking several deep breaths. My fear, once so overwhelming, has vanished completely. Walking farther, I draw my green cloak closer to protect it from the flames inside the pumpkins.

The trees around me shift and morph. The change is so slow, it's almost imperceptible. I lean over a jack-o'-lantern, being mindful of my cloak, and place a hand on one of the pines. A tiny portion of rotten bark breaks away and cracks into glass shards in my fist, but the rest of the tree still stands. And there it is: that death energy I felt in Miranda's arm. Along with a tiny thrum of life. That in-between condition. I stare at the tree in wonder. It is living *and* dead, existing in both states simultaneously.

I back away and start walking down the lit path again. The faces of the jack-o'-lanterns become chaotic, more sinister, with each passing step. Grins turn to sneers, which turn to snarls and fangs. And then, quite suddenly, the pumpkin path ends.

Before me is an old stone wall and wrought iron gate.

The Goodwin graveyard. I suppose it makes sense that it would all end here. At least Celeste and Miranda are far away and safe. It's that thought that guides me forward.

I push on the gate, but it does not budge. Locked. Another push and the gate groans but doesn't swing open. A prickle of fear runs along my neck. The gate always opens for a Goodwin witch. But perhaps the rules are different in the Land Below. I do my best to ignore the fear and confusion. The pumpkins led me here, so it's clearly where the King Below wants me to be. There must be some other option. Angry and annoyed, I rattle the iron bars.

Off to the side of the gate, there is a long, hand-carved wooden table covered with clusters of dried herbs. These bundles of plants look more alive than anything else in the forest.

"What game is this?" I shout out into the darkness, but I receive no response.

I study the herbs. Sage, lavender, rosemary, mugwort, rose petals; there must be over a dozen different piles.

"It's a choice," I whisper to myself.

I have half a mind to choose none, to walk back down the way of the pumpkin path. If the King Below wants to toy with me, see how he likes it when I don't play along.

But I continue to study the herbs carefully. My hand hovers over sage; wisdom would come in great hand during any confrontation. Mugwort maybe—to strengthen my powers? Or perhaps the rose petals, to offer protection to the ones I love.

But my mother's first lesson in the kitchen, nearly twenty years ago, echoes in the back of my mind. I pick up the rosemary.

"There is power in remembrance," I say quietly. The other bundles of herbs disappear, as does the table that held them. A low metallic groaning sounds behind me as the gate to the graveyard finally swings open. It teeters, beckoning me onward.

The usual smell of damp earth and oak moss–covered headstones doesn't greet me in this shadow world. I walk over to the headstone with the most polished granite and a small bundle of dead flowers beside it. I place a hand softly on top.

"Hi, Mom," I whisper.

"Lovely evening, isn't it?" A quiet, wet, and rasping voice sounds out from the darkness. I spin around. In the corner of the graveyard is a mound of boulders, piled twelve feet high, with a figure sitting atop it.

A dark indigo cloak billows in an invisible wind. I shudder, remembering damp hands on my neck. I creep closer. The boulders are not boulders after all, but a precariously piled mass of rotting pumpkins, arranged into a chair-like shape at the very top.

"It would have been lovely, yes. Had I been allowed to celebrate in peace," I say, finding my voice. A wet, guttural laugh vibrates throughout the graveyard.

"You came to me, remember?" the man atop the pumpkin throne says. He leans down toward me, his long silver hair coming into view.

"Your hounds and shadows were invading," I respond. "I hardly had a choice. Besides, I wasn't interested in my sisters seeing me dragged to hell."

"Yes." The man nods appreciatively. "It was a nice surprise when you successfully Shadow Walked here, rather than my Cerberaxi having to take you. It was quite considerate, letting me conserve my energy."

"Happy to be of service," I say sarcastically.

He takes no note of the acid in my voice.

"I am glad you have finally been learning your true craft. It's why I offered you gifts upon your arrival. You will soon come to learn that I enjoy rewarding good behavior, Hecate."

"What gifts?" I ask, mystified.

He blanches from atop his throne and peers down at me disapprovingly.

"I lit your way for you," he says.

"I know how to navigate this forest without a pumpkin path. I'm a hedge witch," I remind him.

"And, of course, I gave you herbs." His voice is growing impatient.

"I can buy rosemary for three dollars at the local supermarket—"

The King Below swoops down from his pile of pumpkins, and before I can move away, those long pale fingers have wrapped themselves around my throat. I let out a strained gasp as he squeezes the air out of me. Up close, he is just as I dreamed him: gaunt, with skin stretched tightly over protruding cheekbones and dark purple shadows under black eyes.

"Try that again, dearest," he seethes.

"Thank you for your very generous gifts," I croak, satisfied when a few droplets of my spit splatter on his face. He releases his grip on me, and I fall to the ground.

"Good. You're a fast learner. I like that," he says, breathing heavily, almost wheezing. He walks back toward the pumpkin throne, but he doesn't ascend again. Instead, he leans against the pile, steadying himself.

"You're weakened," I say, coughing. "You can't even climb your throne."

He looks down at me with disdain.

"I have been without a hedge witch for two hundred years. And the last one—Abigail, was it?" He scoffs. "Well, she was hardly trained at all—a puny little thing. She didn't make it a year before her heart gave out. Very few would last as long as I have without proper help. But yes," he admits, "I am weak."

I smile up at him smugly. "Then perhaps I have a chance in this fight after all." Maybe I could avenge us all. My mother, my father, Abigail Browne, and all the hedge witches who came before me.

The King Below laughs that horrid, raspy cackle. "Who says there needs to be a fight?" he asks, whipping his cloak open with a bit of flourish. He is wearing a black three-piece suit. The only embellishments are the chromatic crown atop his head and the key hanging from a chain around his neck. Around us, the trees in the graveyard explode into flame, but not like they had the night of the hellhound attack. No, the trees are not on fire. Thousands upon thousands of floating candles drift up and down among the leaves, somehow managing not to singe the trees themselves.

"I think you will find I can be quite persuasive." The King Below stares at me hungrily. Memories of my nightmares flash before me. A river full of lost souls. A gaping chasm in the ground. Me, forever bound to a single twisted tree.

"What exactly are you trying to convince me to do?" I ask, unable to keep my voice from shaking slightly.

He opens his arms wide and smiles at me in an eerily friendly manner.

"To be my hedge witch, of course," he says. "Become mine, and I will grant you eternal life. Together we will hold dominion over Death."

There's an awkward moment of silence.

"I get to choose?" I ask uncertainly. The King Below chuckles.

"Yes. The magic doesn't take unless the hedge witch agrees. That's where I've had trouble in the past," he admits with a dark grin.

It's my turn to laugh. I stand up and smile.

"Fine then. Thank you for the opportunity, but I'm afraid I have to decline," I say.

He stares at me for a beat.

"Ah yes. I was afraid you might be of that inclination initially," he mutters, shaking his head. But after a moment, he looks up and gives me another serene smile. "No worries. I came prepared." He twists on his heel to face the throne and snaps his fingers loudly.

A long, glittering gold chain snakes its way down the makeshift arm of the throne. At the edge of the chain, a shimmering translucent specter appears, a golden collar around her neck and a gag in her mouth. Recognizing her eyes immediately, a desperate cry escapes me.

"Yes," the King Below hisses in eager acknowledgment. "Mommy dearest is here to say hello."

He grabs the chain and yanks it toward him. My mother trips over her own feet at the tug and falls to her knees before him. "Don't mind the gag—a necessary evil, I'm afraid. She might have all sorts of ideas to poison you against me, and I can't allow that. But isn't this such a nice reunion?"

I am frozen, rooted between the headstones of two of my ancestors. Knowing retroactively that Margaret had been a wraith has not prepared me to see the spirit of my mother. I want to run to her, push the madman away, and release her bindings. I want to beat against her chest for all the lies she's told and then collapse sobbing into her arms as she strokes my hair. But I know the King Below won't let me within ten feet of her.

"What is this?" I ask, horrified. "You think showing me my mother gagged and chained will soften my heart to you?"

He smirks and shakes his head, his silver hair floating in the air behind him.

"No, no, dearest. Your mother has been waiting quite some time for you. I was ever so surprised when she showed up six months ago. I've been hiding these days. You know, it takes a lot out of me to help spirits cross over. It steals a piece of me every single time, chipping away at my soul, like a bird pecking at a block of seeds, until all that is left is an empty husk. A suffering I wouldn't have to endure if you would *do your job!*"

His shout is the first loud noise I've heard since I began my Shadow Walk. My mother and I both flinch in surprise. There is howling off in the woods behind the graveyard. The hellhounds are close. The King Below collects himself, straightening his tie and clearing his throat.

"My apologies," he says with a curt nod toward me. "I only meant to say that, despite my hiding, I couldn't help but make an appearance for the lovely Sybil Goodwin. My delight over her death was immeasurable. The thorn in my side, the witch who spent years preventing me from claiming you as my own, using the very gifts I gave her to keep me from ascending on Samhain or Beltane. I finally had her in my clutches. I'm sure you can only imagine the reunion we had after being apart for so many years." He grabs my mother by the neck and lifts her up. He plants a wet, sloppy, slurping kiss on the side of her cheek before dropping her back to the ground. My mother glares at him, but he pays her no attention.

"I've enjoyed her company so much, I couldn't bear to actually let her pass on. But for you, I would." He studies my face and must find some satisfaction in my look of horror as I realize what he is saying. He nods happily.

"Say you will be mine. Become my hedge witch, and I will release your mother. She will be free to finally rest."

My mother lets out a series of despairing moans and shakes her head wildly at me. The King Below steps in front of her, blocking her from my view. I swallow the sobs that threaten to escape my lips. I know he must see my despair, must see how he has me trapped. But I can't give into him. I force my face into a glaring frown and look at him with a dead, unaffected stare.

"Why would I sacrifice my life and freedom for a woman who lied to me for thirty years? Who sold me away before I was even born?" I ask him.

The King Below's eyes widen. He looks between me and my mother a few times before breaking out into maniacal laughter.

"Ooh, I do love your cruelty, Hecate! You are going to be marvelous, aren't you? I was worried you wouldn't have what it takes. And yet here you are, gloriously tossing aside the woman who raised you. I would be in raptures if it weren't all in refusal of me." He licks his lips as he stares at me, and fiddles excitedly with the key around his neck. I recoil in disgust.

"Am I free to go now?" I ask. I am not sure what bluff I am playing. I scan the graveyard and nervously twist the strands of rosemary in my hands. Perhaps I can find a way to fend him off while my mother escapes.

"Oh, but do stay! I have one more tactic of persuasion. This one isn't even dead. Yet." he purrs and snaps his fingers again. Another figure, not spectral like my mother, but solid, appears on the opposite side of the throne. The poor soul is wrapped completely in chains. Chains that are red with heat. Glowing hot iron shackles. Beautiful icy-blue eyes stare at me as the body tenses in prolonged agony.

"No," I breathe, rushing toward Matthew.

The King Below flicks his wrist, and the ground beneath me rumbles. Skeletal hands shoot out of the graves and wrap around my ankle. I try to shake them off, but their grip is like a vise, bone cutting into my skin.

"Please," I beg, watching Matthew fall to his knees in pain from the burning irons. "Please stop hurting him."

The King Below tuts.

"You say no to your own mother but immediately fall into line for this creature?" He kicks out a long leg and shoves Matthew's chest into the ground. "Careful, Hecate, you're on the verge of making me wildly blind with jealousy."

"Please," I beg again. I have discarded what semblance of an upper hand I might have had. But I cannot stand the sight of Matthew's anguish.

"You know," the King Below says out loud to all of us in the graveyard, "the Cyphers have been a pain in my ass for nearly half a millennia. My own progeny, so hubristic, so sycophantic. I always knew they would only ever disappoint me. A family of screwups with too much power." The King Below looks back at me. "His sister betrayed me too, you know? Married a mortal man without my approval." He leans down and looks Matthew in the eye.

"You can bet that she's first on my list when I finally walk the land above." He grins demonically.

Matthew fights against his chains, rage seething in his eyes.

The King Below tuts and leans down, coming face-to-face with him.

"I was so eager when you were born, Matthew. So pleased by your innate power and strong will. Finally, I thought to myself, here will be a man worthy of calling himself my descendent. You, the one I entrusted, tasked with making sure my hedge witch was properly trained since her mother refused. The one I gave all the resources to, as well as dreams to guide you, and what did you go and do? You fell in love! And decided to thwart me at every turn from claiming what was *rightfully mine!*"

He lands another kick at Matthew's head this time.

"Stop it! Stop it!" I shriek. I smash the skeletal hand around my ankle. Shards of bone pierce into my skin, drawing blood.

Wriggling free, I run full force toward the King Below. He whips around and grabs me by the throat.

"I will dole out whatever punishment I see fit!" he snarls. "The boy tried to take what was mine. Don't you see, Hecate?" He releases me, his voice growing soft as he strokes my face. "He tried to prevent our union. We could have been together a week ago if not for him. I sent Margaret to you, to test you. To see if you could let a spirit pass through you. I was bitterly disappointed at your failure. I demanded the Cyphers do something about it. The wimp of a patriarch refused to act. But oh, I was so pleased when Matthew ran off toward Ipswich against his father's wishes. I thought surely, he would teach you what you needed to know and then bring you to me. I could have spent the past seven days reveling in your flesh, gaining strength so that I might walk the realm of the living again. Imagine my dismay when he instead cast an insipid little shadow charm to kept us apart." He huffs. "No worries. Such trifling bits of magic will no longer stop me once we become one."

One of his long, spindly fingers strokes my neck. His eyes fall on my lips, and his mouth parts slightly.

"I will destroy you before I ever agree to be your hedge witch, do you understand?" I gasp from under his grip. Tears flow from my eyes. "You will fade and rot away before you see the surface of the living world."

The King Below lets out an aggravated roar and backhands me with surprising force. My skull vibrates from the strength of his hit, and I fly backward. I land forcefully atop one of the gravestones, the wind instantly knocked from me. My ribs crack and I slide limply down the slab of granite, wheezing for air, but no breath will come to me.

My grandmother's name on her tombstone bears down on me. I can hear my mother's sobs as the King Below sighs unhappily.

"Now, look what you made me do," he groans. "You need to be more careful, Hecate. If your spirit is damaged while Shadow Walking, your body could reject it when you try to reenter. Or it will take on the damage itself."

I ignore him, pressing the rosemary in my hand into the carved grooves of my grandmother's name. I try to speak but struggle to find breath.

"If you start behaving, I might find it in my grace to heal you," the King Below sings out happily. "Gwaed is awfully useful for that—just ask your mother."

I manage to suck in a slight breath of air. My ribs burn from the pain of it. I try to remember how it had felt to speak to Margaret's spirit. Of all the darker sides of hedge craft I've learned this week, that one had felt the most natural.

"Please," I rasp, pressing the flowers firmly into the stone. "Please, ancestors, help me." I open my mind the same way I had when healing Miranda's arm. The history and energy of the Goodwin graveyard resonates in the ground around me. Memories of my grandmother's kindness; of my great-aunts sitting together, laughing; old stories I was told of women I'd never met, but whose love and magic still ran through my veins.

"Please, be here with me," I say in an almost silent prayer. My tears fall into the grass as the King Below laughs.

"Be serious," he scoffs. "I am a necromancer, Hecate. You can't turn the dead against me."

"Not their bodies," I croak in agreement.

He frowns. A wind whispers through the grass of the graveyard, and my mother's eyes widen in surprise. Figures, shimmering and translucent, pop in and out of view, all across the rows of headstones. A feeling of belonging, of love, of protection, fills my soul. All my foremothers are here, answering my call.

"Enough!" the King Below bellows. He lets out a snarling yell, raising his hands above his head. The ground shakes heavily. My ribs scream from the jostling movement. Grass splits and clumps of dirt explode from the ground. Graves all around me burst open with necrotic energy. Skeletons begin to crawl out of the earth. Yellowed antique clothes, decomposing flesh, discolored bone. It's all a blur as the bodies of every Goodwin witch emerge from their rest. I stare in horror as they all slowly turn to face the King Below. Waiting for instructions.

"Take control of your spirits, you worthless calcium deposits," he roars.

The whispering all around me increases, growing louder. Skeletons skirt around the graveyard, grasping and clawing at empty air. Shimmering specters swirl above me in a silver tornado. My head is swimming from the lack of breathing. I grip the rosemary tighter.

The frightening mass of ephemeral beings above me rushes down, their wind blowing my hair into a chaotic whirl as they fly together toward the pumpkin throne.

The King Below recoils in horror as he is swarmed. I hear the distinct snapping of chains as my vision begins to blur.

CHAPTER TWENTY-SIX
The Shoulders of Atlas

"I've got you. Don't leave," Matthew's voice calls me away from the gray mist that beckons to me inside my mind. "Kate, if you go back now, you will die in your body. Stay here. Stay with me." His voice is panicked and urgent. My eyes flutter open and look directly into his.

"Matthew," I whisper, scanning his body for signs of injury. He lets out a relieved cry and buries his face in my hair. Other than some blood near his temple, where he'd been kicked, he seems relatively unscathed despite having been covered in burning chains. I want to run my fingers through his hair. Pull him toward me and kiss every inch of him. But I am too weak.

An erratic growling grows louder as one of the animated skeletons crawls quickly across the ground over to us. It reaches out and grabs my ankle, snarling and baring its teeth.

Matthew's fist flies and connects with the creature's head, breaking off the jaw, which lands on my stomach.

"Ugh," I groan at the sight of it, trying not to think which one of my great-aunts it belongs to.

The skeleton still grasps my ankle but doesn't move. Matthew gathers up the shattered jaw and whispers over it. Black shadows pour from his hands and swirl around the disembodied bones. When the inky clouds fade, Matthew yanks the skeleton head toward him and thrusts the jaw back onto the head. A horrifying gasping sound emanates from the corpse.

"Fight my enemy," Matthew says, his voice rough, his eyes an opaque black. The skeleton releases my ankle and turns around, crawling like a spider over the ground, right toward the pumpkin throne. My vision is blurry but flashes of silver and sparks fly all around the graveyard. The sounds of shrieks and howling dogs fill my ears. Specters fly past my field of view with alarming speed. The battle is still ongoing, with Matthew's newly turned thrall joining the fray.

"How . . . ?" I look at Matthew bewildered. He scans the graves around us. No more skeletons are close by.

He turns to me with a knowing smile. "I told you there is power in placing the final piece."

Then, ever so gently, he pulls me up off the ground. "Where are you hurt?" he asks.

"Ribs," I groan, suddenly aware of the excruciating pain searing through my abdomen. I cry out as Matthew shifts me, supporting my back with his knees. He places a flat palm onto my stomach. There is a large rip in my tartan dress. He places his other hand on his own shoulder and breathes deeply. A pleasant warmth fills my stomach, and there are several odd cracks and popping noises as my bones shift back into place. The veins on Matthew's arm turn black, and his skin begins to decay.

"No," I moan, trying to push his hand off my stomach. He presses down more firmly, and a sharp pain from my cracked ribs shoots up my spine. I gasp.

"This isn't up for debate, Kate," he says through gritted teeth.

"You're hurting yourself," I cry. Without a sacrifice to consume, the magic is eating away at him with a ferocious hunger.

"It doesn't matter. None of it matters if you're not okay."
Matthew's breathing is heavy, labored.

The King Below is perched atop his throne in a defensive, crouched stance. Lightning cracks in the sky above him in strange slow motion. At the base of the throne several of my ancestral spirits are trapped in gilded chains, writhing, trying to escape. Others are clutched near their graves, captives of their own bones. A handful still fight. They dodge and swarm, ripping at the King's clothes and hair. Blood drips from his skull and skin, but he is smiling. Cackling.

"We're losing," I whisper, watching as another gold chain shoots from the King's hand and wraps around a spirit. It pulls her instantly to the ground, and her screams join the wails of all my other ancestors.

"We're going to get you out of here. Don't worry," Matthew whispers against my temple, leaning heavily into me. "When you are healed, Shadow Walk back to your body. Hide in your cottage, and don't leave the boundary until sunset tomorrow. By then, it will be too late for him to reach you. He will have to wait until Beltane to try again. If he even survives that long. I will fight him off while you run."

Before he can say more, Matthew is ripped away from me. He lands with a thud in the grass several graves away and doesn't stir. The King Below's indigo cloak blocks my view as he stands above me, wheezing heavily. I bite my tongue to keep from whimpering in fear. The graveyard goes silent. Cracks of lightning still spiral across the sky, but no sound radiates from them. The whispering screams of my ancestors die down as the King Below steps closer to me.

"The Cyphers enjoy making promises they don't end up keeping, my dear," he rasps. He is more corpse than man now, with his ribcage ripped open and exposed. He bleeds from every orifice, and his breath is little more than a death rattle. He sinks to the ground beside me, leaning on his knees, those skeletal eyes staring at me.

"What say you now, little hedge witch? Now that the one you love lies dying. Now that most of your ancestral line, the source of your family's magic, is bound up in chains. The peace of their afterlife shall be sacrificed because you called for their aid. The guilt *must* be eating you alive." He leans closer to me, pressing his bony fingers onto my stomach, and my still unhealed ribs scream in protest. For the first time, I can smell the way he reeks of rotting flesh.

"What say you now?" he repeats with a soft purr, stroking my cheek. My head pounds as I wince at his touch.

The King Below tuts, his eyes appraising me. "A cracked skull and broken ribs. We can't have that. Say you will be mine and rule the lands below and above with me, and I will heal you, sweet."

The wind whips his cloak up for a moment and I catch a glimpse of Matthew crumpled behind him. Blood and bile gather in my mouth as pain and fear are replaced by rage.

"I'm a hedge witch," I say breathlessly. "I can do it myself."

Screaming through the pain, I sit up, shooting a hand out and grabbing the silver chain around his neck, pulling him closer to me before he can move away. I wrap the chain around my hand twice, tethering us together, and firmly place my other palm on his chest, just above the bones of his exposed lower ribs.

He growls at me, his own hand wrapping around my throat, squeezing my airways and trying to push me back down to the grave. At our adversarial embrace, spirits and shadows alike erupt in a writhing panic. The few unbound ghostly figures who remain encircle us, blocking the mutilated hellhounds, who whimper and keel, unable to move closer to their master.

I don't fight against the waves of pain and the burning need for oxygen. I don't let my concentration waver to Matthew or the ancestors circled around me. All my intention, all my focus is on the very center of the King Below's chest, where no heart beats but shadow magic thrums. And just as I had done with the energy and life of Goodwin Manor when I healed Miranda, I begin to pull the shadows toward me.

"What are you doing?" The King Below seethes, his wretched breath sputtering against my face. Bits of dark smoke dribble from his loose jaw. Black flame-like tendrils unfurl from his ribs and curl around my arms, sending sparking electric currents through my body.

There is no air left in my lungs to answer him. I coax every precious dark filament from him, each a thread of the very fabric holding him together. His grip on my throat loosens as shadows pour from his arms, down along my neck, before settling into my skin. I accept them into me, sending them to all the parts of my body that are broken and bleeding. The throbbing of my head eases, the stabbing in my ribs disappears, and my thoughts become sharper as I draw in a quick breath beneath his weakened fingers.

His eyes are wide with surprise and, I can only hope, fear. The hand around my neck crackles as he sends a surge of his own necrotic intention toward me. My vision goes black from the blinding pain. Skin on frozen fire, muscles clenching and shrinking as the blast of energy tries to spread atrophy through my body. For a moment, I know the pain Miranda felt when Matthew destroyed her arm. But I don't let it take root, instead Siphoning this magic as well, pulling it in deeper with the other shadows, letting it mix and dissolve and become a part of me until I can see clearly once again. The King Below's jaw goes slack as he watches me consume his last line of defense.

"Thank you," I say in a low whisper. "I will take all that you are to become whole again." I breathe in deeply, smiling as my lungs expand painlessly into my now healed ribs. He let's go of my neck and tries to scramble away, pushing off my shoulders. But the chain of his necklace is wrapped so tightly around my hand that it keeps him connected to me, cutting into my skin as it does so. I pull more shadows from him and heal those bleeding cuts instantaneously.

I brace myself for more resistance, for another necrotic attack, for something, as I pull the death out of him, thread by thread and morph it into myself, letting it join my own magic. But he ceases all action and smiles. Then laughs.

"Enjoy the fate you've designed for yourself, my dear," he says, his words little more than a whisper. "It would have been more pleasant for you had you just accepted me."

I ignore him, continuing my Siphon as the skin on his face unravels, sloughing away into mist that I, in turn, take into me. He laughs again, the brief chuckle barely an echo on the wind as the last remnants of his skin sag and turn a sickly orange, then brown, and then quickly fade away into dust. All his weight, pressing into me, disappears, leaving me alone on the grave, with the silver chain he wore around his neck still dangling from my hand, the key at one end swinging back and forth like a pendulum.

A groaning rumble sounds out as the pile of rotted pumpkins collapses. I jump away as the entire throne comes tumbling down, the rotten gourds rolling across the graveyard. Lifeless skeletons are strewn about, every grave ripped open and empty. But the hellhounds are gone, and the dozens of chains connected to the demolished throne melt into the grass. The spirits of my ancestors soar into the air and turn into a sparkling mist, free.

After all the commotion, the quiet that has settled over the graveyard is eerie. The night sky still cracks with silent thunder, but the forest does not stir. I've won, but there is no sense of victory inside me—only the memory of the King Below's final words and ghostly laughter as I defeated him. And the growing weight of the chain still in my hands. I pull the key up into my palm, to study it. It's warm to the touch and sparks with the electric current of death magic. My muscles clench with tension. The sense of impending doom has returned.

"Hecate," a voice calls out. I look up as my mother rushes over to me, her feet not leaving any impression in the grass.

"Mom?" I call out, trying to fight the anxiety building in me.

"Oh, sweetheart, I'm so sorry," she says mournfully. Her eyes scan me and she shakes her head.

"What's wrong?" Please, just let her tell me that everything will be all right. That all the secrets are revealed. The fighting finally over.

"This is all my fault, honey. I tried to protect you. To keep him from you." If spirits could cry, I would swear by the tremble in her voice that she was moments from tears. "I agreed to name you as a hedge witch, which is what I had promised. But I never promised to train you. I thought that loophole would save both our lives. But he's had his final revenge on me now. He's signed you off to a fate worse than death."

"He can't hurt you anymore. We can all go back home now." I want to sob. Because nothing has ever felt so far from true.

"Oh, honey," she says softly. "If we do that, everything in the land below will follow behind us. It will be madness. Chaos. You hold the key now. You must accept it into you and become the gate. Before it destroys you."

The key burns, and the edges begin to shimmer and sharpen. It shifts in size, extending into a multichrome dagger in my hand. I can see my face in the reflection of its surface. I try to drop it, but my fingers won't release their grip. An urge builds as I stare at my reflection in the knife's edge, an urge that won't be satisfied until I bring the dagger to my chest and plunge it into my heart.

"Mom?" I ask again, scared and confused, fighting the desire to pierce myself with the key.

"It's all right, sweetheart," she says, shushing me. "I will stay with you through all of it. Until another hedge witch is born and your burden is eased."

I am truly worse than dead. Miranda and Celeste will watch over my sleeping body, which will never wake. I will never see them again. I will never see Merlin, the women of the Atlantic Key, the children of Ipswich—all will only ever see me as a comatose corpse, stored away in some hospital room for the next fifty years until my corporeal body decays.

In the meantime, I will be forced to be the glue that keeps the veils of the worlds in place. This horrid, muted limbo where nothing lives and grows will be my home eternal, for who would ever again name their daughter a hedge witch?

"I am damned," I whisper, horrified.

"No." Matthew's hushed voice is behind me. I turn and let out a gasping sob to see him awake. But his entire right arm is shriveled and black. He walks quietly, slowly, over to me and takes my free hand in his. The coppery scar of his left arm glimmers in the candlelight. He reaches for the dagger but I snatch my palm closed. He sighs.

"Kate," he whispers softly.

I shake my head furiously. "No. No, I won't let you."

"I am dead already," he says, looking down at his arm. "The decay has gone too far."

"You're lying!" I insist. "I could save you. I used Siphoning to fix Miranda's arm. I can heal you like I did her."

Matthew looks at me with admiring surprise and runs his good hand through my hair softly.

"Did you really? Extraordinary," he breathes. "There hasn't been a day since we met where you haven't completely left me in awe."

I lean into his touch but keep my hand closed tightly over the dagger. Its edges are slicing into my flesh. The urge to become one with it is almost unbearable.

"I can save you. I promise," I whisper.

"I have no doubt," Matthew says, putting his forehead to mine. I wrap my free arm around him, holding him to me. His good hand cups my cheek. "But the point is irrelevant. You're not going to stay here. This realm was never meant to be your permanent home. You belong with the living."

"So do you!" I shake my head.

"Listen to me," he says, his lips pressing softly against my cheek. "I have spent the past ten years desperately working to save you. From the moment we met, during those first sips of cinnamon mead, I knew you were too good, too full of life to be subjected to His cruelty. Every day I have worked, invisibly sabotaging His efforts, turning my family against Him. All to keep you from this dark fate. I refuse to come all this way and fail."

"It's not your choice," I insist.

He laughs softly, his breath tickling my neck. He pulls away and looks me in the eye.

"I'm a shadow hexan, Kate, just as he was. It's my fate."

"You were forced to choose shadow magic. You never had a choice," I remind him.

"But I do now," Matthew says, "I want this. Let me choose this."

"Listen to him, Hecate," my mother's spirit insists from behind me. I turn to look toward her, and her eyes are shining, full of hope. I shake my head.

"You don't want this. You can't." I push away from him, but his good hand moves quickly, clutching my waist and holding me to him. The air is dead silent, but there is a screaming cacophony inside my mind.

"I do want it," he says through gritted teeth. "I need it. Nothing is worth anything unless you're happy and safe. I will beg you if I have to." His voice trembles, not from fear, but some other cocktail of emotions.

My whole body is shaking. Drops of blood are running down my palm from where the dagger bites into my skin.

"Please, Kate," he whispers, and leans his forehead against mine again.

I breathe in the scent of him, autumn rain and freshly ground cinnamon. My throat is so tight, fighting against tears, that it's almost agony to speak. I grasp for that perfect calm I feel whenever we're together. But the panic coursing through me is too strong. It would be so easy to rip away from him and plunge the dagger into me. And a part of me wants to, desperately. But Matthew's eyes are pleading. His whole face is tense, waiting.

"I love you," I say, gasping for air.

My palm unfurls, exposing the dagger.

Matthew lets out a sound of strangled relief. My heart shatters as he pulls the dagger away from me. He bends down, slides it out of my palm, and leaves a gentle kiss on my bleeding fingers. A wrenching sob escapes from me. I want to wrap myself around him, prevent him from using the dagger, prevent any harm from coming to either one of us. But he pulls away from me, his eyes suddenly wary, as if he expects me to snatch the weapon back out of his hands.

My mother's cold presence embraces me.

"Thank you," she says, staring off at Matthew as she holds me. And I want to scream at her joy. Matthew stares at me, a soft adoring smile turning up the corner of his lips. He raises the dagger up, and my heart begins to pound, blood rushing like a roaring train through my ears. A shimmering brass chain begins to extend from the blade in Matthew's hands and wraps itself around him. He hovers the dagger above his chest. His eyes meet mine. I can't draw breath.

"This is not goodbye, Kate," Matthew says. "This is the beginning of it all." And then he thrusts the dagger into his chest.

CHAPTER TWENTY-SEVEN
November 1st

I wake with a scream. Miranda and Celeste both shriek above me. I am lying on a couch in the library. The air smells of smoke, and haunting waltz music plays from the ballroom.

"Hecate!"

"You're awake!"

"What the hell happened?"

My sisters talk over each other as I calibrate myself, still reeling from the sight of blood bursting from Matthew's heart.

"You're okay?" I say, looking over both of them. The edges of Celeste's coat are singed and Miranda's arm looks a bit worse for wear, but otherwise they seem unharmed.

They both nod.

"When you collapsed, all the shadows disappeared," Celeste says.

My dress is damp and smells of salt. Incense burns in ceramic pots around me. Tarot cards are spread out in strange orientations on the floor by the couch. And half-empty vials of saltwater sit on the side table.

"What did you do to me?" I say, a crazed giggle escaping my lips.

"You wouldn't wake up," Miranda says with a huff. "We tried everything we could think of. Celeste even tried to cook from Mom's book." She wrinkles her nose at some unpleasant memory.

"How long have I been out?" I ask, listening again to the violins and chatter outside the library door.

"Hours," Celeste says, running a cloth over my face to dry it. "It's well past midnight."

"Why is there music playing?" I ask. My sisters both look at each other.

"Well, when the darkness retreated, everyone else assumed the danger had passed. No one seemed overly concerned that you collapsed. Winifred wouldn't even help us. She just said 'Kate's on her own now,'" Celeste says. She crosses her arms and grimaces. "The coven decided not to waste an evening of celebration."

I blink. "They're partying?" I say aloud. Celeste nods.

"Everyone has been enjoying themselves. They've all been acting a little loopy since Miranda served your birthday cake. But don't worry—she saved the last piece for you." She gestures over her shoulder. Sure enough, over at one of the reading tables, sits a piece of our Samhain china with a thick slice of the chocolate caramel apple cake. "We had to fight several of the elders who wanted it after you passed out. But Miranda protected it fiercely."

Miranda is frowning as she listens to us speak. She neither acknowledges nor denies the efforts that Celeste is claiming.

"I passed out and the elders immediately tried to eat my cake?" Again, I want to laugh.

"Enough," Miranda snaps at me. "Do you want to tell us what exactly happened to you?"

"Miranda," Celeste warns disapprovingly.

Miranda's face is deadly serious as she looks at me, but I can't help the series of laughs that burst from me. I laugh to keep from crying. But tears do come. First one, then two. They spill over between my amused snorts, and then suddenly I can't quite catch my breath. And more tears fall as my laughter turns to heaving sobs.

I am immediately drawn into an embrace. Both of my sisters' arms wrap around me. Miranda sits down next to me on the couch and pulls me into her chest. Celeste, who is sitting on her knees by the couch, lays her head down into my waist. And they both hold me as I sob. Neither asks questions, neither demands I cease.

Every so often, Miranda whispers to me, "It's all right. It will be all right." But soon enough she stops speaking, and I am left to cry in peace. I don't know how long I weep before I start talking, but eventually, with shuddering breaths, I tell my sisters everything that happened in the world below.

"I can't believe we almost lost you," Celeste says shakily. "All while the coven dances blissfully outside the doors."

"Mom was really there?" Miranda whispers, her own eyes wet.

I nod.

"All our foremothers were. I couldn't have defeated the demon without them."

"I misjudged Matthew," she admits. "To subject himself to such a horrid fate to save you. He must truly have loved you."

I wince at her use of past tense.

"How will the Pacific Gate react when they learn their heir is dead?" Celeste asks with a horrified whisper. She and Miranda exchange worried glances at the thought of an inter-coven war.

I bury my face in my hands. I can't bear to think of Matthew as dead. Not yet. But the image of the dagger piercing his heart makes me shudder.

"Hold on," Miranda says to me. She rises from the couch and quickly walks out of the library. Celeste and I wait for her to come back. I notice that the music has stopped, and while there are some random peals of laughter, the general chatter has ceased.

The door opens quietly, and Miranda comes back into the library, carrying a steaming mug. She also picks up the china plate holding my slice of birthday cake and walks back over to the couch.

"Eat," she insists, thrusting the plate toward me. I take it instinctively. More gingerly, she hands me a cup of hot cocoa. Several ghost-shaped marshmallows are floating around in the warm choco-late bath.

I look up at her.

"You're cold and in shock. You need to eat," she says.

"Thank you," I say, surprised. I take a sip of the cocoa. It's an instant packet mix but delicious all the same, and the marshmallows melt slowly in my mouth.

"Come, Celeste," Miranda says. "You need rest. We all do." She stares at me pointedly. "When you've finished, go upstairs and get some sleep."

"I don't want to leave Kate," Celeste says. Miranda glares at her, but Celeste doesn't budge.

"It's all right," I tell her. "I'm tired. No more Shadow Walking tonight. I promise. Sleep well."

This placates her a bit. Reluctantly she rises, letting go of my hand. The past hour may have been the longest I have ever gone maintaining physical contact with my sisters.

"Kate." Miranda's voice interrupts my thoughts. I look up to see her standing at the door. Celeste has already left. "Tomorrow, after we settle everything with the coven"—she stares at me for a moment— "we can go to Salem Library and try to find more about hedge craft. If we can convince the archives to share the Books of the other hedge witches, then perhaps their notes will help train you in the other half of your practice."

My eyes widen with surprise.

"I'd like that," I say to her. She gives me a polite but warm smile before leaving the library and shutting the door.

All alone. My natural state. And yet, the crushing sense of loneli-ness bears down on me. I grab my plate and walk over to the windows that look down toward the sea. I cannot see the ocean; it is much too dark for that. The storm from earlier in the night has cleared, and the stars are shining, but I can sense the huge cloud of fog rolling in off the water. The window is beginning to frost from the rapidly dropping temperature.

The stars blink out one by one from the fog. I take a bite from my slice of cake. The familiar sense of good fortune spreads through my chest. The dark night doesn't seem quite so oppressive after all.

I set the plate down on a stack of books.

I don't want the cake's magic to make me feel better. Not yet. Not when I've lost him. Not when I let him die for me. I sit on the window-sill and watch the inky blackness of the night shift from pitch to indigo, to deep gray. The hours pass. All I know is that if I break my meditation on the sky, the heaviness of it all might become too much. It's not until the first whispers of dawn break through that I come back to myself. I don't want to be in this oppressive house any longer.

I tiptoe out of the library. The manor is silent. All around the entryway there are witches passed out, sleeping happily on the floor. Winifred, Rebecca, and Ginny all lie together on the fainting couch just beside the door. Three generations of Bennet witches sleep soundly, clasping one another's hands. My anger toward Winifred and all her secrets can wait for a different time.

I quietly open the front door and immediately bite my lip at the bitter cold of the morning. It's like ice on my skin. The ground is frozen, and I walk carefully down the hill to my cottage. The entire estate is covered in the densest cloud of fog I have ever seen. The morning is still a deep blue, but the sky is turning brighter. Less than half an hour from dawn.

I wrap my green wool cloak around me more tightly. The fog wets my curls to the side of my face, and my breath comes out as thick as wood smoke. Several of Matthew's carved pumpkins have been carried by drunken revelers down different parts of the path. Their snuffed-out candles and black frozen faces smile up at me as I walk to my cottage. In a bush off to the side of the worn path is my warty devil. He has the sweetest of all the faces. I quickly grab him and tuck him to my chest. A shifting of movement catches my eye.

Winifred.

She stands just a little way down the hill from me. No longer in her large gown, she wears a simple white nightdress with lace sleeves. I turn back toward the Manor. I hadn't heard her follow me out.

"Win?" I say, walking close to her. She stares out at the forest. "Winifred?" I call again.

She turns to look at me, and her hair moves slowly, as if blown in an underwater breeze. Just like Margaret. Just like Mom's.

"Oh my God," I breathe as I stare at her ghost. She gives me a sad but calm smile.

"It is done then?" she asks. "The King Below is gone." Her voice is close and far away all at once.

I nod, still shocked into silence.

"Then my time has come," she says quietly.

"Why is this happening?" I say. My chest constricts as if I am about to cry. But no tears come. Perhaps I have used up all my available tears this night. "Were you sick? Why didn't you tell me?"

Winifred shakes her head. "No, Sweet Pea. This was my deal with that wretched creature. She reaches out to smooth one of my curls, but her hand pauses, and she draws back.

"I could feel my time coming in my late twenties. When Rebecca was only a baby. The meta-magic was getting harder to control. Every time I used it, it took bigger and bigger pieces of me. I couldn't bear the thought of leaving my daughter motherless so early in life. So, I followed in the steps of several other Atlantic Key meta-magic witches. A simple trade. Magic for time."

She bites her lip, hesitating before continuing.

"I begged the King Below to extend my life, to shield me from death. In return, I gave him the unused magic I took from witches during their Containment. It gave him a little strength. Kept him going. Without me, he would have faded decades ago." She stops speaking.

I'm silent for a long moment, tightly gripping the pumpkin in my hands, nails digging into the flesh.

"You're the reason our coven's magic has weakened, aren't you?" I ask eventually. "The Containment—just a ruse?"

No, not just a ruse, but the very cause of our dwindling power. If I hadn't already experienced a barrage of emotional whiplash during the past twenty-four hours, I know I'd be screaming at her.

Winifred won't meet my eyes.

"I did what I thought I had to do to give my daughter a happy life," she says.

"And what of my mother, your best friend?" I snap. The urge to cry has left me, but a hollow ache still pinches the center of my heart.

Winifred nods, expecting the question.

"When Sybil was desperate to save William, I made her the Grimoire and brought her to the King Below. As he had directed me to do."

She looks down at her hands, as if the shame of all her actions has finally hit her.

"She went to him eagerly at first. But after her change of heart, she convinced Margaret and me to help shield you from death. Margaret never thought it was right. She always wanted you to know the full extent of your powers. But Sybil made us promise. For years, your mother and I towed the line. We tried to see how many holes we could poke in our deals without everything blowing up. Not letting him know for certain that we were working against him."

"You played your part well, it seems," I say quietly. "Seventy-five years is an achievement for a meta-magic witch." Fifty years of which had been spent draining our coven of magic. But I don't say that part out loud.

"Indeed," Winifred admits. "But now that he is gone, all the remnants of his magic will fade from the land above. Your mother's book will turn to ash in the coming days if it has not already done so."

"And you?" I ask.

She looks at me for a long moment. "And I must now pass on. Through the veil. If you will let me." Her voice falters on this last sentence, a note of fear and uncertainty in her trembling words. She turns her back to me and stares again at the forest. The fog is heavy, but through the outline of the trees, figures move, ghostly and ephemeral. A soft collective whisper rises above the canopy. Not malevolent or frightening. Welcoming.

I clutch my warty devil to my chest for comfort. Part of me wants to tell her to go rot. But even in the face of all her selfish deeds, I can't punish her in such a cruel way.

"Too many spirits have had to claw their way through the veil these past centuries. Let's allow it time to heal, shall we?" I say gently.

I take a deep breath and rest my hand on Winifred's shoulder. The energy of death swirls through my fingertips, stinging and numbing, but not painful as it had been with Margaret. She lets out a long sigh, and a freezing pressure builds in my limbs. I try to find the same sense of calming rightness that comes over me whenever I Shadow Walk. That same sense of confidence I feel when Siphoning. I close my eyes, breathing through the tight squeeze. My internal fear and resistance give way. The pressure eases.

I know I am alone before I even open my eyes. The foggy hill sits bare of life, save for me and the warty devil. My hand, still outstretched, reaches into empty frigid air.

I gather my arms beneath the fabric of my cloak, trying to find extra warmth, and the moonstone talisman falls free. The all-consuming black mark of necrotic energy is gone. But it is still that same distorted verdant shade I'd seen on Halloween morning. The silver streaks are more apparent now, thicker against the forest green. Yesterday morning, I'd thought the silver flecks were the mark of the King Below, a sign that he was coming for me. But he's gone now. So why are they still present?

I look back out toward the forest, toward the spectral figures shifting through the fog. Three figures, made of the shadow and light between the trees, meld into an embrace before fading into the misty background.

"Rest well, Win," I whisper. Her sins will be revealed in time, and the coven will rebuild.

I look back down at the talisman with its green and silver threads blending together. Maybe the silver isn't from an outside influence at all. Not the King Below. Not a curse.

It's me.

This past week, I've communicated with the dead. I've Shadow Walked. I've Siphoned to heal Miranda's arm and defeat a trickster god. My magic has changed. It's gained dimension and become something new. I run my thumb over the swirling surface of the moonstone and watch as the green and silver dance together, spiraling down into infinity.

The cold air bites at the skin on my hand. I shiver again. A fire will be my first necessity when I get to my cottage. I can only hope Merlin has found some warmth burrowed into the quilts of my bed. Yes. A fire first. Then tears. And perhaps a special tea to help me sleep dreamlessly for a long while.

I quickly run up the steps of my porch and through the creaky wooden front door. I slam it shut and inhale sharply, trying to breathe off the cold. The air inside is not as frigid as I thought it would be, much to my relief. In fact, it's almost warm.

I turn around. The roaring fire crackling in my hearth is the first thing I see. The man sitting on my couch is the second.

"Hello, Kate," Matthew says, gently lifting a dozing Merlin off of his lap. He places my cat onto the adjacent seat and slowly rises. He is wearing the same suit he had worn to the dumb supper. It is perfectly pressed, not a wrinkle in sight, each crease of the seam in its place, but he's rolled the sleeves up his forearms. His hair on the other hand, is wildly untidy, as if he has been running his hands through it, lost in thought.

I can't breathe. He doesn't say anything else as I stare at him. He stands perfectly still in an almost nervous fashion. My feet have a mind of their own, and I give in to the magnetic pull. Slowly, I set my warty devil on the marble coffee table and inch closer to Matthew, studying his face. His eyes meet mine, but we both remain silent.

Is he an apparition? A spirit like Winifred and those I had seen in the woods? He doesn't have the same silvery sheen as them. He looks flesh and bone enough. His right arm isn't even desiccated anymore. It is fully formed and healthy. His left arm still bears the copper scar of his fight with the hellhounds. I reach out and touch the shimmering orange lines that run up his forearm. He's warm. My heart quickens at his soft intake of breath at my touch. I look up at him.

"How?" I wonder aloud, gesturing to his once decayed arm. I almost don't care. Almost. But the impossibility of it stops me from throwing myself into his arms in relief.

"All part of the perks of my new position. Though I did choose to keep your additions," he says appreciatively, admiring the copper grooves that I am currently tracing with one of my fingers. He lifts his arm up. I don't stop him, but I also don't let go. His hand cups my cheek. Tears prick at the corners of my eyes as I feel the familiar rough edges of his skin.

"How are you here?" I ask. I have no strength to speak above a whisper.

"It's Samhain," he whispers, his eyes not leaving mine. Slowly, he runs his thumb over my lips. "The veil is weak. I can walk the realm of the living until sunset."

"And then you will be gone? Until when? Beltane?" A tear falls from me, and it's both in deep relief and deep sadness. At least I haven't lost him forever. But what hell will he be subjected to in the meantime? He studies my face for a moment, brow furrowing.

"Yes. If that is what you wish," he says with a nod.

"Do I get some sort of say in the matter?" I ask.

Matthew smiles again, though it is tinged with uncertainty. "Well, if you agree to be my hedge witch, then I can stay with you." He reaches down and grabs a mug off the coffee table.

"I hope you don't mind, but I took the liberty of brewing the necessary tea. Smoked barberry root bark, damiana, crystalized juniper berries, mugwort powder, *and* moonvine freshly harvested from your garden this morning." He holds the mug out to me in offering. The tea is the color of sun-ripened plums. Strongly steeped with all the ingredients we'd picked up from the Raven & Crone.

I want to erupt with joy. I also want to laugh deliriously at myself for the depression of the last hours.

"All I have to do is drink this?" I ask. "And you'll stay with me?"

"If you would have me, yes. I would stay with you. For the darkest months of the year, I would be by your side in the land above. Keep you company. Keep you safe. Keep your bed warm, if you wish." He chuckles. I can't help my own blissful grin.

"And then come spring?" I ask after a moment.

Matthew frowns.

"Come Beltane, I must return to the land below. But as the hedge witch, you would be free to cross the veil as you please. Any time of year," he emphasizes.

I run a hand down the lapel of his suit, appreciating its silky texture. "Well, I do enjoy my alone time," I say. Matthew laughs quietly, watching my hand fiddle with his outer layer of clothing.

"Yes, I know," he agrees.

"But I often find the summer months are rather lonely," I say, looking up at him. He meets my gaze. "And you are the only person I've met who improves the silence."

His smile widens with pride.

I want to pull him to me, cover his face with kisses until my head swims from lack of air. But there is business to settle.

"I will be your hedge witch," I whisper to him. His smile is so brilliant that my heart aches.

"I want nothing more," I say, taking the mug from him, "than to keep you here with me. To ease your burden. To belong to you. To be yours in every way." I drink. The flavor is bitter and earthy and absolute perfection.

Matthew's smile disappears, and his eyes flash with desire. He is staring at me in the same way he always has since the day we first saw each other. The fire is dying in the hearth. The fog is pressing up against the windows of the cottage so that the world outside doesn't exist. Only we exist. I can't stop myself. I drop the empty mug, ignoring the sound of it breaking against wood. I reach out to Matthew and pull him to me.

I kiss him fiercely, the grief and horror of the previous night exorcized by the feeling of his lips on mine. He wrenches me closer, deepening the kiss. And it's like finally coming home after being lost for days on end.

And then I am grabbing at his clothes, forcefully unbuttoning his shirt, and he helps me as I pull it over his head and throw it to the side. I reach for him again, wrapping my arms around his neck. I want to bury myself in him. But I pause and stare at his naked chest.

Around his neck is a delicate chain with a small key that hangs loosely down to his stomach. It's quite transformed from the gaudy adornment of the previous owner. I reach out to touch it gingerly, my fingers brushing against his stomach. He doesn't move to stop me. It's cold against his warm skin. Tiny letters are inscribed on the blade of the key.

H. G.

My initials.

"To prove I am yours just as you are mine. Partners in guarding the veil. Gate and Key." he whispers as I stare at the necklace.

I look up at him and see my want and feverish desire reflected in his face. We stare at each other, our breath heavy. Then we collide again, desperate after even that briefest of separations. He unties my tartan wrap dress, pushing it off my shoulders. It caresses the length of my body as it falls to the floor. I pull the pins out of my hair and let my wheat waves fall down to my hips.

He grabs my face, pulling me toward him, and kisses me again, desperately. His arms find their way around my hips. With surprising strength, he lifts me off the floor. I immediately wrap my legs around his waist. Every inch of him presses on every inch of me. I am filled with a longing and excitement so exquisite I can hardly breathe.

Outside the cottage the forest has come alive with the rising sun. The morning larks begin their November symphony. Still, only a blanket of white fog can be seen through the windows. I hardly notice any of it as Matthew continues to hold me. I kiss him, thrilling in the way it feels to be wrapped around the heat of his body. For a moment, he pulls away from me, and his eyes meet mine.

"To tell you I love you more than life would be a heretical understatement," he whispers.

"I think the feeling might be mutual," I say with a smile, squeezing my legs around him tightly.

We both laugh and he kisses me again. There is relief in this kiss. That same relief I had seen in his eyes as I let him take the key in the forest. I softly brush my fingers through his hair and run my other hand down his neck and shoulders, thriving in the energies I can sense pulsing through his body. I bend down and place a soft kiss at the base of his throat. His relief disappears and shifts into something more fervent, desperate. His arms tighten around me. He turns away from the fire. And the worlds and veil around us fade away as he carries me into the darkness of my bedroom.

Excerpts From Hecate Goodwin's Herbal

The Duties of a Hedge Witch

Though she will exist on the boundaries of society and coven alike, a hedge witch's role is a vital one. A source of healing, sanctuary, and hope, she is to offer shelter, aid, and an ear to those who need it. Her most sacred duty will be to maintain the boundary between the worlds above and below. And when death comes for a soul, it shall be the hedge witch who offers safe passage across the veil and into eternal rest.

Teas

Somnia

Blend 3 parts peppermint, 2 parts verbena, 2 parts lavender, 1 part catnip, 1 part passionflower. Steep in piping hot water for 5 minutes.
Note to self: Do *not* combine with Tranquilum elixir. Too powerful. May unintentionally Shadow Walk.

Throat Soother

Blend black tea leaves, blood orange peel, cloves, cinnamon (amounts must be adjusted based on severity of sore throat). Steep in boiling water for 6 minutes and stir in your preferred amount of sage honey. Perform a visualization ritual while consuming. Relief should come quickly.

Ipswich Mist

Steep 1 packet of preferred brand of Earl Grey tea in steamed oat milk for 5 minutes. Stir in preferred portions of vanilla syrup and cinnamon syrup. Garnish with a cinnamon stick. May be poured over ice.

Chill-Out Chili

Dealing with difficult people? Hoping to calm everyone down and open their minds to other points of view? Instead of stewing over resentment, whip up a cauldron of this delicious dish, and let the good times roll.

Ingredients

3 lb. ground sirloin
1 yellow onion, chopped
5 cloves garlic, minced
2 tsp. salt
1½ tsp. ground cumin
**7 T. intentional chili powder (the more you use, the calmer your dinner guests will become)
3 80 oz. cans tomato sauce and one can of water
1 6 oz. can tomato paste
2 tsp. sugar
Course ground black pepper to taste

Directions

Heat Dutch oven over medium high.
Add 2 tbsp olive oil to the hot pan and sauté the chopped onion for 1 min.
Add beef and brown.
Ladle out any excess grease.
Add tomato sauce and water.
Stir in all dry ingredients, and bring to a boil.
Add tomato paste, and return to a boil.
Reduce the heat, and simmer for about 1 hour.

Aunt Sophia's Cinnamon Cookies

Have you fallen out of touch with a relative? Is there a loved one you haven't seen in a while? Make these cookies, and expect a call or letter from them within a few days! (*Note:* Will not work if person of interest is cursed or trapped inside a mirror. Cookies will still be delicious though!)

Ingredients

1 cup brown sugar
½ cup granulated sugar
½ cup softened butter, salted
½ cup softened butter, unsalted (this butter ratio is critical. Do not skip)
2 eggs
2½ cups all-purpose flour
1 tsp. baking powder
1 tsp. vanilla
1¼ tsp. intentional cinnamon (for strengthening warm bonds; increase by ¼ tsp if need is urgent)

Directions

Mix flour, cinnamon, baking powder.
In a different bowl, cream butter and sugar.
Mix in eggs, one at a time.
Add vanilla.
Combine dry ingredients with wet until dough forms.

Wallis Kinney

Chill overnight.
Roll dough into balls, and dip in cinnamon sugar.
Bake at 350° for 10 minutes.

Ban-Ban Banana Bread

Though this bread is meant to repel someone away from you, it's anything but repulsive! Whoever it may be that you plan to banish, they will likely thank you for doing it in such a delicious way. The number of miles the banishment extends depends on how many banana chips you lay atop the loaf. The center point will be from where the bread was baked. You will need the hair of your intended target. All others may consume the bread without consequence.

Ingredients

3 bananas, black
½ cup salted butter, melted
1 cup sugar (brown or granulated—your choice)
2 eggs
½ T. vanilla extract
Seeds scraped from 1 vanilla pod
1¼ cup flour
¼ cup cocoa powder
½ tsp. baking soda
¼ tsp. cinnamon
¼ cup caramel chunks
intentional bittersweet chocolate chips (to create repulsion)
banana chips and sweet cream (for garnish and spell specificity)
Optional (for banishing negativity; if not performing spell work, leave these ingredients out): ¼ tsp. each of:
**salt water cursed by a sea witch
**black pepper
**chrysanthemum petals

Directions

Mash bananas with fork in a copper bowl.

Mix in melted butter, brown sugar, egg, vanilla extract, and vanilla seeds.

In a different bowl, combine flour, cocoa, baking soda, and cinnamon.

In 3 batches, add dry ingredients to wet. Stir until just combined.

Mix in chocolate chips and caramel chunks.

Bake in a greased pan for 1 hour at 350°. (If casting a banishment spell, use the flame from a dark blue candle to burn the hair of your target as the bread bakes. Visualize the area you wish to keep them from. You may skip this step otherwise.)

Top with sweet cream glaze and an appropriate number of banana chips.

Stove-Top Simmer

Every good witch should have an arsenal of simmers in her back pocket. They are the easiest way to imbue magic and intention into the walls of your home. They can be used for cleansing disruptive emotions and for protection, and they can also make your house smell wonderful! Once you know the basics of how one is constructed, you may switch up the ingredients list to match whatever your intention may be!

Ingredients

Below is by no means an exhaustive list. Consider carefully, as certain ingredients might react unexpectedly with others despite your best intention. A good rule of thumb is to keep the ingredients of any one simmer to less than five.

Florals: rose petals, violets, marigolds, sunflowers, peonies, sweet peas

Herbs: lavender, rosemary, sage, thyme, basil, bay

Spices: cinnamon (ground or stick), clove, allspice, vanilla, star anise, nutmeg

Produce: any citrus peels, apples, cranberries

Miscellaneous: pine cuttings, almond extract, black tea leaves

Directions

Fill copper sauce pan with water and bring to a boil.

Add desired ingredients into water, boil for five minutes to let aromas develop.

Reduce heat to the barest simmer.

Add additional cup of water every hour to prevent bottom of pan from scalding.

Simmer for as long as you'd like. Once done, remove pot from stove and compost ingredients.

So Cozy Salted Caramel Hot Chocolate

This hot chocolate will keep you warm and dry on a cold, rainy day. The intentional ingredients (whisky and gold flakes) will place a warmth in your home and heart that cannot be extinguished by any outside temperature. One cup will provide an effect for 8 hours. Drink right before bed for sweet dreams and warm blankets. Pair with caramel cinnamon whipped cream for taste.

Ingredients

4 cups whole milk
½ cup heavy whipping cream
¼ cup and 2 T. cocoa powder
1 tsp. ground cinnamon
1 cinnamon stick
7 oz. milk chocolate chips
½ cup salted caramel sauce
1 T. vanilla extract
Optional:
**intentional whisky (for warming)
**intentional gold flakes (for an emotional calm)
Garnish: salted caramel cinnamon whipped cream

Directions

Combine all ingredients, and heat on medium high. Do not bring to a boil, but milk should be steaming and frothing. Stir frequently. Remove cinnamon stick before serving, but garnish each cup with whipped cream, extra gold flakes, and a fresh cinnamon stick, if desired.

Pass-Out Pie

Need to fall asleep quick? This blood orange pie tastes just like a Dream-sicle and the whipped cream is chock full of chamomile. Eat half the pie tin and you're sure to be snoring in no time. It's always best to keep this pie on hand for sleep emergencies, as it does take some time to make.

Ingredients

For the filling:
1 8-inch pie crust
4 blood oranges
1 lemon
4 egg yolks
14 oz can of condensed milk
1 T. vanilla

For the whipped cream:
¼ T. powdered sugar
1 T. honey (orange blossom if you have it)
1 cup whipping cream
2 bags chamomile tea

Directions

Preheat oven to 355°.
Separate the egg yolks from the whites.
Zest three of the blood oranges.
Whisk in the zest with the egg yolks in a small bowl, and set aside for 10 minutes.
Juice blood oranges (aim for just under ½ cup of juice.)
Take juice from half the lemon and whisk into the egg yolk mixture along with the vanilla, orange juice, and condensed milk. Allow entire mixture to sit for 30 minutes. This will help it thicken. Should you like,

meditate during the 30 minutes on what you'd like to dream of once you fall asleep.

Pour into crust.

Bake in oven for 20 minutes. Pie should be set, with the slightest wobble in the center.

Allow to cool and then place in fridge for 2–3 hours to chill.

While pie is chilling, make the whipped cream.

Heat heavy cream and honey in a saucepan on medium low heat. (Do not allow to boil!)

Once steaming, take off heat and place two bags of chamomile tea into the cream (more if your need for sleep is desperate). Allow the tea to steep for 20–30 minutes.

Place in fridge to chill for 1 hour.

Once chilled, whisk cream until stiff peaks form.

Dollop onto surface of chilled pie, and garnish with slices of blood orange.

Put on your pajamas and dig in!

Careful Caramel Apples

A time-honored Goodwin tradition. These caramel apples are sure to help little ones on the night of All Hallows. Gather your best crystals, and fortify your cooking with fresh candles. Be careful! The caramel is tricky, and the spell is finicky. If you take a misstep, it's wise to start over.

Ingredients

5 cups granulated sugar
1¼ cup water
2½ cups heavy cream, warmed
10 T. unsalted butter
salt to taste
apples (for dipping)

Directions

Combine sugar and water in copper cauldron.

Stir 14 times (introducing energy work; for most potent effect, stir clockwise).

Heat on medium-high (no stirring) until the color matches the cauldron.

Slowly incorporate warmed cream. Stir constantly to prevent bubbling over.

Heat until candy thermometer reads 250° (critical energy work; intentions should be of safety and fostering common sense).

Allow to cool slightly, and then dip in the apples. Allow to set for 15 minutes.

Note: The intention from this spell comes from the energy work you do around it, not the ingredients. It is vital to maintain concentration during this recipe. Use candles and crystals to aid you and improve chance of success.

ACKNOWLEDGMENTS

This book exists only because a village of people, far more competent than I, believed in it.

Melissa Rechter, editor extraordinaire, all I ever wanted was for someone to engage with my stories on the levels that you do. Thank you for understanding my characters better than me. The whole team at Alcove, I could not be more grateful for the time and energy you gave turning my manuscript into such a beautiful book. My agents, Ali and Jan, and everyone at Dupree Miller, thank you for opening doors and giving me encouragement at my lowest points.

My parents, Cheryl and Craig Kinney, a list of all the ways you've supported me would make up its own book. No girl has ever been luckier with the people in her corner. And that goes to every member of my extended family. Thank you for your encouragement and love (and for the comfortable couches in your houses where I often write).

Further thanks to:

Katie Ann, Miranda, and Kate, I could not have asked for better beta readers or friends.

Jessica Delaney, you are the reason I had the confidence to try and publish this story.

Kirsten Herman, there were times where it was only your optimism that kept me writing.

Thanks to Alexis Krauss and Kathryn Marshall, booksellers, dear friends, and fonts of wisdom and emotional support.

To the nurses and staff at Dr. Kinney's office in Medical City Dallas: I invaded your workplace for over a year while working on this story and always felt so welcomed.

To the employees of Rebecca's Apothecary in Boulder, Colorado—your store has sparked my imagination for years, and so much of my education about herbalism and magic came from there.

Tieghan Gerard and everyone at the food blog, Half Baked Harvest—to me, you are synonymous with autumnal cooking, and so many of the recipes in this story are inspired by your mouthwatering creations. For any fellow Halloween lovers out there, the cinnamon cookie recipe in the back of the book is indeed inspired by one of my favorite October movies, the Mary Kate and Ashley film *Double, Double, Toil and Trouble*. Liz and Greg Mullen, thank you for letting me share an adaptation of your family's delicious chili. Sarah Kieffer and the community at The Vanilla Bean Blog, thank you for helping me solve the riddle of the Pass-Out Pie. And Davaisha Lamise, you are a saint for helping me test the recipes at the back of the book.

The spirit of this book was born online, and so many people shared their thoughts and opinions on the story as I wrote it. Though I do not know all your names (such is the nature of the internet), I am immeasurably grateful. This is a non-exhaustive list, but I want to thank the people who run the following YouTube channels for their input: Marta, Brenna, Writing Violet, Somberhoney, Susan Monroe McGrath, Singing Sanja, Myownbravado, Nikki Clemmer, Sasha Green, R. K. Stumblingbear, S. D. Hegyes, Rae Kline, Floraandthefaun, Diana Robincheaux, and Rue Roxanne.

And a big thank-you to anyone who has watched the videos on my YouTube channel, Wallisimo.

Stig Dyrdal, and all the troublemakers, thank you for getting me through the pandemic and everything else.

Everyone I met on the Camino de Santiago, you put a pen back in my hand and returned my spirit to me.

And finally, thank you to my beloved older sisters, Jane and Shirley. Without you both, there may as well not be Octobers.